Syd Belton
The Boy Who Would Not Go to Sea

by

George Manville Fenn

Double 9
BOOKS

Syd Belton
The Boy Who Would Not Go to Sea
by George Manville Fenn

ISBN: 978-93-60469-69-6

Published by

DOUBLE 9 BOOKS

2/13-B, Ansari Road
Daryaganj, New Delhi – 110002
info@double9books.com
www.double9books.com
Tel. 011-40042856

This book is under public domain

ABOUT THE AUTHOR

George Manville Fenn was a very productive author of novels, a writer, an editor, and an educator from England. He was born on January 3, 1831, in Pimlico, London. He mostly learned on his own; he taught himself Italian, French, and German. During the years 1851–1854, he went to Battersea Training College for Teachers and then became the head of a state school in Alford, Lincolnshire. In the early 1850s, Fenn started to write short stories and pieces for newspapers and magazines. The Old Forest Ranger, his first book, came out in 1856. Afterward, he wrote more than 100 books, many of them for teenagers and young adults. He was one of the most famous writers of his time, and his books were well-liked and read by many people. He also worked as a reporter and writer for Fenn. Among the newspapers and magazines, he worked for was The Boy's Own Paper, which he ran from 1866 to 1874. He worked hard to make children's books better and was a strong supporter of education and reading. The Englishman Fenn passed away on August 26, 1909, in Isleworth.

CONTENTS

Chapter One

The boy who would not go to sea

"Here you, Syd, pass the port."

Sydney Belton took hold of the silver decanter-stand and slid it carefully along the polished mahogany table towards where Admiral Belton sat back in his chair.

"Avast!"

The ruddy-faced old gentleman roared out that adjuration in so thunderous a way that the good-looking boy who was passing the decanter started and nearly turned it over.

"What's the matter, Tom?" came from the other end of the table, where Captain Belton, a sturdy-looking, grey-haired gentleman nearly as ruddy as his brother, was the admiral's *vis-à-vis*.

"He's passing the decanter without filling his own glass!" cried the admiral. "Fill up, you young dog, and drink the King's health."

"No, thank you, uncle," said the boy, quietly, "I've had one glass."

"Well, sir, so have I. Don't I tell you I'm going to propose the King's health?"

"I'll drink it in water, uncle."

"What, sir? Drink the health of his most gracious Majesty in raw water! Not if I know it."

"But port wine makes my face burn, uncle, and Doctor Liss says—"

"Confound Doctor Liss, sir! Hang Doctor Liss, sir! By George, sir, if I were in active service again, and your Doctor Liss were in my squadron, I'd have him triced up and give him twelve dozen, sir."

"No, you wouldn't, uncle," said the boy, cracking a walnut, and glancing at his father, who was watching him furtively.

"What, sir? I wouldn't? Look here, brother Harry, Liss is corrupting this boy's mind."

"I don't know about corrupting, Tom," said the captain, smiling, "but he certainly does seem to be putting some queer things into his head."

"So it seems. Teaches him to drink the King's health in water."

"No, he didn't, uncle," said the boy, cracking another walnut.

"Yes, he did, sir. How dare you contradict me! Confound you, sir, if I had you aboard ship I'd mast-head you."

"No, you wouldn't, uncle," said the boy, dipping a piece of freshly-peeled walnut in the salt and crunching it between his teeth.

"What, sir?"

"I say you would not," replied the boy.

"And pray why, you young dog?"

"Because you'd know father wouldn't like it."

Captain Belton laughed and sipped his port, and the admiral blew out his cheeks.

"Look here, brother Harry," he cried; "is this my nephew Sydney, or some confounded young son of a sea-lawyer?"

"Oh, it's Syd, sure enough," said the captain.

"Then he's grown into an insolent, pragmatical young cock-a-hoop upstart; and hang it, I should like to spread-eagle him till he came to his senses."

The boy, who was peeling a scrap of walnut, gave his uncle a sidelong look and laughed.

"Ah, I would, sir, and no mistake," cried the admiral, fiercely. "Harry, you don't half preserve discipline in the ship. Here, Syd, it's time you were off to sea."

The boy took another walnut and crushed it, conscious of the fact that his father was watching him intently.

"I don't want to go to sea, uncle," said the boy at last, as he picked off the scraps of broken shell from his walnut.

"What?" roared the admiral. "Here you, sir, say that again."

"I don't want to go to sea, uncle."

"You—don't—want—to go—to sea, sir?"

"No, uncle."

"Well, I am stunned," said the old gentleman, rapidly pouring out and tossing off a glass of port. "Brother Harry, what have you to say to this?"

"That it is all nonsense. The boy does not know his own mind."

"Of course not," cried the admiral, turning sharply upon Sydney, who went on picking the skin from his walnut. "Do you know, sir, that your family have been sailors as far back as the days of Elizabeth."

"Yes, uncle," said the boy, coolly. "I've often heard you say so."

"And that it is your duty, as the last representative of the family, to maintain its honour, sir?"

"No, uncle."

"What, sir?" cried the old man, fiercely.

"I'm not fit to be a sailor," continued the boy, quietly enough.

"And pray, why not, Sydney?" said Captain Belton, frowning.

"Because I'm such a coward, father."

"A Belton!" groaned the admiral, "and says he is a coward."

"A boy to be a sailor ought to be fond of the sea."

"Of course, sir," said the captain.

"And I hate it."

"And pray why?" said the admiral, fiercely.

"Because it's so salt," said Syd, busy helping himself to some more of the condiment he had named.

"Salt?" cried the admiral. "Of course it is, and so it ought to be. Nonsense! He's laughing at us, Harry—a dog."

"No, I'm not, uncle; I'm not fit to be a sailor."

"Then, pray, what are you fit for, sir?" cried Captain Belton, angrily.

"I mean to be a doctor!"

"What!" roared the two officers together.

Crack! crack!

"Put that walnut and those crackers down, sir!" said the captain, sternly. "I am glad your uncle started this subject, for it was time we had an explanation. Do you know that with his interest at the Admiralty and mine you could be entered on board a first-rate man-of-war?"

"Yes, and well looked after, sir," cried the admiral; "so that when you had properly gone through your term, and been master's mate long enough, your promotion would have been certain."

"Yes, uncle, father has often said so," replied Sydney, reaching for another walnut, and taking up the crackers.

"Put that walnut down, sir," cried his father.

Sydney obeyed, and to keep his hands under control thrust them in his pockets and leaned back in his chair.

"Well, sir," said his uncle, "does not that make you feel proud?"

"No, uncle."

"What! Don't you know that you would have a uniform and wear a sword—I mean a dirk?"

"Yes, uncle."

"Well, sir? Why, at your time of life I was mad to have my uniform."

"What for?" said the boy.

"What for, sir? What for? Why, to wear, of course."

"I don't want to wear a uniform. You couldn't climb trees, nor go fishing, nor shrimping, nor riding in a uniform."

"No, sir," continued the admiral, after winking and frowning at his brother to leave the boy to him, "of course not. You would be an officer and a gentleman then, and wear a cocked hat."

"Ha! ha! ha!"

The boy burst into a hearty fit of laughter, and his father frowned.

"Sydney—" he began.

"No, no, Harry, leave him to me," said the admiral; "I'll talk to him. Now, sir," he continued, turning to the boy sternly, "pray what did I say to make you start grinning like a confounded young monkey? I—I—I am not accustomed to be laughed at by impertinent boys."

"I was not laughing at you, uncle," said the boy, dragging one hand from his pocket and making a lunge at an apple.

"Leave that fruit alone, sir," said the admiral, "and don't tell me a confounded lie, sir. You did laugh at me."

"I did not," said the boy; "and that's not a lie."

"What!" roared the admiral, turning purple. "How dare you, sir! To the mast-head at once, and stop there till—"

A hearty burst of laughter from his brother and nephew quelled the old man's anger.

"Ah, you may laugh at that," he said. "Force of habit. But you've got to apologise, you young monkey, for what you said."

"I can't apologise for what I did not do," said the boy, stubbornly.

"What, sir?"

"Steady, steady, sir," said the captain. "He's a confoundedly impudent young scamp, but he could not tell a lie."

"But he laughed in my face, Harry?"

"I was laughing at myself, uncle."

"At yourself, sir?"

"Yes, I was thinking what a popinjay I should look in a cocked hat."

"Well, really," said the admiral, "I am beginning to be glad, Harry, that I never married and had a son. I used to be envious about this boy, and wanted a share in him. But a boy who can laugh at a part of his Majesty's uniform—well! Why, you young whipper-snapper, did I ever look a—a—a popinjay in my cocked hat?"

"Well, you used to look very rum, uncle."

"Harry, my dear boy," said the admiral, fiercely; "we are old men, and this young dog represents us. May I take him into the library, and give him a good caning?"

"No, Tom, certainly not."

"No, of course not, Harry; I beg your pardon. Now, sir—pass that port—and—a—don't fill your own glass. Port like that, sir, is only fit for gentlemen. And you—you want to be a doctor, eh?"

"Yes, uncle," said the boy, pushing the decanter along the table.

"And pray what for, sir?"

"To do good to people."

"What? A doctor do good! Rubbish! Never did me a bit of good."

"Oh, but they do, uncle."

"Never, sir. That Liss has pretty well poisoned me over and over again."

"Oh, uncle, what a—"

"You say that if you dare, sir," cried the old admiral, bringing his hand down bang upon the table, and making the glasses dance. "It's the truth. Always made my gout worse. Colchicum—colchicum—colchicum—and the pain awful. Doctors are an absurd new invention, and of no use whatever."

"Why, you always have a doctor on board ship."

"Surgeon, you young dog, surgeon. Doctor! Bah! Hang all doctors! A surgeon is of some use in action, cutting, and splicing, and fishing a poor fellow's limbs; but a doctor—"

At that moment a rubicund butler opened the dining-room door, and stood back for some one to enter.

"Doctor Liss, sir," he said quietly; and a quick, eager-looking little man in snuff-coloured coat and long, salt-box-pocketed waistcoat entered the room, handing his cocked hat and stick to the butler, and nodding pleasantly from one to the other.

"Who was that shouting for the doctor?" he said cheerily, as he rubbed his hands; then took out a gold snuff-box, tapped it, opened it, and handed it to the captain.

"You, wasn't it, Sir Thomas? Touch of your old enemy?"

"No," grunted the admiral, "I'm sound as a roach. Bah!"

"Thankye, Liss," said the captain, taking his pinch, and handing back the box; "sit down. Syd, pass those clean glasses."

The admiral took a pinch, and then the new-comer took his, loudly snapped-to the box, and drew out a delicate cambric handkerchief to flap off some snuff from his shirt-frill.

As soon as the doctor was comfortably seated the port was passed, and then there was silence, Sydney looking from one to the other, and wondering what was coming next.

The doctor, too, looked from one to the other and formed his own opinion.

"Hullo!" he said. "In disgrace, Sydney? What have you been doing, sir?"

"Eating walnuts," said the boy, mischievously.

"And defying his father and uncle—a dog!" cried the admiral. "Here, Liss; what do you think he says?"

"Bless me! I don't know."

"Why, confound him! says he wants to be a doctor."

"Does he?" cried the new-comer, turning to look at Sydney. "Well, I'm not surprised."

"But I am," cried Captain Belton, angrily.

"And I'm astounded," said the admiral. "A Belton descend to being an apothecary."

"Ah!" said the doctor, dryly, as he held his glass up to the light, "terrible descent, certainly. Wants to save life instead of destroying it."

"Now, look here, Liss," began the admiral, fiercely.

"No, no, Tom, let me speak," said Captain Belton. "No quarrelling."

"No, you had better not quarrel," said the doctor, good-humouredly. "Make you both ill, and then I shall have you at my mercy."

"Indeed you will not," said the admiral, "for I'll call in old Marchant from Lowerport."

"Not you," cried the doctor, laughing; "you dare not. I'm the only man who understands your constitution."

"There, there, there!" cried the captain, "that's enough. But really, sir, it's too bad. As an old friend I did not think you would lead my boy astray."

"I? Astray? Nonsense!"

"But you have, sir. You've taken him out with you on your rounds, and the young dog thinks of nothing else but doctoring."

"And pill-boxes and gallipots," said the admiral, fiercely.

"Now, my dear old friends, you are not talking sense," said the doctor, quietly. "Sydney has been my rounds with me a good deal, and he has certainly displayed so much interest in all my surgical cases, that if he were my boy I should certainly make him a doctor."

"Impossible!" cried the captain.

"Not to be heard of," said Sir Thomas. "He's going to sea."

Sydney, who had been fidgeting about in his chair, gave a sudden kick out with his right leg, and felt something soft as his uncle uttered a savage yell, and thrust his chair back from the table.

"I—I beg your pardon, uncle, I did not know that—"

"You did, sir," cried the old man furiously, as he shook his fist at the boy. "You did it maliciously; out of spite, because I want to make a man of you. Bless me, Harry," he continued, "if you don't take that young scoundrel out into the hall and thrash him, I'll never darken your doors again. Dear—dear—dear—dear! Bless my soul! Ah!"

The poor old admiral had risen, and was limping about when Sydney went after him.

"Uncle," he began.

"Bah!" ejaculated the old man, grasping him by the collar. "Here he is, brother Harry; I've got him. Now then, take him out."

"I'm very sorry, uncle," said Sydney. "I didn't know it was your gouty leg there."

"Then, you did do it on purpose, sir?"

"No, I didn't, uncle. I wouldn't have been such a coward."

"Of course he wouldn't," said the doctor. "But there, sir, sit down; the pain is gone off now."

"How do you know?" cried the admiral. "It's as if ten thousand red-hot irons were searing it. Harry, you've spoiled that boy."

"No, I join issue there," said Captain Belton. "You've indulged him ten times more than ever I have, Tom."

"It is not true, brother Harry," said the admiral, limping to his chair.

"Oh yes, it is. Hasn't your uncle spoiled you, Sydney, far more than I have?"

"No, father," replied the boy, quietly, as he helped the old admiral to sit down, and placed an ottoman under his injured leg.

"Thankye, boy, thankye. And you're not so bad as I said; 'tis quite true, it's your father's doing."

"I think you've both spoiled me," said Sydney, quietly; and the doctor helped himself to another glass of port to hide his mirth.

"Won't do, Liss, you're laughing. I can see you," said the admiral. "That's just what you doctors enjoy, seeing other people suffer, so that you may laugh and grow fat."

"Oh, I was not laughing at your pain," said the doctor, quietly, "but at Sydney's judgment. He is quite right, you do both spoil him."

"What?"

"He has three times as much money to spend as is right, and I wonder he does not waste it more. Well, Syd, my boy, so they will not let you be a doctor?"

Sydney frowned, and cracked a walnut till the shell and nut were all crushed together.

"And so you are to make up your mind to go to sea?"

"Yes," said the admiral, emphatically.

"Certainly," said Captain Belton; and, as soon after the conversation turned into political matters, Sydney quietly left his chair, strolled to the window, and stood gazing out at the estuary upon which the captain's house looked down.

It was a glorious view. The long stretch of water was dappled with orange and gold; and here and there the great men-of-war were lying at anchor, some waiting their commanders; others, whose sea days were past, waiting patiently for their end, sent along dark shadows behind them. Here and there fishing-boats with tawny sails were putting out to sea for the night's fishing; and as Sydney's eyes wandered, a frown settled upon his forehead, and he stepped out through the open window into the garden.

"Bother the old sea!" he said, petulantly. "It's always sea, sea, sea, from morning till night. I don't want to go, and I won't."

As he spoke he passed under an apple tree, one of whose fruit, missed in the gathering a month before, had dropped, and picking it up, the boy relieved his feelings by throwing it with all his might across the garden.

The effect was as sudden as that produced by his kick; for there was a shout and sound of feet rapidly approaching, and a red-faced boy of about his own age came into sight, hatless and breathless, panting, wild-eyed, and with fists clenched ready for assault.

"Who threw—Oh, it was you, was it, Master Sydney? You coward!"

"Who's a coward?" cried Sydney, hotly.

"You are. You throwed that apple and hit me, 'cause you knowed I dursen't hit you again."

"No, I didn't."

"Yes, you did, and you are a coward."

"No, I'm not a coward."

"Yes, you are. If I hit you, I know what you'd do—go and tell your father, and get me sent away."

"There, then! Does that feel like a coward's blow?—or that?—or that?"

Three sharp cuffs in the chest illustrated Sydney's words, two of which the boy bore, flinching at each; but rising beyond endurance by the third, he retaliated with one so well planted that Sydney went down in a sitting position, but in so elastic a fashion that he was up again on the instant, and flew at the giver of the blow.

Then for five minutes there was a sharp encounter, with its accompaniments of hard breathing, muttering, dull sounds of blows and scuffling feet, till a broad-shouldered, red-faced man in a serge apron came down upon them at a trot, and securing each by the shoulder held them apart.

"Now then," he growled, "what's this here?"

"Pan hit me, and I'm dressing him down," panted Sydney. "Here, let go, Barney."

"Master Syd hit me first, father," panted the red-faced boy.

"Howld your tongue, warmint, will you," said the man in a deep growl. "Want to have me chucked overboard, and lose my bit o' pension. You're allus a-going at your pastors and masters."

"Hit me first," remonstrated the boy, as the new-comer gave him a shake.

"Well, what o' that, you ungrateful young porpuss! Hasn't the cap'n hit me lots o' times and chucked things at me? You never see me flyin' in his face."

"Chucked a big apple at me first," cried the boy in an ill-used tone.

"Sarve you right too. Has he hurt you much, Master Sydney?"

"No, Barney; not a bit. There, I was wrong. I didn't know he was there when I threw the apple. I only did it because I felt vicious."

"Hear that, you young sarpint?" cried the square-shouldered man.

"Yes, father."

"Then just you recollect. If the young skipper feels wicious, he's a right to chuck apples. Why, it's rank mutiny hitting him again."

"Hit me first," grumbled the boy.

"Ay, and I'll hit you first. Why, if I'd been board ship again, instead of being a pensioner and keeping this here garden in order for the skipper, I should have put my pipe to my mouth, and—What say, Master Syd?"

"Don't say any more about it. I'd no business to hit Pan, and I'm sorry I did now."

"Well, sir, I don't know 'bout not having no business, 'cause you see you're the skipper's son, and nothing does a boy so much good as a leathering; but if you're sorry for it, there's an end on it. Pan-a-mar, my lad, beg Master Sydney's pardon."

"He hit me first," grumbled the boy.

"Do you want me to give you a good rope's-ending, my sonny?" growled the man; "'cause if you do, just you say that 'ere agen."

The red-faced boy uttered a smothered growl, and was silent.

"Too young to understand discipline yet, Master Sydney," said the man. "And so you felt wicious, did you? What about?"

"They've been at me again about going to sea, Barney."

"And you don't want to go, my lad?"

"No; and I won't go."

"Hear that, Pan, my lad?"

The boy nodded and drew down the corner of his lips, with the effect that Sydney made a threatening gesture.

"No, I'm not afraid, Pan," he cried fiercely; "but I don't want to go, and I won't."

The broad-shouldered man shook his head mournfully, and taking out a steel tobacco-box he opened it and cut off a piece of black, pressed weed, to transfer to his cheek, as he again shook his head sadly.

"I'm sorry to hear that, Master Sydney," he said.

"Why?"

"'Cause it's agen nature. I'm sixty-two now, and from the time I was a little shaver right up to now I never heerd a well-grown, strong, good-looking young chap say he didn't want to go to sea."

"Ah, well, Barney, you've heard one now."

"Ay, ay! and mighty sorry too, sir. Why, there have been times when I've said to myself, 'Maybe when the young master gets his promotion and a ship of his own, he'll come and say to me, Now then, Barney, now's your time to get rid o' the rust; I'll get you painted and scraped, and you shall come to sea with me.'"

"You, Barney? You are too old now. What would you be then?"

"Old! Old! Get out! I don't call myself old by a long way, Master Syd; and if it hadn't been for the captain laying up I should ha' been at sea now. But you'll think better on it, sir; you'll go."

"What, to sea, Barney?"

"Ay, sir."

"No; I mean to be a doctor."

"Then I says it again as I said it afore, Master Syd, there's something the matter with you."

"Matter? Nonsense! What do you mean?"

"Why, what you say sounds so gal-ish and soft, it makes me think as you must have ketched something going out with the doctor."

"What rubbish, Barney!"

"But you going to be a doctor!" cried the old sailor, rubbing his nose with a great gnarled finger. "You, who might be an admiral and command a squadron: no, sir, it won't do."

"It will have to do, Barney."

"Well, sir, it mought and it moughtn't; but it strikes me as you've got something coming on, sir, as is a weakening your head—measles, or fever, or such-like—or you wouldn't talk as you do about the Ryle Navee."

"I talk about it as I do because I don't want to go to sea."

"But it's a flying in the face of the skipper and the admiral. Bobstays and chocks! I wish I was your age and got the chance o' going instead o' being always ashore here plarntin' the cabbages and pulling up the weeds."

"Then you don't like being a gardener, Barney?"

"I 'ates it, sir."

"And so do I hate being a sailor. There!"

"But it's so onnat'ral, sir. Here's your father been a sailor, same as I've been a sailor, and I've drilled up Pan-a-mar o' purpose to be useful to you in the same ship. Why, it's like wasting a season in the garden. I meant him to be your Jack factotum, as the skipper used to call it, and you never heard him say he didn't want to go to sea."

"You said you'd rope's-end me if I did," grumbled the red-faced boy.

"And so I will, you young swab," roared the gardener. "Why, you onnat'ral young galley-dabber, are you going to turn up your ugly pig's nose at your father's purfession?"

"Pan doesn't like the sea any more than I do," cried Sydney; "and I say it's a shame to force boys to be what they don't like."

"Well, this beats all," cried the gardener, helping himself to a fresh piece of tobacco. "What the world's coming to next, I dunnow. Why, if the King, bless him! know'd o' this, it would break his heart."

"Syd! Ahoy there!" came from the dining-room window.

"Aho—"

Sydney was about to reply with a hearty sea-going *Ahoy*! but he altered his mind and cried—

"Yes, father; I'm coming."

This was followed by a savage slap on the leg given by the ex-boatswain, who had settled down with his master the captain at The Heronry, Southbayton.

"Just like a loblolly boy," he growled. "You, Pan, if you was to answer a hail like that I'd—Stop; come here."

"Yes, father, I'm coming," said the red-faced boy, with a grin; and then he dodged while the old boatswain made a blow at his head with open hand.

"Here, I'll speak to the skipper at once about you, youngster. Doing the knives and boots and helping over the weeds is spyling your morals."

"Speak—what about, father?"

"Speak? What about? Why, you swab, do you think I had you chrissen Pan-a-mar, arter a glorious naval victory, o' purpose to have you grow up into a 'long-shore lubber? There, get indoors. 'Fore you're many hours older I'll have you afloat."

Pan went slowly up to the house, followed by his father, who walked along the gravel path with his legs wide apart, as if he expected the ground to heave up; while Sydney went round to the front of the house, and entered by the dining-room window, where his father, uncle, and the doctor were still seated at the table.

"Why, Syd, lad, we did not see you go," said his father; "come and sit down."

The boy obeyed, looking furtively from one to the other, as if he knew instinctively that something particular was coming.

"Ahem!" The admiral gave vent to a tremendous forced cough.

"No, Tom, I'll tell him," said Captain Belton. "Look here, Syd, my boy, at your time of life lads do not know what is best for them, so it is the duty of their fathers to decide."

"Is it, father?"

"Of course it is, sir," growled the admiral, and Doctor Liss wrinkled up his forehead and looked attentively on.

"Now look here, sir. Your uncle has just heard an old friend of his, Captain Dashleigh—"

"Known him from a boy," said the admiral.

"Has been appointed to the *Juno*, one of our finest three-deckers, and he is going to ask him to take you as one of his midshipmen."

"Uncle Tom always said that a boy should commence life either in a sloop of war or a smart frigate," said Syd, sharply.

"If there's one handy," growled the admiral. "*Juno's* a ship to be proud of."

"So, thank your uncle for his promise to exert his interest, and let's have no more nonsense."

"But I want to be a doctor, father," said Syd, looking hard at the visitor.

Crash!

The glasses danced as the admiral brought his hand down heavily.

"No, no, Tom," cried the captain, testily; "I can manage the helm."

"But, Doctor Liss!" said the boy, appealingly.

"Don't appeal to me, my boy," said the doctor, gravely. "You know your father's and your uncle's wish. It is your duty to obey."

"Oh!" ejaculated Sydney, in a tone of voice which seemed to say, "I did think you would side with me."

The doctor took a pinch of snuff.

"You see, Syd," continued the captain, "your uncle has no son, and I have only one to keep up the honour of our family. You will join your ship with the best of prospects, and I hope you will be a credit to us both."

Sydney said nothing, but took another walnut, and cracked it viciously, as if it was the head of a savage enemy.

That night he lay tumbling and unable to sleep, his brow knit and his teeth set, feeling as obstinate as a boy can feel who has not been allowed to have his own way.

Chapter Two

The next morning Sydney Belton rose in excellent time, but not from a desire to keep good hours. He could not sleep well, so he dressed and went out, to find it was only on the stroke of six.

As he reached the garden, there was his self-constituted enemy stretching out before him, far as eye could reach, and sparkling gloriously in the morning sunshine.

"Bother the sea!" muttered the boy, scowling. "Wish it was all dry land."

"What cheer, lad! Mornin', mornin'. Don't she look lovely, eh?"

"Morning, Barney," said the boy, turning to see that the old boatswain had come to work with a scythe over his shoulder. "What looks lovely this morning?"

"Eh? Why, the sea, of course. Wish I was afloat, 'stead of having to shave this lawn, like a wholesale barber. Got any noos?"

"Yes, Barney," said the boy, bitterly; "I'm to go to sea."

"Hurray!" cried the old boatswain, rubbing his scythe-blade with the stone rubber, and bringing forth a musical sound.

"You're glad of it, then?"

"Course I am, my lad. Be the making on you. Wish I was coming too."

"Bah!" ejaculated Sydney, and he left the old boatswain to commence the toilet of the dewy lawn, while in a desultory way, for the sake of doing something to fill up the time till breakfast, he strolled round to the back, where a loud whistling attracted his attention.

The sound came from an outhouse, toward which the boy directed his steps.

"Cleaning the knives, I suppose," said Sydney to himself, and going to the door he looked in.

The tray of knives was there waiting to be cleaned, and the board and bath-brick were on a bench, but the red-faced boy was otherwise engaged.

He was kneeling down with a rough, curly-haired retriever dog sitting up before him, with paws drooped and nose rigid, while Pan was carefully balancing a knife across the pointed nose aforesaid.

Pan was so busily employed that he did not hear the step, and the first notification he had of another's presence was given by the dog, who raised his muzzle suddenly and uttered a loud and piteous whine directed at Sydney—the dog's cry seeming to say, "Do make him leave off."

The glance the boatswain's son gave made him spring at the board, snatch up a couple of the implements, and begin to rub them to and fro furiously, while the dog, in high glee at being freed from an arduous task, began to leap about, barking loudly, and making dashes at his young master's legs.

"Poor old Don—there!" cried Sydney, patting the dog's ears. "He don't like discipline, then. Well, Pan, when are you going to sea?"

"Not never," said the boy, shortly.

"Yes, you are. Your father said he should send you."

"If he does I shall run away, so there," cried the boy.

Sydney turned away, and walked through the garden, his head bent, his brow wrinkled, and his mind so busily occupied, that he hardly heeded which way he went.

"If his father sends him he shall run away."

Those words kept on repeating themselves in Sydney's brain like some jingle, and he found himself thinking of them more and more as he passed through the gate, and went along the road that late autumn morning, kicking up the dead leaves which lay clustering beneath the trees.

"If his father sends him to sea he shall run away," said Sydney to himself; and then he thought of how Pan Strake would be free, and have no more boots and shoes or knives to clean, and not have to go into the garden to weed the paths.

Then by a natural course he found himself thinking that if he, Sydney Belton, were to leave home, he would escape being sent to sea—at all events back to school—and he too would be free.

With a boy's wilful obstinacy, he carefully drew a veil over all the good, and dragged out into the mental light all that he looked upon as bad in his every-day life, satisfied himself that he was ill-used, and wished that he had had a mother living to, as he called it, take his part.

"I wonder what running away would be like?" he thought. "There would be no Uncle Tom to come and bully and bother me, and father wouldn't be there to take his side against me. I wonder what one could do if one ran away?"

"Morning!"

Sydney started, for he had been so intent upon his thoughts that he had not heard the regular trot, trot of a plump cob, nor the grinding of wheels, and he looked up to see that it was Doctor Liss who had suddenly drawn rein in the road.

"Going for a walk, Syd?"

"Yes; but—I—Where are you going, doctor?"

"Into the town. Just been called up. Poor fellow injured in the docks last night."

"Take me with you."

"What?" cried the doctor, smiling down in the eager face before him. "Didn't I get scolded enough last night, you young dog, for leading you astray?"

"Oh, but father didn't mean it. Do take me. Is he much hurt?"

"Broken leg, I hear. No, no. Go home to breakfast. Ck! Sally. Good morning."

The doctor touched the cob as he nodded to Sydney, and the wheels of the chaise began to turn, but with a bound the boy was out in the road, and hanging on to the back.

"No, no, Doctor Liss, don't leave me behind. I do so want to go, and there's plenty of time for me to get back to breakfast."

"But Sir Thomas will declare I am leading you into the evil paths of medicine and surgery."

"Uncle won't know. Do pull up; let me come."

"Well," said the doctor, smiling grimly, "I don't see that it can do you any harm, Syd. Here, jump in."

There was no need for a second consent. Almost before the horse could be stopped the boy had leaped lightly in, and with his face bright and eager once more, and the dark misty notions upon which he had been brooding gone clean away, he began chatting merrily to his old friend, whose rounds he had often gone.

"Yes, yes, Syd, that's all very well," said the doctor, making his whip-lash whistle through the air, "but you don't know what a doctor's life is. All very well driving here on a bright autumn morning to get an appetite for breakfast, but look at the long dark dismal rides I have at all times in the winter."

"Well, they can't be half so bad as keeping a watch in a storm right out at sea. Why, I've heard both father and Uncle Tom say that it's awful sometimes."

"Only sometimes, Syd."

"Well, I can't help it. I hate it, and I won't go."

"Must, my boy, must. Take it like a dose of my very particular. You know, Syd," said the doctor, nudging the boy with his elbow; "that rich thick morning draught I gave you after a fever."

"Oh, I say, don't," cried Sydney, with a wry face and a shudder; "it's horrid. I declare, when I'm a doctor, I'll never give any one such stuff."

"No, Syd, you'll be a captain, and the physic for your patients will be cat-o'-nine-tails."

Sydney frowned, and as they neared the busy town, with its little forest of masts rising beyond the houses, Doctor Liss glanced sideways at the boy's gloomy and thoughtful countenance.

"Why, Syd," he said at last merrily, "you look as gloomy as if you had been pressed. Come, my lad, take your medicine, and then you can have that sweet afterwards that we call duty."

Sydney made no reply, but his face did not brighten, for duty seemed to him then a nauseous bitter.

"Doctor Liss," he said, just as they reached the docks, down one of whose side lanes the patient lay, "if I make up my mind to be a doctor—"

"You can't, Syd. You are too young to have one yet. A man's mind is as strong as if it had bone and muscle. Yours is only like jelly."

Syd was silent again for a minute. Then he began once more—

"If I determined to be a doctor, and wouldn't be anything else, would you teach me?"

"No, certainly not."

"Then I'd teach myself," cried Syd, fiercely.

"Oh, indeed! Humph! I retract my words about your young mind being jelly. I see there is some substance in it growing already. But no, Syd, you are not going to be a doctor; and here we are."

He drew up at a cottage door, where a couple of rough-looking men were waiting about, one of whom held the horse while the doctor descended, and Syd followed into the room, where a poor fellow lay in great agony with a badly fractured leg.

This was reduced, Syd looking on, and handing the doctor splints and bandages as they were required. After this the pair re-entered the gig, and drove back toward the Heronry.

"Just a quarter to nine, Syd. You'll be back in time for breakfast."

"I think I could set a broken leg now," said Syd, whose thoughts were still at the cottage.

"Bless the boy!" exclaimed the doctor. "Take one off, I suppose, if it were wanted?"

"No," said Syd, gravely, "I shouldn't feel enough confidence to do that."

"I should think not, indeed," muttered the doctor, as he gave a sidelong look at his companion. "Why, you morbid young rascal, you ought to be thinking of games and outdoor sports instead of such things as this. Here we are. Ready for your breakfast?"

"Yes, I am getting hungry," said Syd. "How long will those bones be growing together again?"

"Confound you—young dog! Go and pick grilled chicken bones. I'll never take you out with me again. Jump out. Good-bye, sailor."

The doctor nodded and drove off, while Syd walked slowly up to the house, and entered the dining-room just as his father and uncle came down, punctual to the moment.

"Ah, Syd," said his father; "you are first."

"Morning, boy, morning," cried his uncle. "Been for a walk on deck?"

"No, uncle; I've been for a drive."

"Drive! Drive!" said his father. "Who with?"

"Doctor Liss, father."

Bang!

Sir Thomas's hand made the coffee-cups rattle this time, as he said sharply—

"Harry, my lad, if I were you I should take this spark up to town and see Dashleigh at once. I'll go with you."

"Very well. And he can be measured for his kit at the same time, eh?"

"Of course. Mind the tailor makes his clothes big enough, for as soon as he gets to sea he'll grow like a twig."

Syd sat stirring his coffee, and taking great bites out of his bread and butter, as the words of Pan came back to him—"If he does I shall run away, so there!"

Chapter Three

There was something tempting about that idea of being measured for a uniform, though Syd declared to himself he hated it. All the same, though, he went down the garden to where Barney was digging that morning, and after a little beating about the bush, asked him a question he could have answered himself, from familiarity with his father's and uncle's garb.

"I say, Barney, what's a captain's uniform like?"

"Uniform, my lad?" said the old boatswain, seizing the opportunity to rest his foot on his spade, and began rubbing the small of his back, or rather what is so called, for Barney had no small to his back, being square-shaped like a short log. "Well, it's bloo coat, and white weskutt and breeches, and gold lace and cocked hat, and two gold swabs on the shoulders."

"And what's a lieutenant's like?"

"Oh, pooty much the same, lad, only he's on'y got one swab on 'stead o' two. But what's the good o' your asking?—you've seen 'em often enough in Southbayton."

"Oh, but I never took any notice. What's a midshipman's like?"

"Bloo, my lad, and a bit o' white on the collar."

"And a cocked hat?"

"Oh yes, a cocked hat—a small one, you know."

"And a sword, Barney?"

"Well, as to a sword, lad," said the old sailor, wiping a brown corner of his mouth; "it arn't right to call such a tooth-pick of a thing a sword. Sort of a young sword as you may say, on'y it never grows no bigger, and him as wears it does. Dirks, they calls 'em, middies' dirks."

"A uniform and a sword," said Sydney to himself. "A blue uniform with white on the collar, and a cocked hat and a sword!"

It was very tempting, and the boy went on down by the side of the lake, beyond which were the great trees, with the ragged nests of the tall birds which gave the name to the captain's residence, where he had settled to end his days well in view of the sea.

Here where the water was smooth as glass Sydney stood leaning over, holding on by a bough, and gazing at his foreshortened image, as in imagination he dressed himself in the blue uniform, buckled on his dirk, and put on his cocked hat.

It was very tempting, but disinclination mastered vanity, and he turned away to go back toward the house.

"I wonder whether Pan means it," he said to himself. "Suppose we went together to seek our fortunes; he could be my servant, and father and Uncle Tom would forgive me if I came back rich."

But somehow in a misty way as he walked up to the back of the house, half thinking that he would sound the boy, it hardly seemed to be the way to seek a fortune to start off with a servant.

He had nearly reached the yard when a door was thrown open, and the object of his search rushed out, followed by a shower of words and shoes, which latter came pattering out into the yard as a shrill voice cried—

"A nasty, lazy, good-for-nothing young scamp—always playing with that dog instead of doing your work. Not half clean—not fit to be seen."

Syd drew back, thinking to himself that Pan could not be much happier than he was himself with the red-faced cook, who ruled over all the servants, to play tyrant to the boy as well.

"Now what could two lads do if they went right away?" mused Syd. "We couldn't go abroad without going to sea. I don't think I want to be a soldier, and we're not big enough if I did. I know—we'd go to London. People seek their fortunes there."

He seated himself beneath the walnut tree to think it out, but somehow the idea of running away did not seem bright. It was less than a hundred miles to London by the coach-road, and if they walked all the way it did not seem likely that they would have any adventures.

Syd felt in despair, for life seemed as if it must be a terribly dull place without adventures.

He thought he would not run away for two reasons. One that it would look cowardly; the other that it did not look tempting.

"There does not seem any chance of meeting with adventures unless you go to sea," he said to himself. "I wish there was no sea in the world."

A loud voice from the other end of the garden, followed by another, took his attention.

"Poor old Pan catching it again," mused Syd. "Everybody seems to scold him."

The dull sound of a blow, a howl, and then a rushing noise explained by the appearance of Panama Strake, who was dashing helter-skelter across the garden, as regardless of flower-bed and tree as a young colt that had broken through a hedge.

"Hi! Pan, where are you going?" cried Syd.

The boy glanced once in his direction, but did not stop running on as hard as he could go for the front entrance, and directly after the gate was heard to bang.

"Some one must have hit him," thought Syd. "Poor old Pan, he's always in trouble. Why, I kicked him last week," he added remorsefully.

"Seen my boy Pan, Master Syd?" said a hoarse voice.

"Yes; he came running by here like a wild bull. Have you been hitting him?"

"Hitting of him?" growled the ex-boatswain; "on'y just wish I'd had a rope's-end 'stead o' this here," and he held up the handle of the rake he had been using. "On'y time to give him one tap and he was gone."

"Enough to make him go. What was the matter, Barney?"

"Heverythink, Master Syd. That there boy's gettin' worse than you."

"Oh! is he?"

"Growlin' and grumblin' at any mortal thing. Won't do his work, and says he won't go to sea, just the same as you do; and now he's been sarcing the cook."

"For saying the boots and shoes were not clean."

"How do you know, Master Syd?"

"I saw her throwing them at him. You'd no business to hit him with that rake shaft."

"What! No business to hit him? Why, he's my own boy, arn't he? All right then, Master Syd; there's an old wagon rope in the shed, I'll lay up a bit o' that—hard; and on'y just wait till he comes back, that's all. Won't be a sailor, won't he! I'll let him see. If he won't be able to write AB at the end of his name 'fore he's one-and-twenty my name arn't Barnaby Strake."

The old boatswain went off growling; and in the lowest of low spirits, Syd went indoors, to make his way to the library, shut himself in, and begin taking down the books from the dusty shelves, seeking for one which dealt with adventures.

There was no lack of them, but somehow or another all seemed to have the smack of the salt sea. Now and then he came upon some land adventures, but it was always preceded by a voyage to the place; and at last he threw a book down peevishly.

"Any one would think the world was all sea," he grumbled; "that's the worst of being born on an island."

He started from his seat, for the handle of the door rattled, and his father and uncle entered the library.

"Oh, you're here, sir!" cried Captain Belton. "That's right. Your uncle and I have been talking about you."

"Laying down your lines, Syd, so as to turn you out a smart craft."

"Yes," said Captain Belton, merrily. "We've settled about your hull, Syd; and to-morrow morning we're going to take you up to town, and if all turns out right—"

"Oh, that's all right," said Sir Thomas. "Dashleigh would do anything for me."

"If his complement is not made up."

"And if it is. Hang it, Harry; you can always squeeze another boy into a seventy-gun ship."

"Well, I suppose it will be all right," said the captain; "and if it is we'll get you rigged."

"Yes, and if you'll be a good lad, and try and learn your profession, I'll make you a present of your outfit, Syd. The best that can be had," said Sir Thomas.

"And I'd give you a gold watch," said the captain, "only you'd lose it, or get it stolen or broken before you had been to sea a month. There, my boy, no objections. It's all settled for you, and we want to see you a post-captain before we go into the locker."

"Yes, and bring in a few good Spanish prizes, sir. It'll be all right, brother Harry. He thinks he don't like the sea, but he does. Now then, you dog, why don't you come and shake hands?"

"Because I don't want to go, uncle."

"What, you dog! Yah! Get out. I don't believe it."

"Go and shake hands with your uncle, Syd," said the captain, sternly.

The boy walked across to where the admiral was seated on the arm of one of the great easy-chairs, and held out his hand.

"Here, what's this?" cried the bluff, choleric old sailor. "Not a boy's hand, is it. Feels like the tail of a codfish. Shake hands like a man, you dog. Ah, that's better. There, cheer up; you'll soon get used to the sea and love it. You won't be happy ashore after your first voyage."

"Want any money, Syd?" said the captain.

"No, thankye, father," said the boy, gloomily.

"What!" roared the admiral, laboriously thrusting his hand into his breeches pocket and dragging it out again. "Don't believe it. A boy who don't want money is a monster, not fit to be trusted with it. Here you are, boy. Five guineas. Don't fool it away, but buy anything with it you like." — A strange contradiction, by the way, though the old admiral did not notice it. — "Put it in your pocket, and — Pst! Syd," he whispered, "whenever you want any more, write to me. Don't bother the dad. Our secret, eh, you dog?"

"What's that?" cried the captain.

"Mind your own business, sir," cried the admiral, with mock rage. "Private instructions to our young officer. There, be off, Syd, before he begins to pump."

The boy gladly escaped from the library, to dash up into his own room, and fling the money into a corner with a demonstration of rage, before sitting down, resting his chin upon his doubled fists, and staring straight before him.

"It's all over," he said at last. "I wanted to be a gentleman, and do what was right; but — Yes, it's all over now."

Just at the same time Captain Belton was speaking to his brother in the library.

"I'm sorry the boy took it like that, Tom," he said. "I don't like his sulky manner."

"Bah! only a boy," cried the admiral. "Chuffy because he can't have his own way. Wait till he gets his cocked hat and his dirk."

The old man chuckled and wiped his eyes.

"I haven't forgotten the sensation yet, Harry. You remember too?"

"Oh yes, I remember," said the captain, thoughtfully.

"Of course you do. I say, what a pair of young gamecocks we were. Why, I can remember now flourishing the tooth-pick about, with its blade half blue steel and a lion's head on the hilt. Never you mind about Syd; the uniform will set him right."

"I hope so."

"Hope so. Don't I tell you it will! I like the boy; plenty of downright British courage in him. Isn't afraid of either of us. Egad, I like him, Harry; and he'll turn out a big man."

Chapter Four

The rest of that day passed gloomily for Sydney, who was in the garden just before dinner, when Barney came up to him.

"Seen him, Master Sydney?" he said gloomily.

"Seen who? My father?"

"No, my boy, Panama. Strikes me he's cut and run, and when the skipper hears on it there'll be no end of a row."

"Oh, nonsense! He's hiding in the lofts, or one of the outhouses, Barney."

"No, my lad, I've hunted 'em all over with a hay-fork."

"And of course you didn't find him. If he saw you coming with a two-pronged fork what would he think?"

"But I wasn't going to job on him with it, Master Syd."

"How was he to know that, Barney?"

"'Cause I'm allus such a good father to him."

"And hit him with the rake-handle only this morning."

"Well, that would only loosen his skin a bit, and give him room to grow. Do him good."

"Don't see it, Barney. Wouldn't do me any good, only make me wild."

"But you don't think he's cut and run, do you, lad?"

"I dare say he has, but he'll soon come back."

"Only let me get hold of him then."

"If you touch him when he does, I'll tell my father and Sir Thomas you ill-use him."

"What a shame! Master Syd, you shouldn't. But you do think he'll come back, sir?"

"Why, of course."

"That's right. I want him to go along o' you."

"Along with me?"

"Of course. I heared the skipper was going to take you up to town to-morrow to see your new captain."

"Oh!" ejaculated Syd; and he turned sharp round and ran into the house, where he was soon after seated at table with his uncle and father, feeling that the servants were watching him, and expecting every moment to hear some allusion to the next day's journey.

But though no word of the kind was said, Syd cracked no walnuts that night, but sat gloomily over the dessert till his uncle filled his glass, called upon him to pass the port to his father, and then in a loud voice said—

"Here's health and success to Sydney Belton—middy, master's mate, lieutenant, commander, post—captain, admiral."

"Hear! hear!" cried Captain Belton; and Sydney sat feeling more guilty than ever he had felt in his life.

For his brain was full of thoughts that he dared not have laid bare, and his inclination was trying to drag down the balance in which he felt that he hung.

As he sat there holding on tightly by the nut-crackers that he had not used, he felt as if he should have to answer all manner of questions directly, and be put through a terrible ordeal; but to his intense relief, the conversation turned upon an expedition to Portobello, and the way in which certain ships had been handled, the unfortunate officers in command not having done their duty to the satisfaction of the admiral. And as this argument seemed to grow more exciting the boy softly slipped from his chair and went out again to his place of meditation—the garden.

"Shall I—shan't I?" he said to himself. Should he make a bold dash, and go off like heroes he had read of before, seeking his fortune anywhere?

He was quite ready to do this, but in a misty way it seemed to him that there would be no fortune to be found; and in addition, it would be going in direct opposition to his father's and uncle's wishes, and they would never forgive him.

"No," he said, as he walked up and down the broad walk nearest the road, "I must give up and go to sea."

But even as he said this softly, he felt so much on the balance, that he knew that a very little would send him away.

That very little came unexpectedly, for as he walked on down the garden in the darkness, where the short sturdy oak-trees sent their branches over the path on one side, and overhung the road on the other, a voice whispered his name—

"Master Syd!"

"Yes. What is it?"

"Hush! Don't make such a row, or they'll hear you."

"Who is it—Pan?"

"Yes, Master Syd."

"Where are you?"

"Sittin' straddlin' on this here big bough."

"You've come back then, sir. Your father thought you had run away," said Syd sternly.

"So I have; and I arn't come back, on'y to see you, Master Syd."

"Come down, then. What are you doing up that tree?"

"On'y waiting to talk to you."

"But your father says he is going to rope's-end you for running away."

"No, he isn't going to, because I shan't come back."

"But you are back."

"Oh no, I arn't, Master Syd. I'm not going to be knocked about with rake-handles, and then sent off to sea. How would you like it?"

"I'm not knocked about, Pan; but I'm going to be sent off to sea."

"Then don't go, Master Syd."

There was no answer for the moment; then the latter looked up in among the dark branches, where the dying leaves still clung.

"You said you had come back to see me, Pan."

"Yes, Master Syd."

"What for? Because you repented?"

"No; it was to ask you—"

"What for? Some money, Pan?"

"No, Master Syd," replied the boy in a hesitating way. "Hist! Listen! Some one coming?"

"No; I can't hear any one. Why did you come back?"

"You don't want to go to sea, Master Syd, do you?"

"No."

"More don't I, and I won't go."

"Well?"

"I'm going right away, Master Syd, to make a fortune. Come along o' me."

"What!" said Syd, who felt startled at the suddenness of the proposition, one which accorded so well with his own wishes. "Go with you?"

"Oh, I don't mean as mates, only go together," whispered Pan. "You'd always be master, and I'd always clean your knives and boots for you."

"And what should we do, Pan? Where could we go so as to make a living?"

"Make a living?" said Pan, in a wondering tone. "Don't want to make a living—we want to make a fortune."

"But we must have some money."

"I've got two shillings saved up."

Syd's brow puckered. He knew a little more about the necessities of life, and did not feel disposed to set sail on the river of life with no more than two shillings.

"But you've got some money, Master Syd?"

"Yes; eight or nine shillings, and a crown uncle gave me day before yesterday."

"Come along then, that's enough."

Syd hesitated, and thought of the five guineas thrown down in his room.

"If you don't come they'll send you to sea."

That settled it. So evenly was the lad balanced, that a feather-weight was enough to work a change. His dread of the sea sent the scale down heavily.

"Wait here," he said.

"What for?"

"Till I've been and tied up some clean clothes to take with me."

"Never mind your clothes," whispered Pan. "If your father catches you there'll be no chance."

"Look here," said Syd sharply, "if I'm going with you, Pan Strake, I shall do as I like. I'm not going to be ordered about by you."

"No, Master Syd, I won't say nothing no more."

Sydney stood thinking for a moment or two, not hesitating, for his mind seemed quite made up. Then without another word he stepped on to the grass, and ran up the garden, keeping out of sight of the occupants of the dining-room, by interposing the bushes between him and them.

His heart began to beat heavily now, as the full force of that which he was about to do impressed him on hearing his father's voice speaking loudly; and as he crept nearer the window, so as to pass it, behind the bushes, and reach the entrance, he heard the captain say plainly, his words sounding loudly from the open dining-room window—

"Yes, Tom, I've quite made up my mind. It will be the best thing for him. It will be a better school than the one he is at. Time he began to learn the profession, eh?"

"Yes, quite; and good luck to him," said his uncle, gruffly.

Syd stopped to hear no more, but hurried to the front, waited till all was silent in the pantry, and then slipped up to his bedroom, where a few minutes sufficed for him to make up a change of clothes in a handkerchief.

That was all he wanted, he told himself. No: a brush and comb.

"Comb will do," he muttered; "people going to seek their fortunes don't want brushes."

He ran his hand in the darkness along the dressing-table, and touched not a comb, but a tiny pile of money.

Five shillings! And on his dressing-table! How did they come there?

He knew the next moment they were not shillings but guineas, the five he passionately threw down in a corner of the room, and when the maid came up to straighten the place she must have found them and placed them on the table. It was tempting.

Syd was going away out into the wide world with only a few shillings in his pocket, and these guineas, which were honestly his, would be invaluable, and help him perhaps out of many a scrape. Should he take them or no?

Syd pushed them away from him. They were given to him because his uncle believed that he was going patiently with him to see his friend in London. If he took them it would seem despicable, and he could not bear that; so hurrying out of the room, he ran down-stairs lightly and as quickly as possible, so as to get away and beyond the power of the house, which seemed to be all at once growing dear to him, and acting like a magnet to draw him back.

As he cleared the door and made for the shrubs, he heard his uncle's voice as he laughed at something the captain said. Then Captain Belton spoke again, and Syd clapped his hand and his bundle to his ears to stop the sound.

"If I listen I shan't be able to go," he said with a sigh; and he was just about to break into a trot to run down and join Pan, when there was a footstep on the gravel, and the boy stopped short in the shadow cast by a tree.

"Father!" he said to himself. "Can he have found out so soon?"

The step on the gravel came nearer, and Syd knew that it must have passed right under the tree where Pan was hiding.

"Could father have gone down there so quickly?" thought the boy.

Then all doubt was at an end, for he whose steps were heard stopped close at hand, muttering aloud—

"Swears he ketched sight on him in the road to-night, so he must have come home. If I on'y do get howd on him by the scruff of his precious neck, I'll teach him to run away."

A cold chill ran through Sydney, and he shivered. Suppose his father knew that he was going to do this mean, contemptible thing—run away and degrade himself—what would he say? and how would he act? Like Barnaby spoke, his old boatswain and gardener?

Syd shivered again. He was not afraid of the pain, but he shrank from the idea of the degradation. He fancied himself held by the collar and a stick raised to punish him. It was horrible.

"If I don't loosen his hide my name arn't what it is," growled the old boatswain; and he moved on, going close by Sydney, who stood listening with heavily beating heart till Barney had gone right up to the back of the house.

Then only did Sydney run on till he was beneath the tree, and called Pan.

"You there?"

"Yes, Master Syd."

"Did you hear who that was down the garden?"

"Father."

"Did you hear what he said?"

There was a low laugh up in the tree.

"Yes, I heared; but he has got to ketch me first. Ready?"

"Yes, I'm ready, Pan."

"Get up here then."

"Why?"

"You can get out along one of these big branches, and drop out into the road."

"No, no, come down, and let's go by the gate."

"And come upon my father waiting with a rope's-end? Why, when he's wild he lets out anyhow, and in the dark you'd get it as much as me. This way."

Syd listened, and heard the boy creep actively along the bough and drop down on the other side of the fence.

"Catch," he whispered. "Ready?"

"Yes."

He threw over his bundle, and then swung himself up into the tree, got astride the big bough, and was working himself along, when a sound close at hand made him stop short to listen.

It was intensely dark where he sat beneath the thickly-leaved tree, and all was quite still. But he felt sure that he had heard some one approaching, and just as he had made up his mind to get further along, Pan's voice reached him from the other side of the paling—

"Come on."

Hoping that he might have been mistaken, Syd changed his position, so that he hung over the bough, and had just begun to edge along, when there was a quick rustling behind him, and the breaking down of shrubs, as if a man was forcing himself through, and the next minute he felt one of his legs seized.

"My father!" thought Syd, and a cold chill of dread, shame, and misery ran through him as he lay across the bough, silent and motionless, but clinging to it with all his might.

"Got ye, have I, Pan-y-mar?" growled a husky voice. "Now then, let go, and come and take it in your room, or I'll lay on here."

The first sound of that voice sent a warm glow through Syd, and thawed his frozen faculties.

Exulting in the idea that it was only the old boatswain, he drew himself all together as he held on with his arms to the bough, and then he kicked out with all his might; the attack being so unexpected, that as Barney received both feet in his chest, he loosened his hold, grasped wildly at the air to save himself, and then came down in a sitting position with sufficient force to evoke a groan; while by the time he had recovered himself sufficiently to rise and get to the fence, he could hear the rapid beat of steps in the distance.

"Why, there must be some one with him," growled Barney. "All right, my boy, on'y wait a bit. You'll come crawling round the cottage 'fore you're many hours older, and I'll lay that there rope's-end in the tub. It'll make it lie closer and heavier round your back. Oh!"

He had taken a step to go back out of the shrubbery to the path, when an acute pain ran up his spine, and made him limp along to the gardener's cottage at the bottom of the grounds, grumbling to himself, and realising that men of sixty can't fall so lightly as those who are forty years younger.

"But never mind, I'll make him pay for the lot. He shan't play tricks with me. Lor', I wish I was going to sea again, and had that boy under me; I'd make him—Oh, murder! he's a'most broke my back."

Chapter Five

As Syd kicked himself free of Barney's grasp he heard the heavy fall, but he stopped for no more. A couple of vigorous sidewise movements took him clear of the fence, a couple more beyond the ditch, and before Barney had begun to think of getting up Syd had whispered to his companion the magic words—

"Your father!"

The next minute, hand in hand, and keeping step, the two boys were running hard along the road leading away into the country, thinking of only one thing, and that—how great a distance they could put between them and the Heronry.

Fear lent them wings, for in imagination they saw the old boatswain running off to the house, spreading the alarm, and Captain Belton ordering the servants out in pursuit, determined to hunt them down and bring them back to punishment.

Their swift run, in spite of their will, soon settled down into a steady trot, and at the end of a couple of miles this had become a sharp walk. Every hair was wet with perspiration, and as they stopped from time to time to listen, their hearts beat heavily, and their breath came in a laboured way.

"Hear anything?" said Sydney at last.

"No; they've given it up," replied Pan. "Father can't run far now."

"Think they'll get out the horses, Pan?"

"Dunno. If they do we shall hear 'em plain enough, and we can take to the woods. They'll never ketch us now. Arn't you glad you've come?"

Sydney did not answer, for if he had replied he would have told the truth, and he did not wish to tell the truth then, because it would have been humiliating.

For there they were tramping along the dark road going west, with the stars shining down brightly, and, save the distant barking of a dog, all most mournfully still.

Pan made another attempt at conversation.

"Won't my father be wild because he arn't got me to hit?"

Syd was too deep in his own thoughts to reply, for he was picturing the library at the Heronry, and his father and uncle talking together after returning from a vain pursuit. He could picture their florid faces and shining silvery hair by the light of the wax candles. He even seemed to see how many broad wrinkles there were in his father's forehead as he stood frowning; and then something seemed to be asking the boy what he was doing there.

"Getting tired, Master Syd?" said Pan, after a long pause, filled by the *beat beat* of their footsteps.

But still there was no answer. The latter question took too much study, and suggested other questions in its unanswerable-ness.

Where was he going? and why was he going? and why had he chosen this road, which led toward the great forest with its endless trees and bogs?

Sydney could not answer these questions, and by way of relieving the buzzing worry in his own brain, he turned to Pan and became a questioner.

"Where are we going to sleep to-night?"

"Eh?"

"Where are we going to sleep to-night?"

Pan took off his hat and scratched his head.

"I never thought of that," he said.

"We can't go on walking all night."

"Can't we?"

"Of course we can't. We shall have to knock at some cottage, and ask them to give us a bed."

"But they won't," said Pan, sagely enough. "'Tarn't likely at this time o' night; I wish we could find a haystack."

Pan's wish did not obtain fulfilment, and the two lads tramped on along the lonely road for quite a couple of hours longer, when hunger began to combine with weariness; and these two at last made themselves so plainly heard, that Sydney came to a full stop.

"Yes?" said Pan.

"I did not speak, I was only thinking," said Sydney, drearily.

"What were you thinking, Master Syd?"

"That all this is very stupid, and that we should be ever so much more comfortable in bed."

Pan sighed.

"Oh, I dunno," he said. "I shouldn't, on'y my legs ache ever so."

"We ought to have brought a lot of cold meat and bread with us, Pan."

"Ah! wouldn't it be good now!"

"How long do you think it will be before morning, so that we can get to a town, and buy some bread and milk?"

"I dunno, Master Syd. It can't be late yet, and it's ever so far to a town this way, 'cause it's all forest for miles and miles."

They were tramping on again now, but in a more irregular way. There was none of the vigorous pace for pace that had marked the beginning of their flight, and as the road grew more rough their steps began to err, and sometimes one, sometimes the other was a little in advance.

"Don't you wish you were back in your bed, Pan?" said Sydney at last.

"No."

"Why not?"

"Because father would be standing there with the rope's-end."

This was so much to the point that Sydney did not try to pursue that vein of conversation, and they again travelled on in silence till Pan spoke—

"Wish you were back in your bed, Master Syd?"

"No," said the latter sharply.

"Course you don't; 'cause your uncle would be one side o' the bed and the captain the other, and that would be worse than being here, wouldn't it?"

No answer.

"You'd ketch it, wouldn't you, Master Syd?"

Still no answer; and Pan plodded on in silence, wondering whether his young master would always be so quiet and strange.

"What's that?" said Sydney suddenly.

"Rabbud."

The two lads stood listening to the rapid run of feet through the rustling fern, and then tramped on again through the darkness.

Sydney was having a hard fight the greater part of the time with his thoughts, and try how he would, they seemed to be too much for him. In fact, so great a hold did they get at last, that somewhere about three o'clock he stopped short; but Pan went on with his head down till his name was sharply pronounced, when he stopped short with a start.

"Why, I believe you were asleep."

"Was I, Master Syd?" said the boy, blankly looking about him. "I s'pose 'twas because I thought father was making me walk round and round the garden all night for not cleaning the boots."

"Turn round—this way."

"Yes, Master Syd. Where are we going now?"

"Back again."

"Back—again?"

"Yes, to the Heronry."

"What for, sir?"

"Because I've been an idiot."

"But if we go back we shall be punished, Master Syd."

"Of course we shall. But if we go on we shall be punishing ourselves. Oh," cried Sydney, in a voice full of rage against himself, "how could I have been such a donkey!"

"It warn't my fault," said Pan, dolefully. "Father was after me with the rope's-end. I was obliged to go. Let's try another way, Master Syd."

"There is no other way," cried the boy passionately. "There's only one way for us to go, and that's straight back home."

"Oh, there's lots of other ways, Master Syd."

"No, there are not. There's only one that we can tread."

"Which way's that, sir?"

"I told you—home."

"But I dursen't go back, Master Syd; I dursen't, indeed."

"Yes, you dare; and you shall too."

"Well, not till it's light, Master Syd. It do hurt so in the dark, and you have no chance."

But Syd did not answer, only gave an involuntary shiver, and walked slowly back over the ground they had covered during the night.

Chapter Six

A long tramp in silence; but they did not get over the ground very rapidly, for Pan's pace grew slower and slower, and when urged by Sydney to keep up he made no reply.

"Come along," said Syd at last; "do try and make haste."

"I arn't in a hurry," came in a surly growl.

"But I am. I want to get back before it's light; we don't want to be seen."

"Don't matter whether we're seen or whether we arn't; they'll be awaitin' for us."

"Can't help it, Pan," said Syd with a sigh; "we've got to go through it."

"I hope, Master Syd, you won't get no rope's-end."

"I'd take yours for you if I could, Pan."

"Ah, you say so," sneered the lad, as he dragged one foot after the other, "but you know you can't."

"I know I would," cried Syd, hotly. "But it's of no use to talk. We've got to go through it like men would."

"Men don't have no rope's-ending," grumbled Pan.

They went on back for another half-mile, with the stars shining brightly, and seeming to wink derisively at them; and just as Sydney had fancied this, as he gazed up at the broad band of glittering light seen through the dense growth of trees which shut them in on either side, a loud, ringing, mocking laugh smote their ears, that sounded so strange and jeering, that the boys stopped short.

"What's that?" whispered Syd.

"Only a howl. Why, you've heard 'em lots of times."

"But it never sounded like that before."

"You never heard it out in the woods before. There she goes again."

The shout rang out again, but more distant. "Hoi, hoi, hoi, hoi!" sounding now more like a hail.

"Oh, yes, it is an owl," said Sydney, breathing more freely. "Come along."

Pan did not move, but stood with his hands in his pockets, and his shoulders up to his ears.

"Do you hear? Come along, and let's get it over."

No answer—no movement.

"Don't be stupid, Pan. I know you're tired, but you are no more tired than I am."

"Yes, I am—ever so much."

"You're not. You're pretending, because you don't want to come back. Now then, no nonsense."

Pan stood like a stork, with his chin down upon his chest.

"Will—you—come—on?"

It was very dark, but Sydney could just make out that the boy shook his head.

"Then it isn't because you are so tired. It's obstinacy."

No response.

"I declare you're as obstinate as an old donkey; and if you don't come on I'll serve you the same."

Pan did not stir.

"Do you want me to cut a stick, and make you come, Pan?"

Still no reply; and weary, hungry, and disgusted with himself as well as his companion, Sydney felt in that state of irritable rawness which can best be described as having the skin off his temper. He was just in the humour to quarrel; and now, stirred beyond bearing by his companion's obstinacy, Syd flew at him, grasped his arm, gave it a tug which snatched it from the pocket, and roared out—

"Come on!"

Then he retreated a step, for, to his intense surprise, there came from the lad, who had always been obedient and respectful, a short, snappish "Shan't!" which was more like the bark of a dog than the utterance of a boy.

"What!" cried Sydney, as he recovered from his surprise, and felt the blood flush in his face.

"Says I shan't. I arn't coming home to be larruped."

"You are not coming home?"

"No, I arn't. He's waitin' for me with a big rope's-end all soaked hard, and I know what that means, so I shan't come."

Sydney drew a long breath as he reviewed their position, and told himself that it was more his fault than that of the gardener's boy that they were there.

"I know better than he does, and ought to have stopped him instead of going with him, and he shall come back, because it's right."

"Now then, Pan," he said aloud, "I am going back home."

"All right, Master Syd, go home then; but I didn't think you was such a coward."

"It isn't being a coward to go back, Pan; it's being a coward to run away."

"No, it arn't."

"Yes, it is, so come along."

"I shan't."

"Yes, you will, sir; I order you to come home with me at once."

"Shan't come to be rope's-ended, I tell you. I'm going away by myself if you won't come."

"You are coming home with me, and we're going to ask them to forgive us for being so stupid. Now then; will you come?"

"No."

"Do you want me to make you?"

"I don't want no more to do with you; you're a coward."

Sydney made a dart to seize his arm, but Pan dodged, and there was no sign of weariness now, for he bounded aside, and then set off running fast in the opposite direction to that in which his companion wished him to go.

Pan placed half a dozen good yards between them before Sydney recovered from his surprise. Then without hesitation the pursuit began, both lads striving their utmost to escape and capture, and at the end of a couple of hundred yards Syd had done so well that with a final bound he flung himself upon his quarry, and grasped at his collar.

The result was not anticipated. Sydney missed the collar, but the impetus he gave to the boy he pursued was sufficient to send him sprawling in the dirty road; and unable to check himself, Sydney came down heavily on Pan's back.

"Now then, will you come home?" panted Sydney.

"Oh! Ah!"

Two loud yells as Pan wrested himself over, strove to get up, was resisted, and then for five minutes there was a fierce wrestling bout, now down, now up, in which Sydney found himself getting the worst of it; and feeling that in another minute Pan would get free and escape, he changed his mode of attack, striking his adversary a heavy blow in the face, with the natural result that the wrestling bout became a fight.

Here Sydney soon showed his superiority, easily avoiding Pan's ugly rushes, and dealing such a shower of blows upon the lad's head that before many minutes had elapsed Pan was seated in one of the wettest parts of the road, whimpering and howling, while Sydney stood over him with fists clenched.

"You're a coward, that's what you are," howled Pan.

"Get up then, and I'll show you I'm not. Do you hear?"

"How–ow!"

"Don't howl like a dog. Get up, sir, and take your beating like a man," said Syd.

"I didn't think it of you, Master Syd," whimpered Pan.

"Now will you get up and walk home?"

For answer the boy got up slowly and laboriously, went on a few yards in front, and Sydney followed, feeling, as he thought, as if he was driving a donkey home.

For about a mile Pan walked steadily on, with Sydney feeling better than he had since he left home, although his knuckles were bruised, and there was a dull aching sensation in one angle of his jaw. He had gained two victories, and in spite of his weariness something very near akin to satisfaction began to warm his heart, till all at once the figure of Pan began to be visible; and as at the end of another hundred yards or so they came out upon a patch of open forest land, the figure was much plainer. So was his own, as he looked down and saw in dismay that it would soon be broad daylight, that they were some miles from the Heronry, and that Pan was covered with mud, his face smeared with ruddy stains, and that he, Sydney Belton, known as "the young gentleman up at the house," was in very little better trim.

Chapter Seven

The day grew brighter; tiny flecks of orange and gold began to appear high up, then there was a warm glow in the east, with the birds chirping merrily in the woodlands, and then day began.

But as the morning brightened Syd's spirits grew cloudy, and as they reached another patch of wood through which ran a little stream, he stopped short, looking anxiously along the road in both directions.

"We can't go home like this, Pan," he said. "It would be horrid."

"Well, I don't want to go home, do I?" grumbled the boy, in an ill-used tone.

"We shall have to hide here in the wood till night, and we can dry and clean our muddy clothes and have a good wash before then."

"And what are we to get to eat?"

"Blackberries, and sloes, and nuts."

"Oh yes, and pretty stuff they are. One apple off the big old tree's worth all the lot here."

"Can't help it, Pan. We must do the best we can."

"Don't let's go back, Master Syd. You can't tell how rope's-end hurts. Alter your mind, and let's go and seek our fortunes somewhere."

"This way," said Syd, by way of answer; and pointing off the road, the two lads plunged farther and farther into the wood, keeping close to the little stream, which had cut its way deep down below the level; so that it was some time before they came to an open sandy spot, where, with the bright morning sun shining full upon them, they had a good refreshing wash; and soon after, as they sat in a sunny nook where the sand was deep and dry, first one and then the other nodded off to sleep.

It was late in the afternoon before Syd awoke, to look up anxiously about before the full force of his position dawned upon him; and feeling faint and more low-spirited than had ever been his lot before, he sat there thinking about what he had to go through.

As near as he could judge they were about five miles from the Heronry, and two hours before it grew dark would be ample time for their journey.

"I may as well let him sleep," said Syd. "He'll only want to go away, and we can't do that."

Then, in spite of his efforts to the contrary, his mind began to dwell upon home and the various meals. Just about dusk the dinner would be ready, and his father and uncle sitting down, while he—

"Oh, I do feel so hungry!" he muttered. "I'd give anything for some bread and cheese."

He went to the side of the little stream, lay down, and placing his lips to the clear cool water, drank heartily a draught that was refreshing, but did not allay his hunger; and after sitting down and thinking for a time, he put his hands in his pockets and felt his money. But it was of no use out there in the woods.

He sat thinking again, wishing now that they had gone on in spite of their condition, for then the trouble would have been over, and he would have had food, if it had only been bread and water.

"Oh dear! I can't bear this any longer!" he said, suddenly jumping up. "We must get something to eat if it's only nuts. Here, Pan, Pan!"

He touched the boy with his foot, but it had no effect; and bending down, he took one arm and shook it.

The effect was magical. Pan sat up, fending his face with his arm, and apostrophising some imaginary personage, as he fenced and complained.

"Oh, don't! I'll never do so no more. Oh, please! Oh, I say! It hurts!— You, Master Syd?"

"Yes; who did you think it was?"

"My father with the rope's-end and—oh, I say, I am so stiff and sore, and—have you got anything to eat?"

Sydney shook his head despondingly.

"I was waking you up to come and try and find some."

"There's lots o' rabbits about here," grumbled Pan, "if we could catch some."

"Yes, and hares too, Pan, if we had a good gun. Come along."

They rambled along by the stream, finding before long a blackthorn laden with sloes, of which Pan ate two, and Sydney contented himself with half of one. Then they were voted a failure, and the blackberries growing in a sunny, open spot were tried with no better result.

At the end of another quarter of an hour a clump of hazel stubs came in view—fine old nut-bearers, with thickly mossed stumps, among which grew clusters of light golden buff fungi looking like cups; but though these were good for food, in the eyes of the boys they were simply toadstools, and passed over for the sake of the fringed nuts which hung in twos and threes, even here and there in fours and fives.

It did not take long to get a capful of these, and they soon sat down to make their *al fresco* meal.

Another disappointment! The nuts, as they cracked them, were, with a few exceptions, full of a blackish dust, and the exceptions contained in addition a poor watery embryo of a nut that was not worth the cracking to obtain.

They gave up the food hunt in despair, for there was no cultivated land near, where a few turnips might have been obtained; and wandering slowly back they at last reached the road.

The search had not been, though, without result—it had taken time; and when they reached the solitary road the sun was so near setting, that after a final protest from Pan, Syd started at once for home and the scenes they had to face.

The route they had chosen for their flight was the most solitary leading from Southbayton. It was but little used, leading as it did right out into the forest, and in consequence they had it almost to themselves while the light lasted, and after dark they did not pass a soul as they made their way to the Heronry, under whose palings they stood at last to debate in whispers on the next step.

Pan was for flight after they had been on into the town and bought some bread and cheese; but the position in which they were brought out Sydney's best qualities.

"No," he said, "we've done wrong, and I'll face it out."

"But I won't—I can't," whimpered Pan. "How do I know as father isn't waiting just inside the gate with that there bit of rope?"

"You must, and you shall come back, Pan," said Sydney, decisively. "It's of no use to kick against it. Am I to hit you again?"

"I d' know," whimpered Pan. "I'm the most miserable chap as ever was. Every one's agen me. Even you knocks me about, and I didn't think it of you, Master Syd—I didn't; I thought you would be my friend."

"So I am, Pan, only you don't know it. Come now, get up. Go in with me, and let's walk straight in to the dining-room, and ask father to forgive us."

"I would ha' done it at first," whimpered Pan, "but I can't now."

"Why?"

"'Cause I'm so 'orrid hungry."

"Well, so am I. Father will give us plenty to eat as soon as he knows. Come along; it's only a scolding."

"No, Master Syd, I dursen't. You go and ask him to forgive you, and to order father not to hit me. P'r'aps I might be able to come then."

"You are the most horrid coward I ever knew," cried Sydney, impatiently. "Do you think I don't feel how terrible it is to go and tell father I've done wrong? I'd give anything to be able to run right away."

"Come along, can't yer, Master Syd. Never mind being hungry; come on."

"No, Pan, I can't. Now then, don't try to sneak out of it. Come and face them, like a man."

"But I arn't a man, Master Syd, and I can't stir now. Oh dear! oh dear! what will father say?"

"That I've got you at last," roared a gruff voice. "Hi! I've got 'em—here they are!"

Chapter Eight

Barney, the old gardener, had been round the garden that evening, and had paused thoughtfully close to the tree where he had had his adventure the night before; and as he went over the various phases of his little struggle and his fall, thinking out how he would have proceeded had he got hold of that boy again, he fancied he heard whispering.

The fancy became certainty, and creeping inch by inch closer to the palings, without making a rustle among the shrubs, he soon made himself certain of who was on the other side.

Barney's face did not beam. It never had done so, but it brightened with a grin as he slowly and cautiously backed out of the shrubs on to the path, stepped across on to the grassy verge, and set off at a trot in true sailor fashion up the garden toward the house to give the alarm.

"Nay, I won't," he said, as he neared the door. "They two may have cut and run again before I get them two old orsifers round outside. Sure to have gone, for the skipper goes along like a horse, while the admiral's more like a helephant on his pins. Scare any two boys away, let alone them. Lor', if I had on'y brought that there bit o' rope!"

But Barney had left it in his cottage; and as he reached the gate he stood to consider.

"Now if I goes down here from the gate, they'll hear me, and be scared away. I know—t'otherwise."

Chuckling to himself, he circumnavigated, as he would have called it, the park-like grounds of the Heronry, a task which necessitated the climbing of two high fences and the forcing a way through a dense quickset hedge.

But these obstacles did not check the old sailor, who cleared the palings, reached the road at the other side, panting, stopped to get his breath, and then crept along through the darkness on the tips of his toes, treating the tall palings as if they were the bulwarks of a ship, and by degrees edged himself up nearer and nearer till he was able to pounce upon the fugitives in triumph.

Pan uttered a howl, dropped down, and lay quite still; but as the ex-boatswain grappled Sydney by the coat, the lad wrenched himself free and kept his captor at bay.

"No, no," cried Barney; "you don't get away. Hoi! help!"

"Hold your noise, you old stupid," cried Sydney. "Who wants to get away? Keep your hands off."

"Nay, I won't. I've got you, and I'll keep you."

"I tell you I was going home, only Pan wouldn't stir."

"Wouldn't stir, wouldn't he? We'll see 'bout that. Now it's of no use, Master Syd. You're my prisoner, so give in and cry quarter."

"I tell you I have given in; and once more, Barney, I warn you, I'm in such a temper I shall hit you."

"Yah! hit away, Midget, who's afeard! Do you s'render?"

"Yes, yes."

"Then you're my prisoner."

"Nonsense! Make Pan come."

"Make him come? Yes, I just will, my lad. But, I say, to think o' you two cutting yourselves adrift, and going off like that!"

"Don't talk so, but bring Pan along. You needn't be afraid, I shall not try to go."

"Par—role, lad?"

"Yes, parole," said Sydney.

"Ah, well, you are a gent, and I can trust you," said Barney. "Now then," he added, as he stirred up his son with the toe of his natty evening shoe; "get up."

"No, no, no," whined Pan.

"If you don't get up I'll kick you over the palings. Get up, you ugly young lubber, or I'll—"

"Oh!" Pan winced, and rose to his knees, eagerly scanning his father's hands in the gloom to see if the rope's-end was visible.

"And, look here, Barney," said Sydney, quietly, "you are not to hit Pan."

"Not what, my lad?"

"You are not to rope's-end him."

"Who says so?"

"I do."

"Oh, you do, do you? Well, look here, my lad, he's hurt my feelings so that I'm going to lock myself up with him in his bedroom, and then I'm going to skin him."

"Oh, oh!" cried Pan.

"You are not going to touch him, but to bring him before my father."

"'Fore the skipper?" said Barney, in a puzzled voice. "Well, yes, my lad, he's in full command. There is something in that."

"But you shouted, and said some one was coming. Who is it?"

"Oh, that was only a manoofer, Master Syd, just to scare you into s'rending."

"Then there is no one coming?"

"It's par—role, mind."

"Yes, parole, of course."

"And you won't try to cut and run again?"

"No—no!" cried Sydney, impatiently.

"No one. Now then you, Pan, my man, hyste yerself on them two legs o' yourn. On'y you wait till I'm a-handlin' that there bit o' rope."

"You touch him if you dare!" cried Sydney. "My father will punish him."

"Oh, Master Syd!" cried Pan.

"Hold your row, will you, you lubber," growled Barney, seizing his son by the collar, setting him on his legs, and giving him a good shake at the same time.

Pan uttered a low moan, and shuffling his feet along the gravel, allowed himself to be led towards the gate.

Sydney shivered as he felt that he was approaching sentence.

"Is my father in the dining-room?"

"Yes, Master Sydney.—Here you, lift up them pretty hoofs o' yours, will yer!"

"Is my uncle with him?"

"Yes, Master Syd."

"Have they been trying to find us?"

"No, Master Syd. The skipper said as if you was such a young cur as to go and disgrace yourself like that 'ere by running away and desarting the King's colours, he wouldn't stir a step arter yer."

"Oh!" groaned Sydney to himself. Then in a whisper, "What did my uncle say?"

"Said Amen to it, and that he'd been fool enough to give you the money to go with."

"No, no, Barney, I didn't take his money."

"Ah, well, I don't know nothing 'bout that. But here's the gate. On you go first."

"No; go on first with Pan."

"And let you shoot off."

"Am I not on parole?"

"Ay, ay. Forgetted that. Now then, you swab; on with you."

As Barney led the way towards the front door, Sydney noticed that there was a light in the dining-room, whose windows were open, the weather being still warm and fine.

"Stop, Barney," he said, after a sudden thought, "we'll go in there through the window."

"Nay, my lad, nay," said the boatswain; "it'll look as if I was spellin' arter a glass o' wine."

"Never mind. I'll go first, and you bring in Pan afterwards."

"Oh, Master Syd, don't."

"Yah! you swab, be quiet!" said Barney, giving his unfortunate son another shake. "Wait till the admiral's pronounced court-martial on you; and then—"

He did not finish, but followed close behind Sydney, who drew a long breath, walked boldly up to the open French window, looked in a moment on where the two fine old veterans were sitting talking sadly together, and then stepped in.

"What!" roared the admiral, rising from his chair, and oversetting his glass of port.

"You here, sir!" cried Captain Belton. "Why have you come back?"

"Because I've been thinking all night, father," said Syd, quietly, "and I've found out I was a fool."

Chapter Nine

There was a dead silence in the dining-room at the Heronry for some time, during which Syd stood with his head erect gazing at his father, who was erect by the table as he might have stood in old times upon his quarter-deck with some mutineer before him; the admiral dropped back into his arm-chair, stared from one to the other as if astounded by his nephew's declaration, while the light shone full upon Syd, who looked pale, shabby, and dirty, but with a frank daring in his face which kept the two old men silent.

In the background close to the window stood Barney, with all his old training manifest in his attitude—that of a petty officer in charge of a prisoner; for that was the character which his son occupied just then in his eyes. His gardening was, for the time being, forgotten, and he felt that he was in the presence of his commanding officer, not of the master whom he served.

The painful silence was broken by Pan, to whom all this was awe-inspiring. For the moment he forgot all about ropes'-ends, and worked himself up into the belief that he would be sentenced to some terrible punishment. He fidgeted about, breathed hard, looked appealingly from the captain to the admiral and back again, and at last, unable to contain himself longer, he burst forth into a long and piteous howl, dropping down upon his knees, and from that attitude would have thrown himself prone, had not Barney tightened his hold upon his collar and shaken him up into a kneeling position again.

"Stow that!" he growled, as the admiral seized the port wine decanter as if to throw at the boy, but altered his mind and poured himself out a glass instead.

Then the terrible silence began again, and lasted till the captain turned to his brother. But he did not speak, and after a few moments longer Sir Thomas exclaimed—

"You young dog! spent all the money you got out of me, and now you've sneaked back."

"I haven't, uncle," cried Syd, indignantly. "I didn't take it. It's on the table in my room."

This seemed to unlock Captain Belton's lips.

"Well, sir, now you have come back, what do you want?" he said.

"I've told you, father. I've been wrong, and want you to forgive me."

"No, sir: you deserted; and now you come crawling back and want to go on as before. Can't trust you again. Go and be a doctor."

"Will you hold up!" growled Barney, fiercely, as he shook his son, who seemed to want to burrow down out of sight through the carpet.

"Oh, father!" began Syd. But he was stopped by his uncle.

"Hold your tongue, sir! Court hasn't called upon you for your defence. Look here, Harry, put the prisoners back while we talk it over."

"Yes," said the captain, coldly, "you can go to your room, sir, and wait till your uncle and I have decided what steps we shall take."

"Yes, sir, confound you! and go and wash your dirty face," said Sir Thomas, fiercely; "you look a disgrace to your name."

"As for your boy, Strake, take him and punish him well."

"Ay, ay, sir!" growled Barney, with alacrity; but his voice was almost drowned by a howl of misery from Pan—a cry that was checked by his father's fierce grip.

"Like me to do down Master Syd same time, sir?" whispered the ex-boatswain.

"No, father, don't let him be punished," said Sydney, quickly. "I made him come back."

"Yes, sir, he did, he did," cried Pan, eagerly. "You did; didn't you, Master Syd?"

"And I promised him he should not be punished."

"Yes, sir, he did, or else I wouldn't have come back."

"What!" roared the admiral, in a tone which made Pan shrink into himself. "And look here, sir," he continued, turning to his nephew, "who made you first in command with your promises?"

"Don't let him be flogged, father," pleaded Syd. "I'm to blame about him. I did promise him that if he would come back he should not be punished."

"Take your boy home, Strake, and bring him here to-morrow morning," said the captain, sternly. "He is not to be flogged till he has made his defence."

"Ay, ay, sir!" growled the old boatswain; and pulling an imaginary forelock, he hauled Pan out of the room, their passage down the path towards the gardener's cottage being accompanied by a deep growling noise which gradually died away.

"Well, sir," said the captain, coldly, "you heard what I said."

Syd looked from one to the other appealingly, feeling that as he had humbly confessed he was in the wrong, he ought to be treated with more leniency, but his uncle averted his gaze, and his father merely pointed to the door, through which, faint, weary, and despondent, the boy went out into the hall, while the two old men seemed to be listening till he had gone up-stairs.

"A miserable, mean-spirited young scoundrel!" said Captain Belton, angrily, but his face grew less stern directly, as he saw his brother throw himself back in his chair, to laugh silently till he was nearly purple.

"Oh, dear me!" he panted at last, "nearly given me a fit. What a dirty, miserable object he looked!"

"Disgraceful, Tom!" said the captain. "Now, then, what would you do with the young dog? Send him off to some school for a couple of years?"

"No," said the admiral, quietly.

"I don't like thrashing the boy."

"Of course not, Harry."

"But I must punish him."

"What for?"

"What for? Disobedience. This mad escapade—"

"Bah!"

"Tom?"

"I said *Bah*! Punish him? Why, look at the boy. Hasn't he punished himself enough? Why, Harry, we were boys once, and precious far from perfect, eh? I say, I don't think either of us would have had the courage to have faced our old dad and confessed like that."

"Humph! perhaps not, Tom."

"No perhaps about it, dear old boy."

"But I must punish him."

"No, you mustn't. I won't have him punished. I like the young dog's spirit. We said he should go to sea. He said he didn't want to go, and sooner than do what he didn't like he cut and run, till he found out he was making a fool of himself, and when he did find it out he came and said so like a man."

"Well, yes," said the captain, "he did confess, but this must not be passed over lightly."

"Bah! Tchah! Pah! let it be. You see if he don't come the humble to-morrow morning, and want us to let him go to sea."

"Think so?"

"Sure of it, my dear boy. I'm not angry with him a bit. He showed that he had some spirit in running away."

"And that he was a cur in sneaking back."

"Steady there," cried the admiral, "nothing of the kind. I say it took more pluck to come back and face us, and own he was in the wrong, than to run away."

The captain sat slowly sipping his port, and the subject was discussed no more.

Then at last bedtime came.

Syd was seated in his room alone. He had washed and changed his clothes, expecting moment by moment to be summoned to hear his fate, but the hours had passed, and he was sick and faint with hunger and exhaustion.

As he sat there he heard the various familiar noises in the house, each of which told him what was going on. He recognised the jingling of glasses on a wooden tray, which he knew meant the butler clearing the dining-room. He heard the closing of the library door. Then there was a long silence, followed by the rattling of shutters, the shooting of bolts, the noise made by bars, and after another lapse, the murmur of deep voices in the hall, the clink of silver candlesticks on the marble slab, and a deep cough.

"They're gone up to bed," said Sydney to himself, and wearily thinking that he would not be spoken to, and that he had better patiently try to forget his hunger in sleep, so as to be ready for the painful interview of the morning, he rose to undress.

But he did not begin. He stood thinking about the events of the past twenty-four hours, and like many another, felt that he would have given anything to recall the past.

For he was very miserable, and his misery found vent once more as he was asking himself what would be his fate in the world.

"Yes, I've behaved like a wretched, thoughtless fool."

"Pst! Syd!"

He started and looked round, to see that the door had been slightly opened, and that his uncle's great red face was thrust into the room.

"Yes, sir," he faltered—he dared not say, "Yes, uncle."

"Had anything to eat?" whispered the old admiral.

"No, sir."

The door closed, and the boy's spirits rose a little, for with all his fierceness it was evident that the old admiral was kindly disposed. But his spirits went down again. Uncle Tom was only a visitor, and his father was horribly stern and harsh. His voice had thrilled the boy, who again and again had wondered what was to be his fate.

"I'll tell uncle how sorry I am, and ask him to side with me," thought Sydney; and he had just made up his mind to speak to him if he came again, and surely he would after coming to ask him about the food, when the door-handle rattled slightly, and the boy involuntarily turned to meet his uncle just as the door was pressed open a little, and he found himself face to face with his father, who remained perfectly silent for a few moments as Syd shrank away.

"Hungry, my lad?" he said at last.

"Yes, father—very."

"Hah!"

The door closed, and the prisoner was left once more to his own thoughts.

Chapter Ten

"I can't bully him to-night—a young dog!" said the captain. "He must be half-starved. I wonder whether Broughton has gone to bed."

He went down slowly to the library without a light, meaning to summon the butler and make him prepare a tray.

But meanwhile Admiral Belton had provided himself with a chamber candlestick and stolen softly down-stairs, through the baize door at one side of the hall, and along the passage that led to the kitchen.

"Can't leave the poor lad to starve," he muttered; "and I dare say I shall find out the larder by the smell."

He chuckled to himself as he softly unfastened a door.

"Nice game this for one of his Majesty's old officers of the fleet," he said. "Wonder what they'd say at the club if they saw me?"

The door passed, he had no difficulty in finding the kitchen, for there was a pleasant chirping of crickets to greet his ear; a kitcheny smell that was oniony and unmistakable, and a few paces farther on his feet were on stones that were sanded, and all at once there was a loud pop where he put down his foot.

He lowered the light and saw that black beetles were scouring away in all directions.

"Cockroaches, by George!" he muttered. "Now where can the larder be?"

There were three doors about, and he went to the first.

"Hah!" he ejaculated, with a sniff. "Here we are; no doubt about it."

He slipped a bolt, lifted a latch, stepped in and stepped out again quickly, then closed the door.

"Scullery!" he snarled. "Bah! what an idiot I do seem, prowling about here."

He crossed the kitchen, slaying two more black beetles with his broad feet in transit, and opened another door. This he found led into a cool passage, along one side of which was a wirework kind of cage.

"Here we are at last," he said; and opening the door, he found himself in presence of part of a cold leg of mutton, a well-carved piece of beef, and a cold roast pheasant.

"Now then for a plate," he muttered; and this he secured by sliding some tartlets off one on to the shelf.

"Why, I've no knife," he muttered, as he cast his eyes upon the cold roast pheasant. "I must have some bread too."

A huge brown pan on the stone floor suggested the home of the loaves, and on raising the lid he found a half loaf, which he broke in two, secured one piece, and transferred it to the plate.

"Hang it all, where is there a knife?" he muttered. "One can't cut beef or mutton without a knife. 'Tisn't even as if one had got one's sword. Here—I know."

He seized the pheasant.

"Humph! too much for a boy. Don't know, though; dare say he could finish it. Wouldn't do him good. I'll—that's it."

He took hold of one leg, and holding the bird down, pulled off one of its joints; then another; after which he placed the pair of legs thoughtfully on the plate.

"May as well give him a wing too," he said; and seizing the one having the liver, he was in the act of tearing it off, when an exclamation behind made him start round and face the captain.

"My dear Tom!" exclaimed the latter. "Why, my dear boy, didn't you speak, and so have ordered a supper-tray?"

"But you seem to be hungry too," growled the admiral, pointing with the wing he had now torn-off at a plate and knife and fork his brother carried.

"Eh? yes," said the captain, starting and looking conscious. "I—er—that is—"

"Why, Harry!" exclaimed Sir Thomas.

"Tom!" cried the captain. "You don't mean that you have come down to—"

"Yes, I do," cried the admiral, fiercely. "Think I was going to bed after a good dinner to shut my eyes whilst that poor boy was half-starved?"

"But it is a punishment for him," said the captain, sternly.

"Punishment be hanged, sir!" cried Sir Thomas. "Harry, you are my brother, and I am only a guest here, but you are a humbug, sir."

"What do you mean?"

"Mean that you've been bouncing about being strict, and the rest of it, and yet you brought that plate and knife to cut your boy some supper."

"Well, er—I'm afraid I did, Tom."

"I'm not afraid, but I'm very glad you're not such a hard-hearted scoundrel. Poor boy! he must be famished. Here, give me that knife."

The captain handed the knife, but in doing so brushed his sleeve over the flame of the candle he carried, and extinguished it.

"How provoking!"

"Never mind," said his brother; "one must do."

As he spoke, the admiral hacked a great piece off the breast of the pheasant, and added it to the legs and wing.

"There," he said, "that ought to keep him going till breakfast. Must have a bit o' salt, Harry. Hush!"

He stooped down and blew out the remaining candle, as the captain caught his arm, and they stood listening.

For the creaking of a door had fallen upon their ears; and partly from involuntary action consequent upon the dread of being caught in so unusual a position, partly from the second thought to which he afterwards gave vent, the admiral sought refuge in the dark.

"Burglars, Harry," he whispered. "They're after your plate."

"Hist! don't speak; we may catch them," was whispered back, and the two old officers stood listening for what seemed an interminable length of time before they saw the dim reflection of a light; heard more whispering, and then the door leading into the larder passage was softly opened.

"Coming into the trap," thought the captain, as with his heart beating fast he prepared for the encounter which he foresaw must take place. "Be ready," he said, with his lips to his brother's ear.

"Right. They're going to board," was whispered back.

They were not long kept in doubt, for the larder door was suddenly thrown open, and three men dashed in armed with bludgeons and a cutlass. There was a sharp scuffle in the darkness, in which the two brave old officers made desperate efforts to master their assailants, but only to find that their years were against them, and they were completely overcome.

"You lubbers! Do you give in?" cried a hoarse voice—that of the man sitting on the captain's chest, while two men were holding down the admiral, who still heaved and strove to get free.

"Strake, you scoundrel! is it you?" panted the captain.

Barney executed a curious manoeuvre, half bound, half roll, off his master, and brought up close to one of the larder shelves, while one of the other men left the admiral and ran out, to return with a light.

The scene was strange. Barney was standing supporting himself against the larder shelf, with his elbow on the cold sirloin of beef; the footman, in his shirt and breeches, was in a corner; and Captain Belton and his brother, with their clothes half torn-off their backs, were seated on the bare floor, staring angrily at their assailants; while Broughton, the butler, was in the doorway, with the candle he had fetched held high above his head.

"My last tooth gone," roared the admiral. "You scoundrels, you shall pay for this."

"Strake, you rascal!" cried the captain. "Broughton, is this some plot to rob me?"

The men stared aghast, as the captain struggled up.

"Speak, you ruffians! You, John!" roared the captain, as he got his breath again, and stood trembling with passion as he glared at the footman.

"Beg pardon, sir," stammered the frightened servitor.

"No, don't stop for that, sir," cried his master; "tell me what the dickens this means."

"Please, sir, I heard noises down-stairs, and I thought it was after the plate; so I told Broughton, sir, and he sent me after the gardener, sir."

"And then you came and attacked us," roared the admiral. "Here, I'm half killed."

"We didn't know it was you, Sir Thomas," growled Barney.

"Then why didn't you know, you idiot?" cried the captain.

"Didn't think anybody could be down-stairs, sir," said the butler, respectfully.

"Why didn't you show your colours, you scoundrel?" cried the admiral, "and not come firing broadsides into your friends. Confound—I say, Harry, my lad, just look at me."

"I'm very sorry, sir," faltered the butler.

"Hang your sorrow, sir! You've broke my watch-glass, and I can feel the bits pricking me."

"Come to me at ten o'clock to-morrow morning, all of you," cried the captain, fiercely, "and I'll pay you your wages, and you shall go."

"No, no, no," said the admiral; "I think we've given them as much as they gave us, and—haw, haw, haw!" he roared, bursting into a tremendous peal of laughter; "we didn't show our colours either. It's all right, brother Harry; they took us for burglars—but they needn't have hit quite so hard."

"Beg your honour's pardon, sir, sure," growled Barney.

"Beg my pardon, sir!—after planting your ugly great knees on my chest, and then sitting on me with your heavy carcase!"

"Is anything the matter?" said a voice at the door, and Sydney made his appearance, looking startled at the scene.

"No, no, my boy," cried his uncle, cheerily; "only your father and I came down to get you a bit of supper, and then they boarded us in the dark."

"Yes, yes, that was it, Syd," said the captain. "Here, put that plate on a tray, Broughton, and take it into the library. I'm very sorry this has happened."

"All a mistake, sir, I'm sure," said the butler, taking the plate with the hacked and torn-off portions of pheasant.

"Yes; don't say any more about it. Come, brother Tom; come, Sydney."

He led the way, but the jolly old admiral could not follow for laughing. He leaned up against the larder shelf, and stood wiping his eyes; and every time he got over one paroxysm he began again. But at last he beckoned to Barney.

"Here, give me your arm, bo'sun," he said, "and help me into the library; I feel as if everything were going by the board. Oh, dear me! oh, dear me! Wait till I've buttoned this waistcoat. Well, it's a lesson. Done for you, Syd, if you had been going to sea. Never attack without proper signals to know who are enemies and who are not."

The supper was soon spread in the library, and Sydney was ravenous for a few mouthfuls, but after that he pushed his plate away, and could eat no more.

"What!" cried his uncle; "done? Nonsense! I can peck a bit now myself; and, Harry, my boy, I must have a glass of grog after this."

The result was that Syd did eat a decent supper, and an hour later, when all was still, he sat thinking for a time about the coming morning. Perhaps more than that of the fact that neither his father nor his uncle had shaken hands when they parted for the night.

Then came sleep—sweet, restful sleep—and he was dreaming vividly for a time of a desperate fight with the French, in which he boarded a larder, and captured a butler, footman, and a gardener. After that all was dense, dreamless sleep, till he started up in bed, for there was a knocking at his door.

Chapter Eleven

"May I come in, sir?"

"Yes; come in, Broughton," said Syd, recognising the voice, and the butler entered with one hand bound up.

"That, sir? Oh, nothing, sir. Only got it in the scrimmage last night. So glad to see you back again, Master Syd."

"Oh, don't talk about it, Broughton," groaned the boy. "My father down?"

"No, sir; but he's getting up, and your uncle too. I was to come and tell you to make haste."

"Yes, I'll make haste," said Syd; and as soon as he was alone he began to dress hurriedly, with every thought of the blackest hue, and a sensation of misery and depression assailing him that was horrible.

He quite started as he went to the glass to brush his hair, for his face was white and drawn as if he had been ill. But there was very little more time for thought. The breakfast-bell rang, and he hurried down into the dining-room, glad to get off the staircase and through the hall, where one of the housemaids was still busy, and ready to look at him curiously as the boy who ran away from home—and came back.

Syd thought of that latter, for he knew but too well the servants might think it was brave—almost heroic and daring—to run away; to come back seemed very weak and small.

In those few moments Syd wished that ten years would glide away, and all the trouble belong to the past.

His father was in a chair by the window ready to look up sharply, and then let his eye fall upon the book he was reading without uttering a word.

Broughton came in bearing a tray with the coffee and a covered dish or two ready to place upon the table, then he left, and Syd was alone again with his father.

"What will he say?" thought the culprit; but he could not decide in which form his verbal castigation would come.

As he sat glancing at his father from time to time, Syd noted that there was a scratch upon his forehead, and that a bit of sticking-plaster was on one of his knuckles, proofs these of the severity of the past night's struggle.

Then came a weary waiting interval before there was a deep-toned cough outside the door.

"Hah!" ejaculated the captain, rising from his seat as the door opened, and the old admiral stumped into the room.

"Morning, Harry," he said; "morning, Syd."

He closed the door behind him and came forward, and then, odd as it may sound in connection with one who was weak, unwell, and suffering from so much mental trouble, Sydney burst into a hearty fit of laughter. He tried to check it; he knew that under the circumstances it was in the worst of taste; he felt that he would excite his father's anger, and that then he would be furious; but he laughed all the same, and the more he tried the more violent and lasting the fits grew.

"Sydney!" cried his father, and then there was a pause followed by a hearty "Ha, ha, ha!" as the captain joined in, and the admiral gently patted his own face first on one side and then on the other.

"Yes," he said, quietly; "you may well laugh. I look a nice guy, don't I?"

"Oh, uncle! I beg your pardon—but—oh, oh, oh, I can't stop laughing," cried Sydney.

"Well, get it done, boy," said the old gentleman, "for I want my breakfast. Oh, here is Broughton."

The butler entered with a rack of hot dry toast, and as he advanced to the table the admiral exclaimed—

"Now, sir, look here; you've made a nice mess of my phiz. What have you got to say to this?"

The butler raised his eyes as he set down the toast, gazed full in the old gentleman's face, his own seemed frozen solid for a moment, and then, clapping the napkin he carried to his mouth to smother his laughter, he turned and fled.

"And that son of a sea-cook begged my pardon last night, and said he was sorry. Yes, I am a sight. Look at my eyes, Harry, swollen up and black. There's a nose for you; and one lip cut. Why, I never got it so bad in action. And all your fault, Syd. There, I forgive you, boy."

"Well, it's impossible to give this boy a serious lecture now, Tom," said the captain, wiping his eyes, as he passed the coffee.

"Of course. Who wants serious lectures?" said the admiral, testily. "The boy did wrong, and he came back and said he was sorry for it. You've told me scores of times that you never flogged a man who was really sorry for getting into a scrape. Give me some of that ham, Syd, and go on eating yourself. I say, rum old punch I look, don't I?"

Syd made no reply, but filled his uncle's plate, and the breakfast went on nearly to the end before the topic dreaded was introduced.

"Well, Sydney," said his father, rather sadly, "so I suppose I must let you be a doctor?"

"Wish he was one now," cried the admiral. "I'd make him try to make me fit to be seen. Humph! doctor, eh? No; I don't think I shall try to be ill to give you a job, Syd; but I'm very glad, my boy, that you did not take that money."

Sydney bent over his coffee, and his father went on—

"It's like letting you win a victory, sir, but I suppose I must give in. I don't like it though."

"Humph! more do I," said Sir Thomas. "I'll forgive you though if you train up for a naval surgeon. Do you hear, sir?"

"Yes, uncle, I hear," said Sydney.

"Then why don't you speak?"

"I was thinking of what you said, uncle."

"Humph! Well, I hope you'll take it to heart."

"Yes," said his father; "you may as well be a surgeon."

"That's what I should have liked to be," said Sydney, "if I had been a doctor."

"Well, you're going to be, sir. Your uncle and I have talked it over, and you shall study for it, and begin as soon as you're old enough."

Sydney sat still, gazing at his plate; but he raised his eyes at last, and looked firmly at his father, who was watching him keenly.

"Thank you, father," he said.

"No, sir, don't thank me; thank your indulgent uncle."

"No, don't, boy, because I give way most unwillingly; and I'm confoundedly sorry you should want to be such a physic-mixing swab."

"You needn't be sorry, uncle," said Sydney, quietly; "and I'm very grateful to you, father, but I shall not be one now."

"Not be a doctor!" said the captain, sharply. "Then pray, sir, what do you mean to be?"

"A sailor, father."

"What?" cried the brothers in chorus.

"And I want to go to sea at once."

"You do, Syd?"

"Yes, father. I saw it all when I'd gone away, and I came back for that."

"Hurrah!" cried the admiral, starting from his seat, and dropping back with a groan of pain. "Bless my heart!" he cried, "how sore I am! But hurrah! all the same. You'll be a middy, my boy."

"Yes, uncle. I want to be at once."

"And you'll try to make yourself a good officer, my boy?" cried his father, leaning over the table to catch his son's hand.

"Yes, father, as hard as ever I can."

"T'other hand, Syd, lad," cried the admiral; and he grasped it firmly. "Try, Harry?—he won't need to try. He's a Belton every inch of him, and he'll make a ten times better officer than ever we did. Here, where's the port? Who's going to drink success to the boy in coffee? Bah, what does the liquor matter! We'll drink it in our hearts, boy. Here's to Admiral Belton— my dear boy—our dear boy, Harry, eh?"

"God bless you, my lad!" cried Captain Belton. "You've made me feel more proud of you and happy than I have felt for years."

"Here, hi!" roared the admiral; "where's that lubber Strake? I want some one to help me cheer. Sydney, boy, God bless you! I *am* glad you ran away."

"Then you forgive me, father?"

"Hold your tongue, sir," cried Captain Belton, laying his hand on his son's shoulder. "There are things that we all like to forget as soon as we can—this is one of them. Let's blot it out."

"But I want to ask a favour, father."

"Granted, my boy, before you ask."

Chapter Twelve

Sydney Belton, as he felt the pressure of his father's hand, could not speak for a few minutes, and when he did find utterance, he seemed to have caught a fresh cold, for his voice sounded husky.

"I want as a favour, father—" he began, in a faltering voice.

"Here, it's all right, Syd, my boy," said his uncle; "don't bother your father for money. Now then, how much do you want?"

"I don't want money, uncle."

"Eh? Don't want money, sir? Wait a bit then till you get among your messmates, and you'll want plenty."

"I want to beg Panama off from being punished."

"Ah, to be sure. I'd forgotten him," cried Captain Belton; and he went to the fireplace and rang the bell.

The butler answered, looking very serious and apologetic now as he glanced at Sir Thomas. But the old gentleman only shook his fist at him good-humouredly as his brother spoke.

"Send John down to the cottage, to tell Strake to come up directly with his son."

"Look here," said Sir Thomas, chuckling, "don't you two look like that. Pull serious faces, and let's scare the young dog. Do him good."

By the time the breakfast was ended steps were heard in the hall, and the butler came in to announce that the gardener was waiting with his boy.

"Send them in," said Captain Belton, austerely.

The butler retired; Sir Thomas gave his brother and nephew several nods and winks, and then sat up looking most profoundly angry as the door was again opened and a low growling arose from the hall. Then a few whimpering protests, more growling, with a few words audible: "Swab"— "lubber"—"hold up!"—and then there was a scuffle, another growl, and Panama, looking white and scared, seemed to be suddenly propelled into the room as if from a mortar, the mortar making its appearance directly after in the shape of Barney, who pulled his forelock and kicked out a leg behind to each of the old officers before pointing to Pan and growling out—

"Young desarter—wouldn't come o' deck, your honours, and—"

Barney's remarks had been addressed to his master, but he now turned round toward Sir Thomas, and seemed for the first time to realise the old admiral's condition, when his jaw dropped, he stared, and then began to scratch his head vigorously.

"My!" he ejaculated; "your honour did get it last night."

"Get it, you rascal—yes," cried Sir Thomas; "you nearly killed me amongst you."

"And, your honour," said Barney, hoarsely, as he turned to his master, "I hadn't no idee it was you. I thought it was—"

"Yes, yes, never mind now," said the captain. "I sent for you about this lad."

"Oh, Master Syd, sir, say a word for me," cried the boy, piteously. "Father would ha' whacked me if I hadn't run away; then you whacked me when I did; and now I'm to be whacked again. Wish I was dead, I do."

"Eh! eh! what's that?" cried Captain Belton. "You thrashed him, Sydney; what for?"

"Well, father, we did have a little misunderstanding," said Sydney, composedly.

"It was 'cause I wouldn't come back, sir; that's it, sir," whimpered Pan. "I knowd father had made the rope's-end ready for me, and he had."

"What's that?" said the captain. "I said you were not to be flogged until you had been tried."

"Well, your honour, orders it was, and I didn't lay it on him," growled Barney.

"No; but you laid it across me in bed, and you kep' on showing of it to me, and you said that was my supper, and my breakfass, and—and—I wish I hadn't come back, I do."

"Is this true, Strake?"

"Well, your honour, I s'pose it's about it," said the boatswain. "I 'member showing of it to him once or twyste."

"He's got it in his pocket now, sir," cried Pan.

"Ay, ay. That's a true word, lad."

"Let's see," said Sir Thomas, in magisterial tones.

Barney fumbled unwillingly in his pocket, and drew out a piece of rope about two feet long, well whipped round at the ends with twine.

"Humph!" said Sir Thomas, taking the instrument of torture. "So that's what you flog him with."

"Well, your honour, meant to make a man of him."

"Arn't yer going to speak a word for me, Master Syd?" whispered Pan.

"Silence, sir!" said the captain. "Now look here: you ran away from your service, and from your father's house. Then, I suppose, you tried to persuade my son to go with you."

Pan looked up reproachfully at Sydney.

"I wouldn't ha' told o' you, Master Syd. But I don't care now. Yes; I wanted him to *come*."

"Well, I'm glad you spoke the truth; but your companion did not tell tales of you. Now, look here, sir: I suppose you know you've behaved like an ungrateful young scoundrel?"

"Yes, sir," whimpered Pan.

"And you know you deserve to be flogged?"

"Yes, sir, and I want it over; it's like all flogging, and wuss, for him to keep on showing me that there rope's-end."

"Better pipe all hands to punishment, bo'sun," said Sir Thomas.

"Ay, ay, sir," said Barney, thrusting his hand in his breast; and bringing out a silver whistle attached to his neck by a black ribbon, he put it to his lips.

"No, no," cried the captain, "we're not aboard ship now. I wish we were," he added, "eh?"

Sir Thomas nodded.

"Well, sir," continued the captain, "are you ready to take your flogging?"

"Yes, sir," said Pan, dolefully.

"And what will you say if I forgive you?"

"And make him forgive me too, sir?" cried Pan, nodding his head sideways at his father.

"Yes, my lad."

"Anything, sir. There, I'll never run away agen."

"Will you be a good, obedient lad, and do as your father wishes you, and go to sea?"

"No," said Pan, stolidly, "I won't."

"Humph! what are we to say to this, Sir Thomas?"

"Say?—that he's a cowardly young swab."

"Ay, ay, sir; that's it," cried Barney.

"Silence, sir. Look here, boy; we'll give you another chance. Will you go to sea?"

The boy shook his head.

"What! not with my son?"

"What!" cried Barney, excitedly. "Master Syd going?"

"Yes, Barney," cried the boy. "I'm going to be a sailor after all."

The ex-boatswain showed every tooth in his head in a broad grin, slapped one hand down on the other, and cried in a gruff voice—

"Dear lad! There, your honours! The right stuff in him arter all. Can't you get me shipped in the same craft with him, Sir Thomas? I'm as tough as ratline hemp still."

"You going to sea, Master Syd?" said Pan, looking at the companion of his flight wonderingly.

"Yes, Pan; at once. Will you come?"

"Course I will, sir," cried Pan. "Going to-day?"

"There—there, your honours! Hear that?" cried Barney, excitedly. "Aren't that the right stuff too? Here, your honour, begging your pardon, that bit of rope's-end's mine."

He caught up the rope, and gave it a flourish over his head.

"Here, stop! what are you going to do?" cried Sydney, dashing at him, and getting hold of one end of the rope.

"Going to do, Master Syd?—burn it; you may if you like. It's done it's dooty, and done it well. I asks your honours, both on you—aren't that wirtoo in a bit o' rope? See what it's made of him. Nothing like a bit o' rope's-end, neatly seized with a bit o' twine."

"Ah, well, you've a right to your opinion, Strake," said the captain. "There, you can take him back home. I dare say we can manage to get him entered in the same ship as my son."

"And if he's going to do the right thing now," said Sir Thomas, "I'll pay for his outfit too."

"Thank, your honour; thank, your honour!" cried Barney.

"Oh!"

This last was from Pan, who had received a side kick from his father's shoe.

"Then why don't yer touch yer hat to the admiral and say thankye too, you swab?" growled Barney, in a deep, hoarse whisper.

"There," said the captain, "you can go now."

"Long life to both your honours," cried Barney. "Come, Pan, my lad, get home; you dunno it, but your fortune's made."

"Well, Syd, are you satisfied?" said the captain, as soon as they were alone.

"Yes, father."

"Then we'll go up by to-night's coach and see Captain Dashleigh to-morrow. What do you say?"

"I'm ready, father. Will uncle come too?"

"Uncle Tom come too, you young humbug! how can I?" cried the admiral. "No, I'm on sick leave, till my figure-head's perfect, so I shall have to stop here and sip the port."

Chapter Thirteen

A supercilious-looking waiter—that is to say, a waiter who has had a good season and saved a little money—was standing at the door of the oldest hotel in Covent Garden, when a clumsy coach was driven up to the door.

The coach was so old and shabby, and drawn by two such wretched beasts, that the supercilious waiter could not see it; and after looking to his right and his left he turned to go in.

"Here, hi!" came from the coach; but the waiter paid no heed.

"Here, Syd, fetch that scoundrel here."

The door was flung open, the lad leaped out and went at the waiter like a dog, seizing him by the collar, spinning him round, and racing him protesting the while down the steps and over the rough pavement to the coach door.

"You insolent scoundrel, why didn't you come when I called?" said Captain Belton, from inside the fusty coach.

"Don't I tell you we're full!" cried the waiter; "and don't you come putting—"

"Silence, sir! how dare you!" cried the captain in his fiercest tones. "How do you know that we want to stay in your dirty hotel? Take my card up to Captain Dashleigh, and say I am waiting."

The man glanced at the card, turned, and ran with alacrity into the house.

"That's just the sort of fellow I should like to set Strake at, Syd, with his mates and the cat. A flogging would do him good."

The next minute the waiter was back at the coach door with Captain Dashleigh's compliments, delivered in the most servile tones, and would Captain Belton step up?

"Get down my valise and pay the coachman," said the captain. "We shall sleep here to-night, though you are full."

They were shown into a room where a little, dandified man in full uniform was walking up and down, evidently dictating to his secretary, who was busily writing.

Syd stared. He had been accustomed to look upon his father and uncle, and the friends who came to see them, as types of naval officers—big, loud-spoken, grey-haired, bluff men, well tanned by long exposure to the weather; and he wondered who this individual could be who walked with one hand upon the hilt of his sword, pressing it down so that the sheath projected nearly at right angles between the tails of his coat, and as he walked it seemed to wag about like a monkeyish part of his person. The other hand held a delicate white handkerchief, which he waved about, and at each movement it scented the air.

"Ah, my dear Captain Belton, so glad to see you. Lucky your call was now. So much occupied, you see. Sit down, my dear sir. And this is your son? Ah," he continued, inspecting Syd through a gold-rimmed eyeglass, "nice little lad. Looks healthy and well. Seems only the other day I joined the service in his uncle's ship. I have your brother's letter in my secretary's hands. So glad to oblige him if I can. How is the dear old fellow?"

"Hearty, Captain Dashleigh," said Syd's father. "Desired to be kindly remembered to you."

"Ah, very good of him. Splendid officer! The service has lost a great deal through his growing too old."

"We don't consider ourselves too old for service. Timbers are sound. We only want the Admiralty to give us commands."

"Ah, yes, to be sure," said the dandy captain, who seemed to be about eight-and-thirty; and he continued his walk up and down the room as his visitors sat.

"You have succeeded well, Dashleigh," said Captain Belton.

"Well, yes—pretty well—pretty well. Very arduous life though."

"Oh, hang the arduous life, sir," said Captain Belton. "It's a grand thing to be in command of a two-decker."

"Yes," said the little man, who in physique was rather less than Sydney; "the Government trust me, and his Majesty seems to have confidence in my powers. But you will, I know, excuse me, my dear old friend, if I venture to hint that my time is not my own. Sir Thomas said you would call and explain how I could serve him. What can I do? One moment—I need not say that I look upon him as my father in the profession, and that I shall be delighted to serve him. You will take a pinch?"

He handed a magnificent gold snuff-box set with diamonds, and a portrait on china in the lid indicated that it came from one of the ministers.

"Thanks, yes. But, my dear Dashleigh, you should not use scented snuff."

"Eh?—no? The fashion, my dear sir. Now I am all attention."

"Then why don't you sit down as a gentleman would?" said Captain Belton to himself. Then aloud—"My business is very simple, sir. This is my son, whom I wish to devote to the King's service, and my brother, Sir Thomas Belton, asks, and I endorse his petition, that you will enter him in your ship, and try to do by him as my brother did by you."

"My dear Captain Belton! Ah, this is sad! What could have been more unfortunate! If you had only been a week sooner!"

"What's the matter, sir?" said the captain, sternly.

"Matter?—I am pained, my dear Captain Belton; absolutely pained. I would have done anything to serve you both, my dear friends, but my midshipmen's berth is crammed. I could not—dare not—take another. If there was anything else I could do to serve Sir Thomas and you I should be delighted."

"Thank you, Captain Dashleigh," said Syd's father, rising; "there is nothing else. I will not detain you longer."

"I would say lunch with me, my dear sir, but really—as you see—my secretary—the demands upon my time—you thoroughly understand?"

"Yes, sir, I understand. Good morning."

"Good morning, my dear Captain Belton; *good* morning, my young friend. I will speak to any of the commanding officers I know on your behalf. Good day."

The captain stalked silently down-stairs, closely followed by Syd, and then led the way round and round the market, taking snuff savagely without a word.

But all at once he stopped and drew himself up, and gave his cane a thump on the pavement, while his son thought what a fine-looking, manly fellow he was, and what a pleasure it was to gaze upon such a specimen of humanity after the interview with the dandy they had left.

"Syd," said the captain, fiercely, "if I thought you would grow up into such an imitation man as that, confound you, sir, I'd take and pitch you over one of the bridges."

"Thank you, father. Then you don't like Captain Dashleigh?"

Uncle Tom had caught sight of Barney at the bottom of the lawn sweeping leaves into a heap for his son to lift them between two boards into the waiting barrow.

As Barney looked up and saw the admiral signalling from the window, he came across the lawn at a trot, dragging the broom after him.

"Drop that broom and salute your officer, you confounded old barnacle!" roared the old gentleman. "Salute, sir, salute: your master's appointed to the smartest frigate in the service."

Barney struck an attitude, sent his old cocked hat spinning into the air, and then catching it, tucked it under his arm, and pulled his imaginary forelock over and over again.

"Good luck to your honour! I am glad. When would you like me to be ready, sir? Shall I go on first and begin overhauling?"

"You, Strake?" said the captain, thoughtfully.

"You're not going to leave me behind, sir? No, no, sir; don't say that, sir—don't think it, sir. I'm as strong and active as ever I was, and a deal more tough. Ask him to take me, Master Syd."

"Take you, Strake?" said the captain again. "Why, what is to become of my garden?"

"Your garden, captain! What do you want with a garden when you're at sea? Salt tack and biscuit, and a few bags o' 'tatoes about all you want aboard ship."

The captain shook his head.

"It's a long time since you were on active service, Strake."

"Active sarvice, captain! Why, I was on active sarvice when the admiral hailed me; and, I tell you, I never felt more fit for work in my life. Course I'd like to be your bo'sun, captain, but don't you stand 'bout that. You take me, and I'll sarve you afore the mast as good and true as if I was warrant officer once more. You've knowed me a lot o' years, Sir Thomas; say a good word for me."

"I'll say you're a good fellow, Strake, and a first-class sailor," said the admiral.

"For which I thank ye kindly, sir. But you don't say a word for a man, Master Syd. I know I've cut up rough with you, sir, often over plums and chyce pears as I wanted to save for the dessart, but my 'art's been allus right for you, my lad, and never a bit o' sorrow till I see you flying in the master's face and not wantin' to sarve the King. You won't bear malice, sir, and 'atred in yer 'art. Say a good word."

"Yes, Barney. Do take him, father."

"It is a question of duty and of the man's ability. Look here, Strake, if I say no, it's because I fear that you would not be smart enough at your age. It is not a question of the will to serve."

"I should think not, sir. Why, you won't have a man of your crew more willing to sarve you right."

"I know that; but the activity and smartness?"

"Activity, sir? Why, I'm as light as a feather, sir, and I'd run up the ratlines and away aloft and clap my hand on the main-truck long afore some o' your youngsters."

"Well, Strake, I'll take you."

"Why—"

"Stop a moment. It must be with the understanding that you undertake anything I set you to do, for there may be a good boatswain aboard."

"Right, sir; any thing's my work. I'll see about my kit at once."

"Syd, you shall go with me, unless you would like to wait for a chance on another ship."

"No, father, I'll go with you," cried Syd. "And what about Pan?"

"He can come," said the captain. "Now leave me with your uncle, I want to talk to him at once."

A complete change seemed to have come over Barney as he made for the open window, not walking as usual, but in a light trot upon his toes, as if he were once more on the deck of a ship; and as soon as he was in the garden and out of sight of the window, he folded his arms and began to evince his delight by breaking into the first few steps of a hornpipe.

He was just in the middle of it when Pan came silently up behind with a board in each hand, to stand gazing from Syd to his father and back again in speechless wonderment, and evidently fully believing that the old man had gone mad.

All at once Barney was finishing off his dance with a curve round on his heels, but this brought him face to face with his wide-eyed, staring son.

The effect was instantaneous. He stopped short in a peculiar attitude, feeling quite abashed at being found so engaged, and Syd could hardly contain his laughter at the way in which the old boatswain got out of his difficulty.

"Like him, sir? A confounded ungrateful dandy Jackanapes captain of a seventy-four-gun ship! Great heavens! the Government must be mad. But that's it—interest at court! Such a fellow has been promoted over the heads of hundreds of better men. All your uncle's services to him forgotten, and mine too."

"But if there wasn't room in his ship, father?"

"Room in his ship sir?" cried the captain, wrathfully. "Do you think there would not have been room in my ship for the son and nephew of two old friends? Why, hang me, if I'd been under that man's obligations, I'd have shared my cabin with the boy but what he should have gone."

"Yes, father, I think you would. So we've failed."

"Failed? Yes. No; never say die. But I'm glad. Hang him! With a captain like that, what is the ship's company likely to be! No, Syd, if you can't go afloat with a decent captain, you shall turn doctor or tailor."

"Why don't you have a ship again, father?"

"Because I have no interest, my boy, and don't go petitioning and begging at court. But they don't want sea-captains now, they want scented popinjays. Why, Syd, I've begged for a ship scores of times during the past two years, but always been passed over. I wouldn't care if they'd appoint better men; but when I see our best vessels given to such things as that! Oh, hang it, I shall be saying what I shall be sorry for if I go on like this. Come and have a walk. No; I'll go to the Admiralty, and see if I can get a hearing there. If I can't—if they will not help me to place my boy in the service which all the Beltons have followed for a hundred and fifty years, I'll— There, come along, boy, the world is not perfect."

He walked sharply down into the Strand and then on to Whitehall, where he turned into the Admiralty Yard, and sent in his card to one of the chief officials, who kept him waiting two hours, during which the captain fumed to see quite a couple of score naval officers go in and return, while he was passed over.

"Here you see an epitome of my life during the past fifteen years, Syd," he said, bitterly. "Always passed over and—"

"His lordship will see you now, if you please," said an official.

"Hah! pretty well time," muttered the captain. "Come along, Syd."

They followed the clerk along a gloomy passage, and were shown into a dark room where a fierce-looking old gentleman in powder and queue sat writing, but who laid down his pen and rose as Captain Belton's name was announced; shook hands cordially, and then placed his hands upon his visitor's shoulders and forced him into an easy-chair.

"Sit down, Harry Belton, sit down," he cried. "Sorry to keep you waiting, but wanted to get rid of all my petitioners and visitors, so as to be free for a long talk. Why, I haven't seen you or heard of you these ten years."

"Not for want of my applying for employment, my lord," said Captain Belton, stiffly.

"But then I've not been in office, my dear Belton; and, hang it, man, don't 'my lord' me. And who's this?"

"My son, my lord," said the captain.

"Don't 'my lord' me, man!" cried the old gentleman, fiercely. "You always were a proud, stubborn fellow. And so this is your son, is it?" he continued, peering searchingly in the boy's face. "Ah! chip of the old block; stubborn one too, I can see. Shake hands, sir. Now then, what are you going to be?"

"A sailor, sir—my lord, I mean."

"Don't correct yourself, boy. A sailor, eh? Like your father and grandfather before you, eh? Good; can't do better. I wish you luck, my lad. We want a school of lads of your class. The navy's full of milksops, and dandies, and fellows who have got their promotion by favour, while men like your father, who have done good service and ought to be doing it now, instead of idling about as country gentlemen—"

"Not my fault," cried the captain, hotly. "I've begged for employment till I've grown savage, and sworn I would appeal no more."

"Hah! yes," said the old gentleman, sitting back in his chair, and holding Syd's hand still in his; "there's a deal of favour and interest in these days, my dear Belton. John Bull's ships ought to be commanded by the best men in the navy, but they're not; and those of us who would like to do away with all the corruption, can't stir. Never mind that now. Let's talk of Admiral Tom. How is the dear old boy?"

"Like I am—growing old and worn with disappointment."

"Nonsense, Belton; nonsense. We can't shape our own lives. Better make the best of things as they are. Well, my boy, what ship have you joined?"

"None, sir—yet."

"I came up to see Dashleigh, on the strength of his having been under my brother, and asked him to take my son."

"And he wouldn't, of course," said the old gentleman, more fiercely still. "Wrong man, my dear sir. Ladder kicker. And so, young sir, you haven't got a ship?"

"No; and if you could help me, my lord—"

"If you call me my lord again, Harry Belton, I won't stir a peg.—Do you know, boy, that I was once in command of a small sloop, and your father was my first officer? I say, Belton, remember those old days?"

"Ay, I do," said the captain, with his eyes lighting up.

"Remember cutting out the Spaniard at Porto Bello?"

"Yes; and the fight with the big vessel in the Gut."

"Ah, to be sure. How we made the splinters fly! Bad luck that was for those other two to come up. Rare games we had, my boy. We must get you a ship under some good captain."

"If you could do that for me," said Captain Belton, eagerly.

"Well, I can try and serve an old friend, even if he is a lazy one who likes to be in dock instead of being at sea. By the way, Belton, how old are you?"

"Fifty-eight."

"Ah, and I'm seventy. Plenty of work in me yet, though. There, I'll bear my young friend here in mind. Come and dine with me one day next week, Belton, for I must send you off now; you've had half an hour instead of five minutes. Say Monday—Tuesday."

"Thank you, no," said the captain, rising. "I've done all I can, and will get back home."

"Bah! You're a bad courtier, Belton. Stubborn as ever. You ought to hang about here, and sneak and fawn upon me, and jump at the chance of dining with me, in the hope that I might be able to help you."

"Yes, my lord, I suppose so," said the captain, sadly; "but if the country wants my services it will have to seek me now. I'm growing too old to beg for what is my right."

"And meanwhile our ships are badly handled and go to the bottom, which would be a good thing if only their inefficient captains were drowned; but it's their crews as well. There, good-bye, Belton. Don't come to town again without calling on me. I'll try and serve your boy. One moment— where are you? Oh yes, I see; I have your card. Good-bye, middy. Remember me to the admiral."

The fierce-looking old gentleman saw them to the door, and soon after father and son were on their way back to the hotel, and the next morning on the Southbayton coach.

"Ah, Sydney, lad," said the captain, "we shall have to bind you 'prentice to a 'pothecary, after all."

"But Lord Claudene said he would try and serve you about me, father; and I should be disappointed if I didn't go to sea now."

"Indeed?" said the captain, laughing. "You will have to bear the disappointment. There are hundreds constantly applying at the Admiralty."

"Yes, father, but you are a friend."

"Yes, my boy, I am a friend; and yet what I want I should have to be waiting about for years, and then perhaps not succeed."

Chapter Fourteen

"What!" cried Sir Thomas, when he heard the adventures in town, "you mean to tell me that Dashleigh treated you as you say?"

"Exactly," replied his brother.

"My face show the marks much now?"

"No; hardly at all."

"Then we'll go up to town to-morrow."

"What for, Tom?" said the captain. "You'll do no better than I did."

"I'm not going to try, Harry," said the old gentleman, fiercely.

"Then why go? You are comfortable here."

"I'm going up to horsewhip that contemptible little scoundrel Dashleigh, and fight him afterwards, though he's hardly gentleman enough."

"Nonsense, Tom!"

"Nonsense? Why I made that fellow—and pretty waste of time too! And now he's in command of a seventy-four, and you may go begging for a word to get your boy into the midshipmen's berth."

Uncle Tom did not go up to town to horsewhip or fight.

"Never mind," he said, "he's sure to run his ship on the rocks, or get thrashed—a scoundrel! Here, Syd, take my advice."

"What is it, uncle?"

"Never do any one a kind action as long as you live."

"You don't mean it, uncle."

"What, sir? No, I don't: you're right."

A week passed, during which Barney suggested that the proper thing for Captain Belton to do was to purchase some well-built merchant schooner, and fit her out as a privateer.

"I could soon get together as smart a crew as you'd care to have, and then there'd be a chance for your son to get to be a leefftenant 'fore you knew where you were."

But Captain Belton only laughed, and matters at the Heronry remained as they were, till one day with the other letters there came one that was big and official, and its effect upon the two old officers was striking.

"From the Admiralty, Tom," said the captain, as he glanced at the great seal, and then began to take out his knife to slit open the fold.

"I can see that," said the admiral. "It's from Claudene. Syd, lad, you're in luck. He has got you appointed to a ship, after all."

"Bless my soul!" cried the captain, dropping the great missive on the table.

"What is it, my lad?—what is it?" cried Sir Thomas.

"Read—read," cried Captain Belton, huskily—"it's too good to believe."

Sir Thomas snatched up the official letter, cast his eyes over it, and then, forgetting his gout, caught hold of Syd's hands and began to caper about the room like a maniac.

"Hurrah! Bravo, Harry, my lad. I've often grumbled; but I avow it—I am past service, gouty as I am; but you were never more seaworthy."

"Uncle, why don't you speak?" cried Sydney, excitedly. "Has father got a ship?"

"Got a ship, my lad? He's appointed to one of the smartest in the navy— the *Sirius* frigate, and she's ordered abroad."

Captain Belton drew himself up, and his eyes flashed as in imagination he saw himself treading once more the quarter-deck of a smart ship.

"It's too good to believe," he muttered—"too good to believe."

"You haven't read the letter," said his brother, looking wistfully across to the tall, eager-looking man before him.

"No," said Captain Belton. "Hah! from Claudene,"—and he read aloud:—

"My dear Belton, I have managed this for you, and I'm very glad, for you will do us credit. The appointment will clear away the difficulty about your boy, for you can have him in your own ship, and keep the young dog under your eye. My good wishes to you, and kind regards to your brother. Tell him I wish I could serve him as well, but I can't see my way."

"Of course he can't," said the old admiral, quickly. "No; I'm too old and gouty now. But as for you, you dog, why don't you stand on your head, or shout, or something? Here, I am well enough to go up to town after all. Syd and I are going to see about his uniform. The *Sirius*—well, you two have luck at last. Here, hi! you, sir! Put down that confounded birch-broom, and come here."

Uncle Tom had caught sight of Barney at the bottom of the lawn sweeping leaves into a heap for his son to lift them between two boards into the waiting barrow.

As Barney looked up and saw the admiral signalling from the window, he came across the lawn at a trot, dragging the broom after him.

"Drop that broom and salute your officer, you confounded old barnacle!" roared the old gentleman. "Salute, sir, salute: your master's appointed to the smartest frigate in the service."

Barney struck an attitude, sent his old cocked hat spinning into the air, and then catching it, tucked it under his arm, and pulled his imaginary forelock over and over again.

"Good luck to your honour! I am glad. When would you like me to be ready, sir? Shall I go on first and begin overhauling?"

"You, Strake?" said the captain, thoughtfully.

"You're not going to leave me behind, sir? No, no, sir; don't say that, sir—don't think it, sir. I'm as strong and active as ever I was, and a deal more tough. Ask him to take me, Master Syd."

"Take you, Strake?" said the captain again. "Why, what is to become of my garden?"

"Your garden, captain! What do you want with a garden when you're at sea? Salt tack and biscuit, and a few bags o' 'tatoes about all you want aboard ship."

The captain shook his head.

"It's a long time since you were on active service, Strake."

"Active sarvice, captain! Why, I was on active sarvice when the admiral hailed me; and, I tell you, I never felt more fit for work in my life. Course I'd like to be your bo'sun, captain, but don't you stand 'bout that. You take me, and I'll sarve you afore the mast as good and true as if I was warrant officer once more. You've knowed me a lot o' years, Sir Thomas; say a good word for me."

"I'll say you're a good fellow, Strake, and a first-class sailor," said the admiral.

"For which I thank ye kindly, sir. But you don't say a word for a man, Master Syd. I know I've cut up rough with you, sir, often over plums and chyce pears as I wanted to save for the dessart, but my 'art's been allus right for you, my lad, and never a bit o' sorrow till I see you flying in the master's face and not wantin' to sarve the King. You won't bear malice, sir, and 'atred in yer 'art. Say a good word."

"Yes, Barney. Do take him, father."

"It is a question of duty and of the man's ability. Look here, Strake, if I say no, it's because I fear that you would not be smart enough at your age. It is not a question of the will to serve."

"I should think not, sir. Why, you won't have a man of your crew more willing to sarve you right."

"I know that; but the activity and smartness?"

"Activity, sir? Why, I'm as light as a feather, sir, and I'd run up the ratlines and away aloft and clap my hand on the main-truck long afore some o' your youngsters."

"Well, Strake, I'll take you."

"Why—"

"Stop a moment. It must be with the understanding that you undertake anything I set you to do, for there may be a good boatswain aboard."

"Right, sir; any thing's my work. I'll see about my kit at once."

"Syd, you shall go with me, unless you would like to wait for a chance on another ship."

"No, father, I'll go with you," cried Syd. "And what about Pan?"

"He can come," said the captain. "Now leave me with your uncle, I want to talk to him at once."

A complete change seemed to have come over Barney as he made for the open window, not walking as usual, but in a light trot upon his toes, as if he were once more on the deck of a ship; and as soon as he was in the garden and out of sight of the window, he folded his arms and began to evince his delight by breaking into the first few steps of a hornpipe.

He was just in the middle of it when Pan came silently up behind with a board in each hand, to stand gazing from Syd to his father and back again in speechless wonderment, and evidently fully believing that the old man had gone mad.

All at once Barney was finishing off his dance with a curve round on his heels, but this brought him face to face with his wide-eyed, staring son.

The effect was instantaneous. He stopped short in a peculiar attitude, feeling quite abashed at being found so engaged, and Syd could hardly contain his laughter at the way in which the old boatswain got out of his difficulty.

"What now, you ugly young swab!" he roared. "Never see a sailor of the ryle navy stretch his legs afore?"

"Is that how sailors stretches their legs?" said Pan, slowly.

"Yes, it be. Now then, what have you got to say to that?"

"You arn't a sailor, father."

"What? Hear him, Master Syd? That's just what I am, boy, and you too. We're all on us outward bound; and now you come along, and I'll just show you something with a rope's-end."

"Why, I aren't been doing nothing now," cried Pan, drawing back.

"Who said you had, you swab! Heave ahead. Stow talking and get that there rope. I'm going to give you your first lesson in knotting and splicing. Ah, you've got something to larn now, my lad. Go and run that there barrow and them tools into the shed. No more gardening. Come on into the yard, Master Syd, and we'll rig up that there big pole, and a yard across it, and I'll show you both how to lay out with your feet in the sturrup. Come on."

"But, Master Syd, father isn't going to sea again, is he?"

"Yes, Pan, we're all off to join a fine frigate."

"And make men on you both," cried Barney. "Lor', it's a wonder to me how I've managed to live this 'long-shore life so long. Come on, my lads. No, no, don't walk like that. Think as you've got a deck under your feet, and run along like this."

Barney set the example, and Syd laughed again, for the gardener seemed to have gone back ten years of big life, and trotted along as active as a boy.

Chapter Fifteen

"Have they come, Syd, lad?" said the admiral, as the boy walked into the private room of the Red Lion, Shoreport, where the old man had taken up his quarters for the past fortnight, and had spent his time down at the docks, where the *Sirius* was being overhauled in her rigging, and was getting in her stores and ammunition ready for her start to the West Indian station in another week's time.

The coach had not long come in, and on hearing the horn the old sailor, with a twinkle in his eye, had sent the lad to do exactly what he wanted, but would have shrunk from for fear of seeming particular.

"Yes, uncle," he said quietly, "a box has come."

"Well, well, where is it?"

"I told him to put it in my bedroom."

"Well, why don't you go and open it, and see if your outfit is all right?"

"Oh, there's plenty of time, uncle," said Syd, with assumed carelessness.

"Yah! get out, you miserable young humbug. Think I was never a boy myself, and don't know what it means. You're red-hot to go and look at your duds. There, be off and put on your full-dress uniform, and then come down and let's see."

"Put them on, uncle, now?"

"Yes; put them on now," cried the old man, imitating his nephew's voice and manner. "Yes, put them on—now. Not ashamed of the King's livery, are you?"

"No, sir, of course not."

"Then go and put them on, and don't come down with your cocked hat wrong way on."

Syd hesitated, feeling a little abashed, but his uncle half jumped out of his seat.

"Be off, you disobedient young dog," he roared. "If you don't want to see them, I do. There, I'll give you a quarter of an hour."

Sydney took half an hour, and then hesitated about going down-stairs. He peeped out of his room twice, but there was always some one on the stairs, chambermaid, waiter, or guest staying in the place.

At last, though, all seemed perfectly quiet, and fixing his cocked hat tightly on his head, and holding his dirk with one hand to keep it from swinging about and striking the balusters, he ran along the passage and dashed down the stairs.

The quick movement caused his cocked hat to come down in front over his eyes, and before he had raised it again he had run right into the arms of the stout landlady. There was a shrill scream, and the lady was seated on the mat, while by the force of the rebound Sydney was sitting on the stairs, from which post he sprang up to offer his apologies.

"You shouldn't, my dear," said the landlady, piteously, as she stretched out her hands like a gigantic baby who wanted to be helped up.

Sydney's instincts prompted him to rush on to his father's small sitting-room, but politeness and the appeal of the lady compelled him to stay; and after he had raised her to her proper perpendicular, she smiled and cast her eyes over his uniform, making the boy colour like a girl.

"Well, you do look nice," she said; "only don't knock me down again. There, I'm not hurt. They're quite new, ain't they?"

Sydney nodded.

"I thought so, because you haven't got them on quite right."

Sydney stopped to hear no more, but ran on, checked himself, and tried to walk past three waiters in the entry with dignity.

He did not achieve this, because if he had the waiters would not have laughed and put their napkins to their mouths, on drawing back to let him pass.

"Oh, shouldn't I like to!" he thought, as he set his teeth and clenched his fists.

He felt very miserable and as if he was being made a laughing-stock; in fact his sensations were exactly those of a sensitive lad who appears in uniform for the first time; and hence he was in anything but a peaceful state of mind as he dashed into the room where his uncle was waiting, to be greeted with a roar of laughter.

"What a time you have been, sir! Why, Syd, I don't think much of your legs, and, hang it all, your belt's too loose, and they don't fit you. Bah! you haven't half dressed yourself. Come here. Takes me back fifty years, boy, to see you like that."

"Why did you tell me to go and put them on?" cried the boy, angrily, "if you only meant to laugh at me?"

"Bah! nonsense! What do you mean, sir? Are you going to be so thin-skinned that you can't bear to be joked? Come here."

The boy stood by his side.

"I was going to show you how to take up your belt and to button your waistcoat. There! that's better. Flying out like that at me because I laughed! How will you get along among your messmates, who are sure to begin roasting you as soon as you go aboard?"

"I beg your pardon, uncle. I seemed to feel so ridiculous, and everybody laughed."

"Let them. There! that's better. See how a touch or two from one who knows turns a slovenly look into one that's smart. Hallo! some one at the door, my lad; go and see. No; stop. Come in."

The door was opened, and Barney in his uniform of petty officer entered, looking smartened up into a man ten years younger than when he worked in the garden at the Heronry.

As Barney took off his hat and entered, closing the door behind him, his eyes lit first upon Syd, and his face puckered up into a broad grin.

"And now you!" cried Sydney, angrily. "Uncle, I'm not fit to wear a uniform; I look ridiculous."

"Who says so?" cried the old man, angrily. "Here you, Strake, don't stand grinning there like a corbel on an old church."

"Couldn't help it, your honour."

"There, you see, uncle."

"I don't, sir. Going to let the grin of that confounded fellow upset you? If he laughs at you again because he thinks you are a fool, show him that you're not one; knock him down."

"His honour the captain's compliments, Sir Thomas, and he'd be glad to see you on board along o' Master Sydney here."

"Is your master on board, then?"

"Ay, sir; and I've come across in the gig, as is waiting for us with one of the young gentlemen to keep the men in their places."

"Right; we'll come," said the old admiral. "Now, Syd," he whispered, "do you know why people laugh?"

"Yes, uncle, at me."

"Well, yes, my lad; so they did at me years ago. But you don't know why."

"I think I do, uncle."

"No, boy, you do not; you look as if you had got on your uniform for the first time. We're going out now, so look as if you hadn't got it on for the first time. Hold up your head, cock your hat, and if you look at people, don't look as if you were wondering what they thought of you, but as if you were taking his weight. See?"

"Yes, uncle, I think I do. But must I go like this?"

"Confound you, sir!" growled the old man. "Why do you talk like that?"

"Because I look absurd."

"Oh, that's it, is it? Then look here, Syd, I'll prove that you don't."

"If you can prove that, uncle, I shall never mind wearing a uniform again."

"Then you need not mind, boy, for if you looked absurd I wouldn't be seen with you. Now then, hold up your head, and remember you are a king's officer. March!"

The old man gave his cane a thump, cocked his own hat, and stamped along by the side of his nephew. Pan, who was outside waiting for his father's return, staring wide-eyed at Sydney's uniform, and then following behind with Barney, wishing he was allowed to wear a little gilded sword like that.

In this way they walked down to the boat, which lay a short distance from the landing-place, with a handsome boy in middy's uniform leaning back in the stern-sheets, and keeping strict watch on his men to keep them from yielding to the attraction of one of the public-houses, stronger than that of duty.

Barney stepped forward and hailed the boat, which was quickly rowed alongside, the coxswain holding on as the admiral stepped in, followed by his nephew, who found himself directly after beside the good-looking, dark-complexioned middy, who took the helm, and gave the order to give way. The oars fell with a splash, and Sydney felt that he was at last afloat and on his way to join the frigate.

The admiral took snuff, and after a word or two with the middy in charge of the boat, sat gazing silently about him, while from time to time Sydney turned his eyes to find that his companion was examining him closely, and with a supercilious air which made the new addition to the midshipmen's mess feel irritable and ready to resent any insult.

But none was offered, and the men rowed on, till after threading their way through quite a forest of masts the frigate was sighted.

"There she lies, Syd," whispered his uncle; "as fine a craft as you need wish to see. What's your name, youngster?"

"Michael Terry," said the midshipman.

"Ho!" ejaculated the admiral. "Well, this is my nephew, Sydney Belton, your new messmate. I hope you'll be very good friends."

"I'm sure we shan't," said the young fellow to himself. "Too cocky for me. But we can soon cut his comb."

"Arn't you going to shake hands, youngsters?"

"Oh, yes, if you like," said the youth. "There's my hand."

Sydney put out his, but somehow the hand-shake which followed did not seem to be a friendly one, and more than once afterwards he thought about that first grip.

"Ah, that's right," said the admiral; "always be good friends with your messmates."

Syd looked up quickly, and a feeling of angry resentment made his cheeks flush, for his eyes encountered those of the midshipman, and being exceedingly sensitive that day, it seemed to him that Terry was laughing in his sleeve at Sir Thomas.

Syd's eyes flashed, and the young officer stared at him haughtily in return, his glance seeming to say, "Well, I shall laugh at the comical-looking old boy if I like."

The eye encounter which had commenced was checked by Sir Thomas suddenly turning to his nephew.

"There's your ship, boy," he said, "and I wish you luck in her."

Syd looked in the direction pointed out, to see the long, graceful vessel lying at anchor with quite a swarm of men busy aloft bending on new sails, renewing the running-rigging, and repairing the damages caused her in a severe encounter with a storm. And as he gazed with an unpleasant feeling of shrinking troubling him, the boat rapidly neared the side, the oars were thrown up, the coxswain deftly manoeuvred the stern close to the ladder, held on, and Sir Thomas rose and went up the side with an activity that seemed wonderful for his years.

Then with a sensation of singing in his ears, and confused and puzzled by the novelty of all around, Sydney Belton somehow found himself standing on deck facing his father, who came forward to meet the admiral, then gave him a nod and a look which took in his uniform before he went aft, leaving the new-comer standing alone and feeling horribly strange, and in everybody's way.

For the boat's crew were busy making fast the gig in which they had come aboard, and Syd had to move three times, each position he took up seeming to be worse.

He wanted to go after Sir Thomas, but did not like to stir, and he felt all the more uncomfortable as he noticed that people kept looking at him, and talking to one another about him, he felt sure.

"Where can Barney be gone?" he muttered, angrily. "How stupid to leave me standing dressed up like this for every one to stare at! Father ought to have stopped."

He gave a furtive glance to the left, and the blood flushed in his cheeks again as he caught sight of Terry, who was talking to another lad of his own age in uniform, and Syd felt that they must be talking about him; and if he had felt any doubt before, their action would have endorsed his opinion, for they smiled at one another and walked away.

"It's too bad," he said to himself; "they must know how horribly strange I feel."

"Hullo, squire! Who are you?"

Syd turned round to face the speaker, for the words had, as it were, been barked almost into his ear, and he had heard no one approach, for it had seemed to be one of the peculiarities of aboard ship that people passed to and fro and by him without making a sound.

He found himself facing a stern, middle-aged man in uniform, who looked him over at a glance, and Syd flinched again, for the officer smiled slightly, not a pleasant smile, for it seemed as if he were going to bite.

"I am Sydney Belton, sir."

"Eh? Oh, the captain's boy. Yes, of course. In full rig, eh? Well, why don't you go below? You look so strange."

"Does he mean in uniform?" thought Syd.

"Yes, sir," he said aloud. "My father has gone down there."

"Aft, boy, aft; don't say down there. Well, why don't you go below? Seen your messmates?"

"I have seen the young officer who came with us in the boat."

"Eh? Who was that? Yes, I remember. Well, he ought to have taken you down. Here, Mr Terry, Mr Roylance—oh, there you are!—take Mr Belton down and introduce him to his messmates; and, I say, youngster—no, never mind now. Look sharp and learn your duties. Hi! you sirs, what are you doing with that yard?" he yelled out to some men up aloft, and he walked nimbly away just as the two midshipmen joined Syd.

"Thought, as you were the captain's son, you might be going to have your quarters in the cabin," said Terry, with a sneering look in his face. "Be better there, wouldn't he, Roy?"

"I should think so," said the other, looking at the new-comer quizzically.

"My father said I should have to be with the other midshipmen," said Syd, quickly.

"With the midshipmen, not the *other* midshipmen," said Terry, with a sneer. "You are not a midshipman, are you?"

"I suppose I am going to be one when I have learned how," replied Sydney, shortly. "My father said that I was not to expect any favours because I was the captain's son."

"Did he now?" said Roylance; "and what did your mother say?"

Syd winced, and looked so sharply at the speaker that the latter pretended to be startled.

"Wo ho!" he cried. "I say, Terry, this chap's a fire-eater; a bit wild."

"Here, come along down, youngster. Don't banter him, Hoy," said Terry, who had noticed that the officer who had given the order was coming back, and he led the way toward the companion-ladder.

"Who's that gentleman in uniform?" said Sydney. "Eh? That one?" said Terry, looking in another direction. "Oh, that's the purser. You'll have to be very civil to him—ask him to dinner and that sort of thing."

"No, no, I wouldn't do that at first," said Roylance, as they descended. "Ask him to have a glass of grog with you."

"Yes," said Terry. "Get to the dinner by and by. Pray how old are you?"

"Between sixteen and seventeen," replied Sydney, who writhed under his companion's supercilious ways, but was determined to make friends if he could.

"Are you though?" said Roylance. "Fine boy for his age; eh, Mike?"

"Very. Mind your head, youngster. We're going to have all this properly lighted now, I suppose. Our last captain did not give much thought to the 'tween decks. By the way, the young gentlemen of our mess are a bit particular. He ought to show to the best advantage, eh, Roy, and make a good impression."

"Yes, of course."

"Perhaps," continued Terry, turning to Syd, "you'd like to see the ship's barber and have a shave before we go in."

"No, thank you," said Syd, laughing, "I don't shave."

"Remarkable," said Roylance.

"Don't banter, Roy," cried Terry. "The young gentleman is strange, and you take advantage, and begin to be funny. Don't you take any notice of him. By the way though, I didn't introduce you. This is Mr William Roylance, Esquire. Father's not a captain, but a bishop, priest, or deacon, or something of that kind. Very good young man, but don't you lend him money! I say, see that door?"

"Yes," said Sydney, looking at a dimly-seen opening barely lit by a smoky lanthorn.

"Thought I'd show you. Hot water baths in there if you ever wash."

"Ever wash?" said Syd, wonderingly.

"Yes. We do here—a little—when there is any water. Rather particular on board a frigate. Here we are."

He led the way to where in a dimly-lit hole, so it seemed to Sydney, about half a dozen youths were seated beneath a swinging lanthorn busily engaged in some game, which consisted in driving a penny-piece along a dirty wooden table, scoured with lines and spotted with blackened drops of tallow.

The coming, as it seemed, of a visitor, in all the neatness and show of a spick and span new uniform, caused a cessation of the game and its accompanying noise; but before a word was spoken, Sydney had taken in at a glance the dingy aspect of the place, and had time to consider whether this was the midshipmen's berth.

"Here you are, gentlemen," shouted Terry. "Your new messmate: the boy with a belt on."

"Let him take it off then," cried a voice. "Come on, youngster, here's room. Got any money?"

Syd thought of his new uniform and felt disposed to shrink, but he did not hesitate. He had an idea that if he was to share the mess of the lads about him, the sooner he was on friendly terms the better, so he nodded and went forward; but his pace was increased by a sudden thrust from behind, which sent him against the end of the table, and his hat flying to the other side.

"Shame! shame!" cried Terry, loudly, and there was a roar of laughter. "Look here, Roy, I won't have it; it's too bad. Not hurt, are you, Belton?"

"No," said Syd, turning and looking him full in the face; "only a little to find you should think me such a fool as not to know you pushed me."

"I? Come, young fellow, you'll have to learn manners."

He moved threateningly toward Syd, but the latter did not heed him, for his attention was taken up by what was going on at the table, for one of the lads cried out—

"Any one want a new hat? Too big for me."

"Let me try."

"No; pass it here."

"Get out, I want one most."

There was a roar of laughter, and Syd bit his lip as he saw his new hat snatched about from one to the other, and tried on in all sorts of ways, back front, amidships, over the eyes, over the ears, and it was by no means improved when the new hand snatched it back and turned to face Terry.

"Look here, sir," said the latter, haughtily; "you had the insolence to accuse me of having pushed you."

There was a dead silence as Sydney stood brushing his hat with the sleeve of his coat, and without shrinking, for there was a curious ebullition going on in his breast. He did not look up, for he was fighting—self, and thinking about his new uniform in a peculiar way. That is to say, in connection with dirty floors, scuffles, falls, the dragging about of rough hands, etcetera.

"Do you hear what I say, sir?" continued Terry, loudly, and every neck was craned forward in the dim cockpit.

"Yes, I heard what you said," replied Syd, huskily; and then he bit his lip and tried to force down the feeling of rage which was in his breast.

"And I heard what you said, sir," cried Terry, ruffling up like a game-cock, and thinking to awe the new reefer and impress the lads present, over whom he ruled with a mighty hand. "You are amongst gentlemen here, and we don't allow new greenhorns or country bumpkins to come and insult us."

"I don't want to insult anybody," said Syd, in a low tone. "I want to be friends, as my father told me to be."

"But you insulted me, sir. You said I pushed you just now."

"So you did," cried Sydney, a little more loudly.

"What?" cried Terry, threateningly.

"And then shammed that it was that other middy."

A murmur of excitement ran round the mess.

"Why, you insolent young cub," cried Terry, seizing Sydney by the collar of his coat; but quick as thought his hand was struck aside, and the two lads were chest to chest, glaring in each other's eyes.

"Oh, that's it, is it?" cried Terry, with a mocking laugh. "Well, the sooner he has his plateful of humble-pie the better; eh, lads?"

The murmur of excitement increased.

"Then I shall have to fight," thought Syd; but at that moment a gruff voice exclaimed—

"Cap'en wants you, Master Syd. Admiral's going ashore."

Chapter Sixteen

"Why, what was up, sir?" whispered Barney, whose timely appearance put an end to the discussion. "Wasn't going to be a fight, weer it?"

"I suppose so, Barney," said Syd, rather dolefully.

"Then it'll have to be yet, lad; but it's a bit early."

"Yes, Barney."

"They didn't lose no time in 'tackling on yer."

"No, Barney."

"Well, lad, it's part of a reefer's eddication, so you'll have to go through with it. You're a toughish chickin as can whack my Pan; and he knows how to fight, as lots o' the big lads knows at home."

"I don't want to fight," said Sydney, bitterly.

"No, my lad, but you've got to now. Well, that there's a big un, and he'll lick you safe; but you give him a tough job to do it, and then all t'others 'll let you alone."

"Well, Syd, lad; seen your new messmates?" cried a cheery voice.

"Yes, uncle, I've seen them."

"That's right, boy. I'm going ashore now. I'm proud of your ship, Syd, proud of the crew, and proud of you, my lad. Keep your head up, and may I live to see you posted. No, that's too much, but I must see you wear your first swab."

"Am I to go ashore with uncle, father?" said Sydney.

"Hush, my boy, once for all," said Captain Belton. "You are a junior officer now; I am your captain. We must keep our home life for home. No, Mr Belton, you will not go ashore again. You have joined your ship, and your chest will be brought on board by the boatswain."

"Is Barney going to be a boatswain, sir?" cried Sydney, in his eagerness.

Captain Belton gave him a look which said plainly enough, "Remember that I am your captain, sir!"

And feeling abashed, the boy looked in another direction, to see that Barney was winking and screwing up his face in the most wonderful way to convey certain information of the fact that in his inexperience Sydney had not read in his uniform.

"There, good-bye, Syd," said the old admiral, after a few minutes' more conversation with the captain, during which time the boat's crew had been piped away, and Terry had hurried on deck to take charge once more. Then there was a warm grasp of the hand as the old man leaned toward him, his words seeming the more impressive after what had just occurred.

"God bless you, my lad!" he whispered. "You'll get some hard knocks; perhaps it'll come to a fight among your messmates, but if it does, don't have your comb cut. Recollect you're a Belton, and never strike your colours. Always be a gentleman, Syd, and never let any young blackguard with a dirty mind lead you into doing anything you couldn't own to openly. There, that's all, my boy. Drop the father, and never go to him with tales; he has to treat you middies all alike. There! Oh, one word; don't bounce and show off among your messmates, because your father's the captain, and you've got an old hulk at home who is an admiral; but whenever you want a few guineas to enjoy yourself, Uncle Tom's your banker, you dog. There! Be off!"

Syd tried hard, but his eyes would get a little dim as the bluff old gentleman touched his hat to the officers, and went over the side, while the captain put his hands behind him and walked thoughtfully aft, to have a long consultation with the first lieutenant, after which he too went ashore without seeing his son again, and Sydney prepared for his first night on board.

There was so much that was novel that the new middy had no time to feel dull, and he spent his time on deck, watching the return of the boat, saw it swung up to its davits again, and then, after noting the marines relieve guard, and the sentries at their posts, he was going forward, when he encountered the officer who had before spoken to him.

"Got your traps on board yet, Mr Belton?"

"Not yet, sir. My chest is coming to-night."

"That's right. You'll be in a different fig then to-morrow, and I'll have a talk to you. Better pick up what you can from your messmates, but don't quarrel, and don't believe everything they tell you."

He nodded not unkindly to the boy, and went off, while Barney, who had been watching his opportunity, came up and touched his hat.

"Your chest's come aboard, sir, and I've had it put below. Better keep it locked, my lad, for you'll find my young gents pretty handy with their games."

"Thank you, Barney."

"Say Strake, sir, please now, or bo'sun."

"Very well, Strake. Where is Pan?"

"Right, sir. Forrard along with the other boys. Getting his roasting over. What yer think o' the first luff?"

"I haven't seen him yet, Bar— Strake."

"Oh, come now, sir; speak the truth whatever you do, and don't try those games on me. Why, I sin yer talking to him."

"That?" said Sydney, smiling, as one who knows better smiles at the ignorant. "Why, Strake, that was the purser."

"Poof!" ejaculated the boatswain, with a smothered laugh. "Who told you that, sir?"

"That midshipman who brought us off in the boat."

"A flam, sir, a flam. He was making game of you. That's the first luff."

"What a shame!" thought Syd, and then he fell a thinking about the orders he gave him—not to quarrel with his messmates. "And I'm sure to quarrel as soon as I go down. No, I will not. He may say what he likes."

"You speak, sir?" said the bo'sun.

"No, Strake, I was thinking."

"Here, you're wanted below, I think," said one of the warrant officers, coming up and speaking to the ex-gardener.

"Who wants me?"

"That's your boy, isn't it, that you brought aboard?"

"Ay, it is."

"Well, I think he has got into a bit of a row with some of the young monkeys below. Go and stop it at once."

"That's Pan-y-mar gone and showed his teeth, Master Syd," whispered the bo'sun, and he trotted forward, while feeling now that he ought to go and see about his chest, and at the same time wishing that he could go forward and see what was wrong about Pan—but fearing to make some breach of discipline—Sydney once more went below.

Chapter Seventeen

It was impossible to help thinking about the handsome old dining-room at the Heronry as Sydney sat down to his first meal at the midshipman's mess, and however willing he might have been to consider that polished mahogany tables and plate were not necessaries, he could not help comparing the food with that to which he had been accustomed.

As luck had it, he found himself seated next to Roylance, who laughed good-humouredly, and said—

"Don't take any notice of the rough joking, youngster."

He was not above a year older than Sydney, but he had been two years at sea, and seemed to look down from a height of experience at his companion.

"I am not going to," said Sydney, looking up frankly to the other's handsome face.

"That's right. Terry's cock of the walk here, and shows off a good deal. We all give in to him, so be civil too, and it will save a row. The luff doesn't like us to quarrel."

"He told me not to," said Syd.

"Then I wouldn't. If Terry gives you a punch on the head, take it, and never mind."

Syd was silent.

"Got your chest, haven't you?"

"Yes."

"Everything's new, awkward, and fresh to you now, but you'll soon get used to it. You'll put on your undress uniform to-morrow, of course. I'll tell you anything you want to know. Nobody told me when I came on board, and I had a hard time of it."

"Did the others tease you much?"

"They did and no mistake, and I got it worse because I kicked against it; and the *more* a fellow kicks, the more they worry you."

These few friendly advances from a messmate who seemed to be one of the most likely-looking for a companion, sent a feeling of warmth through the new-comer's breast, and in spite of the coarseness of the provisions, which were eked out with odds and ends brought by the middies from the shore, Sydney made a fairly satisfactory meal, the better that Terry was on duty.

"But I've got to meet him some time," thought Sydney; and he wondered how he would feel when he received that blow which was sure to come, and stamp him as one of the subordinates of the lad whom his new friend had dubbed the cock of the walk.

In spite of the novelty of everything about him, Syd had plenty of time to feel low-spirited, and to envy the light-heartedness of his new friend, who in the course of the evening seemed to feel that further apology was due for their first encounter that day.

"I say, Belton," he said, "I am sorry I played you those tricks and sided with Terry as I did. It was all meant for a game. We have such a rough, uncomfortable life here that one gets into the habit of making fun of everything and everybody, from the captain downwards."

"Don't say any more about it," replied Sydney, holding out his hand. "I'm not such a milksop that I mind it."

"That's right," cried Roylance, grasping the extended hand. "You'll soon be all right with us."

"Hi! look there," cried a squeaky-voiced little fellow at the end of the table; "there's old Roy making friends with the new fellow. I say, Belt, don't you believe him. He'll want to borrow money to-morrow."

Bang!

"No, you didn't," cried the little middy, who had ducked cleverly and avoided half a loaf which Roylance threw at his head and struck the bulkhead instead.

"You'll have to be stopped, Jenkins," said Roylance. "You've got off so far because you are such a miserable little beggar."

"Don't you believe him, Belt," cried the little fellow, who had a withered, old-mannish look, and an exceedingly small nose, like a peg in the middle of his face. "Roy's afraid of me. Look at that."

He slipped off his coat, drew up his sleeve, and exhibited his muscle in a pugnacious fashion, which brought forth a roar of laughter.

"Baby Jenks fights best with his tongue," said Roylance, coolly. "We shall have to cut it before he grows civil."

The rattle of the chattering tongues went on till bedtime, and at last, for the first time in his life, Sydney found himself lying in a hammock, tired out but confused, and hardly able to realise that he was down below in a close place, with his face not many inches from the ceiling with its beams and rings. Talking was going on upon each side. The place was very dark, and there was a dim-looking lantern swinging some distance away in the middle of what seemed to be a luminous fog.

He lay there thinking that the hammock was not so very uncomfortable, only he did not feel quite at home with his head and heels high, and as every time he moved he felt as if he must fall, he at last lay very still, thinking how strange it all was, and how he seemed to be completely separated from his father, as much so as if they were in different ships.

Then after coming to the conclusion that he rather liked Roylance, but that he should never care for life aboard ship, the light from the lanthorn swung to and fro a little, and then all was perfectly black where it had hung the minute before.

This did not trouble Syd, for it seemed quite a matter of course that the light should be put out, and so he lay thinking over all that had passed that day—that he was glad Barney Strake and Pan were on board; that Roy lance seemed to be so friendly; then that he should have to stand up and meet Terry before very long and allow himself to be thrashed. Then he thought about nothing at all, for that pleasant, restful sensation that precedes sleep came over him, and all was blank till he felt a curious shock and was wide-awake.

"Here, hi! What's the matter?" shouted a squeaky voice.

"I—I don't know," said Sydney, feeling about him and gradually realising that he was on the floor among his blankets. "I think the rope of my hammock has broken."

There was an outburst of tittering at this, and now it began to dawn upon him that he was the victim of some trick.

"Look here, you fellows," said a voice which Sydney recognised; "the first luff said there was to be no more of these games. Who did it?"

"Baby Jenks," said a voice, and there was a laugh.

"I didn't," squeaked the little middy; "it was one of Roy's games."

"Say it was me again, and I'll come and half smother you."

"Well, they said it was me," protested Jenkins. "I was asleep."

"Who was it?" cried Roylance again.

"Captain Belton, to make his boy sharp," said a voice out of the darkness—a voice evidently disguised by being uttered through a pair of half-closed hands.

There was a hearty laugh here, during which, feeling very miserable and dejected, Syd was groping about, trying to find out how the hammock was fastened, and in the darkness growing only more confused.

"Where are you?" said Roylance.

"Here. It's come untied, I think."

"Untied! You've been cut down."

"Cut?" said Sydney, wonderingly.

"Down. Never mind. It was only at your feet. I'll soon put you right again."

Syd stood there listening to his companions' hard breathing and the whispering and tittering going on in the other hammocks for a few minutes, during which a noise went on like as if a box was being corded. At last this ceased.

"There you are! Where are your blankets?"

"Here; but they're all in a dreadful muddle."

There was a shout of laughter at this, and directly after Sydney heard a gruff voice say—

"Steady there, young gen'lemen. Anything the matter?"

"No; it's all right. Only some one tumbled out of bed."

There was a low grumbling sound, and Roylance whispered—

"Never mind; I'll put 'em right for you. There you are; turn in, and I don't suppose any one will upset you after to-night. If anybody comes, and you hear him, hit out."

"Thank you," said Syd, rather dolefully; "I will."

He climbed into his hammock again, and listened to the rustling sound made by Roylance and the remarks of his messmates.

"Baby Jenks was right. Old Roy means to suck every shilling out of the new fellow," said a voice.

"Does he, Bolton?" cried Roylance. "I know your voice."

"Why, I never spoke. 'Twasn't me," cried the accused.

"Well, it sounded like you," grumbled Roylance, and there was another roar of laughter.

"Look here, youngsters, I want to go to sleep, and I'll come and cut down the next fellow who makes a row."

"Yah!"

"Boo!"

"Daren't!"

These ejaculations came tauntingly from different parts, but in smothered tones, which indicated that the voices were disguised, and after a few more threats from Roylance, there was perfect quiet once more in the berth.

"So I'm not to sleep," thought Sydney, "but keep guard and wait for whoever it was that cut the cords of my hammock. A nasty cowardly trick."

The fall and its following had so thoroughly roused up the sufferer that he felt not the slightest inclination to sleep, and feeling that he could easily keep awake and hear any one approach, he lay listening to the hard breathing on both sides till all grew more and more subdued; and though it was pitch dark the surroundings grew misty and strange, and Syd lay listening to a strange sound which made him turn his head in the direction of the door, towards where he could see a sturdily-built young fellow down on his hands and knees, crawling in as easily as a dog. Now he peered to one side, now to the other. Then he ran on all fours under the hammocks, which seemed to stand out quite clearly with their occupants therein. Then his head appeared, and it seemed, though he could not make out the face, that it was Terry. But the head disappeared again, and as Syd watched he felt that his hammock was the object in view, and in his dread he started to find that all was intensely dark and that he had been dreaming all this.

It was very hot, and there was heavy breathing all around, but not another sound, so feeling once more that it would be impossible to sleep, and that he might as well be on guard, Syd kept his vigil for quite five minutes, and then, as was perfectly natural, went off fast asleep again, to lie until it seemed to him that there was a crash of thunder, and then all was blank.

"Here, hi! Sentry! Bring a lantern. It's a mean, cowardly act, and I'll complain to the first lieutenant."

The roar of laughter which had been going on, mingled with comments, ceased at this, and was succeeded by a low buzzing sound, which seemed to Syd to be close to his ears as he saw a dim light, felt horribly sleepy, and as if his head ached violently.

"It's too bad. The other was only a game. The poor fellow's head's cut and bleeding, and whoever did this is a mean-spirited coward, and no gentleman."

"Shall I go and rouse up the doctor, sir?"

"No; we'll bind it up, and keep it all quiet. There'd be no end of trouble if the captain knew. I only wish I knew who did it, cutting a fellow down by the head like this."

Syd tried to speak, but he was like one in a dream.

"If I knew who it was—" said Roylance.

"What would you do?" said a voice, which Syd seemed to recognise; "go and tell his daddy?"

"No; I'd tell him he was a mean-spirited, cowardly hound," said Roylance, "and not fit for the society of gentlemen."

"Hark at the bishop's boy, I dare say he did it himself."

"Just the sort of thing I should do!" replied Roylance, sharply. "More likely one of Mike Terry's brutal tricks."

"Oh, very well, Master Roy. You and I can talk that over another time. So you mean to say I did it?"

Roylance did not answer, and just then Sydney recovered his voice, the faintness passing away like a cloud. "Was it he?" whispered the boy. "I'm not sure," whispered Roylance. "Don't quarrel because of me. Does my head bleed now?"

"No; I've tied my handkerchief tightly round it. Lie still, you'll be better soon.—Here, marine, knot up that hammock again. You shan't be cut down again, for I'll keep watch."

"There's nothing the matter," said Terry, from the other end of the berth; "it's only one of Miss Roylance's fads. Currying favour with the skipper by making a pet monkey of his boy."

Roylance ground his teeth, and Syd lay very quiet listening, and watching the marine as he knotted together the broken lines, helping him in afterwards, and going away with the lantern.

"Don't wait," whispered Syd; "it's very good of you, but I'm not hurt much. They cut the ropes up by my head, didn't they?"

"Yes; the cowards! But I don't think they'll touch you again now. Shall I stop?"

"No; don't, please. I may as well take my chance."

"Very well," said Roylance, and he went back to his own hammock amongst the remarks and laughs of those who, from liking or dread, had made themselves the parasites of the leader of the mess.

Chapter Eighteen

Syd started into wakefulness in the morning to find that he had been sleeping heavily. His head ached a little, and when he moved there was a smarting sensation, but he felt disturbed mentally more than in body. He turned out of his hammock and dressed as quickly as the new stiff buttonholes of his uniform would allow, all the time suffering from a sensation of misery and discomfort which made his temper anything but amiable.

"How's your head?" said Roylance, who was one of the last to wake.

"Bad—sore—aches."

"Let me look."

Syd submitted himself unwillingly.

"Only wants a bathe, and a bit of plaister. I'll see to that."

The dressing was finished, the hammocks rolled up, and Syd was wondering how long breakfast would be, and what they should have. Terry, who was strolling about the place watching him furtively, suddenly stood aside, the others watching him.

At that moment Roylance came down into his berth with a pair of scissors and some sticking-plaister.

"Here you are," he said. "I'll just cut a little of the hair away, and put a bit of this on. It won't show under your hat."

"All right," said Syd, sitting down in the middle of the place on the top of his sea-chest; "but you needn't have fetched that. I had some in here."

"Do for next time," said Roylance, cutting off a large piece of plaister.

"Oh, nonsense," said Syd, laughing; "a quarter of that would do. I could do it myself if I could see."

Just then Terry came swaggering up, and Roylance winced, the scissors with which he was cutting the plaister trembling a little.

"Oh, look here, Master Roy," said Terry, haughtily. "You made some remarks to me in the night about that cutting down of the hammock. I want an apology from you."

"I'm busy now, Mr Terry," said Roylance; and the irritable feeling which troubled Syd seemed to be on the increase.

"I didn't ask you if you were busy, sir, I said I wanted an apology," continued Terry, while the rest of the mess looked on excitedly at the promising quarrel between the two eldest middies on board the *Sirius*.

"I'm attending to this new messmate's hurt."

"Let him go to the doctor if he is hurt," snarled Terry. "I tell you I want an apology. You as good as said that I cut down this cub's hammock last night."

"If I had quite said it, I dare say I shouldn't have been far wrong," replied Roylance, in a low tone.

"Oh, indeed, miss," sneered Terry, "you always were clever with your tongue, like the long thin molly you are. Now then, take that back before—"

He ceased speaking and doubled his fists.

Syd felt as if he were sitting on a fire, and something within him was beginning to boil.

"I'm not going to apologise now," said Roylance, wincing a little, but speaking more determinedly than before.

"Arn't you? Then I'm going to make you," said Terry. "Bolton, go to the bottom of the ladder and give warning."

"No, no; send Jenks," said the boy addressed, appealingly.

"You go, and do as you're told," said Terry, fiercely; and Syd felt as if he must boil over soon, no matter how much he was hurt.

"Now then, Miss Roylance, if you please, I'm waiting," said Terry, in an offensive way. "You're such a talker that you can easily make a nice apology."

Roylance went on cutting and sticking the piece of plaister.

"Do you hear me, sir?" cried Terry, "or am I to set Baby Jenks to thrash you?"

"Stand up, Belton," said Roylance, quietly. "Now then, turn a little more to the light;" and Sydney rose.

"Stand aside, youngster. I want to give Miss Roylance a bit of sticking-plaister first."

As he spoke he gave Syd, who was between them, a push, whose result astounded him.

"Out of the way will you," cried Syd, fiercely; "can't you see he's busy?"

That which had been boiling in him had gone over the side at last, and Terry stopped short staring with astonishment.

"If you want to talk to him, wait till he has done my head. Better talk to me, for it was you, you great coward, who cut me down."

"Why you—oh, this is too good!" cried Terry, with a forced laugh, as he looked round at the little knot of his messmates. "There, wait a minute till I've done with Molly Roylance, and I'll soon settle your little bill."

Roylance stood looking pale and excited, with the scissors and plaister still in his hand, but on his guard ready to spring back or sidewise if attacked. Then he, like his would-be assailant, stared in astonishment. For Syd had resumed his position between them as if about to lower his head to the light; when, feeling that if he wished to maintain his character he must act sharply against what was to him a new boy in the midshipman's mess, Terry laid hold of Syd's collar and swung him round.

"Out of the way, will you!" he said; and as the road was clear he made a spring at Roylance, but suddenly gave his head a twist, tripped over the new sea-chest that was in the way, and fell heavily.

"Oh, that's it, is it?" he cried, as he sprang to his feet. "Well, the sooner you have your lesson the better."

He began to divest himself of his upper garment as he spoke; and Syd, whose teeth were set, and whose knuckles were tingling from the effect of the blow he had planted on Terry, rapidly imitated him.

"No, no," said Roylance, excitedly; "this is my quarrel. You see fair."

"You want me to quarrel with you?" cried Syd, fiercely; "see fair yourself. Hold that."

He threw his garment to the tall slight lad, and rolled up his sleeves, to stand forth no mean antagonist for the bully, though Terry was a couple of inches taller, as many years older, and better set.

"Be ready to pick him up, Molly Roy," said Terry, sneeringly. "Get a sponge and a basin of water ready, Baby Jenks, and—"

He staggered back. For as he spoke he had begun sparring at one who was smarting with rage, and the thought that the cowardly fellow who had injured him so in the night was before him ready for him to take his revenge. Syd thought of nothing else, and the moment he was facing his adversary, clashed in at him, delivering so fierce a blow that Terry nearly went down.

Then came and went blow after blow. There was a close, a fierce struggle here and there, and both went down just as a pair of broad shoulders were seen at the door beside those of Bolton, who was keeping watch over the fight instead of the companion-ladder, and the broad shoulders and the rugged countenance were those of the new boatswain.

"Arn't lost much time," he growled.

"No. Don't stop 'em," whispered Bolton. "Let them have it out."

"Oh, I arn't agoin' to stop 'em," growled back Barney. "He's got to be a fighting man, so he'd better larn to fight."

"Can he fight?" whispered the middy.

"Seems like it, sir: that was right in the nose."

An excited murmur ran through the spectators, as after a sharp little episode, during which Syd had been a good deal knocked about, Terry went back against the bulkhead and stood with his hand to his face.

"Ready for the sponge and basin, Mike Terry?" squeaked Jenks; and there was a laugh.

"I'll remember that, Baby," cried Terry, squaring up to his adversary again with the full intention of putting an end to an encounter beneath his dignity; and after a sharp struggle Syd's crown struck the bulkhead loudly, and he went down sitting on a locker.

"That's done him," said Bolton, with a sigh, as if he were disappointed.

"Not it, my lad. Master Syd arn't got warm yet. Your chap's got his work cut out to lick him."

"Then he can fight?" whispered Bolton, eagerly.

"Well, it arn't so much his fighting; it's a way he's got o' not being able to leave off when he's wound up, and that tires 'em. Look at that."

The fight had been renewed by Terry rushing forward to finish off his antagonist, who had seemed to be a little confused by the last round.

But Sydney eluded him, and with a wonderful display of activity avoided several awkward blows, and after wearying his enemy managed to deliver one with all his might in unpleasant proximity to Terry's eyes.

The struggle went on with varying success, Syd on the whole naturally getting far the worst of it; but Barney stood stolidly looking on, and when Roylance felt his heart sink as he saw how badly his brave young defender was being beaten, the boatswain said coolly to Bolton in reply to a—

"Now then, what do you think of that?"

"Lot's o' stuff in him yet, young gen'leman. He's good for another hour."

There was encounter after encounter, and close after close, during which Syd generally went down first; but to Terry's astonishment the more he knocked his young antagonist about the fiercer it made him, and at last after delivering a successful blow full in Syd's chest he cried out—

"Take him away, Roy; I don't want to hurt him any—"

Terry did not finish his remark, for the second half of that last word was knocked back by a bang right in the mouth, followed up by several others so rapidly delivered that the champion of the midshipmen's mess went down this time without a struggle.

"What do you think o' that, young gen'leman?" said Barney.

"Hurray!" whispered Bolton, bending down and squeezing his hands between his knees; "he'll lick him."

"Eh? I thought he was your man."

"A beast! He's always knocking us about," whispered Bolton. "Hurray! go it, Belt."

The adversaries were face to face again, and there was a breathless silence.

"Had enough?" panted Terry.

"No, not half," cried Syd, rushing at him.

"Look at that! See his teeth?" said Barney. "That's British bull-dog, that is. Master Syd never fights till he's made, but when he does—My eye! that was a crack."

But it was not Barney's eye. It was Terry's, and the blow was so sharp that the receiver went down into a corner, and refused to get up again, while the subjects of the fallen king crowded round the victor eager to shake hands.

"No, no," panted Syd; "don't: my knuckles are all bleeding. What's my face like?" he said sharply to Roylance.

"Knocked about; but never mind that, Belton; you've won."

"I don't mind," was the reply; "and I don't want to win. Are you much hurt?" he continued, going to Terry's corner, where the vanquished hero was still seated upon the floor with little Jenkins, with much sympathy, offering to sponge his face.

"I'm sorry we fought," said Syd, quietly. "Shake hands."

There was no reply.

"You're not hurt much, are you?"

Terry gave him one quick look, and then let his head down on his chest.

"You'll shake hands?" said Syd. "We can be friends now."

Still no notice.

"Shake hands, Mike Terry," piped little Jenkins. "You've licked everybody, and it was quite your turn."

"Hold your tongue, you little wretch," hissed the other. "I owe you something for this."

"Ha, ha, ha!" laughed the impish little fellow, beginning to caper about with the sponge. "You touch me again and I'll get Belton to give you your gruel. You nasty great coward, you've got it at last."

"Don't you be a coward," said Syd, sharply. "Now, Mr Terry, I'm very sorry: shake hands."

"Here, one of you take that basin and sponge away from Jenks," said Terry, getting up painfully. "He wouldn't have done this if I hadn't hurt one of my arms."

"Well, if I was licked fair like that, I would own to it," said Bolton. "It was fair, wasn't it, Roy?"

"As fair as a fight could be," was the reply.

"Yes," said Barney, thrusting in his head, "that was as fair as could be, Master Syd."

"What you, Barney!"

"Bo'sun, sir. I wouldn't interrupt you afore, 'cause I knowed you wouldn't like it, but the captain wants to see you."

"What!" cried Sydney, as he clapped his hands to his swollen nose and lips. "Wants to see me?"

"Soon as ever he's done his braxfass, sir."

"Oh, what shall I do?" cried Syd.

"Dunno, sir," said the boatswain, grinning, "unless you sends word you're sea-sick, for you do look bad."

"No, no, I can't do that."

"Oh, I dunno, sir," said the boatswain, chuckling. "You was sea-sick months before you joined your ship, so I don't see why you shouldn't be now. My Panny-mar's got it too. Took bad last night."

"What, has he been fighting?"

"Didn't ask him, sir; but he can't see out of his eyes, and when I asked him how he felt, he grinned like all on one side."

"I heard there was a fight with a new boy," piped out Jenkins. "Had it out with Monkey Bill and licked him. Was that your boy, bo'sun?"

"That's him, sir. We all comes of a fighting breed; him and me and the cap'en and Master Syd here. Skipper's awful, and I shall be sorry for the Frenchies and Spanies as he tackles. Well, Master Syd, what am I to tell the captain's sarvant 'bout you?"

"Go and ask to see the captain," said Syd, firmly, "and tell him that I have been having a fight, and am not fit to come."

"Hear that?" said the boatswain, looking proudly round—"hear that, young gen'lemen? That's Bri'sh bull-dog, that is. What do you think of your messmate now?"

The middies gave a cheer, and crowded round Syd as Terry bent over the locker to bathe his swollen face, and he looked up once, but did not say a word.

"Some says fighting among boys is a bad thing," muttered the boatswain, as he went on deck, "and I don't approve of it. But when one chap bullies all the rest, same as when one country begins to wallop all the others, what are you to do?"

Chapter Nineteen

As Bo'sun Strake reached the deck, he came suddenly upon the first lieutenant, and touched his hat.

"Where have you been, my man?"

"Down below, sir."

"I said where have you been, my man?" said the lieutenant, sternly.

"Young gentlemen's quarters, sir."

"What was going on there?"

The bo'sun hesitated, but the lieutenant's eyes fixed him, and he said, unwillingly—

"A fight, sir."

"Humph! The new midshipman—Mr Belton?"

"Yes, sir."

"Got well thrashed, I suppose?"

"No, sir; not he," cried the bo'sun, eagerly.

"Who was it with?"

"Tall young gent, sir, as brought us off in the boat yesterday."

"That will do."

"Hope he won't mast-head the dear boy for this," muttered Barney, as he went aft, found the captain's servant, and asked to see his master.

In a few minutes he was summoned, and found Captain Belton writing.

"Well, Strake; what is it?"

"I had a message, your honour, to take to the young gentlemen's berth."

"Yes; to Mr Belton. Is he here?"

"No, your honour; he's there."

"Well, is he coming?"

"If you say he's to come, sir, he'll come; but he don't look fit."

"Why? Fighting?"

"Yes, sir."

"And been beaten?"

"Beaten, your honour? Well, beggin' your pardon, sir, I'm surprised at you. My boy Panny-mar give it to his man pretty tidy last night, but he's nothing to that young gent below yonder."

"Indeed!" said the captain, frowning.

"Yes, sir, indeed. He do look lovely."

"Who has my son been fighting with?"

"Young gent as was in charge of the boat as brought Sir Thomas and us aboard, sir."

"That will do, Strake."

The bo'sun touched his forehead, and backed out of the cabin.

"So soon!" muttered Captain Belton; and, taking his hat, he went on deck to encounter the first lieutenant directly.

"I find that my son has been fighting in the midshipmen's mess, Mr Bracy," he said. "Please bear in mind that he is Mr Belton, a midshipman in his Majesty's service, and that I wish that no favour should be shown to him on account of his being nearly related to me."

"Trust me for that, Captain Belton," said the lieutenant. "If I made any exception at all, it would be to bear a little more severely upon him."

"And in this case?"

"Well, sir, in this case, from what I understand, he has incapacitated our senior midshipman for duty."

"I am sorry," said the captain.

"I am glad," said the first lieutenant.

"Eh?"

"Cut his comb, sir. Good, gentlemanly-looking fellow, who understands his duty, but a sad bully, I fear."

"Oh! And you will punish—er—them both?"

"Punish, sir?" said the lieutenant; "oh dear, no. I don't mean to hear anything about it, sir. But I congratulate you upon the stuff of which your son is made."

"Thank you, Mr Bracy," said the captain, as they touched their hats to each other most ceremoniously, and the captain went back to his cabin.

For the next week all was confusion on deck, alow and aloft. The captain stayed at the hotel ashore so as to be handy, and the first lieutenant ruled supreme.

The riggers were still busy, and the crew hard at work getting in stores, water, and provisions, including fresh meat and vegetables. Coops and pens were stowed forward, and chaos was the order of the day.

Syd became thoroughly well accustomed to the middies' berth, for he was obliged to keep down all day, mostly in company with Terry, but they kept apart as much as possible, and Syd was old enough to feel that it was a very hollow truce between them.

But as soon as it was dark he was up on deck, where it was not long before he found out that he was the object of attention of the men, who were not slow to show their admiration for the young fellow who had so soon displayed his mettle by thrashing the bully of the mess.

The bo'sun was to answer for a good deal of this, and so it was, that go where he would there was a smile for him, and an eagerness on the part of the crew to answer questions or perform any little bit of service.

This was all very pleasant, and life on board began to look less black, although it really was life in the dark.

"But, never mind, Roy," he would say, in allusion to his nocturnal life; "keeps people from seeing what a face I've got. Don't look so bad to-day, does it?"

"Bad? no. It's all right."

"Oh, is it? I suppose it about matches Terry's, and his is a pretty sight."

During his week Syd was always expecting to be summoned by his father or the first lieutenant, but he encountered neither; they seemed to have forgotten his existence. So he read below a great deal of light, cheerful, edifying matter upon navigation—good yawning stuff, with plenty of geometry in it and mathematical calculations, seeing little of his messmates, who were on the whole pretty busy.

At night, though, he began to acquire a little practical seamanship, calling upon the bo'sun, a most willing teacher, to impart all he could take in, in these brief lessons, about the masts, yards, sails, stays, and ropes. He went aloft, and being eager and quick, picked up a vast amount of information of a useful kind, Barney knowing nothing that was not of utility.

"Never had no time for being polished, Master Syd," he would say, "but lor me, what a treat it is to get back among the hemp and canvas! I never used to think when I was splicing a graft on a tree that I should come to splicing 'board ship again. When are you coming on deck again in the day-time?"

"Not till I look decent, Barney."

"Beg pardon, sir."

"Bo'sun, then."

"Thankye, sir."

The week had passed, and the next day the ship was clear of its dockyard artisans. Shipwrights, riggers, and the rest of them had gone, and leaving the painting to be done by his crew during calms, the captain received his orders, the frigate was unmoored, and Syd watched from one of the little windows the receding waves, becoming more and more conscious of the fact that there was wind at work and tide in motion.

The time went on, and he knew that there was the land on one side and a verdant island on the other, but somehow he did not admire them, and when Roylance came to him in high glee to call him to dinner, with the announcement that there were roast chickens and roast leg of pork as a wind-up before coming down to biscuit and salt junk, Syd said he would not come.

"But chickens, man—chickens roast."

"Don't care for roast chickens," said Syd.

"Roast pork then, and sage and onions."

"Oh, I say, don't!" cried Syd, with a shudder.

"Well, I must go, or I shan't get a morsel," cried Roylance, and he hurried away.

"How horrible!" thought the boy. "I do believe I'm going to be sea-sick, just like any other stupid person who goes a voyage for the first time."

Before evening the frigate had passed high chalk bluffs on the left, and on the right a wide bay, with soft yellow sandy shore. Then there was chalk to right and the open channel to left; then long ranges of limestone cliffs, dotted with sea-birds, and then evening and the land growing distant, the waves rising and falling, and as he went to his hammock that night Syd uttered a groan.

"What's the matter, lad?" cried Roylance, who was below.

"Bad," said Syd, laconically.

"Nonsense! make a bold fight of it."

"Fight?" cried Syd; "why Baby Jenks could thrash me now. How long shall I be ill?"

"Well, if it gets rough, as it promises to, I dare say you'll have a week of it."

"A week?" groaned Syd.

Then some time after, to himself, between bad paroxysms of misery—

"Never mind," he said; "by the time I am able to go on deck again I shall look fit to be seen."

It was about a couple of hours later, when the frigate had got beyond a great point which jutted out into the sea, and began to stretch away for the ocean, that Syd awakened to the fact that the vessel seemed to be having a game with him. She glided up and up, bearing him tenderly and gently as it were up to the top of a hill of water, and then, after holding him there for a moment, she dived down and left him, with a horrible sensation of falling that grew worse as the wind increased, and the *Sirius* heeled over.

"I wonder whether, if I made a good brave effort, I could master this giddy weak sensation," thought the boy. "I'll try."

He made his effort—a good, bold, brave effort—and then he lay down and did not try to make any more efforts for a week, when after passing through what seemed to be endless misery, during which he lay helplessly in his hammock, listening to the creaking of the ship's timbers and the rumble that went on overhead, and often thinking that the ship was diving down into the sea never to come up again, he was aroused by a gruff voice, which sounded like Barney Strake's. It was very dark, and he felt too ill to open his eyes, but he spoke and said—

"Is that you, bo'sun?"

"Ay, ay, my lad; me it is. Come, rouse and bit."

"I couldn't, Barney," said Syd, feebly. "The very thought of a bit of anything makes me feel worse."

"Yah! not it; and I didn't mean eat; I meant turn out, have a good wash, and dress, and come on deck."

"I should die if I tried."

"Die, lad? What, you? Any one would think you was ill."

"I am, horribly."

"Yah! nonsense! On'y squirmy. Weather's calming down now, and you'll be all right."

"No, Barney; never any more," sighed Syd. "I say."

"Ay, my lad. What is it?"

"Will they bury me at sea, Barney?"

"Haw—haw—haw!" laughed the bo'sun. "He thinks he's going to die! Why, Master Syd, I did think you had a better heart."

"You don't know how ill I am," said the boy, feebly.

"Yes I do, zackly. I've seen lots bad like you, on'y it arn't bad, but doing you good."

"No, Barney; you don't know," said Syd, a little more forcibly.

"Why, you haven't been so bad as my Pan-y-mar was till I cured him."

"Did you cure him?" said Syd, beginning to take more interest in the bo'sun's words.

"Ay, my lad, in quarter of an hour."

"Do you think you could cure me, Barney? I don't want to die just yet."

"On'y hark at him."

"But do you think you could cure me?"

"Course I could, my lad; but I mustn't. You've get the doctor to see you. Don't he do you no good?"

"No, Barney; he only laughed at me—like you did."

"'Nough to make him, lad. You're not bad."

"I tell you I am," cried Syd, angrily. "What did you give Pan?"

"I didn't give him nothin', sir. I only showed him a rope's-end, and I says to him, 'Now look ye here, Pan-y-mar,' I says, 'if you aren't dressed and up and doing in quarter hour, here's your dose.'"

"Oh!" moaned Syd.

"And he never wanted to take it, Master Syd, for he was up on deck 'fore I said, and he haven't been bad since."

"How could you be such a brute, Barney?"

"Brute, lad? Why, it was a kindness. If I might serve you the same—"

"It would kill me," said Syd, angrily; and somehow his voice grew stronger.

"Kill yer! You'd take a deal more killing than you think for."

"No, I shouldn't. I'm nearly dead now."

"Nay, lad; you're as lively as a heel in fresh water. Capen sent me down to see how you was."

"He hasn't been to see me, Barney."

"Course he arn't, lad. Had enough to do looking arter the ship, for we've had a reg'lar snorer these last few days. Don't know when I've seen a rougher sea. Been quite a treat to a man who has been ashore so long. See how the frigate behaved?"

"Did she, Barney?"

"Loverly. There, get up; and I'll go and tell the skipper you're all right again."

"But I tell you I'm not. I'm very, very bad."

"Not you, Master Syd."

"I am, I tell you."

"Not you, lad. Nothing the matter with you;" and Barney winked to himself.

"Look here," cried Syd, passionately, as he jumped up in his hammock, "you're a stupid, obstinate old fool, so be off with you."

"And you're a midshipman, that's what you are, Master Syd, as thinks he's got the mumble-dumbles horrid bad, when it's fancy all the time."

"Do you want me to hit you, Barney?" cried Syd, angrily.

"Hit me? I should like you to do it, sir. Do you know I'm bo'sun of this here ship?"

"I don't care what you are," cried Syd. "You're an unfeeling brute. An ugly old idiot, that's what you are."

"Oh! am I, sir? Well, what do you call yerself—all yaller and huddled up like a sick monkey in a hurricane. Why, I'd make a better boy out of a ship's paddy and a worn-out swab."

Syd hit out at him with all his might, striking the bo'sun in the chest, but overbalancing himself so that he rolled out of the hammock, and would have fallen had not Barney caught him in his arms and planted him on the deck.

"Hoorray! Well done, Master Syd; now then, on with these here stockings, and jump into your breeches. I'll help you. On'y want a good wash and a breath o' fresh air, and then—look here, I'll get the cook to let you have a basin o' soup, and you'll be as right as a marlin-spike in a ball o' tow."

Syd was too weak to make much opposition. He had awakened to the fact after his fit of passion that he really was not so bad as he thought. The ship was not dancing about, and there was a bright ray of sunshine cutting the darkness outside the place where he lay, and once or twice he had inhaled a breath of sweet, balmy, summer-like air. Then, too, his head did not swim so much in an erect position, and he let Barney go on talking in his rough, good-humoured fashion, and help him on with some clothes; bring him a bowl of water in which he had a good wash; and when at last he was dressed and sitting back weak and helpless on the locker, the bo'sun said—

"Now, I was going to say have a whiff o' fresh air first, my lad; but you are a bit pulled down for want o' wittals. I'll speak to the cook now, and seeing who you are, I dessay he'll rig you up a mess of slops as 'll do you no end o' good."

"I couldn't touch anything, Barney."

"Yah, lad! you dunno. Said you couldn't get up, and here you are. Think I can't manage you. Here, have another hit out at me."

"Oh, Barney, I am so sorry."

"Sorry be hanged, lad! I'm glad. You won't know yourself another hour."

"But—but I'm going to be sick again, Barney," gasped the invalid.

"That's a moral impossibility, my lad, as I werry well know. You sit still while I fetch you something to put in your empty locker. Didn't know I was such a doctor, did yer?"

Barney stepped out of the door, and went straight for the galley, leaving Syd leaning back in a corner feeling deathly sick, the perspiration standing cold upon his brow, and with an intense longing to lie down once more, and in profound ignorance of what will can do for a sea-sick patient after a certain amount of succumbing.

The threat of the rope's-end had finished Pan's bout. Something else was going to act as a specific for Syd's.

He had been seated there a few minutes when there was a light step, and a little figure appeared surmounted by the comically withered countenance of Jenkins.

"Hallo, Belton!" he cried. "Up again. Better?"

"No; I feel very ill."

"Never mind. You do look mouldy, though. Can I get you anything?"

"No; I couldn't touch a bit."

"Couldn't you? Keep your head to the wind, lad, and get well. Old Mike Terry's getting horrid saucy again, so look sharp and bung him up."

The little fellow popped up on deck, and took the news, with the effect that Bolton came and said a word of congratulation, and he was followed by Roylance.

"Oh, I am glad, old fellow," cried the latter. "You've had a nasty bout. But, I say, your eyes are all right again, and the swelling's gone from your lip."

"Has it?" said Syd, feebly, as if nothing mattered now.

"Yes; you'll very soon come round. We've run down with a rush before that nor'-easter, and we're getting into lovely summer weather. Coming on deck?"

"Too weak."

"Not you. Do you good. But I must go back on deck. Regular drill on."

He hurried away, and Syd was leaning back utterly prostrated, when there was another step, and he opened his eyes to see that the figure which darkened the door was that of Terry, who came into the low dark place, and stood looking down at his late antagonist with a sneering contemptuous smile which was increased to a laugh.

"What a poor miserable beggar!" he said, as if talking to himself. "Talk about the sailor's sick parrot. Ha, ha, ha!"

A faint tinge of colour began to dawn in Syd's face. "Well," said Terry; "what are you staring at?"

Syd made no reply, only kept his eyes fixed on his enemy, and panted slightly.

"Hadn't you better go and ask your father to put you ashore somewhere, miss?" sneered Terry. "You ought to be sent home in a Bath chair."

Syd made no reply, and Terry, who under his assumed nonchalant sneering aspect was simmering with rage at the sight of his conqueror, went on glorying in the chance to trample on a fallen enemy, and trying to work him up to do something which would give him an excuse for delivering a blow.

"*I* can't think what officers are about to bring such miserable sickly objects on board the King's ships to upset and annoy everybody with their miserable long-shore ways. It's a scandal to the service."

Still Syd made no answer, and emboldened by the silence Terry went on.

"If I had my way I'd just take every contemptible sick monkey who laid up, haul him on deck, make fast a rope to his ankle, and souse him overboard a few times. That would cure them."

Syd closed his eyes, for he was giddy; but his breast rose and fell as if he were suffering from some emotion.

"Filling the ship up with a pack of swabs who, because they are sons of captains, are indulged and nursed, and the whole place is turned into a hospital. Why don't you go into the cabin?"

"Because I don't choose," cried Syd, suddenly starting up with his face flushing, his eyes bright, and the passion that was in him sending the blood coursing through his veins.

Terry started back in astonishment.

"I'm not going into the cabin, because I am going to stop here in the midshipmen's berth to teach the bully of the mess how to behave himself like a gentleman."

"What?"

"And not like the domineering cur and coward he is."

"Coward?"

"Yes, to come and talk to me like this; you know I'm weak and ill."

"What? Why, you miserable contemptible cub, say another word and I'll rub your nose on the planks till you beg my pardon."

"Another word, and a dozen other words, Bully Terry. Touch me, coward! I can't help myself now; but if you lay a finger on me, I'll get well and give you such a thrashing as the last shall be like nothing to it. You've got one of my marks still on your ugly nose. Now, touch me if you dare."

"Why, hullo, Master Syd; that you?" said Barney, in his loudest voice, as he entered the place with a basin full of some steaming compound.

"Ha—ha—ha!" laughed Terry. "Here's the nurse come with the baby's pap. Did you put some sugar in it, old woman?"

"Nay, sir; no sugar," said Barney, touching his hat; "but there's plenty of good solid beef-stock in it, the cook says; stuff as 'll rouse up Mr Belton's muscles, and make 'em 'tiff as hemp-rope. Like to try 'em again in a fortnight's time?"

"You insolent scoundrel! how dare you! Do you forget that you are speaking to your officer?"

"No, sir. Beg pardon, sir."

"It is not granted. Leave this place, sir, and go on deck."

"Don't do anything of the kind, Strake," cried Syd, who was calming down. "You are waiting on me."

"Do you hear me, sir?" roared Terry again.

"I can," said Syd, coolly, "and a wretchedly unpleasant voice it is. Go and bray somewhere else, donkey. Let's see, it was the ass that tried to kick the sick—"

"Lion," interrupted Terry, with a sneer. "Are you a sick lion?"

"It would be precious vain to say yes," said Syd; "but I'll own to being the sick lion if you'll own to being the beast who hoisted his heels."

"Bah!" ejaculated Terry, and he turned and stalked out of the place.

"Felt as if I should have liked to go at him again," cried Syd, fiercely.

Barney winked to himself.

"He'll give me one for that, sir. Now then, just you try a spoonful o' this; 'tain't too hot. Not a nyste sort o' young gen'leman, is he?"

"No, Barney," said Syd, taking the spoon.

"His pap was a bit sour p'raps when he was young, eh, Master Syd?"

"An overbearing bully!" cried Syd. "Only wait till I get strong again."

"And then you'll give it to him again, sir?"

"I don't want to quarrel or fight with anybody," said Syd, speaking quickly and excitedly, between the spoonfuls of strong soup he was swallowing.

"Course you don't, sir; you never was a quarrelsome young gent."

"But he is beyond bearing."

"That's true, sir; so he is. Only I mustn't say so. Lor', how I have seen young gents fight afore now; but when it's been all over, they've shook hands as if they'd found out who was strongest, and there's been an end on it."

"Yes, Barney."

"But this young gen'leman, sir, don't seem to take his beating kindly. Hauls down his colours, and you sends your orficer aboard to take possession—puts, as you may say, your right hand in, but he wouldn't take it."

"No, Barney," said Syd, as the bo'sun winked again to himself, "he wouldn't shake hands."

"No, sir; he wouldn't. I see it all, and thought I ought to stop it, but I knowed from the first you'd lick him; and it strikes me werry hard, Mr Syd, sir, that you'll have to do all that there bit o' work over again."

"But I'm weak now, and he may lick me, Barney," said Syd, who was making a peculiar noise now with the spoon he held—a noise which sounded like the word *soup*.

"Weak? not you, sir. Feels a bit down, but you'll soon forget that. I wouldn't try to bring it on again, sir," said Barney, watching his young master all the while.

"Bring it on? No," cried Sydney. "I tell you I hate fighting. I don't like being hurt."

"Course not, sir."

"And I don't like hurting any one."

"Well, sir, strikes me that's foolish, 'cause there's no harm in hurtin' a thing like him. Do him good, I say. You see, Master Syd, there's young gents as grows into good skippers, and there's young gents as grows into tyrants, and worries the men till they mutinies, and there's hangings and court-martials—leastwise, court-martials comes first. Now, Mr Terry, sir, unless he's tamed down and taught better, 's one o' the sort as makes bad skippers, and the more he's licked the better he'll be."

"I shall never like him," said Syd, whose spoon was scraping the bottom of the basin now.

"No, sir; I s'pose not," said Barney, with a dry grin beginning to spread over his countenance. "Nobody could; but I dare say his mother thinks he's a werry nyste boy, and kisses and cuddles him, and calls him dear."

"Yes, I suppose so, Barney."

"And a pretty dear too; eh, Master Syd?"

"Yes, Barney. What are you laughing at?"

"You, sir," cried the bos'un. "Hooray! he's took it all, and said he couldn't touch a drop."

"Well, I thought I couldn't, Barney; but Mr Terry roused me up, and I feel better now."

"Nay, sir; play fair."

"What do you mean?"

"Give a man his doo. It was me roused you up."

"So it was, Barney. I'm a deal better."

"You're quite well, says Doctor Barney Strake, and that's me. Say, Master Syd, what do they call that they gives a doctor wrorped up in paper?"

"His fee."

"Then, sir, that's just what you owes me, who says to you now—just you go on deck and breathe the fresh wind, for this here place would a'most stuffocate a goose."

"Yes, I'll try and get on deck now," said Syd.

"And try means do. Hooray, sir, I'm going to tell the captain as you're quite well, thankye, now, Amen."

"Not quite well, Barney."

"Ay, but you are, sir. But I say, Master Syd."

"What?"

"You never said your grace."

Chapter Twenty

The cure was complete, and two days later Syd had almost forgotten that he had been ill. The weather was glorious, and as they sailed on south and west before a favouring breeze, life at sea began to have its charms.

Every day the ocean seemed to grow more blue; and pretty often there was something fresh to look at, fish, or bird wandering far from land.

But theirs was to be no pleasure trip, as Syd soon realised upon seeing the many preparations that were being made for war.

In his old days of command, Captain Harry Belton's was considered the smartest manned ship in the squadron in which he served, and it was his ambition now to make up for the many deficiencies he discovered on board the frigate. Consequently gun and small-arm drill was almost as frequent as the practice of making and shortening sail. The crew grumbled and grew weary, but all the same they felt an increasing respect for the officer who was determined to have everything done in the best way possible, and when the captain did say a few words of praise for some smart bit of seamanship, the men felt that it was praise worth having.

It seemed rather hard to Syd at times that his father should be so cold and distant. Roylance, who had become great friends with the new middy, noticed it too.

"Were you bad friends at home?" he said to Syd, one day, as they were leaning over the taffrail gazing down at the clear blue sea.

"Oh no, the best of friends; and I always dined with him and Uncle Tom when he was there, and sat with them at dessert."

"Oh, I say, don't talk about it," said Roylance; "late dinners and dessert. Different to our rough berth, eh?"

"Ye–es," said Syd: "but one gets to like this more now."

"Does seem strange though about the captain."

"Takes more notice of the others than he does of me."

"I don't know about more," said Roylance. "Treats us all the same, I think. Well, when you come to think of it, you are one of us, and it wouldn't be fair if he favoured you."

"No."

"Suppose it was promotion? No, you mustn't grumble. — I say."

"Yes."

"I wouldn't trust old Terry too much, Syd."

"Why not? He's friendly enough now; and we don't want to fight again."

"No; but he's too civil to you now, and always looks to me as if he would do you an ill turn if he could."

Syd laughed.

"Ah, you may grin; but you wouldn't laugh if you found he'd just given you a push and sent you overboard some dark night."

"Nonsense!"

"I hope it is, but don't you trust him. I've known Mike Terry three years, and I've always found that he never forgave anybody who got the better of him."

"I'm not going to trust him particularly, nor keep him off," said Syd, carelessly. "I say, though, how funny it is I find myself talking and feeling just as if I'd been at sea ever so long, instead of two or three weeks."

"Soon get used to it. You've been very lucky, though."

"How?" said Syd. "Being beaten nearly to a mummy, and then being sea-sick for a week?"

"Having that fight, and marking Mike Terry. It's made all the fellows like you."

"And I don't deserve it."

"Oh, don't you! Well, never mind about that."

"No; never mind about that," said Syd, carelessly. "I say, where are we going?"

"Don't know. Nobody does. Sealed orders to be opened somewhere. I can guess where."

"Indeed!"

"Yes; at Barbadoes."

"Is that a nice place?"

"Middling. I like Jamaica better."

"And shall we go there?"

"Wait, and you'll see, like the rest of us."

"But do you think we shall have to fight?"

"If we meet any of the enemy's ships, we shall have to fight or run away."

"We shall never run away," said Syd, hotly. "My father would never do that."

Almost as he spoke, the man at the mast-head shouted "Sail ho!" and there was a commotion aboard. Glasses were levelled, and before long a second ship was made out; and before long two more appeared, and by the cut of the sails it was decided that it was a little squadron of the French.

Syd, to whom all this was wonderfully fresh, was eagerly scanning the distant sails, which showed up clearly now in the bright sunshine, when a voice behind him said—

"Of course. How cowardly!"

"What would you do then?" said another familiar voice.

"Face them as a king's ship should."

"One frigate against four—one of which seems to be a two-decker, eh? Well, I say, the skipper's right to cut and run."

"Cut and run from the presence of the enemy—his father going to flee?" Syd felt the blood come into his face, as he listened to the rapid orders that were given, as the ship's course was altered, and in a short time the *Sirius* was rushing through the sea at a tremendous rate.

Syd bit his lip, and felt cold with shame and mortification. It seemed to him that he would not be able to face his messmates down below that evening; and seizing the opportunity he made his way to where the bo'sun was standing, silver pipe in hand, ready for the next order that might come.

"Barney," he whispered, "we're running away."

"Not us, my lad," said the old sailor, gruffly. "Four to one means having our top gear knocked about our deck, and then boarding. Skipper knows what he's about, and strikes me he'll 'stonish some o' them Mounseers afore they know where they are."

"Then, why don't we go and fight them?"

"Good sword-play don't mean going and blunder-headed chopping at a man like one goes at a tree, but fencing a bit till you get your chance. We're fencing, lad. What we've got to do is to take or sink all the enemy we can, not get took or sunk ourselves."

"But the glory, Barney."

"More glory in keeping afloat, my lad, than in going down. You let the skipper be; he's a better sailor than you are, I'll be bound."

Syd, after a further conversation with the boatswain, saw the night come on, with the enemy's little squadron evidently in full chase. He had clung to the hope that his father was manoeuvring so as to attack the ships one by one; but though the frigate had been cleared for action, and the men were full of excitement, there seemed as if there was to be no fighting that night.

The boy was disappointed. He was not free from the natural terror that any one would feel, but at the same time he was eager to see a naval encounter. For home conversation between his father, uncle, and their friends had frequently been of the sea and sea-fights; and he was thoroughly imbued with the belief that a British man-of-war could do precisely what it liked with the enemy, and victory against any odds was a certainty.

And here were they undoubtedly running away, to Syd's great disgust, for he had yet to learn that the better part of valour is discretion, and that a good commander is careful of his ship and men. He was the more annoyed upon encountering Terry soon afterwards discussing the state of affairs with a couple of the lads below, and finding that he ceased speaking directly, and turned away with a laugh.

Syd sat down pretending to ignore what he had seen, but the feeling within him drove him on deck again, where he was not long before one of the hearers of Terry's remarks took care that he should know what had been said. Syd was leaning over the stern gazing away into the transparent darkness, with the stars shining brilliantly overhead, when Jenkins came to his side.

"See 'em now?" said the boy.

"No. It is too dark."

"Then we shan't take any prizes this time. What a pity!"

"Perhaps we should have been turned into a prize, Jenky," said Syd, for he was now on the most familiar terms with all his messmates.

"Yes," said the boy, "perhaps so; but Mike Terry says if our old captain had been in command, he'd have put his helm down when those four frog-boxes were well within range, cut right between them, giving them our broadsides as we sailed, then rounded under their sterns, raked first one and then another as we passed, left two of them with their masts gone by the board, and gone on across the bows of the other two, and raked them from forrard. He says they'd have struck their colours in no time. Then prize crews would have been put aboard, and we should have gone back to port in triumph, with plenty of prize-money, and promotion to come."

"Almost a pity the old captain was not in command, isn't it?" said Syd, bitterly.

"He says it is. He thinks it's downright cowardly to run for it like this. Why, he says even he, young as he is, could have done it."

A sudden snap close at hand made the two lads start and look round, to see a tall dark figure a few yards away in the act of closing a night-glass.

"And pray who is the brave and experienced young officer who would have done all this?" said a cold sarcastic voice, which Syd recognised directly. "No: stop. Don't tell me, but tell him that it is a great mistake for young gentlemen in the midshipmen's berth to criticise the actions of their superior officers, who may be entirely wrong, but whether or no, their critics are more in error."

"It was—"

"I told you not to name him, sir. I don't wish to know. That will do."

The two boys felt that this was a dismissal, and they hurried away.

"Oh, I say, Belt," whispered Jenkins, "did you hear your father come up?"

"No; I think he must have been standing there, using his glass, when you came."

"I did think I saw something black. Oh, I say, Belt, your dad is a Tartar."

This little episode did not tend to make Syd more comfortable, and from that hour whenever he saw any of the men or officers talking together, he immediately fancied that they must be discussing and disapproving of Captain Belton's action in running away.

It was long afterwards that Syd knew that his father's orders were to stop for nothing, but to make all speed for the West Indies, where another vessel of war was lying. Though without those orders it would have been madness to have allowed the enemy to close in and attack.

Syd was on deck at daybreak, eager to scan the horizon, but only to find that those before him of the watch had been performing the same duty with their glasses, and there was not a sail in sight.

Chapter Twenty One

There was plenty of talk during the next fortnight's slow sailing down into the tropics, and the captain's conduct was widely discussed, Sydney every now and then coming upon some knot where those who considered the captain had played a cowardly part were in the ascendant. "Nailed the colours to the mast, and gone down together like heroes," some one said, and Sydney, who did not want to die like a hero if he could help it, but had the ambition of any healthy boy to live as long as possible, went away, feeling very low-spirited, till he came upon another excited group, at the head of whom was the boatswain.

"What!" cried the latter, in answer to a remark made by one of the opposition; "ought to have gone at 'em and give 'em chain-shot in their rigging, when you've got sealed orders. Look ye here, my lads, when you've been afloat as long as I have, you'll know that whether you're able seaman, or luff, cap, or admiral, you've got to obey. Our orders is to go right away to the West Indies, and not stop playing on the road. Strikes me as nothing would have pleased the skipper better than a game of bowls with the Parley Voos. I've sailed with him before."

"Oh, yes; you've often said that," cried one of the men.

"And I says it again, Tom Rogers. And I says this here too—don't you let him hear you say anything o' that kind, or you might have it repeated till it got into the cabin."

"Why, what did I say?" protested the man.

"That our skipper was a coward."

"That I didn't. Never said such a word."

"But you and lots more have said what meant it, and my advice is this here—don't do it again, unless you want your back scratched by the bo'sun's mates."

Sydney felt better after that, and as the days glided by the idle chatter grew less.

It was all wonderfully new to the boy, and sometimes, when the men were allowed to catch a shark, or try to harpoon dolphins, or albicore, beautiful mackerel-like fish, with the pronged implement they called the grains, he found himself wondering why he had objected to go to sea.

Then as his first nervousness wore off, and, with the rapidity common to a fresh young mind, he acquired the ordinary knowledge of his duty, he was always to the front in little bits of routine such as fell to the lot of the middies. So prominent was he in these matters, that one day, after some hours of busy training, Roylance came to him.

"First luff wants to speak to you, Belton," he said.

Sydney flushed, and then the colour faded.

"What have I been doing?" he said, hastily.

"Ah, you'll see," said Roylance, with a very serious shake of the head.

"Belt going up to the first luff," cried little Jenkins. "Oh, my! I'm sorry for you, old fellow."

"What's Belton in for it?" said Bolton. "Never mind, old chap. If it's mast-head, there's a beautiful view."

"And I'll give you a bit of rope to tie yourself on with, so that you won't fall when you go to sleep," whispered Jenkins.

"Ah! and mind you fall when she heels over to leeward," said Bolton, hastily; "then you'll drop into the sea."

"Get some biscuits for the poor beggar, Bolton," cried Jenkins. "Perhaps he'll be kept up there for a week!"

"You'd better look sharp," whispered Roylance. "He don't like to be kept waiting."

"They're only making fun of me," thought Sydney, as he drew himself up, went hurriedly to where the first lieutenant was scanning the horizon with a glass, and waited till he had done, feeling very squeamish and uncomfortable the while.

He stood there for some minutes, glancing behind him once, to see, as he expected, that his tormentors were keeping an eye upon him to see the result of his interview with the great magnate, who seemed to rule the ship—after the captain had had his say.

It was painful work to stand there studying the set of the first lieutenant's pigtail, the cock of his hat, and the seams and buttons of his coat, till the glass was lowered, tucked under this marine grand vizier's arm, and he said angrily, as if speaking to a fish which sprang out of the water—

"I told Mr Roylance to send that boy here."

"*Beg* pardon, sir; I've been here some time," said Sydney, touching his hat.

"And suppose you have, young gentleman; it's your duty to wait, is it not?" said the lieutenant, sharply.

"Yes, sir."

"Don't speak. If you want to be a good smart officer, listen, and don't make remarks till you are asked."

Sydney wanted to say, "You asked me a question, sir," but he held his peace.

"Now, Mr Belton," said the lieutenant, eyeing him severely, "I suppose you know that you occupy a very awkward position on board this ship? Don't answer."

"What's coming?" thought Sydney, who was perspiring freely.

"You are the captain's son."

"Yes, I know that," thought Sydney.

"And of course it naturally creates a little prejudice or jealousy against you."

"Oh, do please put me out of my misery," thought Syd.

"Mr Dallas has been talking to me about you a good deal."

"What have I done to offend the second luff?" thought Syd.

"And I quite agree with him."

"What can it be?" thought Syd.

"Now I am going to give you a bit of advice."

"Yes, sir; thank—"

"I told you not to speak, sir," cried the lieutenant, angrily. "I advise you not to be conceited, not to jump at the conclusion that you are very clever, and not to begin to domineer over your messmates because they flatter and fawn upon you on the strength of your having thrashed Mr Terry. You see I hear all these things."

Sydney felt the colour rising.

"Take that advice and you may, if you attend well to your studies in navigation, become a respectable officer. Life is not all play, my lad, so think that one of these days you will be going up for your examination to pass for lieutenant. Don't waste your time, and find yourself, when a call is made upon you, perfectly helpless and be turned back. It will be years first, but years soon spin round. There, I think that is all I have to say."

"Frightened me nearly into fits, and only wanted to say that," thought Sydney.

"No. Just another word. You think me a very gruff, fault-finding fellow, don't you?"

Sydney was silent.

"I asked you, Mr Belton, if you did not find me a very severe officer. Why don't you answer?"

"Told me not, sir."

"Humph! Yes; I did. But you may answer now. You do find me very severe?"

"Yes, sir; very."

"And you don't like me?"

"No, sir."

"Humph! That's frank, sir. But I like it. Shall I tell you why you don't like me? I will. Because I do my duty rigidly. Now one word more. Don't say a word to your messmates about what I tell you now. It's our secret, Mr Belton; and don't presume upon it, and go backwards."

"I'll try not, sir."

"Good. Then look here. You have been a very short time on board, and I have often found fault with you; but I like to be just. On the whole, Mr Belton, I am very much pleased with your conduct. I felt prejudiced against you, as I was afraid I was to have an addition to my young monkeys in the shape of a spoiled, petted boy. I was ignorant then, for I did not know Captain Belton so well as I do now. There: go to your duties. You are awkward, clumsy, ignorant, and sadly wanting; but you have got on wonderfully, and I think you will turn out a very smart officer before you have done. That will do."

Sydney wanted to say a great deal, but he felt that he was dismissed, and he left the deck and went down below, to avoid his messmates.

Not an easy task, for they were after him directly.

"This isn't the way to the mast-head," cried Jenks.

"Want the rope and the biscuit?" said Bolton.

"What have you been doing?" cried Roylance.

"Nearly everything that's wrong."

"Then he has been wigging you?"

"Yes."

"I know. It's because you didn't touch your hat to him the other day," said another of the boys.

Sydney was going to speak, but he caught sight of Terry lounging towards them, and that made him reticent.

Time glided on, and then came the cry, "Land ho!" with everybody ready to gaze eagerly at the low-looking cloud lying far away on the water where sea and sky met. This cloud gradually assumed the appearance of land, and Sydney gazed wonderingly at the island of Barbadoes, and began to ask himself whether he would be able to get leave to go ashore.

But there was no landing allowed. The stay was too brief, and before long they were sailing away toward the wonderful chain of islands that lie in the intensely blue Caribbean Sea.

Jamaica at last, after a long calm, a name associated in Sydney's mind with sugar, molasses, and rum. But to the great disappointment of all on board, there was to be no landing; even there the middies having to be content to buy cocoa-nuts, oranges, and sweetmeats off the black women whose boats hovered about the anchored frigate.

There was a sister ship lying here, the *Orion*, just fresh in from a cruise round the islands, and the two captains were in constant communication, for here it proved to be, and not at Barbadoes, that Captain Belton was to open his sealed orders and learn definitely what were to be his next steps.

What they were to be troubled the midshipmen very little, for there they were at anchor at what seemed to be a paradise—all waving grass, blue mountain, rivulet, and sunshine. An island of beauty set in an amethyst sea.

"And we can't go ashore," cried Jenkins. "I've a good mind to swim for it."

"One mouthful for the first shark," said Roylance.

"Eh, what? sharks? No sharks here, are there?"

"Harbour swarms with them."

"Gammon!"

"Ask any of the men who have been here before, then," said Roylance.

"But, really, Roy? No gammon!"

"It's a fact, I tell you. Try it, if you doubt me."

"N–no," said Jenkins, coolly; "you see one would have to swim in one's uniform, and get ashore so wet."

"Naturally," said Roylance, laughing.

"No," said Jenkins, "I wouldn't swim ashore naturally. Looks so bad. I'll stop aboard."

"Hullo, Bolton; what's the matter?" cried another of the middies. "Asked leave?"

"Yes."

"What did he say?"

"Said he'd mast-head the next fellow who asked leave to go ashore."

"Strikes me we're off somewhere directly," said Roylance. "Let's send Belton into the cabin to ask his father what he's going to do."

"I shouldn't like to be Belt then," said Jenkins. "Fancy the captain's face. Hullo! What's that?"

"Somebody coming on board."

"No! it's up anchor. We're off again."

"What a shame!" was chorussed; but the disappointment was forgotten directly in eagerness to know their new destination, somewhere else evidently in the deep blue western sea, and as the *Orion* was weighing anchor too, it was likely that they were going to have stirring times.

"Two trim frigates," said Roylance, as they leaned over the taffrail and watched the beautiful receding shore. "Ah, Belt, if we were to meet those Mounseers now, I don't think your father would run away."

Chapter Twenty Two

The fort of Saint Jacques, in La Haute, looked strong enough to keep almost any squadron at bay; and as the *Sirius* lay pretty close in, those on board could see the French flag flying upon the solid square citadel, below which, and running out like arms, were outworks which seemed to bristle with cannon beside the low, cunningly-contrived batteries on the rocks near the entrance of the harbour.

"A strong place, Bracy," said the captain, "and one where they ought to be able to sink any vessels we could bring against them."

"Yes, sir, if we went at it hammer-and-tongs, shot for shot."

"Exactly," said the captain, thoughtfully, as he held his glass to his eye, "and they would have English oak to fire at, while we had to send our shot against stone. Ye–es, a quiet combined attack some night with a few hundred determined men in our boats, and we ought to take the place without firing a shot."

"That's it, sir," said the first lieutenant; "and the only way."

"But I don't like that," said the captain.

"That stone, sir," replied the first lieutenant, as he looked back at an isolated patch of rock which rose up like the top of a mountain behind them about four miles astern. "That would be an ugly spot for annoying us if they had had the gumption to stick a couple of guns there. It would harass the attack terribly."

"The wonder is, that they have not fortified the rock as an outwork to their fort."

"Frenchmen don't think of everything, sir," said the lieutenant, dryly.

"We must seize that rock, Bracy," said the captain, decisively. "I'll communicate with the *Orion* my intentions at once."

Signals were made, a boat lowered down, and communications passed between the two commanding officers; and then Captain Belton gave orders for an exploring party to go and try and land on the rock, and see what its capabilities were for occupation.

The second lieutenant received the instructions; the first cutter's crew was piped up, and as the lieutenant was about to assume his command, he caught sight of an eager-looking face.

"Well, Mr Belton," he said, kindly. "Want to go?"

"Oh yes, sir," said Syd, eagerly.

"In with you, my lad."

Syd wanted no second invitation, and the next minute he was seated in the stern-sheets looking back at the side of the frigate, as the men's oars dipped regularly, and the boat gently rose and fell as she glided over the smooth water.

The rock had a wonderful attraction for Sydney, as it rose clear out of the bright blue water; and as he lay back and half-closed his eyes, it was easy to imagine that it was the ruins of some old castle rising up with walls tier after tier to a height of about a hundred and fifty feet, with only a place here and there shelving down to the level of the water, the rock rising up for the most part perpendicularly from the deep sea which rose against the time and water-worn sides to fall back in sparkling foam.

"What are we coming here for, Mr Dallas?" said Syd, in a low tone.

"To survey the rock, and see if it will do for occupation."

"But nobody would want to live here, sir."

"More likely have to die here, my lad. But we sailors are not allowed to ask questions. We are told to do things, and we do them."

"I only wanted to know," said Syd, apologetically.

"I was not finding fault, Belton. Now, let me see; we've got to land. Where's the best place?"

As he spoke he altered the direction of the boat, which he kept a short distance from where the sea broke, and steered right round the rock, while his companion divided his time between examining the various ledges and gazing into the transparent depths below.

It was soon evident that landing would be rather difficult, only two places suggesting themselves as being feasible; one being like a rough pier, the other a spot where masses of coral rock run down into the sea, with here and there awkward, jagged-looking, scattered pieces showing their heads, sometimes just level with the water, and at others being completely covered.

After the boat had been completely round the rock, which apparently covered a space of some acres, the young officer gave the word, and the lead was thrown over to try for soundings and the possibility of there being good anchorage for a ship that might want to lay off the edge. But the lead went down, down, down to the end of the line wherever it was cast, even close in to the rock, indicating that it rose up almost steeple-like from profound depths.

"Soon settled that point, Mr Belton," said the lieutenant. "The next thing is to land. Back in, my lads, on the swell, and as soon as we jump off pull clear again. I think we can do it yonder where the tuft of green weed is growing."

The men obeyed, and after one or two cautious approaches, the young officer, who had carefully watched his time, sprang from the thwart before him right on to the rock, made a second bound, and was clear of the following wave before it had time to flood the natural pier.

"Now, Mr Belton, can you do that?"

For answer, as the boat was again backed in, Syd leaped out, but did not calculate his time well, and sprang into a few inches of water, which went flying amidst the laughter of the men. But the next spring took him up alongside Mr Dallas.

"A little too soon, Belton," he said. "Now, one of you lads come too. Keep her well off, coxswain; sometimes a good roller comes unexpectedly, and if you are not prepared she may be thrown high and dry, stove in."

"Ay, ay, sir," shouted the coxswain. Then the man told leaped ashore easily enough, and the primary survey of the place began.

It was not an easy task, for from the few square yards of level stone where they stood there seemed to be no means of getting farther, till Syd suggested that if they could get up a bit of wall-like rock there was a ledge from which they could work themselves sideways to a rift in the side over the sea, and from that perhaps they could get higher.

"But we must be careful; it is only a few inches, and if we lose our hold, down we go into deep water."

"It would only be a bathe, sir," said Syd, laughing.

"Oh, I don't mind the bath, Belton. I am thinking there may be hungry sharks about."

"Ugh!" ejaculated Syd, with a shudder, as he glanced at the clear blue water.

"No fear of a fall though, if we are careful."

"Beg pardon, sir; I could get along there," said the man.

"Yes, my lad; but I'll try it first," said the lieutenant; and he was about to start along the perilous little shelf after a short climb, when Syd suggested that they should have a line thrown to them from the boat.

"Good idea, Belton," said the lieutenant, who hailed the boat, now lying fifty yards away, and she came in; the rope was thrown to them, made fast about Syd's chest, and while the lieutenant and the sailor held the slack ready to pay out, the boy clambered on about twenty feet, and then stepped boldly out upon the narrow shelf in the face of the almost perpendicular rock, crept carefully along to the rift, and entered it to come back and shout all right.

With Syd holding the rope tightly round the edge of the cleft, and the sailor keeping it fast, the lieutenant had no difficulty in getting along; the sailor followed, and they passed along a natural passage to where the rock sloped away sufficiently for them to mount again to a fairsized ledge, from the end of which there was a ridge of broken rock giving foothold for climbers. This they surmounted, Syd going up first like a goat, and holding the rope for his officer, and lowering it in turn for the sailor.

"Why, Belton," said Mr Dallas, "this place is a natural fortress. All we should have to do would be to make parapets, and mount some guns. It's a little Gibraltar in its way."

They went on exploring, or rather climbing from block to block and ledge to ledge, till after some little difficulty the summit was reached, from which the lieutenant signalled with a handkerchief, an acknowledgment being seen from the ship.

The top was a slope of some twenty by thirty yards, and from here as they looked about over the edge a better idea of the capabilities of the place could be formed, and they looked down on what only needed a little of the work of man to make the place impregnable so long as there was no treachery from within.

The great peculiarity of the rock was, that from where they stood they could gaze down into a chasm beyond which rose a mass similar to that on which they stood. In fact, roughly speaking, the stony mount seemed to have been cleft or split in twain, giving it somewhat the aspect of a bishop's mitre, save that the lower part between the cleft expanded till it reached the sea.

"Well," said the lieutenant, in a satisfied tone, as they climbed down into the chasm, and gazed from the bottom out at either end toward the sea, in the one case to see the *Sirius* lying with her masts describing arcs on the blue sky; in the other case the white houses and port of Saint Jacques. "Well,

Belton, if I had been set to work to design a rock upon which to plant a fort, I could never have schemed so good a one as this."

"Why?" said Syd, in his outspoken way. "It's very awkward to get up unless you make some stairs."

"The more awkward the worse for an enemy. But can't you see, my lad, we can mount our guns on platforms at either end of this tiny valley; and stow our men, stores, and ammunition there in the bottom of the rift. Nothing can reach them from outside. Gibraltar's nothing to it."

"Isn't it?" said Syd, who felt that he ought to say something.

"No, my boy, nothing. There's one thing though—I don't see water."

"Water?" said Syd, laughing, as he looked round at the sea.

"Drinking water, sir. An enemy would have very little difficulty in taking a fort where the defenders have no water. Must make a cistern and store some up. Come along."

He led the way, and they descended without much difficulty to a spot from whence it seemed possible to mount the other mass of rock, up which they toiled with more difficulty, for in some places it nearly approached the perpendicular. Had it not been for a series of rough cracks or splits in the side, some of which seemed to descend to vast depths, but whose edges gave good foothold, the ascent would have been impossible.

They reached the top, through a little mutual help, signalled again, and after gazing down into the chasm, which the lieutenant looked upon as a splendid find, they slowly went down to the little natural pier, the boat was carefully backed in, the sailor leaped lightly from the wet rock on to the gunwale, and then stepped into his place.

"Now you, Mr Belton," said the lieutenant; "and don't get wet this time."

"No," said Syd, "I'll time it better;" and he let the sea flood the rock as the boat rose high, and then descend twice before he made this attempt.

"Now then!" cried the lieutenant, as the wave glided back from the rough surface, and the boat's stern was seen descending easily a few feet away.

Syd trotted over the wet rock with the water flying up and glittering in the sunshine at every step, reached the edge, and sprang lightly on to the gunwale just as the boat was at its lowest. Nothing in fact could have been better timed, but he had not calculated upon one thing.

The sailor had left the edge of the boat wet, and Syd's shoes were soaked and slippery, so that one of them glided sidewise; there was no chance of recovery, and he went down headlong into the deep. It was so sudden that he was below the surface with the water thundering in his ears almost before he was aware that he had fallen. But he was a good swimmer, and had practised diving often enough, and he knew that he had only to take a few strokes to rise clear of the boat, and then a few more in order to be taken in.

As he swam below after going down some distance he was aware of what seemed to be a black cloud over his head, which he knew was the boat; then he was rising again through the sunlit water, and as his head rose into the sunshine a cold chill of horror paralysed every energy, for he knew that he was almost within the jaws of death.

It was all so rapid that he hardly knew how it took place; but he had been long enough at sea to know that the long, thin, curved shadow approaching him was a huge shark, and that before he could reach the boat the monster would have seized him.

He was conscious of a wild shouting in the boat, of the rapid beating of oars which made the water fly up in fountains; then, as he swam with all his might, of a violent blow on the shoulder followed by a jerk, and then half insensible from the shock he was being dragged over the boat's side.

Amid the babel of voices that ensued, Syd made out a few words here and there.

One man said: "It's broke my arm a'most; the beggar made such a jerk."

"It's broke this oar," growled a well-known voice. "I give it him just in the jaws as he turned over."

"Ah!" said one of the men, "if that had been steel 'stead o' wood you'd ha' gone right through him."

"Yes," growled the boatswain, "'stead o' having a broken oar. Well, if the skipper says I must pay for it, why I must."

"Yah! nonsense!" muttered another. "What, arter saving his boy's life?"

All this brought back to Syd's memory matters which he had seen dimly in the exciting moments during which he was saved from a horrible death; and that which he had not seen, imagination and the men's words supplied. But he could recall something of a sturdy man standing up in the boat and making a thrust at the shark, and while he was realising that this man was Barney, one of the sailors said—

"And if I hadn't ketched hold o' you, Mr Bo'sun, by the waistband o' your breeches, you'd ha' gone overboard, and Jack shark would have had you."

"Ay, my lad, he would," growled Barney; "but I don't believe he'd a liked me, for I must be precious tough by now."

"Say, lads," said another voice, "what's the reward for saving a bo'sun's life?"

"Nothing," said Barney. "'Sides, you've on'y stopped somebody's promotion. Steady there!"

At that moment, as Syd lay there with a misty feeling of confusion troubling him, it seemed from the rocking of the boat that the lieutenant had leaped on board, and the next moment he was kneeling down, and his hands were busy about Syd.

"Belton, my dear lad," he said, excitedly, "where are you hurt?"

Syd looked at him wildly, and saw him through the mist.

"Hurt?" he said, after making an effort to speak, and feeling deathly sick the while, "I—I don't know."

"Great heavens!" cried the lieutenant, "I would sooner it had been me. But I see no blood, bo'sun."

"No, sir; I've been agoin' over him," growled Barney; "and he's got all his arms, and legs, and, yes, his head's all right. You see I shoved that oar in Jack's mouth just as he turned over to grab him."

"But the boy is half dead."

"Ketched him a horful crack with his snout, I think it weer, sir; for, poor dear lad, he were knocked side wise. He'll come round."

All this time it was to Syd just as if the lieutenant and the boatswain were moving about over him in a mist; but as some water was splashed in his face, and his brows were bathed, the mist slowly passed away, and he suddenly struggled up into a sitting position.

"That's better," cried the lieutenant, eagerly. "Are you in pain?"

"Shoulder hurts a little, sir," said Syd, huskily; "but where's the shark?"

"Yonder, sir," said the boatswain, pointing to about fifty yards away, where a something that looked like a thick miniature lateen sail was gliding through the water.

"A narrow escape, Belton," said the lieutenant; "but you are saved, thank heaven. Give way, my men."

"Arn't we going to try and serve out Master Jack, sir?" said one of the men.

"No, my lad. What can we do without bait or line?"

"Like to spritsail-yard him, sir?" said Strake, touching his hat.

"What's spritsail-yarding?" said Syd, who was now trying to squeeze some of the water out of his drenched uniform.

"Ketching your shark and then running a little spar through his nose," whispered the bo'sun, as the men gave way and the boat surged through the water. "This here's lashed so as he can't get it out, and it keeps him from sinking, as he moves it afore him."

"But it's horribly cruel," said Syd, pausing in his wringing process.

"Well, 'tarn't nice for him, sir," said the boatswain; "but then you see it's cruel of Master Jack to be taking off arms and legs, and it stops that, sir."

This argument was unanswerable for the moment, and just then another shark was sighted, and its appearance fascinated Syd, who shuddered as he gazed at the monster, and thought of the horrible fate he had escaped.

"I wonder what father will say to me when he learns of my adventure," he said to himself.

But he had very little more time for thought, the boat soon being alongside; the falls were hooked on, and they were soon after swinging from the davits.

The first person Syd's eyes rested upon was Terry, whose face expanded into a grin as he saw the middy's drenched condition, and the boy turned away angrily, to see if he could catch his father's eye. But he only saw Lieutenant Dallas making his report on the quarter-deck, and his father standing there with a glass in his hand, which he directed at the rock, then seemed to give some orders, and the lieutenant saluted and came away.

Chapter Twenty Three

"Why, Belton, not changing your duds?" said the lieutenant, as he returned from his colloquy with his commanding officer.

"No, sir; just going to. Did my—did the captain know I was nearly seized by that shark?"

"Yes; I told him."

"What did he say, sir?"

"That you were to be more careful."

Syd stared.

"Was that all, sir?"

"Yes, my lad. I think he said something about you'd grow more clever by and by. But go and get on some dry things."

Syd felt crestfallen and hurt, that after such a terrific adventure his father should be so cool.

But down below the news had already spread, and as he went to the berth to change his things, a knot of his messmates were ready and eager to question him for the endorsement of what they had heard from the boatswain and the men.

He told what he had to tell rather unwillingly, and when he had done regretted that he had said a word, for the careless young dogs only laughed.

"That wasn't half an adventure," cried Bolton. "You should have drawn your dirk, dived under him, and slit him up. That's what the niggers do."

"Yes," said Jenkins, "or else have had hold of his tail, and made him tow you. I would."

"Why, Jenky," cried Roylance, "he'd have taken you like a pill."

"I believe," cried Syd, angrily, "that you'd all have liked it better if I'd come back with one leg snapped off."

"Yes," sneered Terry, who was laughing by the door.

"No, no," cried Jenkins, maliciously. "Mike Terry would have liked to see him without any fistusses."

"Why?" said Roylance.

"'Cause he could lick him then."

"I'll put that down in my log, Baby," said Terry, with an ugly laugh. "You're getting deeply in my debt, and you'll have to pay, or I shall have to pay you."

"Oh, lor'," cried the little middy, diving under the table in mock alarm, and then slowly raising his head up on the other side, to peer at Terry. "What would become of me if I hadn't a good banker."

"Who's your banker, Baby?" said Roylance, mockingly.

"Syd Belton there," and there was a laugh.

Terry ground his teeth together, as he turned away and went on deck, followed by a roar of laughter.

"Look here, I say," cried Syd, who bore his honours very mildly, "you shouldn't tease Terry like that, Jenkins; he'll serve you out for it some day."

"He daren't. I should come to you."

"And I shouldn't help you, for you'd deserve it."

"Very well," said the little fellow, "I'd fight my own battle. Who's afraid? Cock-a-doodle-do!"

He gave a clever imitation of a pugnacious game-cock, after clapping his hands against his sides.

"Terry wouldn't touch him," said Roylance, laughing. "Little people are licenced to be saucy. But I say, Belton, what's the rock like?"

Syd described it as well as he could, and he was listened to with eager attention, but it did not seem probable to Roylance that anything further would come of it.

He was undeceived the next morning though, for after signalling and visiting of the two commanders, it appeared that something definite was to be done, and soon after the stir began.

"Here, Belton," said Roylance, "what do you say to this? I believe we're going to attack the town."

Contradiction came the next moment in the excitement on deck.

"This means business," said Roylance, as he stood with Syd, watching the carrying out of certain orders; and in due time two long guns were placed ready, the barge and the launch were lowered down, and gun-carriages and tackle were hoisted down into each.

The men worked well, for this was a change from the monotony of cruising to and fro on the look-out for ships which never came, or which when overhauled only proved to be friends.

The sea was like glass, and in the course of the next few hours the guns were got ashore, shears being erected on the rock, and the heavy masses of metal and their carriages were landed, beside a good deal of other material likely to be useful in occupying the rock.

And all this while great excitement prevailed as to who were to be the lucky ones told off for the garrison, as it was laughingly called. But they were not long kept in doubt, for it was soon whispered that Lieutenant Dallas was to be in charge, with about a dozen men and a junior officer or two.

Who were to be the junior officers, was the question at the mess, the prevailing decision arrived at being that Bolton and Baby Jenks were the pair.

Early next morning the crews of the barge and second cutter were piped away, and a busy scene followed, as barrels and cases were handed down, till the boats were well-laden, and then there was a cessation, the crews evidently waiting for their orders.

It was a glorious day, and after looking at the men selected, Sydney gazed longingly at the stack of things lying on the rock, covered with a couple of sails and some tarpaulin, which, in case of wind arising, were kept down by casks planted on their corners.

The place looked very tempting to Sydney, though he could not help a shudder running through him as he gazed at the little natural pier, which the sea kept flooding and leaving bare.

"I dare say there are plenty of sharks hanging about," he said; and once more the accident seemed to repeat itself vividly.

He had soon something else to think about, for he saw Lieutenant Dallas come out of the captain's cabin, where he had evidently been to receive his orders, which was the case, and they were simple enough.

"The rock would be invaluable to an enemy, Mr Dallas," the captain had said; "and if they occupied it, as the only safe channel to the port lies close by, they could annoy us fearfully, perhaps sink one of our vessels, and to storm such a place would mean terrible loss of life. So you will occupy it and hold it at all hazards. Either I or my consort will communicate as often as we can, and you shall be well supplied with stores before those you have get low."

"I understand, sir," said Dallas; "and I will hold the rock to the last."

"Your courage may not be put to the test, Mr Dallas," said the captain. "*Au revoir*. Make yourself and your men as comfortable as you can. I have been ashore and examined the place."

"You have, sir?"

"Yes, I went in the night, and I am quite satisfied that it can be held against any odds. Good-bye."

He shook hands, and the young lieutenant went out, wondering how the captain could have managed, and then hurried to the side to see if the last arrangements had been made.

He was busy over this, having passed near to Syd without taking any notice of him, much to the lad's annoyance, for he had tried to catch the lieutenant's eye.

At this moment Roylance came along toward where he was standing, but he paid no heed, for something else had taken his attention.

The boatswain had come on deck, and made his way to the side, where he touched his hat to Lieutenant Dallas, and then proceeded to obey some orders which he had received. Syd was about to intercept him, his longing to be one of the party increasing.

"I wouldn't care," he said to himself, "if they'd let me help land the stores. I did go out first, and here I've been left out of all the fun because I slipped and went overboard. It's too bad."

He was hurrying after the boatswain, when something else caught his eye. A member of the mess came fussing up on deck, fuming with importance, and Syd turned and was uttering some angry expression, when he found himself face to face with Roylance.

"Oh, what a shame!" cried Sydney.

"What's the matter?"

"Terry's going in the barge to land the stores."

"And who's going in the second cutter?" said Roylance.

"I don't know; I didn't hear. I did hope they'd order me to go in the barge."

"Why, what a cocky chap you are, Belt! You've had no experience at all."

"I know that, but I want to get it, and I can't learn to take charge of a boat unless they send me. Who's going in the second cutter?"

"I am."

"You? Oh, how lucky you fellows are!"

"I don't think there'll be much luck in it, for the heat will be terrible, and I don't suppose we shall have been there very long before we wish ourselves back on board."

"Oh, I don't know."

"But I do. Think of the work of getting those guns and things up to the top."

"But I thought the party who were going to stay would do that?"

"Of course: that's it. The barge is coming back on board as soon as she has landed her stores, and the second cutter to-night."

"Well, then you'll only have all day."

"Nonsense; I'm going to stop."

"Oh! You're as lucky as Terry."

"Yes, but I wish he was coming back. Not a pleasant messmate to have ashore with me. I'm sure you wouldn't like to be along with him."

"Perhaps not; but I did want to come, for I know so much about the rock.—Oh! I did want to go."

"Better stop on board, lad. I dare say we shall have a good deal of trouble with the men, though they do like Mr Dallas."

"Oh, but I shouldn't mind that," said Syd, thoughtfully. "I say."

"Well."

"Couldn't you manage to smuggle me off in your boat?"

"I could; but look here, you are the captain's son. Go and ask leave to go, even if you have to come back in the boats."

"Oh, yes; I'm the captain's son," said Sydney, bitterly; "and that's the very reason why I should not be allowed."

"What, for fear you should be eaten up by the shark this time?"

"Joke away; you're all right," said Syd, sulkily.

"Don't take it like that, Belton, old fellow," said Roylance, laying his hand upon his arm. "I'd a hundred times rather have you than Terry. I say, look! here's the first luff. I know he likes us fellows to be eager to learn our profession. Go and ask him to let you go."

"Shall I?" said Syd, hesitatingly.

"Yes; go along. He seems always harsh and rough with everybody, but he isn't a bad one when you come to know him."

"But he's busy now."

"Never mind; go on."

It seemed a very simple thing to do to go up to the officer, touch your hat, and ask leave to go with the boats, but there was that peculiar something so hard to get over which keeps lads back from proffering a petition, and saves their elders and those in authority very often the pain of having to refuse.

Syd suffered severely on that occasion from this peculiar form of timidity, till he saw one boat manned and pull off with its load.

In another quarter of an hour the other would be ready, he knew, and then his chance would be gone.

The first lieutenant passed along the deck, and Syd thought he looked very severe. He came back, and he looked worse. It was impossible to ask him, and Syd shrank away and went to where Roylance was busy speaking to the coxswain of his boat.

"I say," whispered Syd, taking him by the sleeve.

"Yes."

"Ask the luff to let me go with you, there's a good fellow."

Roylance gave him a merry look.

"Well, you are a queer one, Belt," he said. "Not afraid to stand up before Mike Terry, and yet daren't go and ask the luff to let you go ashore."

"I'm not exactly afraid," said Syd.

"But you daren't go."

"Yes, I dare," he said; and he went up boldly now.

"Beg pardon, sir," he said, touching his hat.

"Eh? Yes, Mr Belton; what is it?"

"May I go with the second cutter, sir?"

"You? Mr Roylance is going."

"Yes, sir. I wanted to go too."

"Like to take Mr Jenkins as well as Mr Bolton for a good game?"

"Yes, sir; very much," said Syd, eagerly, in astonishment that the severe officer was so amiable.

"Humph! of course. Look here, Mr Belton, do you know what the old proverb says?"

"About idleness, sir?"

"No, not that one. This:—A boy is a boy."

"Yes, sir."

"Two boys are half a boy."

"Yes, sir."

"And three boys are no boy at all. I want some work done, so I send one boy with each boat. Hi! bo'sun; better take another breaker of water; you may not find any, and we do not want to communicate for some hours."

"Ay, ay, sir," cried Strake, and he busied himself about the order.

"Got your arms all right, and plenty of ammunition?"

"Yes, sir," said Roylance.

"May I go, sir?" said Syd, tentatively.

But the lieutenant did not appear to have heard him, and stood giving order after order to the officer and the boat's crew, asking endless questions about the stores they had on board.

"And I should so like to have gone," thought Syd, as he gazed longingly at the rock, standing up grey and brown and green against the deep blue sea, whose waters washed with creamy foam the bottom of the huge mass of stone.

He turned with a sigh to watch the first lieutenant, who was now busily talking to Lieutenant Dallas and Roylance, and Syd knew that in another minute or two the boat, would be pushed off, when the boatswain came up behind him.

"Aren't you going with us, Master Syd?"

"No, Barney," he replied, sadly; "I'm not going."

"Why don't yer ask the luff to let yer go, sir? Be a bit of a change."

"I did ask him, Barney."

"And did he say you warn't to go, sir?"

"No; he seemed as if he wouldn't answer me."

"Didn't say downright as you shouldn't go?"

"No."

"Well, sir, you're a young gent, and the capen's son, and course I wouldn't tell yer to do nothin' wrong; but in the old days when we was goin' to cut out ships from under the guns of a fort, or to land and upset some town, the young gents used to smuggle theirselves into the boat and get down among the men's legs, and the skipper and the luff wouldn't see 'em."

"Wouldn't see them — why?"

"'Cause bein' very young gents they wouldn't send 'em or give 'em leave to go 'cause o' the danger, but they liked 'em to go all the same, 'cause it showed they'd got sperret in 'em."

"Barney!" whispered Syd, looking at the bo'sun searchingly.

"No, sir; I won't say go," was whispered back. "You can't 'spect it. But—"

Syd's eyes sparkled and he gave a cautious look round to see that the captain was on the quarter-deck, and that the first lieutenant had his back to him and was energetically insisting upon something to Roylance.

The next moment Syd was over the side, and down amongst the crew.

"Hide me somewhere, lads," he whispered eagerly. There was a laugh.

"Arn't you scared about meeting Jack Shark again, sir?" said one of the men.

"Hold your row, Jim," said another. "This way, sir." There was a little scuffling about, and the next minute, half fearing that he was playing ostrich and had only concealed his head, Syd was listening. He had hardly ceased moving when he heard the first lieutenant saying something to Lieutenant Dallas, who was evidently descending the side.

"I wouldn't depend too much on that tackle. The guns are very heavy. Now, Mr Roylance; in with you."

"Ay, ay, sir," came in peculiar tones; and Syd felt disgusted that he should not have been able to come down into the boat in the same way, instead of sneaking in like a rat.

"Seems to be a good deal of swell on amongst these little rocks," said the first lieutenant. "You'll land at the other place."

"Oh, yes," said the second lieutenant; and from where he lay Syd could just get a glimpse of him as he stood up in the stern-sheets.

"He must have seen me," he thought; and looking upwards, there right over the side, and quite plainly to be seen, were the head and shoulders of the first lieutenant gazing down into the boat.

Perfectly certain now that he should be shouted at for trying to get off in the boat, Sydney lay perfectly still, waiting for the unpleasant order; but oddly enough thinking at the same time that ignominious as it would be to crawl up the ladder and climb on board, he should be spared one pain— Terry would not be there to sneer at him.

"Might have been worse," he thought, as he gathered himself together, ready to spring out and get the trouble over.

But the order did not come, and he only heard a growling sound as the boatswain said something to one of the men.

"They're waiting for something," thought Syd, as a low talking arose on deck; and he heard a voice reply which he knew was his father's, and the blood flushed to his cheeks.

"Give way, my lads!" came at last, and Syd exultantly exclaimed to himself, as the tension was taken off—

"He didn't see me," and he heard the oars splash, and felt that the boat was gliding through the water.

But Sydney was not quite right, for as soon as the boat had put off, the first lieutenant went aft to where the captain was standing, examining the rock.

"Well, Mr Bracy," he said, as he closed the glass with a snap.

"I thought I'd tell you, sir, that Mr Belton came and asked leave to go in the last boat."

"Did you give him permission?"

"No, sir."

"That's right."

"But—"

"Eh?" said Captain Belton, raising his eyebrows; "he has taken French leave and gone?"

"Yes; he was stowed away there amidships."

"And you forbade his going?" said the captain, frowning.

"Oh, no, I did not forbid him, sir."

"Well, well, Mr Bracy; we were boys once," said the captain, smiling.

"Yes, sir, I'm afraid I did the same."

"And I more than twice, Bracy. One must be a little blind sometimes with a boy of spirit. Bit of change for him. How is he getting on?"

"Capitally. Full of promise."

"Then I hope he will perform. By the way, there was one thing I did not mention to you—a spar for a flagstaff. I should like them to be able to hoist the colours when anything comes in sight."

"I thought of it, sir. They have everything I could think of, and at a pinch ought to be able to hold out for three months."

"I don't think the pinch will come, Bracy.—Ah, they are getting close in."

"Yes," said the lieutenant, shading his eyes. "First boat is landing her additional stores. One comfort at this time of year, there is no fear of rain, so that they need not trouble much about getting covered in to-night."

"No," said the captain, thoughtfully, "but I hope Mr Dallas will get everything covered in all the same."

They were following the second boat, as it rose and fell on the mirror-like surface of the water, till she was cleverly run alongside the rocks, when the captain opened his glass once more, and stood watching—the first lieutenant seeing a smile come over his stern features, and rightly interpreting that he was gazing at his son more than the actions of the men, who were quickly landing the additional stores that they had taken to the rock; the tackle previously rigged up being lowered again and again, and the cases and kegs cleverly swung ashore, the men dipping their oars at the word of command, and every time a box was swung up the boat was drawn out of danger, ready to be backed in when the tackle was once more lowered down.

"Yes," said the captain, thoughtfully, "I have no doubt that Mr Dallas will prove himself most able in this business. Weather seems settled down, Bracy."

"Yes, sir; but you know what it is in these latitudes. A smile one minute and a kick the next, and when it does rain—well, it's a good job it doesn't last, for we don't want another flood."

The captain went on pacing the quarter-deck, looking very cold and stern, but with a glow about his heart.

"He'll make a smart officer," he said to himself,—"one of whom we shall be proud. I'll write and tell Tom about this. How he will chuckle and enjoy it! But I suppose I must lecture the young dog when he comes on board to-night. Discipline must be maintained."

That evening, after the men had been busily helping, the barge came back and was hoisted on board. The captain walked on deck, but recollected that it was in the second cutter that Syd had gone, and he went back to his cabin.

Just at sundown the second boat returned with the coxswain and crew, and she was hoisted up.

"Humph!" said the captain to himself, as he heard the squeaking sound made by the falls, "I will not send for him to-night; I'll have a few words with him in the morning. Let me see, I'll send word to him by Strake. Bah! how absurd. The bo'sun has gone ashore to help putting up the tackle for hoisting the guns."

In the course of the evening, when the stars were blazing overhead, and the rock was invisible in the soft, transparent darkness of the night, the captain was walking up and down, when he encountered the first lieutenant, and they compared notes about the beauty of the night, and how advantageous it was for the unhoused men ashore.

"By the way, Bracy," said the captain, "have you reproved Mr Belton? because, if not, leave it to me."

"Oh, certainly, sir; but of course I have not had a chance."

"What do you mean?"

"I supposed that he had only gone ashore for the day, and would come back with the last boat."

"Well, hasn't he?"

"No, sir; he has stopped ashore."

Chapter Twenty Four

That was a busy day on the rock, which was in places so hot to their bare feet that the men laughed as they stepped gingerly about.

"I say, mate," said one of them in the intervals of hauling up a case, and just as he had noted that Syd was close by, "d'yer know what's for dinner to-day?"

"Ay, lad; cold junk and biscuit."

"Better than that, messmate; on'y it wants the young gen'leman to set to work and ketch some shrimps for sarce."

"What d'yer mean, lad?"

"Fried soles, lad, fried soles," said the other. "Mine's 'most done brown."

Syd was not supposed to be on duty, but he was so much interested in the whole affair that he was as busy as any one, and it was while he was high up on the rock, looking on at the rigging up of a couple of spars, crane-fashion, for hoisting the stores, that he came across the lieutenant, who gave him a peculiar look and a smile, and then went on giving a few orders before going higher to re-inspect the chasm, prior to getting the stores and light things in there.

"Couldn't see yer, Master Syd," whispered the boatswain. "'Stonishing how invisible young gents is sometimes."

But there was little time for talking. Work was the order of the day, and so clever were the contrivances for hoisting, and so well did the men work, that by sundown all the light things were under cover in the chasm, and only the guns, barrels, and heavy cases down by the natural pier. These latter were covered in turn, and made fast with pieces of rock piled upon the edge of the tarpaulins, after which the men of the barge embarked and went back to the ship, the crew of the second cutter following, and the garrison being gathered in their new quarters, high up in the cleft of the great rock, for a hearty meal, to which Sydney came down from the bare fork of the cleft, ravenously hungry, and at once fell to.

He was partaking of his portion with eager zest, when Roylance, who had been busy below seeing to the covering of the barrels, came up.

"Why, Belt," he said, in a whisper; "not gone back?"

"No," said Syd, laconically.

"But I thought you'd gone back in the second cutter."

"No," said Syd, with his mouth full; "I did mean to, but I've been exploring, and when I came back the boat was gone."

"What are you doing here?" said a sharp voice.

"Eating," said Syd, without looking up.

"Don't be insolent, sir. I am one of the officers of this expedition, and on duty. You have no business here."

"Look here, Terry," said Syd, eating away in the most nonchalant fashion; "I'm hungry, and don't want to leave off and spoil my dinner. I don't want to quarrel to-night."

"This is insufferable," cried Terry, who felt clothed in authority as second officer of the expedition, and striding away, he found out the lieutenant, and stated what he had seen.

"He had no business here, Mr Terry," said the lieutenant, quietly; "but of course we can do nothing to-night."

"If we signalled for a boat, sir?"

"One would come and fetch him off, but would create unnecessary alarm. And look here, Mr Terry, is it not time you forgot old sores, and became good friends with your messmates?"

"I don't understand you, sir," said Terry, haughtily. "Then I'll try and be plainer," said the lieutenant, rather sharply. "Don't you think it is a pity that you should let your enmity to Mr Belton make you jump at a chance to do him a bad turn?"

"I came here, sir, to do my duty, and I reported misconduct on the part of one of the midshipmen."

"Who once gave you a good thrashing, Mr Terry, for playing the bully. There, there, my good lad, forget and forgive, and don't try and usurp my duties here. I will look after Mr Belton."

"Such confounded favouritism to the captain's son!" muttered Terry; but it was loud enough for the lieutenant to hear, and he exclaimed, hotly—

"And if you dare to say such a thing as that again, sir, I'll clap you under arrest, and put Mr Belton in your place." Terry slunk off and stood about sulking till the men had finished, and were then set to work to make a temporary shelter for the night, which was quickly done by tying the edges of the sails they had brought to some spars, and resting these against the perpendicular side of the rock in the cleft, thus forming a lean-to, which was spacious enough to cover the men and the stores and ammunition already protected by the tarpaulins thrown over them.

Roylance and Syd were standing together in the darkness, watching the men arranging the spars and hauling the canvas tight, when Syd laid his hand upon his companion's arm.

"Don't speak or move," he whispered; "but look down to the right. There's some wild beast crawling up from the west end of the gap."

Roylance gripped Syd's hand to indicate that he saw the creature, and they remained silent, watching it creeping nearer and nearer, till it reached the spot where the men had been making their meal, and there it seemed to pause for a few minutes before returning the way it came.

It was so dark that its motions were more those of a shadow than of some living creature, and at last it seemed quite to die away among some loose rocks, just where the gap ended in a precipice.

"Gone," said Sydney, drawing a long breath; "why, it was after the provisions."

"Evidently. I couldn't have thought that there were any live creatures here."

"Looked like a great monkey."

"Well, I thought so once—an ape, but it couldn't have been."

"I say," whispered Syd; "was it a man, and they're going to play some prank on us from the ship to see if we are on the look-out?"

"What's that?" said a voice behind them, and the two lads started to find that the lieutenant had come up to them unawares while they were talking earnestly.

"We just saw something come up from that end of the gap, sir," said Syd; "it was like a monkey."

"And Mr Belton here fancies it might be a spy from the *Sirius* to see if we were on the watch," said Roylance.

"Impossible! they would not play us such a trick. Stop, it might be from the enemy—a boat landing men to see what we are about. But where?" he said, excitedly. "They couldn't have landed where we did, because there are two men on the watch, and I don't think there is any other place. Let's see."

Orders were given, the men seized their arms, and after a few admonitory words had been whispered, a search commenced, anything but an adequate one, for the task was one of risk, and the men had to proceed with the greatest caution, so as not to make a false step and go over the side, either into the sea or down one of the cracks and rifts into which the rock was cleft.

This went on for a couple of hours, during which the men on the watch were certain that no one had landed, and at last the weary sailors felt ready to endorse the remark of Terry, which somehow became spread among them, that it was only a trick of the captain's son to set them on the alert.

At last this came to the lieutenant's ears, and he called Syd and Roylance aside.

"Was this some prank?" he said, sternly.

"I would not be guilty of such a trick, sir," said Syd, warmly. "It would have been unfair to the men, who were tired, and an insult to you, sir."

"Of course it would, gentlemen," said the lieutenant. "I beg your pardon."

He went away, feeling rather uneasy, and set watches in two more places, with orders to fire at the slightest alarm. Then in turn with Terry he visited the posts during the early part of the night, and in turn with Roylance during the latter part, the anxieties of the new command keeping him on the alert.

As for Syd, he sat talking to Roylance for a time after going up to a point where on the one side they could see the lights of the ship as she lay to in the offing, and on the other, very dimly, the distant lamps of the town of Saint Jacques, or those at the head of its harbour.

It was a strange experience up there in that cleft, under the shelter of the tent, with the distant murmur of breaking waves upon the rocks. The low buzz of the men lulled for a time, then ceased, and Syd lay gazing at a great bright star which he could see peering through a slit between two outstretched sails. Then that star passed out of sight and another moved in, followed by another, which grew dim, then dimmer, and finally disappeared, for the simple reason that Syd's eyes had closed and he was fast asleep.

Chapter Twenty Five

The bustle about him at daybreak woke Syd up to find that it was a glorious morning, but a sharp breeze had arisen; the sea was alive with breaking waves, and great rollers kept coming in to thunder upon the rock, sending up the broken water so far that it was evidently the first duty to get all the tackle and raise the remainder of the cases and barrels to the level of the cleft.

Willing hands worked well at this, and at last everything was got up in safety on the first platform ready for running into the cleft, all save the two dismounted guns and their carriages, which were not likely to hurt, and the raising of these was deferred till after the breakfast, which one of the men who acted as cook had prepared.

"There'll be no communication with the ship to-day, gentlemen," said the lieutenant, "unless the wind drops. Why, she must be three miles farther away, and I can't see the *Orion*. Bad job for you, Mr Belton."

"Yes, sir," said Syd, quietly going on with his breakfast, and glancing at Terry, who scowled.

"Well, I shall make you work. That's the only plan in dealing with stowaways."

"Oh, I'll work, sir," said Syd. "When I've done break fast," he added to himself.

"I tell you what," said the lieutenant; "we shall all be busy getting up and mounting those guns, so I shall set you to find your mare's-nest."

"My what, sir?"

"Mare's-nest, my lad. You shall have two of our most active lads well-armed. Take pistols yourself, and be careful with them. Go and search every hole and cranny you can. Find the thing you saw last night, and bring him or it to me. I'm satisfied it was no one from the *Sirius*, and it may be some young black sent across and landed to find out what he can."

As soon as the morning meal was ended Syd set about his task, meeting with a lowering look from Terry as he passed him. Two smart young fellows were his companions, and the fact that he had a brace of loaded pistols stuck in his belt making him feel more important than ever he had felt before, till he came upon Strake, who was busy at the very part where he had seen the dark figure pass, and strengthening and adding to the tackle which was to be used to get up the guns.

"Mornin', Mr Belton, sir," said the boatswain; and stepping aside so as to be out of hearing, he said in a low voice, "'Member what I says to you when I was cleaning the cap'in's pistols?"

"Yes, I remember, Barney," said Syd, in the same low tone.

"Then I says it again, sir, that's all."

"I'll take care," said Syd; and he went on in advance of his men, but feeling as if the old boatswain had been cutting his comb.

An isolated mass of rock some eight or ten acres in extent does not suggest that there would be much difficulty in the way of search; but before they had gone many yards Syd realised that he had a very awkward task, and that a rope would be a very acceptable article for helping one another. This had to be fetched, and then once more they started, with Syd beginning to feel the responsibilities of his work, and the necessity for showing that he possessed energy and determination if he wished the men to obey.

They had not gone much past their first halting-place when he stopped and hesitated, for there were cracks and holes large enough to conceal any one, in all directions. As he stood looking round him, one of the men whispered to the other, and they both laughed.

This seemed to stir Syd up. He had inherited enough of his father's habits to feel nettled at any doubt of his ability, and he rather startled the men by saying sharply —

"You, Rogers, go yonder to the left; Wills, you take the right. Both of you keep as close to the sea as you can, and I'll take the centre of the rock. Keep both of you to about my pace, and whenever I'm out of sight wait till you see me again, for I'll keep on the high ground as much as I can. Now then, off and search every hole you see. If you feel that you have run the enemy to earth, stop and fire as a signal."

"Ay, ay, sir," they cried together. "But what's the enemy like, sir?"

"Find him and see," said Syd, sharply. "Now off."

The men separated at once, and the toilsome job began, with the sun beating down with tropical power, but the brisk wind reducing the ardour to bearing point.

"Nice job this," thought the boy, as leaving the cleft centre of the rock a little to his left, he began his arduous clamber. "Why, it's as bad as being an ant in a loaf-sugar basin. Given myself the hardest job."

But he persevered, searching diligently every rift, and amongst great blocks of stone over which he afterwards clambered, seeking the highest point so as to get a sight of one or the other of his two men, who were as active as he; but they all reached the edge of the rock at the point furthest from where they had landed without making any discovery.

"Well," cried Syd, wiping the great drops of perspiration from his brow, "found anything?"

"Lots of holes, sir," said one.

"Cracks big enough to hold a ship's crew, sir," said the other.

"Back again, then," cried Syd. "There's either a monkey or a man in hiding somewhere about the place, and we've got to find him."

"Ought to have said *it*" thought Syd, as he started back, shouting to the men to take lines a little nearer to him, while he too altered his course, making straight now for the cleft rock which rose like the citadel of the place.

As he climbed along he found rift after rift, some so close that he could not get his hand down, others so wide and deep that he hesitated at the task of leaping over them, wondering what would be the result if he slipped and fell. The fact grew upon him as he went on, that small as the place looked from the ship's deck, there was plenty of room for an enemy or fifty enemies to hide; but he became more certain that the natural pier was the only place where an enemy could land; the two men having confirmed the opinion formed when Lieutenant Dallas rowed round.

"Strikes me," said Syd to himself, as he kept on peering down into chasm after chasm, "that if we want to catch our friend we shall have to set a trap for him."

He climbed on and came to another eerie-looking place, more forbidding than any he had yet seen. It was only a jagged crack of a couple of feet across, but it sloped outward directly, so that a vast hollow was formed, and when he shouted down it there was a deep reverberating sound which died away in a whisper.

Boy nature is boy nature all the world over, and Syd could not resist the prompting which led him to drag a great piece of stone to the edge of the crack and push it in.

He shrank back, startled at the effect of what he had done, for no sooner had the stone disappeared than it seemed to strike on the side and rebound, to strike again and then again and again, raising an echoing, booming roar, which ended as suddenly as it had begun.

Syd Belton | 161

"I can't go down a place like that," he said, impatiently, as he shrank away; and then he stood staring, for the noise began again. But not below ground, for it was as if the rock had come crashing out in front of him a hundred and fifty feet away, to be followed by a hurried shouting; and on climbing a block of stone to his right, he made out one of his men looking out for him, and waving his hand and shouting—"Back! Back!"

Something was wrong. Perhaps it was an attack; and he clambered higher so as to attract the attention of the other man, who also shouted and waved his hand before pointing at the citadel in front.

"Something must be wrong," thought Syd, and he hurried panting on, to get in sight of the end of the chasm at last, but he could see nothing, only that the spars rigged up crane-fashion were not there.

He was now on the highest part of the ridge, which ran down from the centre rock to the end; and as he clambered along he gazed seaward in search of the frigate, but it seemed to be gone. The next moment, though, he caught sight of her top-gallant spars, and realised that she must be sailing right away.

The heat was tremendous as Syd struggled on, finding that he had selected a far worse piece of the rock than had fallen to his men, and that his task would prove hopeless without the whole party turned out to help.

All at once, after getting over a block of rugged limestone, which seemed full of coral, he found that he must let himself right down into a deep crack, or else clamber to right or left, where the difficulties were far greater, even if they were surmountable.

He paused for a few moments to wipe his streaming face, and looked up overhead longingly at where the wind was whistling among the blocks of stone, and then lowered himself carefully down some thirty feet, stood listening to a curious sound which came whispering up from where the chasm he was in contracted to a mere crack, and after coming to the conclusion that it must be caused by there being some communication with the sea, he crossed the crack, and began to climb up the other side, where before he was half-way up one of his two men appeared peering over the edge, and looking down with a scared face.

"Oh, there you are, sir," he cried; "we was getting frightened, and thought you'd tumbled."

"No: give me your hand. Thank you. Phew! how hot it is down there!" cried Syd, as he climbed out and stood in the comparatively cool sea-breeze again. "But why did you hail me?"

"Don't know, sir. There's some'at wrong up yonder."

"Something wrong? Not attacked, are they?"

"Dunno, sir."

"Where's your messmate?"

"Here he comes, sir," said the man, waving his hand; and following their young leader, the two sailors made for the end of the great chasm where the guns were to be hoisted up, and Strake had been so busy with the tackle.

For some minutes, as they climbed over or round the obstacles, there was nothing to be seen; but after creeping round a bold corner of rock, Syd suddenly found himself looking down on the whole party from the ship gathered in a knot round what seemed from the rope and tackle to be one of the guns.

"Got it up, and it slipped and fell," thought Syd, as he lowered himself down and made his way to Roylance, whom he touched on the back.

"What's the mat—"

He did not finish, for as the midshipman turned Syd caught sight of the gun and ropes, with some handspikes which had evidently been used as levers.

All that was at a glance. Then he pushed his way forward to sink down on one knee beside the lieutenant, who was lying on his back, his face haggard and ghastly, his teeth set and his eyes closed, while the great drops of agony were gathering on his brow.

He saw no more, for a piece of sail was thrown over his legs.

"Mr Dallas," he cried, "what is it? Are you ill?" A low murmur ran round the little group, and at that moment the boatswain appeared with a pannikin of water from one of the tubs.

As the lieutenant heard the lad's voice, he opened his eyes, looked round wildly, and then his gaze rested on Syd's anxious face.

"Ah, Belton," he said in a hoarse whisper, "bad job. The gear gave way—confounded gun—fell—crushed my legs. Ah!"

He uttered a groan full of anguish and fainted away.

"It's horrible!" cried Roylance, as every one looked on helplessly. "No surgeon; the gale increasing, and the ship out of sight. Here, some one get some brandy or rum. Ah, Belton!" he whispered, with the tears in his eyes, "such a good fellow, and I'm afraid it's all over."

Syd heard this as if in a dream, as a deathly feeling of sickness came over him, and there floated before his eyes a scene in a grand old beech-wood near home, with a group of men standing round, helplessly as these were, the sun shining down like a silver shower through the branches, beneath which was a doctor's gig and a man in a smock frock holding the horse's head. There on the moss, where scattered white chips shone out clearly, lay a fine, well-built young man close by the trunk of a tree which he had been helping to fell, but had not got out of the way soon enough, and the trunk had crushed his legs.

The scene died away, and he was gazing down again at the unfortunate lieutenant instead of at the woodman, with the doctor on his knee and a boy by his side; and as the deathly sickness passed off he was brought more to himself by hearing the haughty domineering voice of Terry.

"Stand away, some of you—all of you!" he cried. "Mr Belton, do you hear me? Go away, sir; you are keeping the air from the wounded man."

Accustomed to obey, fresh ashore from the ship where the discipline was of the strictest, Syd drew back; but as he did so a hysterical sob burst from his throat, and he stepped forward again.

"Confound you, sir! do you hear me?" cried Terry. "I am in command now. Stand back, or I'll put you under arrest."

As he advanced threateningly, Roylance touched Syd's sleeve.

"Don't make a row now, for poor Dallas's sake. Look! He's dying."

Syd looked at him quickly, and then turned back to face Terry, as he said in a dreamy way—"Is there no help?"

"Will you stand back, sir?"

"No doctor? No one who understands—"

"Here, bo'sun—Strake; seize Mr Belton, and take him away."

No one stirred, but a murmur ran round the group as with a bitter cry of agony Syd stepped forward so quickly that Terry drew back, expecting a blow. But the lad did not even see him, and he was in the act of sinking on his knees to take the lieutenant's hand, when his eyes rested on the piece of sail-cloth thrown tightly over the injured man's legs, where a ruddy patch of blood was slowly spreading.

"He's bleeding to death," he cried excitedly; and a change seemed to come over the boy, as he bent down and quickly drew away the sail-cloth.

"This is too much," cried Terry. "You meddling young fool!"

Syd flushed for a moment into anger. "Roylance! Strake!" he cried, "take that idiot away." As he turned from the astounded middy, he threw off his jacket, gave one glance at Dallas, whose eyes were fixed upon him in a wild despairing way; and then knife in hand he was down upon his knees.

"Here, Barney," he said, in cool firm tones, as recollections of what he had seen in the wood at home played once more through his brain; "down on your knees there by his head, and bathe his face with the cold water. Keep back on the windward side," he continued. "Mr Roylance, let four men hold a sail over us to keep off the sun."

His orders were so full of the force which makes men obey, that they were acted upon at once; and all the time Syd was on his knees busy.

Without a moment's hesitation he had inserted his sharp knife at the left knee-band, and slit up the garment right to the groin, laying bare a ghastly wound that seemed to go right to the bone, and from which the blood came in one spot with a regular throb, throb, which Syd knew meant death before long if it was not stopped.

"Water, here!" he shouted.

"I must protest against this boy's meddling," cried Terry. "Mr Belton, let him die in peace."

"Mr Roylance—" came in faint tones from the white lips of the wounded man, "take—Mr Terry—"

He fainted as he spoke, but it was enough. At a word from the midshipman two of the sailors secured Terry by the wrists, and he was forced away, while two other men ran for a bucket of water.

"Leave his head now, Barney," cried Syd, in a quick, decided voice. "Your neckerchief, man. Quick, roll it up."

This was handed to the young operator, who passed it under Dallas's limb far up, tied it round in a knot, called for a jack-knife, and then shouted to the willing man who handed it to shut it up. This done he passed the knife inside the neckerchief, pressed it down on the inner part of the thigh, and then took his sheathed dirk from his belt.

This he also passed under the neckerchief, and began to twist round a few turns, drawing the bandage tightly down on the knife-handle, which, as he still twisted, was forced firmly home, pressing the artery against the bone.

This done, and the dirk secured so that it could not twist back, Syd turned to the gaping wound, from which the blood still welled, but sluggishly. The water was ready, and scooping some on to the wound, it was more plainly revealed as a great clean-cut gash, extending many inches.

Syd's fingers were soon busily employed searching for and finding the ruptured artery, and in spite of the horrible nature of the gash, he uttered a sigh of satisfaction as he discovered it and pressed it between his finger and thumb.

"Now one of you—no, you, Strake," he cried, "off with my handkerchief, and tear it across so as to get me a couple of strips, which roll up fine as twine."

This was done, but the pieces were rejected as too thick.

Two more were prepared and laid ready.

"Now," he said, "a little more water here, over my hands."

He was obeyed, and with deft fingers, taught by Doctor Liss, he rapidly tied the artery, and the main flow of blood was stopped amid a low murmur of satisfaction, the patient, who had revived, lying perfectly motionless with his eyes fixed upon his surgeon.

And now for a few moments the lad paused, with his brow wrinkled up, thinking.

He wanted silk and a large needle, and the latter was unattainable.

"Has any one a pin or two?" he said.

There was an eager search, and the result was that five were found, of which the boatswain produced three; and then stared as he saw his young officer unbutton and strip off his white linen shirt, to kneel there half-naked beneath the rough awning the men held over them, and rapidly slit and tear it up into bandages.

By this time Roylance was back, and taking his cue from his friend, he did not hesitate to follow his example.

"Now quick, Strake," said Syd; "lay me up a few more strips of silk as fine as you can."

"Ay, ay, sir!" and the boatswain's fingers were soon busy, while by means of a couple of broad bandages Syd drew the edges of the wound together, and gave the ends of the bands to two men to hold, while first in one place he cleverly thrust a pin through the skin of one side of the wound and out at the other, then holding the lips of the gash together he quickly twisted a fine thread of silk over the pin-head on one side, over the point on the other, and so on, to and fro, till the wound was closed there.

Over this a temporary bandage was secured, and he proceeded to draw the wound edges together in another place in the same way till this was also fast and temporarily bandaged over. The other three pins were similarly utilised, and then broad fresh bandages of linen were wrapped firmly round, the temporary ones being removed by degrees, and again used in a better manner, till the horrible wound was properly secured; then as Syd ceased his efforts, as if moved by one spirit, a hearty English cheer burst from every one present; and the men whose hands were not occupied threw their hats in the air.

"Hush! pray!" cried Syd, looking up angrily, as, taking his knife once more, he cut through the knee-band of the other leg, slit it up in turn, and then softly drew down the stocking.

Here he paused, and looked anxiously up at his patient, whose pallor was terrible.

"Keep on moistening his lips with a little spirit-and-water, Roylance," he whispered, "or he will not be able to bear the pain."

He was obeyed without a word, and after waiting a few moments the lad, clumsily enough perhaps, but with a show of some of the skill that he had seen displayed by Doctor Liss when out with him upon his rounds, began to make his examination.

The leg was terribly scraped and bruised, but this was not the trouble. Syd's eyes were sufficiently educated to detect what was wrong, and a few delicate touches satisfied him.

"Got off a bit there, hasn't he, Master Syd?" whispered the boatswain.

"Got off, Barney? No," said the lad, sadly. "His thigh-bone is broken, and his leg too, just above the ankle."

"Lor' ha' mussy!" muttered the boatswain, "who'd ha' thought o' that!"

Syd was silent, for he was face to face with another surgical problem. He wanted splints, bandages, and brown paper, and he had none of these. What was to be done?

"Two of you take your knives," he said, "and split up the lid of one of those cases. I want half a dozen strong thin laths of different widths."

"Ay, ay, sir!" came back; and there was the rending sound of wood heard.

"Now for bandages, Barney. Ah, I see. But I want some linen first to go next the skin."

"Oh, you can have all the men's, sir, and welcome, I know."

"Yes, poor fellows. But I want some long narrow ones. You must cut them from one of the sails."

"Ay, ay, sir!"

All worked hard at these preparations, while Syd had the longest lid of any case they had brought to him, and this, after being covered with a piece of sail-cloth, was carefully slipped under the broken limb. Then there was a certain amount of trimming and measuring required over the splints before the young surgeon was satisfied, a sensation of shrinking keeping him from beginning what was another crucial task. Fortunately the fractures were simple, and he had no very great difficulty in bringing the broken bones into their proper positions, after which he bandaged and applied the splints, making all fast, a low moan from time to time being all that escaped from the sufferer.

At last. The final bandage was secured, and a horrible weight was removed from Syd's breast, for he knew that he had set the bones rightly even if his surgery was rough, and so far his patient had not sunk under the operation.

"Shall we carry him up yonder now, sir?" said the boatswain, touching his forelock.

"Move him? no," cried Syd. "Rig up something over his head. He must not be touched." Then, turning to Dallas, he went down on one knee and took his hand. "Are you in much pain?" he said.

The poor fellow was conscious, and he looked full in the speaker's eyes; his lips moved, but no sound came, and the horrible feeling of sickness which had first troubled Syd came back, increasing so fast that the lad rose quickly and staggered a few yards.

"Give me something—water—quick!" he muttered; and all was blank.

Chapter Twenty Six

When Syd opened his eyes he was lying down, with Roylance kneeling by his side, and a curious feeling of wonderment came over him as to what all this meant.

"What's the matter?" he said, sharply.

"You fainted. Are you better now?"

"Some people do faint at the sight of a drop of blood," said a familiar voice, followed by a sneering laugh.

It was medicine to Syd, and he felt better directly, and sat up.

"Give me my jacket and things," he said; and paying no heed to Terry, who was standing close by the two men who had been placed over him, busily helping with the rough tent they were fitting over the lieutenant, he walked to his patient, to find him lying so passive that he shuddered, and wondered whether the poor fellow was dead.

"Did I do wrong?" Syd asked himself. "Would he have got better if I had left him alone?"

He felt his ignorance terribly as he asked himself these questions; but the answer was ready for utterance as Roylance said, looking white as he spoke—

"Oh, Belt, old fellow, what a horrible job to have to do!" And then, "Would he have got right without?"

"No. If he had gone on bleeding from that artery he would by now have been a dead man."

"But how did you learn all that? The lads can do nothing else but talk about it."

"Hush! come away," said Syd. "Let him sleep, and"—he shuddered— "let one of the men bring me a bucket of water."

It was well on in the middle of the day, and there was no sign of the ship. The men had greatly improved the shelter up in the chasm; but though the carriages were up one at each end near the positions they were to occupy, the two guns which should by this time have been mounted lay on the rock, the first one having brought down the tackle, and bounded from a sloping stone on to the unfortunate lieutenant, pinning him to the ground before he could get out of the way.

After seeing that his patient was carefully watched by one of the men who had been his companion that morning, Syd was trying to drive away the miserable feeling of faintness and exhaustion from which he suffered by partaking of a little refreshment, when, just as he was thinking of his father's orders, and that those guns ought to be mounted, the boatswain came up, touched his hat to him and Roylance, and was about to speak, when Terry strode up, and ignoring his brother midshipmen, said sharply—

"Look here, bo'sun; that was all nonsense this morning. Mr Dallas is wounded, and incapable. I am senior officer, and the captain's orders must be carried out. Call the men together, and I'll have those guns up at once."

"Ay, ay, sir!" cried Strake; his whistle sounded shrilly against the sides of the rock, and the men came running up.

"All hands to hoist up the guns," cried Terry. "Now, bo'sun, have that tackle fixed better this time."

"Ay, ay, sir. Now, my lads, be smart, and we'll have that gun up in a jiffy."

The men were all gathered together in a knot, but no one stirred; and they began muttering to themselves.

"Now, my lads; what is it?" cried the boatswain. "You don't mind a bit o' sunshine, do you? Come, bear a hand."

Not a man stirred, and Syd and Roylance exchanged looks.

"What is the meaning of this?" cried Terry, in a bullying tone. "Do you hear, men? I want these guns up directly."

Still no one stirred, and Terry grew pale. His one hand played about his sword, and his other hand sought a pistol.

"Bo'sun!" he cried, "what is the meaning of this insubordination?"

Strake shook his head.

"D'ye hear, my lads? Mr Terry wants to know the meaning of this ins'bordination."

Not a man spoke.

"Look here," cried Terry, drawing his dirk, "I am not going to be trifled with. I order you to help hoisting up those guns. What do you mean? Are you afraid of another accident?"

"No," cried the men with one consent, in quite a shout.

"Then look here, my lads," cried Terry, drawing a pistol, "I'll stand no nonsense. Will you obey?"

"Look here, Terry," said Roylance, sharply, "there is no occasion for violence. The men think they have some grievance; ask them what it is."

"Mind your own business, sir," cried Terry, sharply; but as Roylance drew back with a deprecating gesture, he spoke to the boatswain.

"Ask the mutinous scoundrels what they mean," he said.

The boatswain went up to the knot of men.

"Now then, you swabs," he growled; "what's these here games?"

"We arn't going to have him playing at skipper over us," said one of them. "The luff put him under arrest for interferin'."

"Ay, ay," growled the others; "we don't want he."

"S'pose you know it's hanging at the yard-arm for mutiny, my lads?" said the boatswain, gruffly.

"Mutiny? Who want's to mutiny?" said another. "We're ready enough to work, arn't we, messmates?"

"Ay, ay," came in chorus.

"Then lay hold o' the rope, and let's have them guns up yonder."

"Ay, to be sure; we'll get the guns up," said another man; "but Mr Terry's under 'rest."

"Then you won't haul?" said the boatswain.

"Not one on us. He arn't an officer till he's been afore the skipper."

"Well, what am I to tell him?"

"What yer like," said one of the first speakers.

Strake gave his quid a turn, rubbed his ear, and walked back.

"Won't haul, sir," he said, laconically.

"What! Then it's mutiny. Mr Roylance, Mr Belton, draw your swords. Bo'sun, run and get a cutlass and pistols."

"I don't want no cutlass to them, sir; I've got my fists," growled the boatswain.

"What, are you in a state of mutiny too?" cried Terry.

"Not as I knows on, sir?"

"Then arrest the ringleader."

"Which is him, sir?"

"That man," cried Terry, pointing with his dirk to Rogers, one of the smart young fellows who had been Syd's companion in the morning. "Bring him here. Oh, if I had a file of marines!"

"Which you arn't got," muttered Strake, as he strode back to where the men were together.

"Here you, Ike Rogers," he said; "I arrests you for mutiny."

"No, no," growled the men together.

"All right, messmates," said Rogers, laughing. "Can't put us in irons, for there arn't none."

"Come on," said Strake, clapping him on the shoulder. "Mr Terry wants you."

"What for?" said Rogers, eyeing the middy's dirk; "to pick my teeth?"

In the midst of a burst of laughter the boatswain marched the man up to where Terry was, strutting and fuming about.

"Now, you scoundrel," he said; "what does this mean?"

"Beg pardon, sir; that's what we want to know."

"Then I'll tell you, sir; it's rank mutiny."

"There now, bo'sun; that's just what we thought," said Rogers, turning to him. "I know'd it was, and that's why we wouldn't come."

"You scoundrel! You're playing with me," cried Terry.

"Nay, sir; not me. Wouldn't ketch me play with a orficer with a big sword in his hand."

"Then tell me what you mean. You said it was mutiny, and so you would not come."

"That's it, sir. Sworn to sarve the King; and when a young orficer, which is you, sir, breaks out of arrest, and wants to lead a lot of poor chaps wrong, 'tarn't me as 'll risk my neck."

Terry's jaw dropped at this unexpected reply, and Roylance burst into a roar of laughter, in which he was joined by Syd, while Strake stood with his face puckered up like a year-old pippin, and rubbed his starboard ear.

"Mr Roylance!" cried Terry at last, "how is discipline to be preserved while you encourage the men in this tomfoolery? I shall report it to the captain, sir."

"Look here, Mr Terry," said Roylance, firmly; "the man is, in his way, quite right."

"Ay, ay, sir," cried the others, who had closed in, following their messmate.

"Quite right?"

"Yes; Mr Dallas put you under arrest."

"Mr Dallas is ill—dying, and unable to give orders, sir. I am your senior."

"Oh, you're welcome to take command for me," cried Roylance. "I don't want the responsibility."

"Once more, my lads, I warn you of the consequences. Will you go to your work?"

There was no reply, and the men drew back, while Terry stood looking along their faces with his pistol raised.

"Mind that there don't go off, please, sir," said Rogers, dryly. "You might hit me."

There was a roar of laughter at this, and Terry stamped with rage.

"Shall I go and try and bring 'em to their senses, sir?" said the boatswain.

"No—yes," cried Terry.

"Which on 'em, sir?" said the boatswain, dryly.

"Yes. Go and see, and tell them I'll shoot down the first man who disobeys."

"Oh, Lor'!" groaned Rogers, with mock horror, and there was another laugh, while Syd turned away unable to keep his countenance, and went to where the lieutenant lay asleep.

"Look here, my lads," growled the boatswain; "it's no use kicking agen it. Come on; lay to at the ropes, and let's get the work done."

"We arn't going to be bully-ragged by a thing like that," said the oldest man present. "If he was a chap with anything in him, we would. But he's a bully, that's what he is. Let Mr Roylance take command."

"Says as Mr Roylance is to take command, sir," shouted Strake.

"No," said Roylance, "I will not undertake the responsibility."

"Look ye here, messmates," cried Rogers, as Syd hung back from the little tent, "Capen Belton's our skipper."

"Ay, ay," shouted the men.

"And he arn't here, and the luff's in orspittle."

"Well, we know that, Iky," said one of the men.

"Ay, lad; but here comes the son. I says let young Captain Belton take command."

"Ay, ay!" thundered the men, and they gave three cheers.

"There you are, sir," said the boatswain. "Men says you're to take command."

"I?" cried Syd; "nonsense. There's Mr Roylance."

"No, no," cried the men; and Terry stood grinding his teeth, and looking threateningly at Syd.

"Look here, my lads," cried Syd; "the captain wants those guns mounted, and this place held."

"Ay, ay, sir; we'll do it and hold it again anybody," cried Rogers.

"Very well put, Belton; very well," cried Terry.

"Your officer is helpless. Will you obey Mr Terry, and do your duty like men?"

"No!" came with a roar.

"Then let Mr Roy lance take command. Come, be men."

"We arn't got nothing agen Mr Roylance," shouted a voice; "but we want you."

"Go on, Belton; take command. The ship will be back perhaps to-night, and we must have those guns up," said Roylance.

"Will you back me up?"

"Of course," cried Roylance, heartily.

"All right, then, my lads," cried Syd. "Now then, with a will."

"Ay, ay. Hooray!" shouted the men.

"Man signalling from the tent, sir," said Roylance.

"Oh!" ejaculated Syd, as a cold chill ran through him, and he shrank from learning what it meant. "Go and see, Roy."

Roylance was already half-way there, and he came back directly.

"Mr Dallas says you are to take command, Mr Belton," he cried, loud enough for the men to hear; "and he begs that at any cost you will get the guns in position before dark."

"Ay, ay," yelled the men, and then there was dead silence.

"I am only one against you all, Mr Belton," said Terry, in a low, snarling tone, "and the moment the *Sirius* comes back, I go to the captain and tell him the whole truth."

"Do," said Syd, quietly; "only tell him all."

Chapter Twenty Seven

"Barney, keep near me, and tell me what to do," whispered Syd; "I feel such a fool."

"You dear lad," said the old man, softly. "Why, I've been that proud on you to-day as never was, and been wishing the capen was here."

"Nonsense! Now about getting up these guns. I can't tell the men what to do."

"Yah! you're right enough. All you've got to do is to look on and say, 'Now, my lads, with a will!' and, 'Come, bo'sun, don't play with it!' And, 'Altogether, my lads!' and you'll see them guns mounted in no time. Steady; here's Mr Roylance coming."

"But it seems to be only playing at captain, and I don't—"

"Ay, ay, sir," roared the boatswain. "You're right. Parbuckle it is. Be smart, my lads, and get down a cask. One o' them as the stores was in."

There was a hearty assent, as Syd said to himself, "What does he mean by 'parbuckle'?"

"Cast off these here ropes, sir," shouted Strake again. "Ay, ay, sir. Now, my lads, off with them."

The men trotted here and there with the greatest of alacrity, and by the time the ropes were unfastened from the first gun, a cask was rolled to the end of the gap, lowered down, and placed by the end of the gun.

The boatswain came to Syd's side again.

"Get the gun inside, and then pack her round with tarpaulin and doubled-up sails, wouldn't you, sir?" he said.

"Yes, if it's best," replied Syd; and the boatswain went off again to the men.

"Talk about a lad!" he said. "My! he is the right sort. Now then, in with that handspike, boys."

The men placed one end of the tough ash staff into the muzzle of the gun, then laid hold and lifted it high enough for a block to be placed under it. Then the men depressed the muzzle, the leverage given by the handspike enabling them to raise the breech; and the cask was run over it right up over the trunnions, a little more hoisting and heaving getting the gun right in, when it was easily packed round with doubled-up sails, and wedged tight in the centre.

After this the task was comparatively easy. Four ropes were made fast to a mass of rock in the gap, brought down and passed under the cask, taken back over the top, and from thence into the gap, where, with Syd now comprehending, and wonderfully interested in the task, giving orders, all the strength of the detachment was brought to bear, and the cask was hauled up the slope without a mishap.

A burst of cheers greeted this, and it was then rolled on over the rough ground with handspikes, till it was at the upper end of the gap by its carriage, which was ready on a rough platform.

Then the unpacking began, Syd needing no instructions now the cask and packing were rolled back, and the second gun was brought up with greater ease than the first.

The rigging up of a kind of tripod, and hoisting each gun up into its place on the carriage, was a mere matter of every-day detail, and before dark Syd had the satisfaction of seeing his father's wishes carried out, and each piece ready with its pile of shot and ammunition stowed under the shelter of a niche in the rock which made an admirable magazine.

He had been alone part of the time, but admirably seconded by Strake, who kept up his bit of acting at first with a show of reality that was admirable, till he saw that his young master had grasped the requisite knowledge, and in his excitement began to order and dictate till the work was done; for Terry had gone off with a glass to sweep the horizon in search of the frigate, getting under shelter of a great piece of stone, the wind blowing almost a gale.

But he searched in vain. For some reason the *Sirius* had sailed right away; and he crept down at last with the unsatisfactory feeling that he had been superseded, and that it would be some time before the frigate returned.

But long before he descended, Roylance—who had set the sailor free, and was watching in his place by the lieutenant's side—had communicated with Sydney, and asked him to come and look at his patient.

It was a sad sight. The poor fellow lay motionless and breathing feebly and hurriedly, for there was a suggestion of the fever that was pretty sure to come; and a feeling of helplessness came over Syd as he bent over his patient, and wondered what he could do more to save his life.

After the guns had been dragged up, a portion of the men were at liberty to help in other ways, and a good deal more had been done to the shelter up in the gap.

It was quite time, for with the coming night it was evident there would be a storm. And it became a matter of certainty that if the wind did rise, the rough tent set up with a sail thrown over a spar, for the lieutenant's use, would be exposed to the higher waves, and must inevitably be saturated by the spray.

It was no use to sigh, the task had at all risks to be done, and the question arose how the wounded man was to be transported to the gap.

"Can't we do something to keep him here?" suggested Syd; "build a rough wall of rock to shelter him."

The answer came at once in the shape of a large roller, which seemed to glide in, and after deluging the little pier broke with a heavy, thunderous noise, and sent a tremendous shower of broken water over the canvas of the rough tent, nearly driving it flat, and proving that the position where Mr Dallas lay would not be tenable much longer.

"I think I can manage it, sir," said the boatswain, touching his hat, "if I may try."

"What will you do?"

"This here, sir."

There was no time to waste; and with all the handiness of a sailor the old man set to work, took down the sail, and folded it till it was in the form of an oblong, some eight feet by four.

"Now two on you," he said, "draw that under the lufftenant while we eases him up. Not that way, you swabs: folded edge first."

The doubled sail was reversed, and as Mr Dallas was gently lifted the canvas was drawn under him; Syd feeling a chill run through him as the poor fellow lay perfectly inert, not so much as giving vent to a moan.

"Now, one at each corner," said the boatswain. "Mind and not shift that there board under his leg. Steady—altogether."

The men lifted, and the wounded man was borne close up to the slope below the gap, where the spars and tackle were erected at the edge some fifteen feet above their heads.

It was none too soon; the men were in the act of lowering their burden gently down, when, with a noise like thunder, another wave broke, and it was only by making a rush through the foam that the spars, canvas, and rope lying by the rough tent were saved by the men from being carried away.

"Just in time, Roy," said Sydney; "but how are we to get him up there, bo'sun?"

"Oh, that's easy enough, sir; I can work that."

Taking a small boat-mast, the boatswain rapidly lashed the ends of the temporary hammock fast to the spar, and then ropes were carried and secured to the tackle-block in a way that, when all was ready, there was no difficulty in hauling the spar horizontally up, with the temporary hammock and its burden swinging from the spar like a palanquin.

All this was cleverly managed, and willing hands seized one end of the spar as soon as it was up to the end of the gap, drew it in till the other end could be reached and shouldered, and then the hammock was borne right up to where the shelter had been previously prepared.

As soon as the patient had been carefully laid down, Sydney knelt beside him to place his light hand upon his heart, trembling the while in anticipation of his worst dread being fulfilled, and a cold chill came over him again, as it seemed to him that there was no movement.

He shifted his hand to the pulse, and still there seemed to be no sign, till he lifted the fingers up a little and drew a catching breath, for there was certainly a feeble throbbing sensible.

"Can't s'pect much, sir," whispered the boatswain. "Man's awful weak when he's like that. Bimeby, though, he'll turn hot and fev'rish; they generally does."

"But he is alive," said Syd, softly; and he proceeded to examine his bandages, thankful to find that the bleeding had stopped, and the splints, thanks to the board beneath the sufferer's leg, unshifted.

Breathing a little more freely now, and enforcing silence among the men, Sydney left the temporary tent, and took a look round with Roylance, previous to making dispositions for the night.

Everything was rather chaotic, but the guns were in position, the men's arms arranged, and the tackle drawn up, so that they were all secure in a natural fort, whose approaches could easily be defended, there being only one place where an enemy was likely to approach. Here a watch was set, and orders given for a meal to be prepared, in anticipation of which a tot of rum was served round to the tired men, and a bit of tobacco handed to each by Sydney's orders.

The effect was miraculous. Five minutes before the men looked worn-out and dull in the gathering gloom; now there was a burst of subdued laughter and talk from the group gathered round the fire which the cook had prepared, the light shining on the face of Terry, who stood leaning against a piece of the perpendicular rock, his arms folded, and a heavy scowl upon his brow.

"I don't like that, Roy," said Syd, in a low tone; "it's miserable work being bad friends."

"Yes; I hate it."

"I've a good mind to go and ask him to shake hands."

"If you do he'll think you are afraid of him."

"He wouldn't be so stupid, would he?"

"Yes: make him come to you."

"I suppose that would be best," said Syd, with a sigh. "Let's go up here and look out for the lights of the frigate. What are you laughing at?"

"You. Come; you're a capital doctor, but not much of a sailor yet."

"Oh, I'm no doctor. I couldn't have done that, only I used to go along with a friend of my father on his rounds, and saw what he did."

"Well, you've saved poor Mr Dallas's life."

"Think so, Roy? Ah, if I could only feel sure! But why," added Syd, after a pause, "did you say I was no sailor?"

"To talk about seeing the frigate's lights. She couldn't have beat up near here in such a gale as this. Whew! it does blow."

They had been walking carefully along the gap towards the point where the further gun was mounted, and gradually clambered up higher till they were beyond the shelter of the side of the southern cleft, when Roylance had just time to clap his hand to his head and save his hat, which was starting on a voyage into the black night.

The next minute Syd was beside him, holding on to the rocky edge of the cleft, high up above the guns, catching the full force of the wind. Down below they were in complete shelter. Here the gale had such power that it was impossible to stand securely. The wind shrieked about their ears, and seemed to come at them in huge waves, each throwing them back against the rock, and now and then making what felt like a snatch to tear them from where they stood, and hurl them down the rocks, or blow them away to sea.

"I say," cried Roylance, panting to get his breath, and holding his lips close to his companion's ear, "they must be having it pretty rough on board to-night."

"Think there's any danger?" shouted Syd.

"Not if they keep well out to sea. Eh? What?"

"I didn't speak," roared Syd; "it was the wind howling."

"Hadn't we better get down? I feel as if I was going to be blown right off."

"Wait a bit. I say, I think I'll have a man posted here by this gun."

"What, now?"

"Yes, at once."

"Nonsense, man; there's no one on the rock but ourselves, and no enemy could come near us in this gale."

"No," shouted Syd; "suppose not. But—"

He had to cease speaking and hold on, for the wind rushed at them now with redoubled violence, and for a minute neither thought of anything but the danger.

"It does blow," panted Syd at last, as the wind lulled a little. "I was going to say—do you feel sure there is no one else on the rock?"

"Yes, of course."

"I don't," said Syd, decisively; "I know I saw something, or some bird."

"A goat left on the rock."

"No; it could not have been a goat; it must—"

Whoo! The wind rushed at them again, and once more they held on, longing to get down below, but fascinated by the awful din. Below them the darkness seemed profound; only now and then they saw a gleam, as if one of the waves—which broke with a roar like thunder on the rock, and sent a fine cloud of spray floating about their faces—contained some kind of light living creatures, or it was only a reflection on the smooth curve, before it broke, of the stars overhead. For there all was clear enough, save that the stars looked blurred, though bright, and were quivering and vibrating beyond the rushing wind.

"Oh!" ejaculated Syd. "Hear that?"

"Hear it!" was the reply; "I could feel it. Shan't have the whole rock swept away, shall we?"

There was a lull in the wind just then, but the two lads had clung there, completely awe-stricken, as a huge hill of water had heaved up, and fallen on the outer buttresses of the rock, which quivered under the shock. Then there was a roar of many waters, a wild rushing and booming sound, and the wind blew harder.

They looked out into the awful blackness, which seemed transparent, glanced up at the quivering stars, once more paused to listen again to the tremendous impact of the waves that came regularly rolling in, and then, taking advantage of a lull, they descended to where the gun had been mounted.

The change was wonderful. They had not descended fifty feet, but it was into complete shelter. The wind was rushing over their heads, and the waves were thundering in far below, but the noise sounded dull and distant, and they sat down, breathing freely, and rubbing their spray-wet faces.

"No," said Syd, quietly; "no fear."

"What of?"

"The rock being swept away; it would have gone before now."

"Well, I'm beginning to think we're safer here than on board," said Roylance.

"Don't say that," cried Syd, excitedly. "You don't think there's any danger to the frigate, do you?"

"No," said Roylance, sharply. "Come on down now, and let's get something to eat."

They walked steadily back towards where the fire was glowing and burning briskly in the sheltered depth of the chasm, casting curious lights and reflections on the rocks to right and left, and showing plainly the figure of the man on the watch beside the farther gun, and the spars rigged up at his side.

"Looks as if he were going to be hung," said Roylance, quietly.

"Yes, the spars have an ugly look with that rope hanging down. I almost wish I had put a man up by the other gun."

"What for? I tell you we can go to sleep in peace to-night."

"With poor Mr Dallas like that?"

"Forgotten him for the moment. No; of course one of us will take the watch, unless Terry comes down and turns civil. There, hi! look at that! look at that."

Bang! — The report of the sentry's pistol as Syd and Roylance had started trotting down towards the gun at the lower end.

In an instant the men about the fire had leaped up, and stood ready for any action by their arms.

"Did you see it, my man?" panted Syd.

"Ay, ay, sir; came running along like a big tiger from up yonder by the fire, and I fired at it, and then it was gone."

"Did you see which way it went?"

"No, sir, 'cause o' the smoke."

"It seemed to me to disappear among these rocks," said Roylance.

"No; I saw it come out from behind there, and then it leaped off into the darkness just below the gun. Here, spread out, my lads; it didn't go that way. Keep a smart look-out, and go steady down to the edge. It couldn't have jumped off, and must be here."

A thorough search took place, and this was easy enough, for the space within the gap or chasm was comparatively small. But there was no result, and at last a few burning brands were thrown down from the edge just below the gun to light up the rocks there, in the hope that some animal might be lying killed by its fall.

There was nothing visible, and at last, after making their arrangements for the night, Roylance and Sydney sat together, talking in low tones about the mysterious appearance seen now twice.

"Here, I'll keep watch," said Roy, after they had taken another look at the injured man.

"No, I'll take the first half," said Syd, quietly.

"Well, you're in command," said Roylance; "but I don't feel comfortable about going to sleep with a wild beast dancing minuets all over one in the night."

"I shall be watching," said Syd.

"Oh, very well: I'll lie down. Poor Terry's got the best of it; he has been fast asleep for an hour."

Roylance lay down under the sail, covering himself with his boat-cloak, and was asleep directly; while Sydney, after another glance at Dallas, who seemed to be sleeping quietly, placed his pistols in his belt, and went out to visit the watch.

Chapter Twenty Eight

As Syd stood outside the effect was very curious. The wind was blowing with hurricane violence, and in a dull distant way the sea was breaking wave after wave against the rocks, but where he stood there was hardly a breath of air. Then with the novelty of his sensations increasing, and feeling that all this seemed to him like a dream from which he would awake in the morning, he walked to where the watch was posted, and started a little on seeing two figures in the darkness instead of one.

"On'y me, Mr Belton, sir," came in the boatswain's gruff growl. "Rogers here felt it a bit lonesome like with no company but a long gun. And look ye here, mate," he whispered to the man, "don't you never forget to reload arter you've fired your pistol."

"Seen or heard anything more?" said Syd, making an effort to keep up his new dignity.

"No, sir. Fancied I did once, but it warn't nothing."

"Blowing very hard, bo'sun."

"Well, sir, tidy, tidy; most a capful o' wind. Thought I'd come and stay with him, sir," he whispered, as they walked aside to gaze out to sea; "bit scared like arter seeing that there thing again."

"There was something, Barney, I'm sure."

"Steady, Master Syd, sir, steady," growled the boatswain. "You can't lower yourself to call me Barney now you're commander of a fort, and a werry strong one too."

"Oh, very well, bo'sun. But about that thing, whatever it was. What do you think it could be?"

"Well, sir, I don't see how it could get here; but it's either a monkey or some small kind o' nigger as lives nateral like on rocks."

"But what could he live on?"

"Dunno, sir; lickin' on 'em p'r'aps."

"But there's no water."

"No, sir; that's what puzzles me. The worst on it is it scares the lads."

"Well, it is startling. He did not hit it, I suppose?"

"Hit it?" said the boatswain, contemptuously; "not him, sir. Get's thinking it's— there, I arn't going to say what he thinks. Sailors has all kind o' Davy Jonesy ideas in their heads till they gets promoted, and then o' course they're obliged to be 'bove all that sort of thing."

"When do you think the frigate will be back?"

"Can't say, sir. Not so long as the wind's blowing like this."

"Oh!" ejaculated Syd; "so unfortunate. Just as we want the surgeon so badly."

"What for, sir?"

"Mr Dallas, of course."

"Surgeon? What do he want with a surgeon? You mended him a deal better than I've seen poor chaps patched in the cockpit during an action, when the surgeon and his mates was busy. Look ye here, Master Syd, I've knowed you ever since you was a bit of a toddlin' thing as held on to my finger—this here one—and couldn't get your little dumpy things right round it; and you know me, sir, I wouldn't say a word to praise you as I didn't mean."

"Oh, I don't know, Strake."

"Then you may know, sir; I wouldn't—theer! And I says to you now as a honest man as never took nothin' worse than one o' them yaller gummy plums off the wall—them as crack right open like wide mouths, and seems to be putting out their stones at you laughin' like, and sayin', eat me if you dare. Well, sir, I say as a honest man, if ever I'm wounded I don't want no surgeon but you."

"Oh, nonsense, man! There'll be a long serious time yet when he wants the surgeon's attention."

"Not him, sir. No: we'll do all that."

"I hope so, Strake. But now we are alone, tell me what I am to do to-morrow."

"Just what you like, sir. If it was me I should mast-head Master Terry, if he come any of his games."

"Without a mast-head?"

"No, sir; you'll have to set up one o' them spars, the one with the little truck for the halliards right a top o' the highest pynte, to fly the Bri'sh colours, and you can send him there."

"But about this place, and men?"

"Oh, I dunno, sir. If it was me I should set the lads to level the gun-platforms a bit, and some o' the others to build up two or three walls with the loose rocks for us to roof in. One for the men, one for the orficers, and one for the stores."

"Yes, I thought of doing that."

"Why, of course you did, sir. And then you could give the men some gun-drill, and arter that wait till the enemy comes."

"Yes, and when the enemy comes?"

"Send him back with a flea in his ear. No room for no Frenchies here."

"I hope they won't come," said Syd, half to himself.

"Now, now, now, sir; no yarns to an old sailor," said the boatswain, chuckling. "I can believe a deal, but I can't believe that."

"Don't talk nonsense, Strake. Look here, is there anything else to be done?"

"Well, sir, it seems to me, going over it all as I have been, that you've been thinking that we've got our prog here, and some water, and not enough of it till the frigate comes back, so that you might put the lads on 'lowance so as to make sure."

"Ah, I had not thought of that."

"Beggin' your pardon, sir, you had, only it hadn't come up yet. That there was a thing to be thought on by a commanding orficer, and course you thought on it, on'y talking to me promiskus like you forgetted it. Then there's another thing. The skipper never thought 'bout going far away from here, I s'pose, and there's precious little wood, so I'll tell the cook he's to let it off easy, if so be as you says I am."

"Yes, of course, Strake. Tell him."

"Ay, ay, sir. We may have the luck to get some drift timber chucked up among the rocks; but if we do it'll want a deal o' drying 'fore it's good to burn."

"No, we must not reckon on that."

"Arter seeing to these two or three little things 'cordin' to your orders, sir, I should say that you've got as snug a little fort to hold as any one could wish, and all you'll want then is a sight o' the enemy to make you quite happy."

The boatswain ceased speaking, and Syd stood laughing to himself, but treasuring up what had been said, as the wind swept overhead, and the waves kept on thundering in over the natural pier; though strangely enough the noise of the waves at this end of the gap also passed right up and away, so that it was possible to talk in a low tone, and hear the slightest sound anywhere near.

They had been standing like this for some time when Syd suddenly laid his hand on the boatswain's arm.

"What's that?" he said, in a low whisper.

"Dunno, sir," whispered back the boatswain. "Trying to make out. I heard it twyste afore. What did it sound like to you?"

"One stone striking against another."

"That's it, sir, exact. Don't say any more here. It'll only scare yon chap. Sailors is easily frightened 'bout what they don't understand."

They stood listening for some few minutes, but there was no farther sound, so they bade the man on guard keep a sharp look-out, though for what Syd could not have said, and turned to go up to the tent and see if Mr Dallas was awake.

As they approached the place where the fire had been, a faint waft of the wind passed down the gap, and as it swept over the embers they brightened up, and shed sufficient light for Syd to see something creeping softly by the spot.

Syd caught the boatswain's arm, and a gentle tap from the rough fellow's hand seemed to express that he knew, and had noticed. This was so evidently the object that had twice before been seen, that now was the time to convince themselves whether it was human, or some quadruped dwelling on the rock.

"If I whisper," thought Syd, "it will take alarm, I know."

He caught the boatswain's arm again and tried to draw him away back into the darkness. For the moment Strake resisted, then he gave way and allowed himself to be drawn toward the man on guard.

"Now we shall lose him, sir," said the boatswain in a gruff whisper. "I'd got my eye on him, and was just a-going to give a pounce when you stopped it."

"Yes; but look here, Strake," whispered Syd. "Each time it has been seen it came up this way from somewhere close to the gun. If we stop here we shall trap it."

"But will it come back by here?"

"Yes, I feel sure. It goes up there to prowl about and get food, and then it comes back to hide somewhere here in these cracks among the rocks."

"Werry good, sir; I dare say you knows best. What shall I do—shoot it, or give it a chop with the cutlash?"

"No; it may be a man—and we don't want to shed blood."

"Right, sir. Then we watches here?"

"Yes," said Syd, taking his place behind a block of stone, though it was so dark there was hardly need to hide. Strake followed his example, and they crouched down, with their ears on the strain, satisfied now that the clicking sound of stones striking together was made by this creature, whatever it was.

"You must be on your guard, sir," whispered Strake. "Whatever it is, it'll be sure to scratch or bite. But so sure as you make a grab I shall be there, and he won't kick much with me atop of him. Hist!"

Syd listened, but there was no sound, and he waited so long that he was going to speak to the boatswain and say, "We'll give up now," when a curious crunching noise fell upon his ear, and the next moment something dark was evidently trotting by them, looking in the darkness like a great dog.

With one bound the young midshipman was at it, but it eluded his grasp, and ran right at Strake, who was the next moment down on his face.

"Stand, or I fire!" came from a short distance away.

"No, no. Avast there; it's the captain—I mean Mr Belton and me, my lad," growled Strake, getting up. "See that, Mr Belton, sir; I'd just got it when it went right through my legs, and I was down. Which way did it go?"

"Don't know. I did not even feel it."

"It's a big monkey, sir, or else—I know, sir, it's one o' they small bears, and that was biscuit he was chawing. We'd better shoot him. They bites as well as scratches and hugs, besides being very good eating, so they say."

"Well, it's of no use to try to catch it now. Better hunt it from its hole by daylight. Isn't it time Rogers was relieved?"

"Gettin' nigh, sir; on'y it's all on the guess.—Look here, sir, I know; we'll smoke the beggar out."

"A capital way," said Syd; "only we've first got to find the hole."

Chapter Twenty Nine

The sea was terrific when Sydney took his first look-out next morning, after a good restful sleep, and he felt terribly low-spirited, for he was experienced enough to see that Mr Dallas was in a very low and dangerous state. He was feverish, and lay wild-eyed and strange, evidently recognising no one, but talking in a low, muttering way.

"It's too much to be on my shoulders," Syd said to himself, despondently, as he took off his hat, and stood letting the cool morning air fan his forehead. "Mr Dallas wanting a surgeon, Terry setting me at defiance, the men half mutinous, and the whole charge of everything on my shoulders."

One of his remarks was hardly fair, for the men greeted him with a smile and a cheery aspect every time he went near them, and after their breakfast worked most energetically to make the improvements suggested overnight, so that about sundown Strake smiled in his grim way, and touched his hat.

"There, sir," he said; "the captain may come back and land now if he likes. I shouldn't be ashamed to show him round."

"No, Strake; everything is beautifully neat."

"Yes, sir; decks cleared for action. We're ready for anybody now."

"Have you looked in on the lieutenant lately?"

"Half-hour ago, sir. Mr Roylance was with him, watching closely."

"Well, don't you think he looks very bad?"

"Yes, sir; purty well. Bad as one's officer could look to be alive."

"And you talk of it in that cool way."

"Well, sir, how am I to talk? He's no worse than lots more I've seen."

"But do you think he's dying?"

"Nay: not he, sir. Lots of life in him yet. And look here, sir, what do you say to that?"

"A bit of biscuit?"

"Yes, sir; that's it. Monkey, sir, or a bear?"

"I don't understand you, Strake."

"Picked it up, sir, just where we tried to catch him last night. I'm going to lie wait for that gentleman, and give him a pill."

"Oh, never mind about that, Strake; there's so much else to think about. I've been in twice to Mr Dallas, and he doesn't know me."

"Dessay not, sir. Lost a deal of blood, you see. He's all right, I'm sure. Why, I've seen lots o' men worse than he, ever so much; legs off, both on 'em, an' an arm took off fust by a shot and then afterwards by the doctors, and they've come round."

"But, Strake—"

"Now, look here, dear lad," whispered the boatswain, speaking earnestly. "I wouldn't say what I do if I didn't think it. Mr Dallas is going to be purty bad, I dessay, for a month, but he'll come round."

"But I feel, Strake, as if I have done wrong by him."

"Nat'rally, dear lad; but I feel that you haven't."

"If I could only think that."

"Oh, well then, I'll soon make you. Let me ask you a question, sir. S'pose you hadn't touched Mr Dallas?"

"Well?"

"Nobody else would, of course. We didn't know how."

"I suppose not."

"Very well then, dear lad, what would have happened?"

"I'm afraid—he would have died."

"And how soon, sir?"

"He would have bled to death. I can't say how soon. Before night."

"Exactly, sir. Well, then, you came and set to work in a way as made every Jack here feel as if he'd do anything for you, sir; and it's to-morrow now, and the lufftenant arn't dead."

"No, Strake; not yet."

"Nor arn't going to be; what more do you want? Come, rouse up, my lad, and hold your head higher. Don't be skeered. Let go at us; call us swabs and lubbers, anything you can lay your tongue to; the men 'll like it from you. And as to Mr Terry, as has gone up where I planted the flagstaff this morning, don't you fret about him. He daren't hardly say his soul's his own."

"You've planted the flagstaff?"

"Yes, sir; right on the top, fastened it down between some rocks, and got guys out to other rocks. I didn't hyste the colours, for this wind would tear the bunting all to rags."

Sydney took a few steps to one side.

"Can't see it from here, sir, or you'd see Mr Terry too, getting hisself such a blowing as never was. He's a-looking out for the frigate, him too as studies navigation with the master. He ought to know better."

"What do you mean?"

"As we shan't see the *Sirius* for a week to come, if we do then."

"Then I must go on as if we were to stay some time," thought Syd; and that day was spent in adding to the comfort of their quarters and the security of the magazine, in case rain should follow the gale of wind.

Another stormy day followed, and toward night, after spending some time by the lieutenant's bedside, Sydney was relieved by Roylance, Terry having made no offer to aid, and when asked by Roylance, having replied that he was under arrest, and exonerated from such duties.

"What's the weather going to be, bo'sun?" said Syd, meeting that officer on the upper platform.

"Don't see no prospect o' change, sir."

"Because as soon as we possibly can, I want the rock properly gone over by a strong party, so that we can make sure that there is no other landing-place. We may run down that bear of yours."

"Yes, sir. He was here again last night."

"Did you see it?"

"No, sir; or I should have spoke."

"No, no; unless the beast proves dangerous, I will not have it shot."

"But the beggar carried off a whole lot o' biscuit last night, sir, and a lump o' cold junk."

"Well, that must be stopped at any rate. What do you say to half a dozen men being told off to lie in wait for the brute to-night?"

"No, sir; it's what do you?"

"I say yes," said Syd, and the boatswain brightened up.

"With pistols, of course, sir?"

"No, certainly not," replied Syd, decidedly. "If we have firing in the dark there may be some accident. Select five men. There will be yourself, Mr Roylance, and I shall be there too. Eight of us ought to hold him if he comes."

"And come he will, sir. You'll go over the island to-morrow?"

"Yes."

"But you didn't say you'd have another thing found."

"What?"

"Water, sir. If the *Sirius* is going to leave us here, water must be had."

That was a serious matter. With the gale blowing there was nothing to mind as to the sun, but Syd felt that the heat would be felt terribly as soon as the wind sank, and with no slight feeling of uneasiness he went to his rough quarters, looked into the hospital, where the lieutenant lay muttering in his delirium, and beckoned Roylance to come and join in the meal.

"Takes one's appetite away to see that poor fellow lying there," said Roylance, summoning one of the men to take his place.

"But we must eat to work," said Syd, firmly. "Here's Terry, I'll ask him to come and victual. I hate seeing him keeping aloof. Mr Terry, coffee is served. Will you join us?"

Terry started a little, and his face relaxed into a smile.

"Yes," he said quietly, "I am very hungry."

The ice was broken, and the three young fellows sat down to their rough meal, one which was, however, thoroughly enjoyed—Terry seeming quite to have forgotten the trouble that had caused the estrangement.

But Roylance had not, and that night he said to Syd—

"Don't trust him."

"Trust whom?"

"Terry. I may be wrong, but if ever a fellow's eyes looked one thing and meant another, his did this evening."

"Fancy. He's beaten, and he has given in, and so, I dare say, we shall be fairly good friends for the future."

"Perhaps so," said Roylance, dryly; "but I say, don't trust him all the same. Keep on your guard."

"Can't. Impossible; and I couldn't go on suspecting every one I saw."

"No, not every one—this one."

"Never mind that. Don't suppose I shall have any cause to distrust him."

"I hope you will not," said Roylance, prophetically.

"Come along."

"Where? It will be impossible to stand out of shelter."

"We are not going to. Ah, here is Strake. Now then, have you got your men ready?"

"Ay, ay, sir; but won't you alter your mind about the pistols?"

"Certainly not. Use your fists, and take the creature, whatever it is, alive."

"Ay, ay, sir," said Strake; and leading the way down to the lower gun, the men were posted among the rocks, and in the midst of the utter darkness, with the dull roar of wind and sea coming in a deep murmur, the watch was commenced.

Chapter Thirty

It was strange work keeping that watch, and Syd could not help feeling a sensation of dread master him at times. He knew that Roylance was close at hand, that he had but to speak and the old boatswain would come to him, while the men were scattered here and there; but all the same it was terribly lonely.

For what were they watching? It might be some wild beast with teeth and claws that would rend him if he were the one who seized it, and the longer he waited the more reasonable this seemed to be. It was a creature that lived in a cave, or some deep rift among the rocks by day, and came prowling out by night in search of food. Such a creature as this must be dangerous.

But the next moment he laughed to himself as he recalled that rabbits and many other creatures sought their food by night, and were innocent and harmless as doves. Yet still the feeling of dread came back, and he longed for an end of the watch.

"I like danger that I can see," he thought, as he began involuntarily rubbing his shoulder that had been struck by the shark, and had taken to aching in the moist cool night.

He shivered a little as he recalled the scene that day when he first realised the danger of the hideous fish marking him down; and try how he would the scene kept growing more vivid.

"I never half thanked those men for saving my life," he said to himself. "The brute would have had me if they had not stabbed at it with the oars. What's that?"

He strained his eyes to watch something which appeared to be crawling along among the blocks of stone close by, but he could not be sure that it was anything alive.

"A stone!" he said, and he went on thinking, not liking to draw attention to what most likely was only imagination. "It would be so stupid," he said; "and would alarm the brute and keep it from coming, if I was wrong."

So he sat there, crouched up together, his back against the stone, and his arms round his knees, which formed a resting-place for his chin, till quite a couple of hours of watching and listening to the roar of the wind overhead and the beat of the sea beneath had passed away.

"I wonder how Mr Dallas is," he thought at last; and as the scene in the rough canvas-covered shelter came to his mind's eye, with the tallow candle stuck in a corner of the rock, some of its own fat sealing it there, as they had no candlestick, he saw again the sunken cheeks and wild, fevered eyes of the wounded man, and pictured his white, cracked lips, and the tin pannikin of water placed ready on a box by where he lay.

There was some biscuit too, ready to soak and give him a few bits. He thought—"I wonder whether that man has given him any."

Another half-hour passed, during which Syd had forgotten everything but his patient, and at last, full of anxiety, he felt that he must go and see him.

"No, I will not," he muttered, and he began watching again.

"How contented these sailors are," he said after a time; "how silently they sit keeping guard. I hope they are not asleep."

He crept softly in the direction where Strake was posted, and as he neared it he thought to himself that it was a good job he had told the boatswain not to bring firearms; but as the thought came he oddly enough regretted it.

"If the brute is dangerous it is not fair to the men. I was wrong. But they must be all asleep, or they would have heard me."

Click, click!

The cocking of a pistol close by.

"Strake! Don't shoot."

"You, Master Syd!" growled the boatswain, "I thought it was that there bear. Why, you shouldn't come crawling up like that, sir, I might have shot at you."

"But I told you not to bring pistols." "So you did, sir; but as I thought as the brute might stick his teeth into me, I felt as you wouldn't like me to be hurt, and so I brought 'em. You see, sir, you've only got one bo'sun, and it would be awkward if I was killed."

"Look here," whispered Syd, "I'm going up to see how Mr Dallas is. Don't make a mistake and fire at me as I come back."

"Don't you be scared about that, sir," growled the boatswain; "I'll take care."

"Are the men all awake?"

"Trust 'em, sir. They've got open eyes."

"I shall not be long," said Syd.

"Right, sir."

"And be careful with that pistol, Strake. You may use it, though, if there is danger."

"Thankye, sir," said the boatswain, and then to himself, "I'll use both sooner than have my eyes clawed out, and my nose chawed off."

Syd crept quietly along among the high blocks of rock which dotted the chasm, gazing up at the quivering stars once and wishing they gave more light, and thinking of what shelter these rocks would give if the French ever did attack them and were in such numbers that they took the lower gun, and came swarming along into the gap.

"We could keep them off after all, I dare say," he said. By this time he was close up to the rough shelter which the men had dubbed the hospital. Drawing aside the canvas hung down over the doorway, he was about to step in when there was a rush, the candle was knocked down, and by its feeble glimmer, where it lay on the rocky floor, he caught a glimpse of something dark which rushed at him, drove him backwards, and disappeared in the darkness.

"You stupid idiot!" cried Syd, in a loud whisper. "Frightened him, I suppose, going in so quickly."

He once more stepped into the rough place, to see with astonishment the sailor who had been placed there to relieve Roylance, in the act of picking up the candle from where it lay flickering on the floor.

"Tumbled down, sir," said the man, confusedly.

"Tumbled down!" cried Sydney, in an angry whisper; "why, you lazy rascal, you were asleep!"

"Sleep, sir?"

"Yes. Who was that in here just now?"

"Here, sir; and banged out o' the door there! Wasn't it you?"

"No—no," whispered Syd, who grasped the position now; "it must have been that beast we are trying to catch. Yes; he has taken the biscuit that lay there while you slept."

"Very sorry, sir; been hard at work, and—"

Sydney heard no more. He had dashed out of the canvas-covered hut and run swiftly down toward the lower gun.

"Look out, Roylance! Strake!" he shouted; "it's coming your way."

Bang!

A pause as the shot echoed among the rocks. Then there was another report, and a wild cry. Then silence, broken directly after by the muttering of men's voices.

"Got it," cried Syd.

"Yes; Strake has brought it down. It came with a rush between us, and he fired, and then fired again."

"Yes, I heard. What is it—a bear?"

"Don't know; we want a candle. I'll fetch the one from Mr Dallas's place and shade it with my hat."

Roylance went on toward the hospital, while Sydney cautiously felt his way among the rocks, full of excitement and eagerness to learn what the strange creature might be.

"Hi! where are you?" he shouted.

"This way, sir," answered a voice, which he recognised as that of Rogers.

He hurried on, the shout coming from close by the lower gun, and as he reached the spot he made out the group of figures, and heard the boatswain's gruff voice groaning out—

"Oh, lor'! Oh, lor'! Oh, lor'!" Then in angry tones—"It sarved you right. No business carrying on games like that."

"What's the matter?" cried Syd. "Is any one hurt? Haven't you shot the bear?"

"It warn't no bear, sir," said Rogers, excitedly; "it was young Pan Strake, and his father's brought him down."

Chapter Thirty One

"Ha' mussy on us! Here, Mr Belton, sir, quick," cried the boatswain, hoarsely. "You said I warn't to bring pistols. Wish him as 'vented 'em had been drowned first. Look ye here, sir; is no one going to bring a light? Mr Belton, sir; Master Syd; pray make haste. I've made you another job."

All this in a wild, excited manner, as, trembling now with horror, Sydney knelt down by a dark-looking object on the rocks, lying quite motionless, and for a few moments he could not collect himself sufficiently to render any aid.

"Ha' mussy on us!" groaned the boatswain. Then with an angry burst, "I want to know how he got here."

"Stowed hisself away in the boat," said one of the men, "when we corned away, but I thought he'd gone back again to the ship."

"Brought him down. My own boy," groaned the boatswain. "Ah, here's the light."

"Quick! Stand round so as to shelter the candle," cried Syd, who was now recovering himself and trying to act in a calm, business-like manner; and directly after he was kneeling there in the centre of that ring of anxious faces, and proceeding by the light of the candle, which the boatswain held down, to examine the boy, who lay curled up in a heap.

To all appearances he was dead, so still did he lie; but the moment Syd took hold of one hand to feel the injured boy's pulse, there was a sudden spasmodic jerk and a loud yell which went echoing up the valley.

"Hah!" ejaculated Syd, for he knew it was a good sign. "Hold still, Pan," he continued, gently; "let me see where you are hurt."

"Let him be, sir. I've killed um, I know I have!"

Syd tried to find where the boy was wounded, but at every touch Pan shrieked out as if in agony, and kicked out his legs and drew himself up again as if trying to make himself into a ball.

"It's all over with the poor lad, sir," groaned Strake. "Better let him die in peace, and I gives myself up, sir. Nothin' but misfortun' here."

"Try and bear it, Pan," said Syd, gently. "I must see where you are hurt before I can do you any good."

But the boy shrieked out wildly every time he was touched, and after many essays, Syd felt ready to give up in despair.

"Ha' mussy on us!" groaned the boatswain. "Where's he got it, sir?"

"I'm afraid it is somewhere in the body, Strake," replied Syd, softly; "but I don't like to give him pain.—Is the hurt in your chest, Pan?"

The boy shrieked again, as a hand was slid into his bosom.

"I'm afraid it is there, Barney; I ought to examine him and stop the bleeding."

"Yes, sir; course you ought; but I don't like to see you hurt the boy."

"No, it is very terrible, but I'll be as gentle as I can. Come, Pan, lad, be a man, and let me see where you are hurt."

Syd touched him again, but there was another yell and kick, not before the boy pressed his chin down in his chest, and cried out more wildly than ever.

"Is his spine injured?" cried Roylance.

"Can't be," replied Syd, "or he could not kick out like he does."

"And for the same reason his legs must be all right," said Roylance.

"Spine of his back and his legs," said Strake; "well, that's something to be thankful for."

"The bullet must have lodged in his chest," said Syd, "and I dare say perhaps has injured him fatally. No blood visible; he must be bleeding inside."

There was a pause after a couple more attempts to inspect the injury.

Then, after a little thought, Syd said, firmly—

"Pan, I must examine your wound."

The boy curled up more tightly.

"It is of no use, Strake," continued Syd, firmly, and unconsciously imitating Doctor Liss with a stupid patient on the south coast; "it is my duty to examine your boy's wound. He may bleed to death if it is not done. Two or three of you must hold him."

A yell burst from Pan at this announcement, and Syd and Roylance exchanged glances.

The patient was evidently quite sensible.

"Smith, hold his legs," said Syd; "Strake, you and Rogers each take an arm. I will be as tender as I can."

"Hadn't we better let him die in peace, sir?" groaned the boatswain.

"No; not till everything has been done to try and save him."

"Oh!" yelled Pan.

"Now then, as softly as you can. Once I see where he is injured, I shall be able to know what to do."

"Very well, sir," said the boatswain, piteously. "There, my poor boy, I won't hurt you much," and he took Pan's arm.

A shriek made him let go and jump away to begin wiping his brow.

"Again: quick, and let's get it done, Strake," whispered Syd. "Ready? Now then, all together."

"Oh!" yelled Pan, but the men held on, and Syd was about to tear open the boy's shirt, when Rogers exclaimed—

"Sleeve's all wet here, sir," and he pointed to the fleshy part of the boy's arm.

"Oh lor'!" groaned Strake.

"Ah, let me see," cried Syd, eagerly; and he took out and opened his knife.

Pan's eyes were wide open now, and he stared in a horrified manner at the blade.

"No, no, no," he yelled. "I won't have it off; I won't have it off."

"Hold the wrist tight," said Syd.

Rogers obeyed, and with the boy shrieking horribly, the point of the knife was inserted and his sleeve ripped right up to the shoulder.

"Hah!" exclaimed Syd, closing his knife, as he caught sight of the wound in the thick of the arm. "It has not bled much. Hold the light here more closely."

"No, no," yelled Pan. "I won't have it off."

"The bone is all right," said Syd, continuing his examination; "but the bullet must be there. Look: here it is!"

In fact there it was, lying in the sleeve, having passed clean through, and of course making a second wound.

"There, that will not hurt," said Syd, coolly. "Now let's see about his chest."

"No," yelled Pan, bursting into a fit of blubbering; "there arn't nothing there. T'other one missed me."

The boatswain drew himself up and seemed to be taking a tremendously long breath.

"I'm very glad, Pan," said Syd. "Now, come, be a man. I'm just going to put a little pellet of rag over those two holes, and bind them up tightly. I won't hurt you much."

"No, no, no," howled Pan; "you'll take it off. I won't have it cut off."

"I tell you I'm going to bandage your arm up, and you'll have it in a sling."

"No, no," yelled Pan.

"And on'y winged him arter all," cried the boatswain in his familiar gruff tones.

"Will you be quiet, boy?" cried Sydney, almost angrily now.

"Sit up, you swab," roared the boatswain; and Pan started into a sitting position on the instant. "You, Rogers, go up to the stores and get me three foot o' rope, thickest you can find.—Look ye here, Panny-mar," he continued, rolling up his sleeve and holding out his enormous fist close to the boy's nose, "see that?"

"Yes, father."

"You turned yerself into a stowaway and comed ashore without leave; you've been turning yerself into a bear and a monkey, and living in the holes o' the rocks by day, and coming out and stealing the prog by night."

"I was so hungry, father," whispered Pan, who forgot his wound.

"Yah! hungry indeed! And then you've been giving your father the worsest quarter of a hour he ever had in his life, and making his heart bust with haggerny. You shammed dead at first, then you made believe as you was hurt, when there was nothing the matter with yer but a little bit of a hole through one arm."

"Oh!" moaned Pan, turning his eyes upon his white arm, where a bead of blood was visible.

"And then you kicked out as if all your upper rigging was shattered with chain-shot, and every kick went right through me. So now, look here: your young captain's going to bandage that there bit o' nothing up, and if you give so much as one squeak, you'll have my fist fust and the rope's-end arter till you dance such a hornpipe as never was afore."

"Oh!" moaned Pan.

"Ah!"

There was silence for a moment, and then all present burst into a roar of laughter, so great was the relief that the boy was not very bad.

"Ah, you may laugh, my lads," said the boatswain, looking round; "but I do declare I'd sooner have a leg off with a shot than go through all that again. Thought I'd shot him."

"So you did, father," cried Pan, with a vicious look.

"Yah! Hold your tongue! Call that shot? No more than having a sail-needle slip and go through yer."

"But it hurts like red-hot poker."

"Good job too. Nothing to what you made me feel as I see yer lying there.—Lying! Yes, that's the word, for yer did lie, yer shamming young swab."

Pan began to cry silently, as Syd busied himself bandaging his hurt.

"And now he's a piping his eye like a great gal on Shoreport Hard. Panny-mar, I'm proud o' you, I am; but I feel that bad, Mr Belton, sir, that I'd take it kindly if you'd order me a tot o' rum."

"Take him up and give him one, Mr Roylance," said Sydney, quickly; and while he went on bandaging the arm which Rogers held for him, Roylance and the boatswain went up to the chests and kegs which formed the stores, and filled a little tin.

"Thankye, sir," said Strake, holding out one of his great gnarled hands for the tin, but drawing it back, for it trembled so that he could not take the rum; but he turned sharply round, laid his arm against the rock, and laid his face upon it, to stand so for some minutes before he turned back, wiping his eyes on the back of his hand.

"Bit watery, sir, that's all," he said, with a smile. "Don't tell Mr Belton, sir, what you see. Most men got their soft bit somewhere. I dunno, though. I've knowed Master Syd from a babby, and I wouldn't mind if you told he; but pray don't say a word before Mr Mike Terry. Thankye, sir.—Hah! That's good rum, as I well knows. Here's success to yer, sir, and may you never know what it is to be a father." With which doubtful wish the boatswain drained the tin and smacked his lips.

"Well, sir, since you are so kind, I—No, put it away, my lad. No more to-night."

The rum was replaced, and they rejoined the group near the lower gun, just as the finishing touches were being given to Pan's wound by means of a handkerchief being tied loosely about his neck to act as a sling.

"Got that bit o' rope, lad?" said the boatswain, and then, "Thankye," as it was handed to him. "Beg pardon, sir, ought this here boy to have his fust dose to-night or to-morrer morning?"

"Not till I prescribe it, Strake," said Syd, smiling, and the old man coiled up the piece of rope and put it in his pocket, very much to Pan's relief.

Chapter Thirty Two

"And where have you been?" said Syd next day, after examining his second patient's injury.

"Down in a big hole yonder," said the boy. "It's on'y a sort o' crack, but as soon as you gets through there's plenty o' room; and when I'd got a blanket and a bit o' sail to sleep on, it beat the straw corner up in the tater-loft at home all to nothing, on'y I was getting very tired o' nearly always biscuit. I say, Master Sydney, sir, you won't let father give me the rope's-end will you?"

"You deserve it for smuggling yourself on shore."

"Didn't you smuggle yourself ashore too, sir?" said Pan, innocently.

Sydney and Roylance exchanged glances, and went to see how Mr Dallas was getting on.

The morning had broken bright and fine, the wind had gone down, though the sea was still fretting and breaking on the rocky islet; but the high spirits in which the lads were became damped directly as they stood gazing down at the wreck of the fine handsome man lying there before them, hovering as it were between life and death.

"I wouldn't care, Roy," said Syd, "if I could only do anything but attend to those wretched bandages."

"You do a good deal," was the reply.

"Oh, it seems like nothing. One gets no further, and I always go in to see him feeling as if it was for the last time."

Partly to get rid of his painful thoughts Sydney worked hard with the men till everything possible under the circumstances had been done. Rocks had been shifted, breastworks built, and the place was so added to, that if an enemy should come, the scaling of the cliff over the landing-place and capture of the lower gun did not mean defeat. There was quite a little fort to attack half-way up the gap, and then there was a stout wall built across behind the second gun, which could be slewed round ready for an attack from the land side.

Two mornings later, just after Sydney had been again combining the duties of surgeon and commander, Strake came up to him.

"Going to order that boy a rope's-ending now, sir?" he said.

"Not yet, Strake."

"Done with him, sir?"

"Yes."

"Then I'd like a word with you in private."

The privacy consisted in a walk to the upper gun, where, after a look round in the calm sunlit sea in search of the frigate, the boatswain said —

"Enemy's here, sir."

"Where?" cried Syd, excitedly, looking out to sea again. "I was up at the flagstaff an hour ago, and Mr Terry's there now. He has not given the alarm."

"Didn't look in the right place," said the boatswain, oracularly. "I did."

"Don't play with me, Strake; where is he?"

"In the tubs, sir."

"What!"

"On'y water enough to last four more days."

Syd looked at him aghast.

"We must have sails and casks ready to catch every drop when the rain comes," cried Syd.

"Ay, sir, when it comes; but it don't come."

"Then what shall we do?"

"I ought to say die o' thirst, sir, on'y it sounds so unpleasant."

"But my father, surely he'll be here soon. He knows how we are situated, and the other ship knows too. They will be sure to come."

"I don't want to upset you, sir, but I do say the captain's a long while coming."

"What's to be done, Roy? Hi, Mr Terry, will you join here?" said Syd, who had gone in search of his companion.

Terry came up smiling pleasantly.

"I have bad news for you. The water is nearly done. Can you make out why it is the frigate does not come?"

Roylance shook his head, and Syd turned to Terry.

"Of course I cannot say," replied the latter; "and I don't like to make you uncomfortable; but the captain seemed to me to be such a particular man, that I fear something has happened."

"Happened?"

"Yes; his frigate has either been taken by the enemy, or gone ashore in the storm."

"Oh!" ejaculated Sydney, with an agonised look at Roylance. "You don't think this?"

Roylance was silent.

"Why don't you speak?" cried Syd, excitedly. "It's absurd to pretend to help one, and then stand and stare at him like this."

"I did not want to hurt your feelings," said Roylance, quietly.

"Never mind my feelings; speak out."

"I have thought so for the past two days," said Roylance, gravely. "When Captain Belton put us ashore here, he meant to be in constant communication with the rock. He knew that we could do little without his help, and his being close at hand."

"But the storm made him put to sea," said Syd, excitedly. "I know enough of navigation for that, though I've not been a sailor long. I've heard my father and my uncle talk about it; and he has not had time yet to come back."

His two companions were silent.

"Do you hear what I say? He has not had time to come back."

Still there was no reply, and Syd turned sharply away to go to the stores and make out for himself how long their provisions would last. But in his bewildered state, with the cares of his position increasing at a terrible rate, the task was more than he cared to see to, and asking himself what he should do, he took his way up the higher side of the gap, climbing slowly, with the heat making him feel faint, higher and higher, till he stood where the well-guyed flag-pole rose up with its halyards flapping against the side.

"It seems too much for me," he thought, "and I may be wrong, but Terry looked pleased at my being so worried. No water; the provisions running out; my father's ship lost—no, I will not believe that. He's too clever. It only wants the enemy to come out now and attack us to make it more than I can bear."

He stood with one arm round the flagstaff, gazing at the distant port of Saint Jacques, wondering whether the people there knew of the English occupying the rock, and if they did, whether they would make an effort to drive them out.

But though he gazed long at the houses, which looked white in the sunshine, there was nothing to be seen, and he swept the horizon once more to see the dazzling blue sea everywhere, but no sail in sight.

He sighed as he let his anxious eyes rest on the deep soft blue of the water, close in, and became interested directly, for in one spot a cloud of silver seemed to be sweeping along—a cloud which, from his south coast life, he was not long in determining to be a great shoal of fish playing on the surface, and leaping out clear every now and then as they fed on the small fry that vainly endeavoured to escape.

Syd's countenance cleared directly.

"Why didn't I think of it before? I ought to have known that a rock is of all places the best for fish. We need not starve."

He hurried down to find the boatswain, and propose to utilise some of the men, who were idling about in the shade cast by the overhanging rocks, and met the old sailor looking more serious than before.

"I say, Strake," cried Syd, "why should not some of the men fish?"

"Got no boat, sir."

"Then let them fish from the rock."

"That's just what Rogers has gone off to do, sir, by that patch o' rocks where we landed, and Mr Roylance and Mr Terry's gone to look on."

"Mr Terry should be on duty," said Sydney, colouring slightly.

"Ought he, sir? I thought he was under arrest."

"We are not in a position here to study such things as that, Strake. Mr Terry is friendly now, and we want his help."

Syd walked straight to the lower gun, descended a rope-ladder, which had been made and slung down for their convenience, and found the little group on the natural pier.

"Mr Terry, a word, please, with you."

"With me? yes," said the midshipman, looking at him wonderingly as he followed his young companion aside. "What is it?"

"You have forgotten that you are under arrest, sir," said Syd. "I know it may seem absurd," he added quickly, as he saw Terry smile, "but it would be the captain's wish that good discipline should be kept up on the rock. Be good enough to stay with the men."

"Oh, this is too—I beg your pardon, Mr Belton," cried Terry, mastering an outbreak of passion, and speaking in a cold, formal way. "You are right, sir; I'll go back."

He went off at once, with Syd watching him till he had mounted the rope-ladder, where he paused to speak to the men by the gun, and then went on up the gap.

"One don't feel as if he was to be trusted," said Syd to himself, wearily. "He is too easy and obedient, and I'm afraid he hates me. I wish he was in command instead. It would be much easier for me, and I feel such a boy."

A shout behind him made him start and look round, to see that Rogers, who had been seated on the edge of a piece of stone waiting patiently, had now started up, and was playing at tug with a fish he had hooked—one which was splashing about on the top of the water as the man began to haul in his long line.

All at once, as the silvery sides of the fish were seen flopping about, the water parted and a long, lithe, snaky-looking creature flashed out like lightning, seized the hooked fish, and flung itself round it in a complete knot, making Rogers cease hauling, and watch what was going on in dismay.

"Haul, my man, haul! You'll get them both," cried Syd, excitedly; and two other men who were looking on ran to help.

But as they drew hard on the line, there was abundant floundering, the water flew up in a shower of silver, and then the line came in easily, for the captive was gone.

"Look at that now," said Rogers, good-temperedly. "They're beginning to bite, though, and no mistake."

He rebaited his hook, and threw out as far as he could, beginning to tighten the line directly after, and then hauling in rapidly, for the bait was taken at once, and though some longish creature made a savage dash at it, the sailor was successful in getting a good-sized mullet-like fish safe on the rock.

"Got him that time, sir," he said, merrily, as he rebaited and threw in again.

Syd was delighted at the man's success, and stood watching eagerly for the next bite.

"I don't know what it is," said Roylance, who was examining the capture, "but it must weigh four pounds, and it looks good to eat."

"Here you are again, sir," cried Rogers, hauling away, with another fish at the end of his line. "You've brought me good luck, sir. Hah! Look at that!"

For there was another splash and a sudden check, followed by a battle between the sailor and some great thing which had seized his captive.

"'Tarn't one o' them snaky-looking chaps this time, sir. Hooray! he's gone. — Well, now, I do call that mean."

For he hauled in about a third of the fish he had hooked, the other two-thirds having been bitten off.

"Cut a piece off the silvery part and put on your hook."

"To be sure, sir; but hadn't I better cut off all but the head, and leave that on?"

"Try it," said Syd, who forgot all his cares of government over the sport.

The man whipped out his knife and cut through the remains of his fish just at the gills, throwing out the bright silvery lure, and the moment it touched the water, all fresh and bleeding, it was seized by a heavy fish, which he dragged in successfully, for it to be flapping about with its scales as large as florins flashing in the sun, all silver and steely blue.

"Ten pounds, if he's an ounce," cried Roylance. "I say, Rogers, are you going to have all the fun?"

"No, sir. Have a try," cried the man. "I'll soon put you on a good bait. Look here, sir, this head's on tight. Try it again."

Roylance threw in his line, but there was no answering attack; and he waited a few minutes, with the waves carrying it here and there.

"No good," he said. "Cut a fresh bait."

But as he spoke there was a jerk which made the line cut into his hand, followed by a desperate struggle, and another, the largest fish yet, was landed; one not unlike the last caught, but beautifully banded with blue.

"Why, here's provision for as long as we like to stay," cried Syd.

"And how are we to cook it? We have not much more wood?"

"We'll dry it in the sun, if we can't manage any other way. Now throw out just to the left of that rock."

Roylance was already aiming in that direction, the bait falling a couple of yards to the left; and if it had been aimed right into a fish's mouth, the answering tug, which betokened the getting home of the hook, could not have been more rapid. Then followed a minute's exciting play, a tremendous jerk, and the hook came back baitless and fishless.

"Never mind, sir; try again. Strikes me it's sharks is lying out there, waiting to get hold of all we ketches, 'cause the weather's too hot for 'em to do it themselves. There you are, sir; as shiny silver a bait as any one could have."

There was another cast, and in less than a minute a fresh fish was hooked, and this escaped the savage jaws waiting to seize it, and was hauled in.

"There, that's the biggest yet," cried Syd. "Fifteen pounder, I know."

"You try now," said Roylance, and for the next half-hour, with varying success, they fished on, for there was to be quite a feast that evening, the men hailing with delight so capital a change from their salt meat diet; while there was supreme satisfaction in Sydney's heart, for he had solved one of the difficulties he had to face—the sea would supply them with ample food.

"If we could only find water, and get some drift-wood, we could hold on till my father comes back."

As he said these last words, he saw a peculiar look of doubt in his companion's eyes—a look which sent a chill of dread through him for a few minutes.

"No," he said, "I will not think that; he'll come yet, and all will be right."

Just then Pan came down from the hospital, where he had been placed to keep watch by Mr Dallas's rough bed and call if there seemed any need.

"Mr Dallas says, sir, will you come to him directly."

"Mr Dallas—he said that?" cried Syd, joyfully.

"Whispered it, sir, so's you could hardly hear him, and then he said, 'Water!'"

"Water!" thought Syd, with the feeling of despair coming back, "and we have hardly a drop left."

As he thought this, he hurried up to the little canvas-covered place.

Chapter Thirty Three

As Syd entered the place he was startled by the change visible in the young lieutenant, and his heart smote him as, forgetting the long nights of watching and his constant attention to the injured man, he felt that he had forgotten him and his urgent duties and responsibilities to go amusing himself by fishing off the rocks.

"Ah, Belton!" greeted him; "I am glad you have come."

"Why?" thought Syd, with a feeling of horror chilling him—"why is he glad I've come?" and something seemed to whisper—"is it the end?"

"I'm afraid I am impatient; my leg hurts, and I've been asleep and dreaming since you dressed it so cleverly yesterday."

"Dressed it yesterday!" faltered Syd, as he recalled the days and nights of anxiety passed since the injury.

"Yes; you thought I was insensible, but I heard everything," said the lieutenant, slowly. "I saw everything; felt everything."

"You knew when I dressed it yesterday, with the boy standing here?"

"No, no; out yonder below the place where that wretched gun was to be mounted, and the sun came down so hot."

Syd laid his hand upon the young officer's brow, but it was quite cool.

"I am terribly weak, but I don't feel feverish, as so many men are when they are wounded. I suppose I bled a great deal."

"Terribly; but don't—don't talk about it now."

"But I want to talk about it a bit; and then I am hungry, but I don't feel as if I could eat salt meat."

"A little fish?" said Syd, eagerly.

"Ah! the very thing."

"Wait a minute," cried Syd, and running out, he gave orders to one of the men for one of the fish to be cooked for the invalid.

"Fish, eh?" said Mr Dallas, when Syd returned.

"Yes, sir; I've been—we've been fishing this morning, and caught a good many."

"That's right, but the men must not idle; I want to give some instructions to you about getting up that gun."

"Hadn't you better lie still and let me talk to you?" said Syd, smiling.

"No, my boy; I must not give up, in spite of being weak. It was very unfortunate—my accident yesterday. It was yesterday, wasn't it—not to-day?"

"No; not to-day."

"Of course not; I've been asleep, and had terribly feverish dreams. But business, my dear boy. First of all, though, let me thank you for your clever doctoring."

"Oh, don't talk about it, sir," said Sydney, quickly.

"But I must talk about it. How did you learn so much?"

Syd told him.

"A most fortunate thing for me, Belton; I should have bled to death. But now about that gun. Call the bo'sun, and I'll have it up at once; it is an urgent matter."

"It is up, sir."

"What!—How did you manage it?"

"The boatswain had it packed in a cask, and it was rolled up."

"Excellent! How quick you have been! The other must be got up too, the same way."

"They are both up, Mr Dallas."

The lieutenant stared.

"Is this some trick?" he said, excitedly; "a plan to keep me quiet?—because if so, Belton, it is a mistake. It makes me anxious about the captain's plans."

"Don't be anxious, Mr Dallas. I did not like to tell you at first, for fear it should trouble you. Don't you understand that you have been lying here for many days and nights, quite off your head?"

"No!"

"And we thought you would die; but—but—" cried Belton, in a choking voice, "you are getting better, and know me now."

The lieutenant lay with his eyes closed and his lips moving for some minutes before he spoke again, and then his voice was very husky.

"No, my boy," he said, "I did not understand that. But it is quite natural; I could not have been so weak without. Tell me now, though, what has been done."

"Everything, sir. The guns are mounted; there are good platforms; we have built rough covering walls and mounted a flagstaff. Everything that Strake, Mr Roylance, and I could think of has been done."

"But the captain—did he send the surgeon ashore, and some one else to take command here?"

"No," said Sydney, and he explained their position.

"It is very strange," said the injured man, thoughtfully, and soon afterward Strake appeared, bringing in the freshly-cooked fish, of which the invalid partook; and then, seeming to be drowsy, he was left to sleep.

The next morning Sydney explained more fully their position, and the lieutenant listened eagerly.

"I can't be much use to you, Belton," he said.

"Oh, yes, you can, sir; you'll command, and we'll do what you tell us."

"No, my dear fellow, I shall not even interfere. You are in command; you have done wonders, and I shall let you go on. But I hope you will let me be counsellor, and come to me for advice."

"No, no, sir; you must take command now."

"Men do not obey a commander well if they cannot see him," said the lieutenant, smiling. "Ah, Roylance!" he continued, as that individual came to the door of the tent; "I'm telling Mr Belton he must go on as he has begun. I'm getting better, you see, only I shall have to be nursed for weeks. As soon as I am a little stronger you must have me carried down to the rocks, and I'll catch fish for you all."

"No, sir, you will not," said Roylance, laughing, "unless you want to be pulled in; the fish are terribly strong sometimes. Has Belton told you everything about how we stand?"

"Yes."

"About the water?"

Sydney hesitated.

"I did not mention the water," he said at last.

"Then you have found no water?"

"No, sir."

"And the supply is giving out?"

"Almost gone, sir."

The lieutenant was silent for a few moments.

"It cannot be long before the *Sirius* returns. Of course Captain Belton put out to sea. It would have been madness to have stopped in these reef-bound channels. Had you not better call the men together, and thoroughly search all the crannies among the rocks for a spring, Mr Belton?"

"Already done, sir, twice."

"Yes, of course; you would be sure to do that. Then there is only one thing to do; we must wait patiently for help. Had we been provided with a boat, of course we could have searched for water on the nearest island. But keep a good heart; the *Sirius* cannot be long."

Chapter Thirty Four

But the time seemed terribly tedious upon that parched rock, where not a single green thing grew. The heat was terrific, and the men sat and lay about panting, and glad of the relief afforded by the tobacco they chewed. It was impossible to hide the fact from them that they were using the last drops of the water; but there were no murmurs, not a mutinous voice was heard against the tiny portion that was served out so as to make what was left last for another forty-eight hours. After that?

Yes; no one dared try to answer that question. A man was always on the watch by the flagstaff. But he swept the offing with the glass in vain. There was no ship in sight that could be signalled for help, and no sign of movement in the direction of the town.

"It's seems horribly lowering to one's dignity," said Roylance, "coming here to occupy a rock and set the enemy at defiance, and then be regularly obliged to give up and say, 'Take us prisoners, please,' all for want of a drop of water."

"If it would only rain!" cried Syd, as he thought of how bitter all this would be to his father.

"Never will when you want it."

"It is degrading," said Syd. "But we must wait. What does Terry say?"

"Nothing. He has taken to chewing tobacco like the men, and I don't want to be hard upon him, but he seems on the whole to be pleased that we are in such a scrape."

"But you are too hard on him," said Syd. "There, let's go and sit with poor Mr Dallas. We must keep him in good spirits."

"I haven't the heart to go," said Roylance, sadly. "He is suffering horribly from the want of a drop of cold water, and we have none to give him."

The long day dragged by, and was succeeded by a hot and pulseless night. The last drop of water had been voted by common consent to the sick man, and the sailors were face to face with the difficulty of passing the next day. It would be maddening, they knew, without water on that heated rock. They had tried to quench their thirst by drawing buckets of water down on the natural pier and drenching each other, for they dare not bathe on account of the sharks; but that was a poor solace, and the poor fellows gazed at each other with parched lips and wild eyes, asking help and advice in vain, and without orders climbed up high and perched themselves on points of vantage to watch for a sail, the only hope of salvation from a maddening death that they could see.

The look-out man by the flagstaff was ready with the bunting for signals; and when he hauled it, all knew now that it would be no flaunting forth of defiance, but an appeal for aid. But no ship came in sight all that next long day.

"It's all over, Belt," said Roylance, as the sun rose high once more, and his voice sounded harsh and strange. "I shall die to-day raving mad. We must go, but let's write something to your father to find when he does come."

"I have done it," said Sydney. "I wrote it last night before I turned so queer and half mad-like with this horrible thirst."

"Did you turn half mad?"

"Yes, when I was alone after I had done it.—I told my father that we had all tried to do our duty, and had fought to the last; and said good-bye."

"Where did you put it?" said Roylance, as they walked slowly to the upper gun, while Terry lay beneath a rock seeming to watch them.

"Put what?" said Sydney, vacantly.

"The letter to your father."

"What letter to my father? Has Uncle Tom written to him?"

"Belt, old fellow, hold up," cried Roylance, half frantically. "Don't you give way."

"Oh, I did feel so stupid," said Syd, with a loud harsh laugh. "Said I wouldn't go to sea, and ran away, and then came sneaking back with my tail between my legs. Oh, there's Barney."

"No, no, my dear fellow; there's no one here."

"Yes, there is," cried Syd, angrily, as he stared with bloodshot eyes straight before him. "Barney, what does the dad say? Is he very cross?"

"Oh, Belt; don't, don't," groaned Roylance.—"I must get him under shelter."

He took his friend's arm.

"No, no, you shan't," cried Sydney. "I won't be dragged in before them. I'll go in straight when I do go, and say I was wrong. Touch me again, Barney, and I'll hit you."

"It is I, Belt. Don't you know me?"

"Know you?—of course. What made you say that?"

"I—I don't know."

"Roy, poor fellow, you are suffering from the heat. There's no ship in sight, but you and I mustn't give up; we must set an example to the men.—No, no, Barney, I tell you I will not go."

"Terry, Mike Terry, come and help me," cried Roylance; but the midshipman did not stir from where he lay under a shadowing rock.

"Not for a hundred of you I would not go. Eh! Water—where? Ah, beautiful water! Can't you hear it splashing? Plenty to-night. Rain."

"Come into the shade, Belt," said Roylance, who felt now that their last day had come, and that there was nothing to be done now but lie down and die.

"No," said Syd, sharply, "I want to see the men. How are the poor fellows?"

He staggered down to where the men not on duty were lying in the shade cast by the rocks, and the boatswain, who seemed to have been talking to them, rose.

"Sad work, sir," he said, touching his hat; and several of the men rose and saluted, others lying staring and helpless, their lips black, and a horrible delirious look in their eyes.

"No ship, Barney," whispered Syd, huskily.

"No, sir. We must give it up, sir, like men; but it do seem hard work. Seen my boy Pan-y-mar?"

"On board, on board," said Syd quickly.

"What, sir?"

"I did not speak," cried the boy, shaking his head, and Roylance and the boatswain exchanged glances.

"Yes, yes, I spoke—you spoke," said Syd, strangely. "I know now, but my brain feels hot and dry, and I can't breathe. Yes. Pan. He's with Mr Dallas in the hut."

The boy sank down on a stone, and placed his elbows upon his knees to make a resting-place for his head.

"Poor lad! Oh, Mr Roylance, sir, I'd give my last drop o' blood if I could save him."

Syd started up and then looked round wildly, as he made a desperate effort to ward off the delirium that was attacking him.

"Keep in the shade, my lads," he said. "Please God we shall get rain to-night, or help will come."

The men stared at him in stupid silence, all but Rogers, who feebly hacked off a bit of a cake of tobacco, and struggled up to offer it.

"Take a bit, sir. Keeps you from feeling quite so bad."

"No, my man," said Syd, smiling feebly, "keep it for yourself."

Then turning to Roylance, he looked at him wonderingly.

"Did I dream you said something about writing?"

"No. You told me you had written a despatch."

"No. No: I wrote nothing," said the boy, vacantly. "It ought to be done, to say that we held out to the last."

"My father will see that," said Syd, gravely. "Amen!" cried the boatswain, in his deep hoarse voice, and he drew back, and then staggered forward to drop down for a few moments. He rose again.

"Worst o' being an orficer, Mr Roylance, sir," he said. "Don't matter what happens we mustn't give way."

How that day glided on none could tell. It was like some horrible dream, during which the sun had never been hotter to them, and the rock seemed to glow. Three times now in a half delirious way Syd had been into the hut, to find Mr Dallas sleeping, for though he suffered terribly, his pangs did not seem so bad as those of his stronger companions in adversity.

But at last Syd passed Terry lying with his eyes closed; and with Roylance staggering after him almost as wild and delirious as he, they paused by the hut where Mr Dallas lay. Syd passed his hand over his eyes to clear away the mist which hung before him and obscured his sight, and then, fairly sane for the moment, he looked about him to see that every man was prostrate, and that his faithful henchman, Barney Strake, was leaning against a rock, helpless now.

He saw it all; it meant the end. Had there been a cool, moist night even to look forward to, they might have lived till another day, but there were many hours of pitiless sunshine yet in the hottest time when the glare was right along the gap.

"It is the end," he said, half-aloud. "Roy, lad, I should like to shake hands first with Terry."

He took a step or two toward where the midshipman lay, but had to snatch at the rock to save himself, and he gave up with a groan.

"I do it in my heart," he said. "Come and bid Mr Dallas good-bye."

"Are—are we dying, Belt?" whispered Roylance, and his voice sounded very strange.

"Yes; it can't be long. But I hope we shall go to sleep first and wake no more."

He staggered in at the open doorway, for the canvas had been drawn aside, and stood gazing down at the lieutenant, who feebly raised his hand.

Roylance remained there, leaning against the rough entrance, and on a case sat Pan, with his head resting against the wall and his eyes half-closed.

That grip of the hand was all that passed, save a long, earnest look of the eyes, and an hour must have passed over them in the almost insupportable heat. There was not a breath of air, and the poor fellows felt as if they were being literally scorched up, and that before long it would be impossible to breathe.

They had silently said good-bye, and Syd sat now on the floor with his hand in Mr Dallas's, thinking of his father, and of how he would come some time and find him lying there dead, and know by the work about that he had done his duty.

"And poor Uncle Tom," he said to himself. "How sorry he will be! I liked Uncle Tom."

Then there was a wave of delirium passed over, in which as in a dream he saw sparkling waters and bright rivers dancing in the sunshine, and all was happiness and joy, till he started into wakefulness once more at a low groan from Roylance, who lay close beside him.

The hideous truth was there: they were all dying of thirst, and Syd's last thought seemed to be that he had forgotten to ask help from above till it was too late, and he could not form the words.

It was but a half delirious fancy, for he had prayed long and earnestly. But the idea grew strong now, and he tried to repeat the Lord's prayer aloud.

No word came but to himself, and he went on sinking fast into unconsciousness till he came to "Give us this day—"

He started up, for something seemed to strike him, and he gazed wildly at the boy Pan, who had fallen from where he sat upon the box, and now struggled to his knees.

"Water!" he gasped—"so thirsty. Master Syd—water—water—I know where there's lots o' water—lots!"

He literally shrieked the words, and some one who had been leaning against the entrance stumbled in, electrified with strength as it were, as he shouted hoarsely—

"Water, my boy, water; where?"

Pan gazed about him wildly in the delirium that had attacked him in turn, and did not seem to understand.

The straw of hope that had been held out faded away again, and a mist came back over Syd's eyes till he heard Strake's voice, as he shook his son, shouting—

"Water, d'yer hear, Pan? to save us all."

"Water," said the boy, hoarsely; "water. Yes, I know," he yelled. "I used to get lots—down there."

"Where—where, boy?" cried the boatswain, wildly.

"Down—where—I hid—father," he whispered. "Big hole—cave in the rocks. Plenty—water—give—water."

He lurched over to the left, and lay insensible upon the floor.

If it was true! The last hope gone unless the boy could be revived sufficiently to guide them to the spot.

"He was mad," said the boatswain, slowly; and he looked wildly round with his bloodshot eyes.

But the boy's words had brought hope and a temporary strength to Syd, who pressed his head with his hands and tried to think.

"Would a bucket of sea-water revive him to make him tell us, Strake?" he croaked, more than spoke.

"No, no, no; good-bye. It's all a dream."

"It is not," cried Syd, wildly. "I know—the place. Heaven, give us strength. I know it now."

"You're mad, sir, mad," groaned the boatswain.

"No, Barney, do. Help, come. Water—I know—I can find it now."

Chapter Thirty Five

It seemed too late as Syd rose to his feet, tottered to the looped-back opening of the hut, and crawled out with his eyes starting, his dry mouth open, and every breath drawn with a wheezing, harsh sound that was horrible to hear.

Before he had gone far down the slope toward where the men were lying beneath the rock, and the rope-ladder hung over the rocky wall below the lower gun, he stopped short panting, with the sinking sun scorching his brain and everything swimming round. He looked backward, and had some idea that the boatswain was crawling after him, bringing a vessel that rattled on the loose stones as he came.

But Syd could think of but one thing as he made his way toward the rope-ladder, and that one thing was the fluid which should give them all back their life. He crawled on slowly and painfully, and then a black cloud came over his brain, and everything was gone for the time.

Then the recollection came back, and he knew why he was there. Water—he knew where there was water if he could keep on recollecting till he reached the place. And could he reach it? His hands and arms gave way, and he lay prone, sobbing hoarsely in his misery and despair. There was water, plenty of water, if he could reach it—if his mind would only hold out, and his strength last till he had taken one long deep draught of the cool, sweet drink. And he could reach it and bury his face in the gushing flood, he could save everybody who lay dying there. But he could go no farther, only lie down moaning on that hot rock.

"Master Syd!—the water—where?"

There was a hot breath upon his face, a great hand was grasping his arm, and he turned to look wildly at the boatswain, and tried to speak, but there was only a harsh inarticulate sound from his parched throat.

"Master Syd. Where—the water?"

He tried again, but no words would come. The few minutes lying there, though, had given him strength to crawl on again till he was abreast of the men, only one of whom close by unclosed his wild eyes to stare at the couple crawling toward the edge of the rock wall.

Syd stopped again panting, and once more all seemed over, for the black cloud had settled down over his understanding; and though he could see the men lying only partly in shadow now, for the sinking sun was scorching them, he did not know why he had struggled so far till the hot breath was upon his cheek again, and the harsh high-pitched voice cried—

"Master Syd!—water—where?—the water?"

"Water!"

It was another voice uttered that word, and without knowing how or why, Syd was aware that the young sailor who had been so much mixed up with his adventures—Rogers—was gripping his hand. Syd stared at him wildly as with a fierce harsh cry the man tore at him as if he were holding the precious fluid back. A hoarse groan escaped from Syd's throat, and he struggled hard to think of what it all meant, while the mental confusion and insensibility grew upon him as he lay face downward on the burning rock, staring at that imaginary black cloud.

"Water—water!" Who said water? It was not Strake, but this wild-eyed, fierce man, whose fingers were pressed into his arm.

Yes, he knew that now, and the burning sun shone through the black cloud again. Water—yes, he had come to get the water, and he began once more to crawl on toward the rope-ladder below the gun, with the boatswain and Rogers hunting him, and nearly as feeble as he, pursuing him with their harsh repetition of that one word—*water*!

At last close to the edge of the rocky platform with the gun above him on his right, straight before and below him the rope-ladder fixed to a great mass of rock, and down there the natural pier, with the beautiful clear blue sea flooding it, and looking so calm and tempting. If he could reach that and lie and let the waves flow over him, how pleasant and refreshing it would be! No more pain or suffering, only rest and sleep.

He felt a thrill of horror run through him like a spasm of pain, and he shrank away, for there above the clear water was gliding the triangular back fin of a shark—two—three, and one monster's long, black, rounded muzzle rose up; the creature curved over and dived down under one of its fellows, showing its soft white under-parts, and telling the miserable being on the rock above that it was no peaceful sleep he would find there, but an end of unutterable horror.

That spasm of dread seemed to clear Syd's mind for the moment, as he drew himself back a little just as Strake gripped his shoulder again, and Rogers uttered the one word in a harsh snarl—

"Water!"

For the moment Syd's head was clear, and he knew why he was there. His lips parted to speak, but only a harsh sound came, and the black cloud began to loom over him. But he had the momentary strength which enabled him to fight it back, and raising his left arm he pointed along the ridge of tumbled rocks full of rifts and hollows toward where on the day of the accident he had been struggling back, when Rogers had climbed up to his side.

"Water!" gasped the man, showing his teeth like some savage beast, and his eyes glared wild and bloodshot at his young officer.

Again Syd tried to speak, but only that harsh sound came; and he pointed still at the rugged backbone of the islet which ran from the natural citadel, and descended slowly toward the far end by the sea. The young sailor stared back, then turned his head in the direction pointed, but no answering look of intelligence came. But Syd's finger still pointed, and the man turned his head and stared again.

"Water!" he snarled; "dying—water."

The hand was still extended toward the furrowed ridge with its chaos of tumbled rocks; and after gazing in the direction once more, the man uttered a harsh groan, and crawled to the very edge of the rocky platform, lowered himself over as he clung to the rope-ladder, and would have fallen headlong had not his hands been cramped now so that the fingers were hooked, and he descended half-way before his strength failed, and he fell ten or a dozen feet, rolled over, and struck against one of the two buckets that lay there close up, as the men had left them after dipping for sea-water to bathe with, as they could not venture in.

Rogers lay there for a few minutes half-stunned, and with his brow cut, and bleeding freely. Then he rose to his hands and knees to begin climbing up to the left, while Syd and Strake, with hot staring eyes, watched him as he went up slowly and painfully foot by foot.

What for? Syd found himself thinking. Was it to fight back that black cloud of confusion which would keep coming and going, as now clearly, now as through a mist, he could see the young sailor climb and crawl higher and higher, and further away; now he was behind some great rock, now he was in sight again; now he descended into one of the crevices of the slope which looked red-hot in the glow of the setting sun. Then there came a blank, of how long Syd could not tell, for the black cloud was over him. But his eyes opened wildly again, and he saw that Rogers was somewhere close by the edge of the great rift where he had stood and listened, and then it seemed that the man had fallen, for he disappeared suddenly, and Strake uttered a low harsh groan.

Was it a dream, or was it really the young sailor coming back? He could not tell; he did not even know that the hoarse, harsh, rattling sound came from the boatswain who lay by his side; but in an indistinct way he saw the man coming down quickly till he was where the two buckets stood, and he shouted something to him whose sound fell like a blow upon his brain.

All was blank again, and he saw no more till hands were touching him, and he felt himself lifted up till his chest was reaching over the edge of something hard, and directly after there was cold delicious water at his lips, water that he tried to drink, but which only entered by his nostrils, and he gasped and choked, as it seemed suddenly to have turned to boiling lead.

But the water was at his lips again, and this time, though it was almost agony, he drew in one great draught of the cool, sweet fluid, and then felt himself lifted and thrown roughly aside, to lie panting on the rock, and watching, with his senses returning fast, the acts of the man by him, who was bending over Strake, where the boatswain lay staring, and with his black lips apart, apparently dead.

The man was Rogers—he recognised him now—and he saw him dip one hollowed hand into the bucket and let the water he scooped out trickle slowly between the boatswain's parted lips. Then he stopped quickly, and took a quick deep draught himself—a draught which gave him strength to go on trickling more of the fluid between the apparently dead man's lips before turning to Sydney.

"I'll help you, sir," he whispered, faintly. "Drink again."

Hah! Water, delicious cold pure water; a long deep draught that sent life fluttering through Syd's veins once more, and he half lay there, watching as some more water was trickled between the boatswain's lips.

"I spilt—a lot," said Rogers. "More down there."

The power to act came back to Syd with his senses, and he loosened the handkerchief the boatswain wore from about his neck, plunged it into the bucket, and drew it out full of water to hold over Strake's mouth, and let the water drip down as the poor fellow kept on making spasmodic, choking efforts to swallow.

There was an intense desire on Syd's part to drink again, but he could think now, and he pointed up the gap toward the hut, where he knew that his brother officers and the boy lay dying.

"Can you carry this up—to them?" whispered Rogers. "I'll go down and get the rest. There's quarter of a bucketful below here."

Syd nodded.

"I'll try and get it up. Give him some more, and take the rest to my mates."

Syd looked his assent and tried to get up, but fell down. His second effort was more successful, and he took the bucket, which contained nearly a quart of water, and reeled and staggered up the gap, past the men who lay apparently dead to his right, and then on with his strength returning, and with an intense desire to kneel down and drink the precious fluid to the last drop.

It was a hard fight, but he conquered, and staggered on to where the opening into the hut gaped before him, ruddy in the last rays of the setting sun.

Were the inmates dead, and was he bringing that which would have saved them, too late?

He tottered in and he shuddered as he gazed at their wildly distorted faces. Dallas lay gazing up, and Roylance was on the left, perfectly motionless, but Pan was lying on his back, rolling his head slowly from side to side.

There was a tin pannikin, the one that had held the last drops of the water, on the floor close to the case which had served as a table, and as Syd stooped to reach it, a horrible dizziness seized him, and he nearly fell and scattered the precious burden.

But he saved himself by snatching at the stone wall, and brought down one of the little blocks of which it was composed. Then dipping about a tablespoonful of the water with the pannikin, he let a few drops fall in Roylance's mouth, then in the lieutenant's, and lastly in Pan's, and as the water was absorbed, for neither seemed to have the power to swallow, he repeated this twice, his own powers returning more and more, and bringing that intense desire to drink in a way that was terrible.

But he controlled it successfully, and went on giving a few drops of the precious life, as it were, to each, and setting his heart throbbing and a hysterical feeling rising in his throat, as he found that he was not too late.

He wanted to drink the last drops himself, then he wanted to sit on the floor and weep and sob like a child. Then he felt that he must cry out and yell and kick like a mad creature, and all these desires had to be fought down, so that he could go on now trickling slowly the cold water between the white and blackened lips, over which he passed his wet finger from time to time, jealously careful lest a drop should be lost, till the whole quart was gone, and the last drop drained from the bucket into the tin.

"More, more!" panted Syd, as he looked wildly from one to the other of the sufferers, whom he found making spasmodic efforts to swallow, and taking pannikin and bucket, he went feebly out and down the gap to where he had left Rogers and Strake.

The sun had gone down and the short twilight would soon be passed. They must get more water before it was too dark.

"No," he thought, "it can never be too dark for that;" and he went on to find Rogers bending over Strake.

"That's the last drop, sir," said the young sailor. "I've give all of it to 'em."

"And will they all live?" faltered Syd.

"Dunno yet, sir. It was a near toucher. Now you stop with him, and I'll get some more.—No," he added; "I can't go without a light."

"How did you find it? I could not tell you where to look."

"Don't quite know, sir. I was off my head. But I recollect you pynted, and I climbed up and up to where I found you t'other day, and then I tumbled, 'most cut to pieces with they rocks. And when I tried to get up I could hear the water gurgling, and went mad to get to it and drink it. Look here, sir—no: feel, sir; wet through with slipping in. But, oh!"

He drew a long deep breath, and then caught up the bucket.

"Let's go and drink as long as we can, sir; but we shall want the lanthorn now."

It was quite true, for the darkness which falls so rapidly in the tropics was quickly coming in.

"Didn't think I was going to do this no more, sir," said Rogers, as the pair struggled up to the quarters, and with trembling hands managed to strike a light and set the lanthorn candle burning.

"Quick!" whispered Syd, as there came a low moaning from the hospital. "If I go in they'll be expecting water."

"Which they shall have, sir, before long," replied the sailor, and going back down the gap, they picked up the buckets, Syd stopping to speak to Strake.

"Yes, sir; coming round, sir, I think," he said, hoarsely. "Is there a drop more water?"

"There'll be plenty soon. Only wait."

"Now, sir, you take the lanthorn; I'll take the buckets. Lor', how swimmy I do feel. Not from having so much water, is it?"

The man's words jarred on Syd. They sounded so careless from one who but a short time back was dying. But with a sailor, as soon as the danger is past, he is careless again, and the man was all eagerness now to help his messmates.

Syd did not find it easy to descend the rope-ladder, but he got down in safety, and then the difficult ascent of the rocks began.

It was now dark, and he trembled lest they should miss their way and be wandering about for hours, while the poor creatures they had left were still in agony.

But after one or two false slips they hit upon the right gap, as they thought, and were about to descend when Syd stopped short.

"This can't be the place," he said; "I don't hear the water gurgling."

"That's what I've been thinking, sir," said Rogers. "Let's try again."

Weak and weary as he was, Syd's heart sank, but their next attempt was successful, the faint sound of water trickling far below acting as their guide, and they found the place, descended carefully, not seeing their danger, to where the water gurgled musically from the rock into a little pool some five feet long.

Here both drank long and deeply of the delicious draught, after filling their buckets, finding it no easy task to climb back with them to where they stood in the bright, clear star-shine, and begin their journey back down to the bottom of the rope-ladder, where Rogers set down his pail, climbed up, lowered down a rope, and hauled both the buckets up without spilling a drop. Then while he attended to the men with one, Syd hurried up to the little hospital with the other, to find his patients sufficiently recovered to drink with avidity as much water as he would let them have.

There was no sleep that night, but many a prayer of thankfulness was sent up from the darkness of that black gap toward where, in all their tropic splendour, the great stars twinkled brightly.

"And we shall see the light of another day," said Syd, aloud, "and— Roylance—Roy, are you awake?"

"Yes. I was listening to what you said."

"We've forgotten poor Terry."

Chapter Thirty Six

It was a false alarm, for Terry had been tended by Rogers, and seemed one of the strongest of the party that sat eating their morning meal a few hours later.

But an enemy would have found an easy capture of the place that day had he come; though, as there really was no illness, the recuperation was rapid enough, and all congratulated themselves on the find.

"It warn't nice while it lasted, but you see it was an eggsperens like, sir," said Strake; "only what puzzles me is, why you and Pan-y-mar didn't think of the water afore."

"I was thinking about it all night, Strake," said Syd, "and it was as great a puzzle to me. I heard the gurgling of water that day when Mr Dallas was hurt, and thought it must be the sea coming in through some crack, and I never thought of it again till I felt that I was dying. Then it came like a flash."

"Dying! Lor' now, we warn't dying," said the boatswain cheerily. "But thirsty I will say though, as I never was so thirsty afore. I've been hungry, and had to live for a week on one biscuit and the wriggling things as was at the bottom of a cask, but that's heavenly to going without your 'lowance o' water."

"Don't talk about it," said Syd; "it was a horrible experience."

"Well, come, sir, I like that," growled Strake, who soon seemed quite himself again; "it was you begun it, not me."

"I?" cried Syd, angrily; "why, didn't you come to me, sir, and say that you always thought as long as a man had a biscuit and plenty of rum he could do without water?"

"Why, so I did, Master Syd, sir. Of course I'd forgotten it. Got so wishy-washy with so much water, that I can't think quite clear again yet."

"Never mind; you know better about the rum now."

"Yes, sir; and if I gets back home again well and hearty, you know, there's a good cellar under the cottage at home."

"Yes, of course, I know. What of that?"

"Well, sir, I'm going to set Pan-y-mar to work—his fin 'll be strong long afore then—to wash all the empty wine-bottles I can find up at the house, and I'm goin' to fill 'em at the pump, cork 'em up, and lay 'em down in the cellar same as the captain does his port wine."

"And give up rum altogether?"

"Give? Up? Well, no, sir; I dunno as I could quite do that."

"Never mind talking about it, then," said Syd; "but as soon as the men are well enough, let's have all the water-casks well-filled."

"Beg pardon, sir."

"Well, what?"

"Water's lovely and sweet and cool where it is; wouldn't it be better to have it fetched twice a day as we want it?"

"Yes, Strake," said Syd, "if you are quite sure that no enemy will come and try to oust us. Suppose they land, and we are shut up here; are we to go on suffering for want of water again?"

The boatswain hit himself a tremendous blow on his chest with his doubled fist.

"Think o' that now, sir. Must be the water. Head's as wishy-washy as can be. Sort o' water on the brain kind o' feeling, sir."

"We'll have the casks all filled and stored in that cave near the powder, and be secure from it, but have the water for use fetched twice a day from the spring."

"O' course, Master Syd, sir. Never struck me till this instant. Well, I'm proud o' you, sir, I am indeed, and it's a comfort to me now as I did have something to do with teaching of you."

"What's that mean? What does Rogers want?"

"Dunno, sir. Caught a big 'un, I s'pose, or lost his line. You give him leave to fish, didn't you?"

"Yes.—Well, Rogers, what is it? Got any fish?"

"Lots, sir. But here's a big boat, sir, close in; floating upside down."

"Boat?" cried Strake. "Ay, ay, my lad; that means firewood for the hauling up; soon dry on the rocks."

The news brought Roylance from Mr Dallas's quarters, and Terry hurried down, the little party finding that the current had brought a water-logged boat as big as a small schooner close in to the rock, by which it was slowly floating some forty yards away.

"If we could only get a rope made fast on board," cried Syd, excitedly, as he gazed at the swept decks, and masts broken off quite short.

"I'll swim off with a line, sir," said Rogers.

"Ugh! sharks!" ejaculated Roylance.

"I could swim off with a line and make it fast," began Syd.

"Do, then, Belton," said Terry, eagerly; "the boat would keep us in firewood for long enough."

"But I should be afraid of the sharks, and should not like to let a man do what I would not do myself."

"P'r'aps there are no sharks here now," said Terry, with an aggravating smile, which seemed to say, "you're afraid."

"I'm not going to risk it," said Syd, quietly, "badly as we want the wood."

"But that little vessel may be valuable," said Terry, "and mean prize-money for the men."

"I don't think the men would care for prize-money bought with the life of their captain's son," said Syd, coldly.

"I wouldn't for one," muttered Rogers, as a murmur ran round the group of watching men.

"Pish!" said Terry, with a merry laugh.

"Why don't you try it, Mr Terry?" said Roylance.

"Because I should order him not to go, and would not allow it, Mr Roylance," said Syd, firmly.

"Brayvo, young game-cock!" muttered Strake, who was busy with a line. "My, what a orficer I shall make o' him."

"It would be too dangerous a job for any man to attempt. The sea swarms round the rock with hungry fish, and I don't mind saying I should be just as much afraid to go as I should be to let one of my men go."

"There, sir, I think this here 'll do it," said Strake, coming forward with a ring of line and a marlin-spike tied across at the end. "If you'll give leave for me to go with half a dozen o' the men along yonder, we may be able to hook her as she comes along."

"Come along, then," said Syd. "But will not that marlin-spike slip out?"

"That's just what I'm afraid on, sir. Ought to be a little tiny grapnel as would hold on, but this is the best I can think on."

The party climbed along the rocks, which formed a perpendicular wall from thirty to forty feet high, till they were some twenty yards beyond the derelict. Place was given to the boatswain, who had the line laid out in coils, and while he waited he carefully added to the stability of the marlin-spike with some spun-yarn.

And all this time, rising and falling, the water-logged boat came on, the current drawing it in till it was only some thirty yards away from the cliff where they stood, and the men whispered together as to the possibility of the boatswain throwing so far. At last she was nearly opposite.

"Stand by," growled the boatswain, gruffly. "Hold on to the end o' that line, Rogers, my lad, and stick to it if there comes a tug; then tighten easily, for we've got to check her way if my grappling-iron does take hold."

"Stand clear all," said Syd, as the old man made the marlin-spike spin round like a Catherine wheel at the end of three feet of the line. The speed increased till it produced a whizzing sound; then, letting it go, away it flew seaward right over the derelict, and the men gave a cheer.

"Well done, Strake," cried Syd, making a snatch at the line.

"Nay, nay, sir," whispered the old man; "you're skipper here; let me do this."

"Yes; go on," said Syd, colouring at his boyish impetuosity, as he resigned the line to the boatswain's hands. "Haul steadily! that's the way. Now, then, will it hold?"

There was another cheer, for, as the rope was drawn upon, the marlin-spike caught somewhere on the far side among the broken stays of the foremast.

But the wreck was not secured yet. It was gliding along slowly with the tide, but with great force, while it required a great deal of humouring and easing off to succeed for fear that the hold should break away. The consequence was that the men who held on by the rope had to follow the little vessel for some distance before it began to yield, and then they towed it slowly and steadily along. No easy task, for the towing-path was one continuous climb, and the men had to pass the line on from one party to the other.

But they towed away till the spot was reached whence the line had been thrown, and now that the boat was well in motion, the task grew more and more easy.

"Steady, there, steady!" growled the boatswain. "You arn't got hold of a nine-inch cable, and it arn't hard and fast to the capstan. Steady, lads."

For the men were getting excited, and were stamping away. They calmed down though, and towed on and on till Syd began to give his orders, looking hard at Strake the while, as if to ask if he was doing right.

"You, Rogers, have a line ready and jump aboard as she comes close in by the pier. Make it fast round the stump of the bowsprit."

"Nay, nay, sir," growled Strake; "take a turn or two round the foremas', my lad, run the rope out through the hawse-hole, and then chuck it ashore here."

"Ay, ay, sir," shouted Rogers, picking up one of the rings of rope they had ready, and throwing it over his shoulder, as he stood barefooted on the rock.

"Don't jump till you are quite sure, Rogers," cried Syd, "and 'ware sharks."

The men laughed, the little vessel came nearer and nearer, and the excitement increased; when all at once, just as she was within a dozen feet of the rocks where the officers stood and the men were hauling steadily away, there was a yell of disappointment; the marlin-spike came away, bringing with it some tow and tarry rope, and the prize stopped, yielded to the pressure of the current, and began to glide away again.

"Never mind, sir, I'll make another cast," cried Strake, gathering in the line; but before he had got in many feet there was a splash, a quick scattering of the water, and after rapidly making a few strokes, Roylance was seen to climb over the side of the little vessel, which was nearly flush with the water.

As he did so there was a shriek of horror, for a couple of sharks, excited by the sight of prey standing so near the edge of the waves that ran over the natural pier, made a swoop down upon the young officer, who in his hurry and excitement let loose the ring of rope he had snatched from Rogers, and it was seen to descend through the clear water.

"Why, he has no rope! He'll be carried away with the boat. Jump back now; never mind the sharks."

"Stay where you are," cried Syd, as loudly as he could call out above the hurry and excitement. "Now, Strake, quick!"

The boatswain was being quick, but it was hard work to get the line free from the tangle that it had dragged ashore. There was no other line handy, and it began to seem as if the brave young fellow, who was a favourite with all but Terry, would be carried off to sea to a horrible lingering death, for all knew that it was impossible for him to swim ashore.

"Who told him to go on board?" said Terry, coolly.

"No one," replied Syd, who was now as excited as his companion was calm. "It was his own rash idea. Oh, bo'sun, bo'sun, be smart!"

The boat had drifted some distance, before the old man, who, though really quick, seemed to be working with desperate deliberation, was ready to gather his line up in rings, and climb along the rocks till he was abreast, and could make his cast.

The climb was difficult, as we have seen, and half a score of hands were ready to snatch the rings from his hands, and try to go and cast them.

But discipline prevailed. It was Strake's duty, and he clambered up, followed by the men who were to haul; while on the vessel Roylance stood with his arms folded, waiting, the water rolling in every now and then nearly over his knees, and—horror of horrors!—the two sharks slowly gliding round and round the boat, their fins out of the water, and evidently waiting for an opportunity to make a dash at the unfortunate lad and drag him off.

"Now, now!" was uttered by every one in a low undertone that sounded like a groan, as the old boatswain stopped short, raised the ring of rope, holding one end tightly in his hand, and cast.

The rings glistened in the sun like a chain as the main part went on, and there was a groan of horror, for the end of the last ring fell short with a splash in the water.

"He's gone!" muttered Syd. "Oh, my poor brave, true lad!"

But even as he uttered those words, with sinking heart the boatswain was gathering the line up into rings again, with the most calm deliberation, climbing along the edge of the cliff as he went, till he was again well abreast of the vessel, when he paused to measure the distance he had to throw with his eye, for it was farther than it was before.

The line, too, was heavy with its fresh drenching, and a murmur once more arose as it seemed to them that the old man was losing confidence, and letting the time go by; for though he would be able to follow along right to the end of the rock, the line of coast trended in, and the current was evidently setting out, and increasing the distance.

"Oh, Strake! throw—throw," whispered Syd, who was close behind.

"Ay, my lad," said the old man, calmly; "it's now or never. Safety for him, or the losing of a good lad as we all loves. Now, then—with a will! stand clear! Hagh!"

He uttered a peculiar sound, as, after waving the rings of rope well above his head, he looked across at Roylance, who stood in a bent attitude, close to the side, forgetful of the sharks; and then, with everybody wishing the cast God-speed, the rope was thrown.

Chapter Thirty Seven

The excited party burst into a hearty cheer as the rings of wet rope flew glistening through the sunshine, and a fresh burst broke forth as they saw the outermost deftly caught by Roylance. But the cheer changed to a yell of horror as it was seen that in his effort to cast the line far enough, the old boatswain had overbalanced himself and fallen headlong down the cliff, which was, fortunately for him, sufficiently out of the perpendicular where he fell to enable him to save himself here and there by snatching at the rugged blocks of coral, checking his fall cleverly enough till, as his companions breathlessly watched, he stopped altogether, hanging, almost, on a ledge about six feet above the waves, and only keeping himself from going farther by grasping the stones.

The intense interest was divided now between Roylance on the slowly drifting boat and the boatswain clinging for dear life.

"Who can climb down to him," cried Syd, "before the rope tightens and he is dragged off? Here, I will."

"No, sir; I'll go," said Rogers, eagerly; and without waiting further orders he began to lower himself down as actively as a monkey, now hanging by his hands and dropping to a ledge below, now climbing sidewise to get to a better place before descending again.

"Give the rope a turn round one of the blocks as soon as you get hold of it, Rogers," cried Syd.

"Ay, ay, sir."

"Can you hold on, Strake?"

"Ay, my lad, I think I can," growled the boatswain. "Nuff to make a man hold on with them sharks down below."

"The rope—the rope!" shouted Roylance from the derelict boat.

"Yes. We're trying," cried Syd. "Here, what are you doing? Don't tighten that; you'll have Strake off the rock."

He yelled this through his hands as he saw Roylance stooping down and hauling away at the rope hand over hand.

"Perhaps he knows what he's doing," thought Syd; and he turned his attention to the boatswain and the man going to his help.

"Can any other man go down to assist?" he said. "I'm afraid that Rogers will not be able to hold on, and the boat will go."

"You'd better go, Belton," whispered Terry. "I'll take command here. Mustn't lose poor Roylance."

Syd turned upon him sharply, and was about to follow the suggestion, when a shout came from Rogers.

"The rope—the rope!"

For a moment or two Syd stood there half-paralysed as he grasped the fresh trouble that had come upon them, and saw the explanation of Roylance's action. It was plain enough now: in the boatswain's headlong fall he had either loosened his hold of the end of the rope, or retained it so loosely, that as he clung to the rock for his life it had dropped into the waves, and by the time Syd quite realised what was wrong, Roylance had hauled it on board, and was standing with it in his hand, fully awake to the peril of his position, and seeing that no help could come now from the rock.

Syd's throat felt dry, and a horrible sensation of fear and despair ran through him as he stood there motionless watching his friend and companion drifting slowly away. Another minute and his position would be hopeless unless some vessel picked him up. So desperate did it seem that Syd felt as if he could do nothing. Then he was all action once more, as he saw what Roylance intended. His lips parted to cry out "Don't! don't!" but he did not utter the words, for it was Roylance's only chance; and all on the rock stood with starting eyes watching him as he seemed to be examining the rocky wall before him, and they then saw him turn his back, bend down, lift a loose coop, bear it to the side of the boat furthest from them, raise it on high, and heave it with a tremendous splash into the smooth sea.

Before Syd could more than say to himself, "Why did he do that?" Roylance was back to his old place, had let himself down softly into the water, and was swimming hard for the rock.

"It was to attract the sharks," said a voice behind him, as some one else grasped the meaning of the act, and to Syd's intense delight he heard a panting sound, and another of the sailors came toiling up with a fresh ring of rope which he had been to fetch.

"Can you save Strake, Rogers?" shouted down Syd.

"Ay, ay, sir. I'll help him all right."

"Come on, then," panted the young midshipman, and setting off he led the way, climbing along the edge of the rock so as to get level with Roylance, who was rapidly drifting to the end of the rock.

"He is bringing the rope ashore," said Syd to himself, as he saw the end in his companion's teeth; and they climbed on, encouraging each other with shouts, and steadily progressed; but as they climbed it was in momentary expectation of hearing a wild shriek, and seeing Roylance throw up his hands, as one of the ravenous monsters dragged him under.

And as they climbed to get level with him, Roylance swam steadily on through the clear blue water; and though every eye searched about him for a sight of some shark, not one was visible, though the back fins of no less than four could be seen gliding about in the neighbourhood of the floating hutch on the far side of the boat.

By making almost superhuman efforts the party on the rock managed to get abreast of Roylance just as he was half-way between the boat and a patch of rugged boulders which had seemed to promise foothold till help could reach him from above, and still the brave fellow swam on with the rope in his teeth, ring after ring slowly gliding out over the boat's side.

"Now," cried Syd, as he grasped mentally the spot where his companion would land. "A man to go down."

The sailor who had been his other companion on the day when Syd had attempted to explore the rock stepped forward, a loop was made in the rope, the man threw it over his head, and passed it below his hips.

"Ready," he cried, and he was lowered down over the edge to be ready to give Roylance a helping hand, and try to make fast the line the latter was bringing ashore.

"Ah!" shrieked Syd, suddenly, for it seemed to him that the end had come. For as he gazed wildly at his messmate, he saw that he was swimming with all his might, but making no way. Worse: he was being drawn slowly and surely out to sea, and the reason was plain; the rope that should have continued to give over the side had caught somewhere in the broken edge of the bulwarks, and all Roylance's risks and efforts had been thrown away.

"Let go, and swim for it!" yelled Syd, and Roylance answered by throwing up a hand.

"Can you see the sharks?" said Syd, half-aloud.

"No, sir, not yet," said one of the sailors. "They're cruising about the boat."

"Roylance—Roy! Let go of the rope and swim," cried Syd, in an agony of dread.

But the young middy turned on his back, loosened the rope all he could, and gave it a shake so as to send a wave along it. This had no effect, for it was too tight, and to the honour of those on the rock they saw him deliberately turn and take a stroke or two back toward the boat before giving the rope another shake. This time it had its due effect, for the wave ran along the line and shifted it out of the rugged spot where it had caught, so that it once more ran out freely as Roylance turned to swim for the shore.

"Hist! Don't make a sound," whispered Syd, as a murmur of horror ran through the group on the top of the cliff.

For something had caught the eyes of all at the same moment. To wit, one of the triangular back fins, which had been gliding here and there about the coop on the far side of the boat, was seen to be coming round her bows, and the next thing seemed to be that the monster would detect the position of the midshipman, and then all would be over. In imagination Syd saw the voracious creature gliding rapidly toward Roylance, dive down, turn over showing its white under-parts, and then there was the blood-stained water, the wild shriek, and disappearance. But only in imagination, for as he made an effort all this cleared away from his excited brain, and the midshipman was there still swimming vigorously, and with a slow steady stroke, toward the rock, towing the line. But there was the shark between him and the boat, quite round on his side now.

"Hadn't you better let go?" said Syd, in a voice he did not know for his own.

"No," came back rather breathlessly, "there's plenty of line, Belt. I made the other end fast and—can't talk now."

A sudden thought struck Syd.

"I must not say any more," he said to himself; "a word would frighten him and make him lose his nerve. Here, quick! My lads," he whispered, "get some big lumps of rock ready to throw down."

The men scattered, and in less than a minute they were back, and a little heap of stones from the size of a man's head downwards were ready at the edge of the cliff, where Syd was gazing down fifty feet or so at his friend, who still swam on toward where the sailor was waiting, and in happy ignorance of the nearness of one of the sharks. Syd could see right down into the clear water whenever the disturbance made by the lad's strokes did not ruffle the surface, and his starting eyes were plunged down into the depths in search of fresh dangers.

"Oh!" he said to himself, "if he only knew how near that savage beast is! Swim, Roy, swim, lad! Why don't you let go of the rope and save yourself?"

He dare not shout aloud; and though he was high up in safety, he felt once more all the agony of horror and fear which had come over him when he was himself escaping from a shark, and he shuddered as he heard a murmur about him, and the men stood ready each with a great stone.

"Couldn't no one go and help him with a knife?" whispered one of the men. "Oh! look at that."

"Hullo! Caught again?" cried Roylance, as the rope jerked.

No one replied. It was as if their mouths were too dry to utter a word, for the party on the top of the cliff plainly saw the shark thrust the rope up with its muzzle and glide under it.

Just then the horrible secret was out, for the sailor down below at the end of the rope shrieked out—

"Swim, sir! swim for it. One of those devils is coming at yer."

Roylance was not a dozen feet from the speaker now, and they saw him give a violent start, and glance wildly over his shoulder.

The fright did it. He could no longer swim calmly now, but began to throw out his arms hand over hand to reach the rock, splashing the water up into foam, and in an instant this brought the shark in his track.

"Ready with the stones?" cried Syd, seizing one himself, and poising it above his head.

The others obeyed, and what followed seemed afterwards almost momentary.

The shark scented its prey, and came on steadily now toward where Roylance was struggling desperately. In another minute the poor fellow would have been seized, but a shower of great stones came whirling down in dangerous proximity to the swimmer, only one of which struck the shark, but that one with so good effect that it was for the moment disconcerted, and turned round as if puzzled. But directly after it saw its prey, went down, and rose in the act of turning over to seize its victim.

But there's many a slip between the cup and the lip, even in the case of sharks. Many a one has had a knife ripping it open just as it has anticipated enjoying some juicy black; and others have had their prey snatched from their lancet-studded jaws, or tasted with it a hook.

It was so here. Syd had hurled his stone, and was watching its effect before stooping for another, when he realised what the sailor in the loop below was about to do.

"No, no," he cried, quick as thought. "No more stones, stand by with the rope."

Syd threw himself down upon his chest and strained over the edge to watch what was going on, while, with the rapidity taught by discipline, the sailors seized the rope, and stood ready and waiting the next order.

It was not for them to think for themselves, but to act as their officers bade, and Syd was already one whom they trusted and flew to obey.

All this takes long to describe, but the action was quick enough.

The sailor at the end of the rope had, as Roylance drew nearer, spun himself round rapidly till the loop was tight about him as he sat astride in the bight, and then he began to swing himself to and fro, describing a longer and longer arc till he found that he could reach. Then with a sudden desperate movement he flung himself forward and grasped Roylance round the waist, seizing the line the midshipman held with his teeth, too; and then as, with the horror of despair, Roylance exerted his failing strength to get a grip of the bight of the hanging rope, Syd loudly shouted —

"Now, my lads, run them up." It was just in time.

In spite of the rocks and dangerous nature of the top of the cliff, the men, who had been waiting, started away from the edge, the rope hissed in running over the limestone, and Roylance and his brave rescuer were literally snatched up ten feet as the shark made its second attack, but only to fall back into the sea with a mighty splash.

"Haul now!" cried Syd, excitedly, for the men could go no farther.

"No, no, avast! avast!" came up hoarsely from between the sailor's teeth, as he and Roylance swung to and fro just above the maddened shark, which began to swim in a circle.

"Stop!" roared Syd. "Can you hold on, sir?" said the sailor. "Yes," said Roylance. "Then here goes. Loose the line, sir." His hands were free, and he had taken the tow-rope now from his teeth.

Hardly knowing what he did Roylance obeyed, and with the rapidity taught by much handling of hemp, the sailor passed the end of the tow-rope through the bight of that which supported them, and then sent it through again, and secured it with a knot.

It was just in time, for as he drew through the end and tugged at it, the line began to tighten, and draw them out of the perpendicular, then more and more away from the rock as the boat still glided away.

"All right, sir, I've got you now," cried the sailor, clasping Roylance about the waist. "Now then, get your legs 'cross mine, and put your arms round my neck and the rope too. That's your sort. Glad I saved your end from going after all that trouble."

"Ready below?" cried Syd, as he looked down. "Well, no, sir," said the sailor, "I wouldn't haul yet, or t'other line might part.—Did you make it well fast aboard the boat, sir?" he continued to Roylance.

The latter nodded his head, and sat gazing down, shuddering, at the shark.

"Then you'd best wait, sir," shouted the man, as they were drawn up higher and higher, swinging gently like a counterpoise. "You see our weight eases it off like on the boat, and we may get her yet."

It seemed possible, for its rate was checked, but the slow deliberate glide still went on a little, flattening the curve formed by the two lines extending from the deck of the boat to the top of the rocks, fifty feet above the sea.

"One moment, Mr Roylance, sir," said the man, as coolly as if he were in the rigging of the ship, and not suspended by a thin rope over the jaws of a monstrous shark. "I want to get my legs round facing that cliff there. That's your sort. Now if your line gives way, as I'm feared it will—one minute: yes, the knot's fast; that won't draw—I say, if the rope gives way we shall go down again the rocks with a spang, but don't you mind; it'll only be a swing, and I'll fend us off with my feet. My! we're getting tight now. Look out, sir, we're going."

But the rope did not break, for seeing how dangerous the strain was becoming, Syd ordered the men behind him to ease off a little, and then a little more and a little more, till the progress of the water-logged vessel was gradually checked, and as they felt that the worst of the strain was over, the men on the cliff gave a cheer.

"Steady there, steady!" cried Terry, angrily, and the men murmured.

"Silence there!" cried Syd. "Now, my lads, I think you may begin to haul."

The men obeyed, and by the exercise of a great deal of caution the first rope was drawn slowly hand over hand up the cliff till Roylance's head appeared. Syd extended his hands to his help, and the midshipman climbed over the edge and sat down in the hot sunshine in his drenched clothes, looking white and haggard, as one looks after a terrible escape from death.

The next minute the sailor was on the cliff, looking none the worse for his adventure, but pretty well drenched by contact with Roylance's dripping clothes.

Then a little more hauling took place, till the men could get a good hold of the line Roylance had brought ashore, in the midst of which the latter suddenly sprang up, looked over the edge of the cliff, and catching sight of his enemy, he picked up the biggest piece of stone he could lift and hurled it down. It fell with a mighty splash in the water, and as chance had it, for little could be said for the aim, right down upon the shark, which turned up directly after, and then recovered itself and swam laboriously away.

Chapter Thirty Eight

"You made me feel horribly bad, Roy," whispered Syd, hastily. "How could you do such a fearfully dangerous thing?"

Roylance smiled feebly and pointed down at the boat, which was yielding slowly to the drag kept on it by the men.

"That may be the means of saving our lives," he said.

"Are you going to leave those other two poor fellows to fall off the rock as food for the sharks, Mr Belton?" said Terry, who had been put out of temper by the action of the men.

"I think you can answer that question yourself, Mr Terry," said Roylance, flushing up angrily.

Syd made no reply, but quietly gave his orders.

"Mr Roylance," he said, "are you well enough to take charge of the men here, as they haul the boat along, while I go and see to the bo'sun and Rogers being got up the cliff?"

"Well enough? yes," cried Roylance, upon whom the short encounter with Terry had acted like a stimulus.

Terry turned pale with rage at being passed over, and he followed Syd and four of the men as they hurried along with the rope set at liberty coiled up.

It was with no little anxiety that the party approached the spot where Rogers had gone down, while Terry, who had expressed so much interest in the fate of the two men, oddly enough hung behind.

Syd was the first to reach the place, and looked over to be greeted by Rogers with a hail.

"Is Mr Strake all right?"

"Ay, ay, sir; all but my bark," said the boatswain. "Don't say, sir, as you haven't got Mr Roylance off the boat."

"Got him off, Strake, and they're towing the boat along."

"Hurrah!" shouted the two men, whose position in an indentation of the rock line had prevented them from seeing what was going on.

The rope was lowered down with the loop all ready, and Strake was hauled up first, his appearance over the side being greeted with a cheer, and plenty of hands were ready to help him into a sitting position, for it was evident that he could not lift one leg.

"Never mind me, my lads," he said, quietly. "Get Rogers on deck first."

This was soon effected, the smart young sailor displaying an activity as he scrambled over the edge of the rocks that contrasted strangely with the boatswain's limp.

"Now, Strake," said Syd, as soon as he had seen Rogers safe, "are you hurt?"

"Hurt, sir? Did you say hurt?"

"Yes, yes, man."

"Well, I s'pose I am, sir, for I feels as if I'd got a big sore place spread all over me. Mussy me, sir, that's about the hardest rocks to fall on as ever was."

"But no bones broken?"

"Bones broken? Nay. I've got none of your poor brittle chaney-ladle kind o' bones; but my head's cut and the bark's all off my right leg in the front. Left leg arn't got no bark at all, and I'm reg'larly shaken in all my seams, and stove in on my starboard quarter, sir. So if you'll have me got into dock or beached and then overhaul me a bit, I'd take it kindly."

"Of course, of course, Strake; anything I can do."

"Ahoy!" cried the old man, raising a hand as he sat in the sunshine upon the rock, but lowering it directly. "Oh, dear; I wanted to give them a hearty cheer yonder, but, phew! it's bellows to mend somewhere. Yes, I'm stove in. Old ship's been on the rocks; all in the dry though."

A cheer came back, though, as Roylance and his men caught sight of the two who had been rescued, while they towed the boat slowly along.

"How are we to get you back to the huts, Strake?" said Syd, anxiously.

"Oh, never mind me just at present, my lad," said the boatswain; "what I want to see is that there boat got alongside o' our harbour—on'y 'tarn't a harbour—and made fast with all the rope you can find. Maybe she's got a cable aboard. I should break my heart if she weer to break adrift now."

"Mr Roylance has her in charge, Strake, and I'll see to you. Where are you in pain?"

"Ask me where I arn't in pain, Mr Belton, sir. I got it this time."

"I'm sorry for you, Strake."

"Thank ye, sir; but I'm sorry for you. There's a big job to patch me up and caulk me, I can tell you. It's horspittle this time, I'm feared."

"But how are we to move you without giving you pain?"

"I'll tell you, sir. Sail again, and some un at each corner. We shan't beat that."

The sail was procured, and the injured man was carried as carefully as possible back to the foot of the gap, hoisted up, and then borne into the hospital.

"Strake! Hurt?" cried the lieutenant.

"Oh, not much, sir; bit of a tumble, that's all, sir. Don't you be skeared. I arn't going to make no row about it. No, no, sir, please," continued the boatswain, "not yet. I don't feel fit to be boarded. Just you go and give your orders to make that there boat safe, and then I'm ready for you. One word though, sir."

"What is it?"

"Have that there boat well fended, or she'll grind herself to pieces agen the rock."

Syd hesitated, but being full of anxiety to see the boat that had cost them so much thoroughly secured, and feeling perhaps that after all a rest after his rough journey would make the boatswain more able to bear examination and bandaging, he hurried off to find that he need not have troubled himself, for Roylance was doing everything possible, and the vessel was being safely moored head and stern.

But he was in time to have the boatswain's proposition carried out, and a couple of pieces of spar were hung over the side to keep her from tearing and grinding on the edge of the natural pier.

As Syd was returning he came upon Terry, looking black as night, and held out his hand.

"I'm sorry there should have been any fresh unpleasantness," he said. "Can't we be friends, Mr Terry?"

"That's just what I want to be, Belton," cried Terry, eagerly, seizing the proffered hand. "I'm afraid I did interfere a bit too much to-day."

"And somehow," mused Syd, as he went on to the hospital, "I can't feel as if it's all genuine. It's like shaking hands with a sole and five sprats. Ugh! how cold and fishy his hand did feel."

The lieutenant was lying in the hospital with his eyes closed, and Pan was bathing his father's brow with water, using his injured arm now and then out of forgetfulness, but putting it back in the sling again as soon as it was observed.

"Arn't much the matter with it, I know, Pan-y-mar," the injured man whispered, as Syd halted by the door to see how his new patient seemed, trembling terribly in his ignorance at having to put his smattering of surgery to the test once more.

"Ah, you dunno, father," grumbled the boy. "You've ketched it this time. I don't talk about getting no rope's-ends to you."

"No, my lad, you don't. I should jest like to ketch you at it. But you won't see me going about in a sling."

"Ah, you dunno yet, father."

"Don't I? You young swab; why, if I had my head took off with a shot, I wouldn't howl as you did."

"Why, yer couldn't, father," said Pan, grinning.

"What, yer laughing at me, are yer? Just you wait till I gets a few yards o' dackylum stuck about me, and you'll get that rope's-end yet, Pan-y-mar."

"Oh, no! I shan't," said Pan in a whisper, after glancing at the lieutenant, who was lying with his eyes closed. "You'll be bad for two months."

"What? Why, you sarcy young lubber, if the luff warn't a-lying there and I didn't want to wake him, I'd give yer such a cuff over the ear as 'd make yer think bells was ringing."

"Couldn't reach," said Pan, dabbing his face.

"Then I'd kick yer out of the door."

"Yah!" grinned Pan. "Can't kick. I see yer brought in, and yer couldn't stand."

"Keep that water out o' my eye, warmint, will you," whispered the boatswain. "Water's too good to be wasted. Give us a drink, boy."

Pan rose and dipped a pannikin full of the cool water from a bucket, and held it to his father's lips.

"Wouldn't have had no water if it hadn't been for me coming ashore," he said.

"Ah, you've a lot to boast about. Just you pour that in properly, will yer; I want it inside, not out."

"Who's to pour it right when yer keeps on talking?" said Pan, as he trickled the water into his father's mouth.

"Ah, you're a nice sarcy one now I'm down, Pan-y-mar," said Stoke, after a long refreshing draught. "But you may be trustful, I've got a good memory for rope's-ends, and you shall have it warmly as soon as I'm well."

"Then I won't stop and nuss yer," said Pan, drawing back.

"You just come on, will yer, yer ungrateful swab."

"Shan't," said Pan.

"What! Do you know this here arn't the skipper's garden, and you and me only gardeners, but 'board ship—leastwise it's all the same—and I'm your orficer?"

"You arn't a orficer now," said Pan, grinning. "You're only a wounded man."

"Come here."

"Shan't!"

"Pan-y-mar, come here."

"Say you won't rope's-end me, and I will."

"But I will rope's-end you."

"Then I won't come."

The boatswain made an effort to rise, but sank back with a groan. Pan took a couple of steps forward, and looked at him eagerly.

"Why, you're shamming, father," he said.

The boatswain lay back with the great drops of sweat standing on his face.

"I say, you won't rope's-end me, father?"

There was no reply.

"Why, you are shamming, father."

Still all was silent, and the boy darted to the injured man's side and began to bathe his face rapidly.

"Father," he whispered, hoarsely, "father. Oh, I say! Don't die, and you shall give it me as much as you like. Father—Oh, it's you, Master Syd. Be quick! He's so bad. What shall I do?"

"Be quiet," said Syd, quietly. "Don't be frightened; he has fainted."

"Then why did he go scaring a lad like that?" whimpered Pan, looking on.

"Hush! Be quiet. There: he is coming round," said Syd, as the injured man uttered a loud sigh and looked wonderingly about him.

"Just let me get hold—Oh, it's you, sir. Glad you've comed. I'm ready now.—Stand aside, Pan-y-mar, and give the doctor room.—Say, Master Syd," he whispered, "don't let that young sneak know what I said, but I do feel a bit skeared."

"You are weak and faint."

"But it's about my legs, Master Sydney. Don't take 'em off, lad, unless you are obliged."

"Nonsense! I shall not want to do that. You are much bruised, but there are no bones broken."

"Ay, but there are, my lad," said the boatswain, sadly. "I didn't want to say much about it, but I am stove in. Ribs."

"How do you know?"

"Feels it every time I breathes, my lad. Bad job when a ship's timbers goes."

Sydney knew what to do under the circumstances, and sending Pan for Rogers to help him, he proceeded to examine his fresh patient, to find that two ribs were broken on the right side, the rest of the injuries consisting of severe bruises and grazings of the skin. In addition there were a couple of cuts on the back of the head, which called for strapping up.

Part of these injuries had been attended to by the time Pan returned with Rogers, and then the ribs were tightly bandaged with a broad strip of sail-cloth.

"I say, sir," growled the boatswain, "not going to do this all over me?"

"No! Why?"

"'Cause I shan't be able to move, and my boy's been a-haskin' for something hot 'fore you come."

"That I didn't, father."

"Oh, yes, you did, my lad. You didn't ask with yer mouth, but have a way of asking for what you're so fond on without making no noise."

Pan screwed up his face, and the lieutenant, who had been lying apparently asleep, burst into a loud laugh.

"Come, Strake," he said, "you had better leave that, and think of getting better."

"Ay, ay, sir; but I hope I see you better for your nap."

"I wish you did, my man, and I wish you the same. But there, we've such a skilful young doctor to look after us, we shan't hurt much."

"Not us, sir. I am't nothing to what you was, and see what a job Mr Belton's made o' you."

"Yes; it's wonderful. I can never be grateful enough."

"Beg pardon, sir," said Sydney, "but I want to finish bandaging the boatswain; and if you keep on talking like that I can't."

"I am silent, O doctor!" said the lieutenant, laughing. "And so you've got a boat, have you?"

"Such as it is, sir."

"Then if the captain does not come back we shall have the means of getting away from this place. No; that will not do, Mr Belton: we must hold it till we are driven out. Keep to it to the very last. I say we: you must, for you are in command. I suppose it will be months before I am well."

"I'm afraid it will," replied Syd.

"Then you must hold it, as I said."

"Hurrah!" cried Strake, and then screwing up his face—"My word! that's bad. You're all right, Pan-y-mar. There won't be no rope's-end for you this week."

"No," said Syd, merrily, "I think he's safe for quite that time."

"And when may I move, doctor?" said Mr Dallas, smiling.

"As soon as you can bear it, sir, I'll have you got out in the morning to lie in the shade and get the fresh sea-breeze before it grows hot."

"Ah! thank you, my lad," he said, with a longing look. "I'm beginning to think I would as soon have been a surgeon as what I am."

Syd started and coloured up, as he wondered whether the lieutenant knew anything about his life at home.

Chapter Thirty Nine

The same reply always from the look-out man by the flagstaff; no ship in sight, and the town of Saint Jacques slumbering in the sun. But there was so much to do that Syd and Roylance could spare very little time for thinking.

As soon as the patients had been tended there were a score of matters to take Syd's attention; but he was well seconded by Roylance, who, to Terry's disgust, threw himself heart and soul into the work of keeping the fort as if it were a ship.

The lieutenant progressed wonderfully now that the feverish stage was over, and one day he said—

"I can't work, Syd, my dear boy, for I am as weak as a baby, and I shall not interfere in any way, so go on and behave like a man."

Pan forgot to use his sling to such an extent that there could be no mistake about his wound being in a fair way to heal, and were other proof needed it was shown in the way in which he tormented his helpless father. For though the boatswain pooh-poohed the idea of anything much being the matter with him, it was evident that he suffered a great deal, though he never winced when his injuries were dressed.

"Serves me right," he used to say. "Arter all my practice, to think o' me not being able to heave a rope on board a derrylick without chucking myself arter it. There, don't you worrit about me, sir. Give me a hextry fig o' tobacco, and a stick or a rope's-end to stir up that young swab o' mine, and I shall grow fresh bark over all my grazings, and the broken ribs 'll soon get set. How are you getting on with the boat?"

"Not at all, Strake," replied Syd. "We can't pump her out because there's a big leak in her somewhere, and I don't like to break her up in case we think of a way of floating her so as to get away from here."

"What? Who wants to get away from here, sir? Orders was to occupy this here rock, and of course you hold it till the skipper comes back and takes us off."

"Yes; but in case our provisions fail?"

"Tchah! ketch more fish, sir. There's plenty, aren't there?"

"Yes; as much as we can use."

"And any 'mount o' water?"

"Yes."

"And the only thing you want is wood for cooking?"

"Yes."

"Then that boat, which seems to ha' been sent o' purpose, has to be got ashore somehow to be broke up. Now, if you'll take my advice you'll just go down to the rocks there and think that job out. I can't help you much, sir, 'cause here I am on my beam-ends. Go and think it out, lad, and then come and tell me."

"Strake's right," said the lieutenant, who had been lying in the shade outside the hut. "Captain Belton will either be back himself or send help before long. You must hold the place till he comes."

Those words were comfortable to Sydney. They were like definite orders from his superiors, and he could obey them with more satisfaction to himself than any he thought out for himself. So he went down to the pier, meeting Roylance on his way, who had just been his rounds, and had a few words with the men on duty by the upper and lower guns, and at the flagstaff.

"My orders are to go and see to getting the wreck ashore for firewood, Roylance."

"Orders?" said the midshipman, laughing. "Well, it does seem a pity after the trouble we took."

"And risk," interpolated Syd.

"To get her moored here to be of no use."

"Come, and let's see what can be done."

The two youths descended the rope-ladder beneath the lower gun, and spent some time in examining the vessel, but were compelled to give up in despair. She was securely moored so that they could easily get on to the water-washed decks, where there were a couple of fixed pumps, but these had been tried again and again; and, as the men said, it was like trying to pump the Atlantic dry to go on toiling at a task where the water flowed in as fast as it was drawn out.

"There's no getting at the leak even if we knew where it was," said Roylance.

"I think the same," said Syd, "so we may as well get all the wood out of her we can, and lay it on the rocks to dry."

This task was begun, and for two days the men worked well; some cutting, others dragging off planks with crowbars, while the rest bore the wood to the foot of the rocky wall, where it was hauled up and laid to dry in the hottest parts of the natural fort.

It was on the third day from the beginning of this task, as the pile of dripping wood they had taken from the wreck began to grow broad and high, while endless numbers of riven pieces were ranged in the full sunshine, and sent forth a quivering transparent vapour into the heated air, that Syd, who was standing ankle-deep in water on a cross-beam directing the men, and warning them not to make a false step on account of the sharks, suddenly uttered a cry —

"Look out!" he shouted, and there was a rush for the rock, where as soon as they were on safely the men began to roar with laughter.

"Beg pardon, sir," said Rogers, touching his hat, as he stood axe in hand; "but seeing as how he tried to eat me, oughtn't we to try and eat he?"

The "he" pointed to was a long, lean, hungry-looking shark which had been cruising about the side of the vessel, whose bulwarks had all been ripped off and deck torn up, so that she floated now like a huge tub whose centre was crossed by broad beams. So open was the vessel that it had needed very little effort on the part of a shark to make a rush, glide in over the ragged side, and then begin floundering about in the water, and over and under the beams which had supported the deck.

"I don't know about eating him, Roy," said Syd; "but as I'm captain I pass sentence of death on the brute." Then to the men — "How can you tackle the wretch?"

"Oh, we'll soon tackle him, sir," said Rogers; "eh, messmets?"

There was a growl of assent at this, and the men looked at their young leader full of expectancy.

"Well," he said, "be careful. What do you mean to do?"

"Seems to me, sir," said the man, "as the best thing to do would be to fish for him."

"No, no," cried Roylance; "fetch a line with a running knot, and see if you can't get it round him, and have him out."

Rogers gave his leg a slap.

"That's it, sir. Pity you and me can't be swung over him like we was off the rocks. Easily run it across his nose then."

Roylance could not help a shudder, and he glanced at Syd to see if he was observed.

"I get dreaming about that thing sometimes," he said. "I wonder whether this is the one."

"Hardly likely, but it's sure to be a relation," said Syd, laughing, as they stood watching the movements of the shark, which seemed to be puzzled by its quarters, and was now showing its tail as it dived down under a beam, now raising its head to glide over and disappear in the depths of the ship's hold.

The men were not long in getting the line that had been used to tow the vessel to its moorings, and a freely running noose was prepared and tested by Rogers, who suddenly threw it over one of his messmates' heads, gave it a snatch, and drew it taut. Taking it off, he lassoed another in the same way.

"That's the tackle," he said, smiling. "Next thing is to get it round the shark."

"Yes," said Roylance, "but it's something like the rats putting the bell on the cat's neck. Who's to do it?"

"Oh, I'm a-going to do it, sir," said Rogers, shaking out the rope. "Lay hold, messmates, and when I says 'now!' have him out and over the rocks here.—P'r'aps, sir, you'd like to have an axe to give him number one?"

"How do you mean?"

"One on the tail, sir, to fetch it off; only look out, for he's pretty handy with his tail."

"That's what some one said of the man who had his legs shot off," whispered Roylance, laughing, "that he was pretty handy with the wooden ones."

"We're ready, sir," said Rogers, "when you likes to give the word."

"But about danger, my man?" said Syd, who half-wondered at himself, as he hectored over the crew, and thought that he was a good deal like Terry, who was contemptuously looking on.

"Theer's no danger, sir," said Rogers. "I don't know so much about that," said Syd; "suppose you slipped and went down into the hold?"

"Well, in that case, sir," said Rogers, grimly, "Master Jack there would have the best of it, and none of his mates to help. Wonder whether a shark like that shovel-nosed beggar could eat a whole man at a meal?"

"Ugh!" ejaculated Syd, with a shudder. "It's too risky. Better give it up." But the men looked chapfallen.

"But the brute will put a complete stop to our work," said Roylance, who was watching the restless movements of the self-imprisoned shark. "Don't stop them, Belton," he continued, in a low tone, "I want to see that monster killed."

"For revenge?"

"If you like to call it so. It or one of its fellows made me pass such moments of agony as I shall never forget."

"I shall never forget my horror either," said Syd, as he too looked viciously at the savage creature, which just then rose out of the water and glided over one of the beams. "There, go on, Rogers, only take great care."

"I just will that, sir," said the man, as his messmates cheered; and taking the noose in his hand he stepped along the plank leading from the rocks to the vessel. "When I say '*now*, lads,' mind you let him feel you directly; and haul him out."

"Ay, ay!" cried the men; and then every eye was fixed upon the active young fellow, whose white feet seemed to cling to the wet planking upon which he stood, and from which he stepped cautiously out upon one of the beams that curved over from side to side.

Hardly was he well out, and stooping down peering into the water, than Syd uttered a warning cry, and the man bounded back as the shark, attracted by the sight of his white legs, came up from behind, and glided exactly over the spot where he had been standing.

"Ah! would yer!" shouted Rogers; and the men roared with laughter. "This here's fishing with your own legs for bait," continued the young sailor. "Well, it's got to be who's sharpest—him or me."

"I think you had better not venture," said Syd, hesitating again.

"Oh! don't say that, sir. We shall all be horrid disappointed if we don't get him."

"But see what a narrow escape you had."

"Well, yes, sir; I wasn't quite sharp enough, but there was no harm done."

"Go on," said Syd, unwillingly, as he caught Roylance's eye; and hurrying by for fear that the permission should be withdrawn, the man stepped quickly back on to the beam, keeping a sharp look-out to right and left.

"I see you, you beggar," he said; "come on."

The shark accepted the invitation, and made quite a leap, passing over the beam again, diving down, snowing his white, and swam twenty feet away, to turn with difficulty amongst the submerged timber forward, and returned aiming clumsily at the white legs which tempted him, but missing his goal, for the young sailor nimbly leaped ashore.

"I shan't get him that way," he said. "Here, give us something white."

There was nothing white handy but blocks of coral, and Rogers solved the difficulty by selecting a hat and taking a handspike.

He tried his plan at least a dozen times without result, and lost two good chances; but the man was too clever for the shark at last. Rogers had scanned pretty accurately the course the brute would pursue, and had noted that when once it gave a vigorous sweep with its tail to send itself forward, there was no variation in its course.

So waiting his time, standing in the middle of the cross-beams with the noose in his hand, he fixed his eye upon his enemy, threw the hat ashore as a useless bait, and depending once more upon himself, he waited.

It was not for long. The brute made at him, and as it glided out of the water to seize its prey, Rogers, by a quick leap, spread his legs wide apart and held the noose so cleverly that the shark glided into it as a dog leaps through a hoop; and it was so ingeniously adjusted that the rope tightened directly, almost before the young sailor could shout *Now* while the shark went over and down between two of the cross-beams behind his fisher, as, from a cause upon which he had not counted, Rogers took an involuntary header into the part of the water-logged vessel from which the shark had come.

The cause upon which the young sailor had not reckoned was the rope, which, at the shark's plunge as soon as noosed, tightened the line which crossed Rogers' leg, snatched it from under him, and down he went, to the horror of all present.

In a moment the water all about where the shark had plunged began to boil, and the next moment there was a quick splashing as Rogers' head appeared.

"Hold on to him!" he shouted. "Don't let him go. Where's he ketched?"

"Don't talk," yelled Syd, running along the planks to stretch out a hand. "Here, quick, let me help you out."

"Oh, I'm all right, sir, so long as the rope holds," cried the young sailor, coolly. "He won't think of me while he's got that bit of line about him." But he climbed out all the same, and stood rubbing his shin.

"Never thought of the rope hitching on to me like that," he said. "Whereabouts is he ketched, mates?"

"The rope has slipped down pretty close to his tail," cried Roylance, as he watched the creature's frantic plunges in the limited space.

"Something like fishing this, Roy," said Syd, excitedly, while the men held on, and they could see amid the flying, foaming water the long, lithe body quivering from end to end like a steel spring.

"I'd haul him out, sir, 'fore he shakes that noose right over his tail."

"Yes. Look alive, my lads. Now then!" cried Syd, "haul him out. Quick!"

The men gave a cheer, and hauling together, they ran the writhing monster right out of the water, and over the edge of the natural pier, fifty feet or so up among the loose rocks, where it leaped and bounded and pranced about for a few minutes in a way which forbade approach.

Then there was a loud cheer as Rogers seized his opportunity, and brought down the axe he had snatched up with so vigorous a stroke on the creature's back, about a couple of feet above the great lobe of the tail, that the vertebra was divided, and from that moment the violent efforts to get free lost their power.

It was an easy task now to give the savage monster its *coup de grâce*, and as it lay now quivering and beyond doing mischief, the men set up another cheer and crowded round.

"There," cried Rogers, "that means shark steak for dinner, lads, and—"

"Sail ho!" came from above; and the shark was forgotten as the words sent an electric thrill through all.

"Come on, Roylance!" cried Syd, climbing up the rope-ladder to run and get his glass.

"Ay, ay," cried Roylance, following.

"Let's get a better hold with the rope, mates," said Rogers, "and haul the beggar right up on deck. They're artful beggars is sharks, and if we leave him here he'd as like as not to come to life, shove a few stitches in the cut in his tail, and go off to sea again."

The men laughed, and the prize was hauled right up to the perpendicular wall below the tackle, willing hands making the quivering mass fast, and hauling it right up into the gap, and beyond all possibility of its again reaching the sea.

Chapter Forty

A good deal had been done to make the way easy, but still it was an arduous and hot climb up to the flagstaff, on his way to which Syd had found time, in case they had not heard, to announce the sail in sight to Mr Dallas and the boatswain.

There it was, sure enough, a vessel in full sail right away in the east; and as Syd gazed at it through the glass, his spirits sank.

"It isn't the *Sirius*," he said, as he handed the glass to Roylance.

"No, sir," said the man on the look-out; "she's a Frenchy, I think."

"How do you know it isn't the *Sirius*?" said Roylance, as he used the glass.

"Because her masts slope more than those do," replied Syd, and then he felt how ignorant he was, and how old Strake would have told the nationality of a vessel "by the cut of her jib," as he would have termed it. His musings were interrupted by Roylance.

"Yes, I think she's a French ship," he said. "Bound for Saint Jacques, evidently, and I dare say she'll come by here."

"Well, we can't stop her," said Syd, shortly, for he felt annoyed that his companion should know so much more of seafaring matters than he.

"No," replied Roylance; "but she can stop us perhaps. I should not be surprised if she is coming on purpose; for the people, you see, must know we have taken possession of this rock, and that is why all shipping has kept away."

"Perhaps so," said Syd, a little more testily, for it was painful to be so ignorant. "Well, I suppose we can do nothing."

"Do nothing? Well, you are at the head of affairs; but if it was my case I should go and have a word with the lieutenant, and take his advice."

These were his words of wisdom, and Syd hurried down to the hospital and reported.

"And me a-lying here like a log," muttered the boatswain.

"In all probability a French man-of-war come to see what we mean by settling down here. Well, Mr Belton," said the lieutenant, "I do not suppose it means fighting; but, if I were you, I should get out my ammunition, and have it well up to the guns."

"Why don't you tell me to do it, sir?" cried Sydney, humbly.

"Because the command has fallen upon you, my lad; and I'm only a poor feeble creature, hardly able to lift an arm. Come; you have no time to spare. Draw up your ropes, beat to quarters, and if the enemy does come near, and send a boat to land, you can warn them off."

"And if they will not go, sir?"

"Send a shot over their heads."

"And if they don't go then?"

"Send one through their boat."

"But that will hurt somebody, sir."

"I hope so," said the lieutenant, dryly. "Why, Strake, what are you doing?" he continued, excitedly, as the boatswain slowly sat up, uttering a groan as he lowered down his feet.

"On'y going to see to that there ammunition, sir. There's no gunner aboard, and some one ought to do it."

"But you are too weak and ill, my man."

"I shall be weaker and iller ever so much, sir, if I stop here," said the boatswain. "Oh, I arn't so very bad."

"But really, my man—"

"Don't stop me, your honour, sir. How could I look his father in the face again if I didn't lend a hand just when it's wanted most?"

"Well, I cannot stop you, Strake," said the lieutenant. "I only wish I could stir. I could do nothing but take up the men's strength, and make them carry me about. Go on, Mr Belton; play a bold part, and recollect you are acting in the King's name."

Syd flushed up, and went to work at once. The preparations did not take long. The rope-ladder was hauled up and stowed away, the men were called to quarters, ammunition served out under the boatswain's orders, and the guns loaded. Every man had his cutlass, and the British colours had been laid ready for hoisting at a moment's notice.

When these arrangements had been made, Syd took Roylance and Terry into consultation, and asked them if there was anything else that could be done.

Neither could suggest anything, for the water-casks were filled, the stores were up in safety, and the men had a supply of fresh fish, in the shape of the shark just caught—a toothsome dainty that some sailors consider excellent for a change.

All was ready; every man at his post; and after buckling on his dirk, Syd thought to himself, "What an impostor I am! What impudence it is for me to pretend to command these men!"

But as he went out amongst them, somehow it did not seem as if they thought so. There was a bright eagerness in their faces, and whenever he spoke it was to be answered with a cheery "Ay, ay, sir!" and his orders were executed with alacrity.

It was a small party to command, if this should prove to be a French man-of-war come to dispute the right of the English to this rocky speck off their possessions.

But the matter was soon to be proved. From time to time Syd climbed to the flagstaff to watch the stranger, which was approaching fast, and also to sweep the distant horizon in search of help in what promised to be his dire need.

And here it may as well be stated that in planting his garrison on the rock, it had been the intention of Captain Belton—an idea endorsed by his consort—to let a party of his men hold the place, so as to keep any party from Saint Jacques from taking possession, and from thence annoying his ships. Such a venture could only be made with boats from the town, and these he felt that it would be easy for the little garrison to beat off. It never entered into his calculations that the rock could be attacked by a man-of-war, for he and his consort would be there watching the channel which led up to the town, and theirs would be the duty to repel any formidable attack.

The gale, which had risen to a hurricane, changed all this, and that upon which the captain did not count had come to pass.

For a French frigate was sailing steadily up the broad channel—a vessel whose captain was evidently quite at home among the coral reefs and shoals which spread far and near, and its nearing was watched with eager eyes.

From time to time Roylance was sent to report the state of affairs to Mr Dallas, who lay on his rough couch, apparently quite calm and confident, but with a red patch burning in either cheek, as he bitterly felt his helplessness and inability to do more than give a word or two of advice. But this advice he did give, when the frigate was about a mile off.

"We are so weak here," he said to Roylance, "that Mr Belton had better keep his men well out of sight, and not invite inquiry or molestation. The vessel may not be coming here, and if they see no one will pass on."

Roylance communicated this to Syd.

"But there is one thing they will see," he said.

"What?"

"The flagstaff."

"Yes; I had forgotten that, and it is too late to take it down; the men would be seen."

All this time the frigate was steadily approaching, for if her course was to reach the town that slept so calmly in the sunshine, she would come within about half a mile of the rock as she passed.

The orders were given for the men to keep out of sight at the lower gun, the heavy piece being drawn back from the opening in the stone wall built up in front; and Roylance, who had charge there, lay down behind a piece of rock, where he could watch the vessel's course.

Syd went on himself to the upper gun, after bidding the man at the flagstaff keep out of sight.

Terry was walking up and down impatiently as the lad approached, and the latter looked at him wonderingly, for only a short time before they had parted apparently the best of friends.

"Look here, Mr Belton," said Terry, losing not a moment in developing his new grievance, "I want to know why Roylance has been sent down to the lower gun, where the work is of more importance than this."

"More importance?" said Syd.

"Yes; I suppose you have been advised to do it as a slight upon me. You would not have done it of your own accord."

"I was not advised to do anything of the kind," said Syd, quietly; "I did what I thought was best. If there is any difference in the two posts, this is the more important, because every one would have to retreat here in case the lower gun was taken."

"Surely I ought to know which is the more important, sir," cried Terry, loudly, "and I see now it is a question of favouritism or friendliness. But I shall protest against it, and so I tell you."

"There is no time to discuss such a matter as this now, Mr Terry," said Syd. "You are to hold this gun in readiness to cover the retreat if the lower work becomes untenable; and now you must keep yourself and men hidden, and the gun drawn back."

"What for?" said Terry, with asinine obstinacy.

"I cannot stop to explain why."

"But I insist, sir. Am I to play the part of coward without having the privilege of knowing why such a distasteful course is to be adopted? I am sure if Mr Dallas knew—"

"Do as you're told, sir," cried Syd, warmly. "Not a man is to be seen. Run that gun in, my lads."

Then, as the order was obeyed, much to Terry's disgust, Syd said quietly—

"The men are to keep out of sight, so that the French ship may pass on. You understand?"

"Oh, yes: I understand," sneered Terry, as Syd went away, and then crept up under the shelter of the side of one of the rifts to the flagstaff, where he lay down beside the watch and opened his glass, so that he was able to examine the coming vessel at his ease.

Twenty-eight guns he counted, and as he kept on watching he could even see the movements of the men on deck. All calm and quiet there; the men in knots, the officers seated, or leaning over the side. There could be no doubt about it; the man-of-war was on a peaceable mission, as far as the rock was concerned, and would pass on.

Once or twice Sydney saw an officer glance in his direction, but only to turn away again. But he made no report to any one else, and the frigate sailed on in the hot evening sunshine.

Syd felt his spirits rise. He had proved himself to be no coward, though he shrank from the awful responsibility of giving orders or committing acts which might cause the shedding of blood. The Frenchman was sailing steadily on, and the lad drew his breath more freely, as he said, almost unconsciously, to the man watching by his side—

"There'll be no fighting, my lad."

"Well, sir," replied the man, who happened to be Rogers, "I dunno as I want to fight. If I'm told to, course I shall, but it takes a lot with me to get my monkey up; and I'd rather look like a coward any day than have to fire at a man or give him a chop with my cutlash."

"Quite right, Rogers. I don't think those who bounce most are the bravest. How bright and clean it looks on board ship! I wonder how soon the *Sirius* will come back. Ah, there she goes," he continued, as he used the glass, "sailing straight away for Saint Jacques; one could almost like to be in her for a change. Hallo!"

He looked eagerly through his glass at the passing ship, and became suddenly aware of the fact that something had attracted the attention of the officers of the French frigate, for one of the men went up quickly to an officer on the quarter-deck, and through the glass Sydney could see the gold lace of his uniform glisten as he raised one hand and pointed at the rock.

"How vexatious!" said Syd, aloud; "that officer must have seen the flagstaff."

"No, sir; I don't think so," said Rogers.

"Nonsense, man! they have seen it. Look, they're throwing the ship up in the wind, and—yes—they're going to lower a boat. Look at the men swarming across the deck like ants. They must have seen the flagstaff. What a pity it was not taken down!"

"Beg pardon, sir; I don't think it was the flagstaff."

"What, then? They couldn't see the guns."

"No, sir; but they could have seen Mr Terry."

"How? Why?"

"He got up on the gun-carriage, and stood down below there, staring out to sea."

Syd lowered the glass and changed his position, so that he could look down into the little stone-built fort, where the upper gun was placed, and there, sure enough, was Terry in the act of getting down from the gun-carriage.

"Why, what can he mean by that?"

"Dunno, sir," said the man, bluntly. "He's a orficer; but if it had been one of us we should precious soon know."

"What do you mean?" cried Sydney, uneasily.

"Only, sir, as you orficers would call it treachery, and it might mean yard-arm."

Chapter Forty One

Treachery or only spite, which could it be? Syd felt a sensation of cold running through him as he raised the glass again and watched the frigate, for he felt that perhaps after all he might have been mistaken, and the sailor lying by him too. Terry was an officer and a gentleman. He had a horrible temper; he was as jealous and overweening as could be, but it seemed impossible that he could so degrade himself as to be guilty of an act that was like a betrayal of his brother officers and the men.

But it was no mistake as far as the frigate was concerned. She had rounded to, her sails were beginning to flap, and amidst the scene of bustle on deck a boat was lowered, and the next minute it was seen gliding away from the vessel's side, filled by a smart crew whose oars seemed to be splashing up golden water as the sun sank and got more round. There were two officers in the stern, and now and then something flashed which looked like weapons, and a second glance showed that they were the swords of the officers and the guns of the marines.

"We are seen, sure enough," said Syd. "Be ready with the colours, Rogers," he added aloud. "Hoist them the moment you hear me shout."

"Ay, ay, sir. But it may only be a bit o' *parley voo*, and no fighting arter all."

"I hope not," thought Syd, as he hurried down the rift, avoiding Terry's work, and making straight for the lieutenant's quarters, where he flinched from telling of Terry's actions, and contented himself by saying what he had seen.

"Well, Mr Belton," said the lieutenant, with a slight flush coming into his pale face, "you are a King's officer in command, but you know the captain's wishes; and, boy as you are, sir, you must do what we all do under such trying circumstances — act like a man."

"And —"

Syd ceased speaking, and asked the remainder of his question with his eyes.

"Yes, sir, fire upon them, if necessary. If that boat is from a French man-of-war, her men must not land."

Syd drew in a long breath, nodded shortly, and was going out without a word.

"Stop!" cried the lieutenant. "Take off that plaything, my dear lad, and buckle on my sword. That's right, take up a hole or two in the belt as you go. Here's a motto for your crest when you sport one, 'Belton—Belt on'! Now God bless you, my lad! Do your duty for your own and your father's sake."

There was a quick grasp of the hand, and Syd ran out, fastening on the sword-belt as he went, and feeling rather a curious sensation in the throat as he mentally exclaimed—"I will."

The men were lying down by the breastwork of the lower gun as he trotted over the slope, and to his surprise he found the boatswain seated on a piece of stone with his face puckered up, watching Pan whom he had just sent up to the magazine.

"Well: what news?" said Roylance, eagerly. "Are they gone?"

Every eye was fixed on Syd, as he replied—

"No; a boat is coming ashore, and they must make for here. We can hear what they have to say, but they must not land."

A thrill seemed to run through the men, who lay ready to jump up and work the gun, and at a glance Sydney saw that their arms were all ready, and half the men were stripped for action.

"It is a French frigate?" said Roylance. "Yes."

"Then who is to talk to them? Can you?"

"I know the French I learned at school."

"Well, I know that much," said Roylance. "I can make them understand, but I don't know about understanding them."

"Begging your pardon, gentlemen," said Strake, with a grim smile, "you needn't trouble 'bout that 'ere. I've got a friend here as there isn't a Frenchy afloat as don't understand."

"Whom do you mean, Strake?" said Syd, as he looked sharply at the boatswain.

"This here, sir," he said, patting the breech of the cannon. "On'y let her open her mouth and bellow; they'll know it means keep off." The men laughed. "Is the gun loaded?"

"Yes, sir, with a round shot; but I've got grape and canister ready."

This began to look like grim warfare, and Syd stood there waiting in silence, and gazing out seaward for the coming of the boat.

From the little battery the extent visible was rather limited, for the rock rose up high to right and left. The French frigate was right behind them, plain to be seen from the upper gun, the steep slope downward shutting it out from the lower.

A full half-hour glided by, but there was no sign of the enemy, and the men lay waiting with the sun now beating full upon them with such power that the rock grew almost too hot to touch.

"If they don't look sharp and come," said Strake, moving the lantern he had with him more into the shade, "my candle here will melt into hyle, and that there gun 'ill begin to speak French without being touched."

"Surely the sun has not power enough to light the charge, Strake."

"Well, sir, I never knowed it done yet," said the boatswain, dubiously.

Another quarter of an hour passed away, and Roylance exclaimed—

"Can there be any other place where they could land?"

"No," said Syd, "I feel sure not."

"Then why are they so long?"

"Don't know the rock, and they are rowing to search all round for a place, the same as we did."

Still the long-drawn-out space of time went slowly, and doubts began to intrude which made Syd glance anxiously up to right and left, as he thought how helpless they would be should they be taken in rear or flank.

"Make a good fight for it all the same," said Roylance, who read his looks. "But I don't see how they could land anywhere round the rock without men on the cliff top to help them."

"Terry would not do that," thought Syd, and he glanced sharply round to gaze above him at the upper gun.

He blushed at the thought, as he saw the young officer there, evidently engaged in looking out to sea.

"Think the man up yonder by the flagstaff can see them?" said Roylance, after another weary wait.

Sydney shook his head.

"I say, oughtn't we to hoist the colours, Belton?"

"Rogers will run them up when I make him a signal. We don't want to challenge them to fight, only to defend the rock against all comers."

"Gettin' hungry, mate?" whispered one of the men to the lad next him.

"No: why?"

"'Cause this side o' me's 'most done."

There was a laugh.

"Silence!" cried Syd, and then in the same breath, "Here they are!"

For the bows of the frigate's boat, which had been right round the rock, suddenly appeared from the left with one of the officers standing up in the stern-sheets; and as they came on he suddenly pointed toward the natural pier, and the men, who had just been dipping their oars lightly, gave way.

As they came on the party in the little battery could see the French officers searching the opening with their eyes, and eagerly talking together; but they did not hesitate, apparently not realising that the place had been put in a state of defence, for the gun was drawn back, and the embrasure was of so rugged a construction that it did not resemble the production of a military engineer.

They ran their boat close alongside of the little pier, and one of the officers was about to spring out, when Syd shouted forth deeply as he could, as he stood on the breastwork.

"Hallo!"

The officer looked up sharply, smiled, waved his hand, gave an order to the sailors in the boat, and a dozen well-armed men sprang out.

"*Halte!*" shouted Syd again.

"*Aha!*" cried the French officer, leading his men forward. "*Nous sommes des amis.*"

"Oh, *êtes-vous?*" cried Syd. "I dare say you are, but you can't land here. Back to your boat. *Allez-vous-en!*"

"*Mais non!*" said the French officer politely, and he still came on, smiling.

"This rock belong to his Britannic Majesty, the King of England. *Waistcoat à nous, Monsieur. Allez-vous-en.*"

"*Mais non,*" said the French officer. "*En avant!*"

"*Nous allons donner le feu*—Fire at you—Fire!" shouted Syd, and he leaped backward into the fort perfectly astounded. For Strake did not understand French, but he thoroughly comprehended English, and as he heard his commanding officer say *fire!* and then more loudly, *fire!* he clapped his slow match to the touch-hole of the cannon, whose mouth was about a foot from the embrasure; there was a burst of flame and smoke, a deafening roar which threatened to bring down the rocks to right and left, and as Syd looked through the smoke he could see the French officer and his men running back to the boat.

"Strake, you shouldn't have fired," he cried, excitedly.

"You give orders," growled the boatswain; "and there was no time to haim. Shot went skipping out to sea.—Be smart, my lads," he continued, as the men who had sprung to their places wielded sponge and rammer, and this time ran the gun out so that its muzzle showed over the rough parapet.

By this time Syd had made a sign, and Rogers quickly ran the colours up the flagstaff, where they were blown out fully by the breeze.

"Don't find fault," whispered Roylance, wiping the tears from his eyes. "What a game! See that little French officer fall down?"

"No."

"He caught his foot in a stone. Look at them now."

Syd looked down at where on the pier the French officers were gesticulating and talking loudly; the gist of their debate being, should they try to take the battery or put off, and the majority seemed to be in favour of the latter proceeding. For as they eagerly scanned the little battery they could see now the frowning muzzle of the gun, and the heads of a number of English sailors apparently ready to fire again, this time probably with better effect.

One officer seemed to be for coming on. The other thought evidently that discretion was the better part of valour, for he looked up at the colours on the flagstaff, then down at the battery, and then finally gave orders to the men to re-embark. But this was too much for the spirit of the other, who after a few sharp words took out a white handkerchief, tied it to the blade of his sword, and held it up, advancing with it in his hand till he was just below the gun, and at the foot of the cliff wall.

"Messieurs," he said, politely, "I speak not ze Angleesh as you do. I you make me understand?"

"*Oui*—yes," said Syd, who had again mounted the rough wall.

"It is good," said the French officer. "You make fire upon us. Yes?"

"Yes; we fired."

"You—you teach me yourself, vat ze diable you make here?"

"We hold this place as a possession of the King of England," replied Sydney. "Can you understand?"

"*Parfaitement*, sare. Zen I tell you I go back to my sheep, and me come and blow you all avay. *Au revoir*!"

"*Au revoir*, Monsieur," said Syd, exchanging bows with the French officer, who went back to the boat, sprang on board, the men pushed off, and the little garrison gave them a cheer.

"Thank goodness that's over," said Syd, taking off his hat to wipe his brow, as he leaped back into the battery.

"Over?" said Roylance, "not till they have been back and blown us all away."

"Beg pardon, sir," said the boatswain, "but I 'member now nuff of my old work years ago to be able to send a round shot right through that there boat, if you'll give the word."

"No, no, Strake. — There, you keep your men ready in case they do come back, Roy," whispered Syd; "I'll go up and report matters to Mr Dallas."

Chapter Forty Two

"Could not have happened better," said the lieutenant, as he was put in possession of all particulars. "The accident happened well, and gave them a lesson in our strength that may make them think twice before attacking us."

"Then you think they will attack us?"

"Sorry to say I have no doubt about it, and since I have been lying here I have come to the conclusion that it would be better to bring that upper gun down, and mount it about twenty feet from the other. The attack must come from the lower end. If, however, they could land, and tried to scale the rocks at the top of the gap, you would have to defend the upper battery the best way you could. Even if you had a gun there you could not get more than one shot. Haul it down at once."

Syd went off and communicated the result of his conversation to Roylance and Strake.

"Yes, I think he's right," said the former. "Eh, Strake?"

"Right, sir; why of course he is. I felt that when we got the guns up, only it warn't for me to give my 'pinion. Speaking in parabolas like, what I say is, that the t'other gun's worth twopence up there, but down here it'll be worth a hundred pound or more. Start at once, sir?"

"Yes, directly.—Roylance, will you see to making a platform and running up a breastwork, while the bo'sun gets down the gun?"

All hands were soon at work, and meanwhile Syd had gone up to the flagstaff with a glass to see that the boat was half-way back to the French frigate.

"What will they do?" thought Syd. "Make sail and come and batter us with their guns, or send out three or four boats?"

He waited patiently till the Frenchmen were alongside, and he watched the officers through the glass go on the quarter-deck and make their report to their captain.

"Now, then," said Syd, half-aloud, "which is it to be—boats, or come up abreast of us?"

"Make sail, sir," said Rogers. "They're coming down on us to give us a dusting with their guns. There'll be some chips o' rock flying far to-night.—And something more for you to do, my lad," he muttered to himself, as he recalled the lieutenant's injury.

Syd made no answer, and stood watching the French vessel's sails gradually begin to fill and make her careen over.

"Here she comes," said Rogers; then, respectfully, "They won't have half time to get that gun into place, will they, sir?"

"No, Rogers, no," said Syd, thoughtfully; "but look, she's changing her course."

It was so indeed, for the French frigate curved gracefully around, and went off on her old course toward the town of Saint Jacques.

Syd rubbed his eyes and stared, while Rogers in his excitement slapped both his legs, shouting derisively—"Yah! Cowards! G'ome!" and then darted to the flagstaff and began to haul the colours down a few feet, and just as his young officer was about to stop him, seized the second line and jigged them up again in a sort of dance that was intended in mockery of the captain and crew of the departing frigate.

"That will do there," cried Syd, sharply.

"Beg pardon, sir," cried the sailor, starting away from the flagstaff; "but for them to go away like that. The old chaps aboard were always bragging that they could lick three Parlyvoos, but arter what I've seed to-day, I'm ready to tackle six. I don't say I'd lick 'em, but I'd have a good try."

"Don't judge them too soon," said Syd, quietly; and he went down to the hospital and reported everything to the lieutenant.

"Well," he said, "what do you think of it, Mr Belton—that you've frightened them away with one gun?"

"No, sir; I think they've gone for help."

"Or else to report, and perhaps deliver despatches."

"Yes, sir; think we shall have them back?"

"Not a doubt about it, Mr Belton. We laugh at and brag about our superiority over the Frenchmen; but with all their chatter and gesticulation and show, they know how to fight, and can fight bravely and well. Get your other gun ready and keep the sharpest of look-outs, as they'll be down upon you before you know where you are. What's the matter yonder," he continued, raising his head and listening; "Mr Terry in hot water again? We don't want trouble among ourselves. You are wanted there, commandant."

Syd hurried out and found Terry up by the battery he had had in charge, furiously refusing to let the men under Roylance remove the gun.

"Ah, you are there," he cried, savagely, and with his face convulsed with passion. "It is a trick of yours to deprive me of my chance of distinguishing myself in this wretched hole."

"It is nothing of the kind, Mr Terry," said Syd, quietly; "but are you mad to go on like this before the men?"

"I should be mad if I held my tongue, and let every puppy of a boy be placed over me to insult me. I say the gun shall not be moved."

"It is for the proper defence of the place."

"It is a piece of insolence to annoy me."

"You would have charge of the gun in its fresh place."

"I don't believe it," cried Terry, in his rage. "This is the gun's place. It shall not be moved."

"Silence, sir!" cried Syd, flushing up, and something of his father's stern way giving him an older and firmer look. "I gave orders for the gun to be taken down. Mr Roylance, be smart with your men."

"It shall not be done," cried Terry. "I say—"

"And I say, sir," said Syd in an angry whisper, "that if you are not silent, I'll put you in arrest; yes, and tied hand and foot for your treachery of an hour or two ago."

Terry's jaw dropped, and he turned ashy in hue as he shrank away.

"Look here, sir," continued Syd, "you will no longer have charge of that gun, but act under Mr Roylance's orders when I am not there. Fight like a man, and do your duty, and I may forget to report your conduct to the captain. Go on as you are behaving now, and everything shall be known."

A curiously vindictive look shot from Terry's eyes as his hand involuntarily played with the butt of the pistol he had in his belt.

Syd saw it, and continued—

"Another such threat as that, sir, and you will be disarmed."

Terry walked away and stood aside, gazing out to sea, while Syd could not help thinking that if his messmate had a favourable opportunity and could do it unseen, he would not scruple to use his pistol, or to push him over the steep cliff.

The thoughts were dismissed directly and forgotten in the busy toil, the men rigging up the tackle, dismounting the gun, and packing it once more in one of the water-casks, ready for rolling down to the new platform, which was slowly progressing, but not yet ready for its reception. So the one party was piped to refreshments, after which, the place being declared sufficiently advanced, the second party took the place of the first for rest and food, while with a cheer the gun-carriage was dragged below, then the tackle was rigged over it, and the gun rolled down, hauled into its place, and by the time darkness had quite set in, the fresh one-gun battery was in working order.

"Where's Terry?" said Syd, about this time.

"Sulking," said Roylance, laughing. "What did you say to him? You are getting an awfully great fellow, Belton, to calm him down like that. I say, how old are you?"

"Nearly seventeen. Why?"

"Are you sure it isn't a mistake?"

"Quite."

"Because you are going on over this like a fellow of twenty-seventeen. What do you think one of the men said just now?"

"How should I know?"

"He said that when this little job was over you ought to be promoted and have a ship of your own, and old Strake turned upon him sharply to say, 'Well, why not?'"

"I? A ship!" laughed Syd; "and this is my first voyage. Why, you have been three."

"Yes, but then your people have always been sailors, and it's born with you. My father's a clergyman. Well, when you do have a ship by and by, if you don't have me for first luff, I'll call you a brute."

"Wait twenty years, then, till I get my ship," said Syd; and he went off to see to the watch.

Chapter Forty Three

That was an anxious night; and after a sort of council of war at the hospital, in which the lieutenant, Roylance, and Strake took part with Syd, it was determined to have all ready for a retreat to the upper battery, and in case that should be taken, provisions and water were to be carried at daybreak up to the flagstaff, where a breastwork had already been made, plenty of broken masses of rock lying about to strengthen it, so that it would be a fresh position for the crew of the French frigate to attack.

Syd was not at all surprised soon after daybreak—when the men were busy strengthening the empty battery, and others were building up the breastwork about the flagstaff and conveying up stores—to see the frigate coming back in full sail.

There was plenty of excitement as the enemy was seen, and the men thoroughly realised the fact that the day's work before them would be no light task.

"Seems to do one more good, though, Master Syd, sir," said Strake, as they were together alone. "Lying down, and bein' helped, and strapped and lashed 's all very well, but the sight o' one's nat'ral enemy 'pears to spurt you up like, and if it had only been a month longer, strikes me as we should have had the lufftenant helping of us again."

"Have you seen Mr Terry about?"

"No, sir; 'pears to have struck work like. Beg pardon, sir; but seeing as some on us may be gone to Davy Jones's locker 'fore night—not meaning you, o' course, but him—wouldn't it be handsome-like to go and make friends, and offer him your hand?"

"I have done so more than once, Strake," said Syd, sternly, as he recalled the midshipman's action on the previous day, "but I can't do it again."

"All right, sir, you knows best, o' course," said the boatswain, and he went off to his duty.

The men worked hard, and by the time the frigate was close in there were the provisions and water in the upper battery, and a good supply in the works about the flagstaff.

"You can do no more, Belton," said Mr Dallas. "I don't want to discourage you, but without help from sea we can only manage to hold out as long as possible, and give the enemy a tough job, for Old England's sake. Are the colours flying well?"

"Yes, sir, splendidly."

"That's right, then. Now, one word of advice; don't fire a shot at the frigate. With your two guns you can do her very little harm. Save your powder for the boats—round shot when they are coming to the shore, and grape as they are landing. Keep your men cool, and only let them fire when there is a good chance."

Bang!

The first shot from seaward followed by a crash, and the sound of stones falling as the frigate tried her range, and sent a heavy ball against the side of the gap.

"Did not know she was so near," said the lieutenant.

"But about you, sir? Shall I have you carried up to the flagstaff?"

"Certainly not, my lad, never mind me. Go and do your duty. God save the King!"

"God save the King!" echoed Syd, as he shook hands with the lieutenant, and hurried down to the little battery, to find that the frigate had drawn as close in as she could, but dared not come right in front of the gap, for her boat out sounding had discovered a reef right opposite. So after firing a few shots obliquely, all of which struck the north side of the gap, she made sail and went round to the other side of the reef, where disappointment again awaited her captain; for here again he could only fire obliquely, and send the stones rattling down on the south side of the gap.

But he went on firing for about an hour before shifting his position once more, and then feeling his way in exactly opposite, but quite out of range.

This was an unexpected change in favour of the defender, for though when they were freshly come it had been noticed that the sea ran high a quarter of a mile out from the lower end of the gap, the existence of a reef was not suspected, and it was some time before the defenders could thoroughly believe that the frigate could not get into position for sweeping the little gully from end to end.

Again the frigate's position was changed, and fire opened.

"We ought to shake hands on this," cried Roylance. "Fire away, Monsieur, knock down the rocks; it's all good for the powder and ball trade."

"And doesn't frighten us a bit," added Syd, who for the moment forgot his important position, and its seriousness. "Haven't you seen Terry yet?"

"No."

"And I arn't seen my boy Pan, gen'lemen," said the boatswain—"My word, that was a good one," he interpolated, as a heavy shot struck the rock about twenty feet below the flagstaff, and a good ton of stones came rattling down—"strikes me as that boy's a-showing the white feather, gen'lemen, and it goes home to my 'art."

"The boy's wounded, Strake; don't be too hard on him."

"Not so bad but what he might ha' done powder-monkeying with one hand. But there's a deal o' vartue in rope's-ends arter all, and if I gets through to-day—"

"You'll forgive him. What are they doing now?" Syd shouted to the man at the look-out, for the frigate was once more close in, south of the little pier, and had for half an hour been blazing away, but doing not the slightest harm.

"Getting her boats out, sir."

"Preparing to board, sir," cried Strake. "Round shot first as they come on?"

"But the boats will be close in before we can get a shot at them, and there will not be time to reload," said Syd. "It is not as if they were going to row straight in, so that we could see them for some time first. It must be grape."

"Grape it is, sir. Right," cried Strake, and the guns were charged accordingly.

The men's orders were that they should wait till the enemy were well in by the little pier, then to fire, and as there would not be time to reload, they were to seize their cutlasses and pikes and be ready for the attacking party, who would undoubtedly swarm up to the foot of the rock wall, provided with spars, or something in the way of tackle, to enable them to scale the place, when the desperate fighting must begin.

They were not long kept in waiting after the guns had been depressed, and their muzzles brought to bear well upon the only spot where the boats could land their men—the wreck moored close in limiting the space. And it turned out as Syd had imagined: the boats—three—came as close in as the submerged rocks would allow, and they were still out of sight when the defenders heard a shout, and first one and then another rowed into sight, making for the landing-place. Then came the third, as, thinking it a pity to have to give so terrible an order, Syd shouted "Fire!" with the result that the closely-packed charge from the first gun went right through one boat, leaving her crew struggling in the water; and the shot from the second gun completely tore off the bows of the third boat, but not until her crew was so near land that they were able to pilot the boat a few yards farther before she sank, her men literally tumbling one over the other into the deck-less hull of the water-logged wreck.

The other boat got up to the pier in safety after her crew had held out oars and boat-hooks to their drowning comrades, and so all got to shore; the rush and beating of the water, and its churning up by the grape-shot having scattered the sharks for the moment.

All this gave the occupants of the battery more time than they had anticipated, and this was utilised in reloading, which was almost completed, when there was a word of command, a shout; and armed with cutlass, pistol, and boarding-pike, the Frenchmen dashed up gallantly to the wall, some stopping back to fire at the defenders, who were, however, too well sheltered to be hurt.

"Be ready with your arms, my lads," cried Syd, as he recalled stories of fights he had heard his father relate.

"Ay, ay, sir."

"Throw them back as fast as they get up."

"Ay, ay, sir!" came again heartily; but the enemies' heads did not appear above the edge, and though the loud buzzing and shouting of orders came up, there was no adversary.

It was not the men's fault, for they were at the bottom of a vast natural wall, which towered up from fifteen to twenty feet, and so smooth that there was not the slightest foothold to enable them to climb.

The officer who had come up to it before with a flag of truce had in his excitement omitted to notice the difficulty, and consequently neither rope nor spar had been brought; and though the men clambered and shouted and made brave efforts to mount upon each other's shoulders, fortunately for them they were not able to get up far enough to be sent down with a cut on the head.

The shouting and confusion lasted for some time, during which the defenders crouched in safety behind their breastwork, and waited.

At last, just as the officers were deciding upon withdrawing their men, and asking themselves what their fate would be if the English began to play upon them during their retreat to the one boat which was left, there was another cheer, and a reinforcement from the frigate appeared.

Strake sprang up to alter the level of the gun and take aim, but Syd stopped him.

"This one hasn't come to attack," he said, as he saw that the boat was only half manned; the captain having seen the misfortunes that had befallen his other boats, and sent this one on to afford his men a means of retreat.

For the attack was hopeless, and the officers gathered their men together, and despatched them in two parties to the little pier, the men moving with the greatest of regularity; and while a few kept up a running fire against the battery, the others embarked.

"Now then, sir, give the word," whispered Strake, who was hoarse with excitement; "I can send a shot right through that there boat."

"What for?" said Syd, coldly. "They are retreating, and we don't want to stop them and make them prisoners."

"But they're our mortial enemies, sir," cried the boatswain, aghast.

"Let them go," said Syd; and as the boats pushed off, with the frigate recommencing its useless fire to cover the retreat, the defenders of the little natural fort gave a hearty cheer.

"We don't want a lot of bloodshed, Roy," said Syd, as they congratulated one another over the refreshment they were glad to take.

"No; but I suppose we ought to have slaughtered a lot of them. We could."

"My father used to tell my uncle, the admiral, that he was the greatest commander who could achieve a victory with the smallest loss of life."

"Yes, sir," said a gruff voice behind him; "but I've know'd your father send some awful broadsides and rakings into the enemy's ships. Why, when we've gone aboard arter to take the furren captain's sword, I've seed their deck all slippery with blood."

"And I'm glad those stones are not."

"Very well, sir, if you're satisfied, I am; but I want to know what's gone o' my Pan. Hasn't hidden hisself in that water-cave, has he?"

"I have not seen him," said Syd, and with Roylance he climbed up to the flagstaff to see the enemy's two crowded boats return to the frigate's side, after which the French captain made a slight change in his position; and as they watched they saw two fresh boats lowered and row away, and then they were recalled.

Then came a long spell of waiting in miserable inaction till toward sunset, when the two boats put out again, spent a little time sounding close up to the rocks where Roylance was rescued, and were again recalled.

"What does that mean, sir?" said Syd, as he told all this to the lieutenant, who, as he lay helpless, eagerly listened to every word.

"I don't quite see, my lad," he said. "A trick, probably, to take off your attention. But be well on your guard, for, depend upon it, they will try to surprise you to-night, and come prepared with ladders of some kind for the escalade."

Chapter Forty Four

The night was brilliant starlight, and the strictest watch was kept, but hour after hour went by, and there was not a sound; no dark shadow creeping over the water from the frigate, which lay anchored, with her lights showing reflections on the smooth sea.

Everything was in readiness to give the enemy a good reception if they came, and in spite of his weakness, the boatswain rose from where he lay on a folded-up sail beside one of the heaps of ball, to see if the light in the lanthorn by his head was burning, and handy for the slow matches to fire the guns.

"That there swab has gone down into his old hole by the water, sir, so as to save his skin," said Strake, on one of the occasions when Syd was going his rounds, "and here he might be o' no end of use saving his poor father. You won't say I arn't to use the rope's-end arter this, sir."

"Hadn't you better go up to the hospital and lie down, Strake?" replied Syd; "you are tired out."

"So are you, sir: so's all on us. But if I went and had a caulk just when the enemy might come, what should I say arterwards when I met the skipper?"

"But your injuries are such as sent you into hospital."

"Where I warn't going to stay, sir. Been up to the flagstaff, sir?"

"I have just come from there, and I have been with Mr Roylance, and had a talk with Mr Dallas. All's well."

"Seems well, Mr Syd, sir," whispered the boatswain, so as not to be heard by the men; "but I'm sure all aren't well. They're trying to dodge us, sir, and you see if they don't come and board us just afore daylight, when they think we're asleep. Tell them chaps at the look-out to keep their eyes open, and be on the kwe weave, as the Frenchies call it, for boats sneaking up in the dark. You've got two there."

"Yes, Strake, and each man has a glass, and those very instructions."

"What a horficer he will make," muttered the boatswain; and then the watch went on, with the men peering through the transparent darkness at the waves heaving over the little natural pier, and the bright stars broken up into spangles on the smooth surface of the sea.

"Rather queer about Terry," said Roylance in a whisper, as Syd joined him where he was leaning over the rough parapet, watching the surface for the first sign of the enemy.

"Very," said Syd.

"I can't understand it."

"I can," thought Syd, as he recalled what he had seen; and in the full belief that his messmate was heartily ashamed of his treacherous conduct of the previous day, he went softly up to find the lieutenant sleeping peacefully. He stood looking at him for a few moments, and then went up to the empty battery, to stand looking down over the precipice, before gazing up towards the flagstaff.

"All well, Rogers?" he said in a low, distinct voice.

"All well, sir," came back from far on high. "Nothing left the ship. We could ha' seen by the broken water. It brimes to-night, and we should have seen their oars stirring the water up."

Note: "brimes" means "is phosphorescent."

Syd went thoughtfully back, feeling so exhausted and drowsy that twice over he stumbled, and shook his head to get rid of the sleepy feeling, for it had been a terribly trying and anxious time.

"I'll go and talk to Strake," he said to himself; and pulling out a biscuit, he began to nibble it to take off the sensation of faintness from which he suffered, as he began wondering whether the French would attack them that night, or come prepared the next day with ladders to scale the natural wall which was their chief defence.

"All well, Strake?" he said, as he reached the place again where the boatswain was lying down.

"Ay, ay, sir."

"Halt! who goes there?"

"On'y me," cried a hoarse, excited voice, in a whisper, accompanied by a panting noise. "Where's father?"

"What, Pan-y-mar?" growled the boatswain. "Just you come here, you ugly-looking young swab."

"Hush, father!" whispered the boy, coming out of the darkness. "Give's a cutlash; the French is coming."

"What? Where?" said Syd, eagerly. "To your guns, my lads."

"No, no," cried the boy, in a hurried whisper. "Not that way; they're coming over the top there."

"He's been dreaming," growled the boatswain. "What d'yer mean, you dog?"

"I arn't been asleep," cried Pan, angrily; "and I'm so hungry."

"Tell me: what do you mean?" cried Syd.

"I've been a-watching o' Mr Terry, sir. He went down on the rocks over yonder, and I lay down and see him make signs to the French ship, and two boats come out and rowed in close to where he was a-hiding down in one o' them big cracks like I hid in and found the water."

"Yes; go on," whispered Syd, whose heart sank with apprehension.

"And he talked to 'em, and they talked to him, and then rowed back to the French ship."

"What did they say?"

"I dunno; I was too far off to hear."

"Well, go on."

"I thought he was up to some game, and I lay there and watched him, and I've been watching of him ever since, till to-night he crawled into the stores, after hiding all yes' afternoon and to-night, and I see him come creeping out again with a rope, and he put it over his shoulder. And then he climbed up one o' those cracks, and I went arter him, and he got right out there past the water-hole, and then crep' all along till he got to the place where you hauled Mr Roylance and t'other sailor up with a rope. And I crep' up close as I could, and lay there watching him hours till three boats come round from the other side, and then Mr Terry tied the end of the rope round a big block, and let the other end down, and I see a French sailor come up, and then another, and another, and they let down more rope, and they're all climbed up, and they're coming right up yonder over the top by the flag-post."

"How do you know?"

"'Cos I come that way first, and they was all coming close up arter me all the time, and I had to come on my hands and knees."

"Why didn't you come the other way, and give the alarm in front?"

"'Cos they've got lots o' fellows there with swords and pistols. I heard 'em cock."

"Yah! it's all a fancy," growled Strake; "he's scared, and dreamed it."

"I didn't," cried the boy.

"Couldn't climb up there," growled Strake.

"Yes, they could, Strake," cried Syd, excitedly. "Once they were on the rock they could climb up, and—yes, they'd come over by the flagstaff."

"I tell yer the young swab dreamt it."

"Ahoy! help!"

Bang! bang! Bang! bang!—Pistol-shots from high up by the flagstaff; and as the men seized their cutlasses and pistols, and, with Syd and Roylance at their head, advanced up the gap to meet this treacherous attack from the rear, there was the clash of steel, the sounds of struggling, then a momentary silence, followed by a few sharp orders, and the rattling noise of stones told that a strong party of men were coming down the rough path from the flagstaff.

"Forward, my lads!" cried Roy lance; "we may beat them back."

The men gave a cheer, and advanced quickly, the excitement of all taking them from the battery, which was left defenceless.

As they advanced, the old feeling of terror that he had always felt when about to engage in a school-fight was for a few moments in Sydney's breast; then the eager excitement carried all away, and, sword in hand, he ran on with his men.

Directly after there was the shock and confusion of the two parties meeting, with stray shots, the clatter of sword against sword, with sparks flying in the darkness, and the shouts and cheers of contending men.

What he did Syd never knew, for everything was centred in the one idea that he was leading his father's men, and that he must try and be brave. And if being brave meant rushing on with them right at the descending Frenchmen, he was brave enough.

So vigorous was the rush, and so desperate were the little English party at being surprised in so sudden a fashion, that the first group of the enemy were driven backward toward the path by which they had climbed down. But more and more were hurrying from above to their help, the officers threw themselves to the front, and the flight was stayed, while quite a series of single combats began to take place.

"Give it 'em, boys! Old England for ever!" was yelled out in the darkness, close by to where Syd was cutting and thrusting at an active little Frenchman. Then there came a groan, and the same voice said hoarsely—

"Oh, if I had my strength!"

"Hurrah, boys! they're giving way!" shouted Roylance. "Keep together, and over with them."

For in spite of the bravery of their officers, the French were yielding ground once more, and being slowly driven up the narrowing path. But there was a fresh burst of cheering, the hurry of feet, and about twenty of the French frigate's crew, who had taken advantage of the little garrison being attacked from the rear, and crept up to the cliff wall to scale it with a spar, one man going up with a rope which he had secured to a gun, soon turned the tables again.

With enemies before and behind triple their strength, and taking them in each case so thoroughly by surprise, the *mêlée* did not last long. Syd was conscious of seeing sparks after what seemed to be a loud clap of thunder above his head, and the next thing he knew was that Roylance was saying—

"Belt, lad, do, do try and speak."

"Speak? yes," he faltered. "What's the matter?"

"Matter! don't ask."

"But what does it mean? Where are we? Has Terry won?"

"My poor old fellow, you haven't been fighting Terry—yes, you have—a coward! he is with the French."

"And—" cried Syd, sitting up, "are we beaten?"

"Yes! no!" cried Roylance. "They're all down or prisoners—but eight of us here."

"Where are we?" said Syd, who felt sick and dizzy.

"Up in the little top battery, and they're coming on again. Stand by, lads!"

Syd rose to his feet as the men cheered, and stood with his sword hanging by the knot to his wrist, holding on by the rough stone wall, looking over into the starlit gloom at a body of French sailors apparently about to attack. Just then an officer stepped forward, and said, cheerily—

"*Rendez-vous, mes braves. Parlez, vous!*" he continued, turning to some one at his side.

"Here, you there!—the French officer says it's no use to fight any longer; he has taken the place, so give up."

"Terry!" cried Roylance; "you miserable traitor!" and the men around burst into a loud groan, and hooted the renegade.

"Yes, traitor!" cried Syd, excitedly; and forgetting his wound, "coward!"

"Coward yourself!" cried Terry. "Do you think I was going to stay in a service which compelled men to serve under a contemptible boy like you? Here, my lads, it's no use to resist. Give up, and you will have good treatment as prisoners. Come out."

"Do you hear, lads?" cried Roylance. "Will you do as the new English-French deserter says?"

"No!" roared the men; and Rogers' voice rose above them—"Say, lads, it's yard-arm for a desarter, eh?"

"Yes."

Terry turned away savagely, and they saw him saying something to the French officer—saw him dimly, as it seemed, then more plainly, for day was breaking with the rapidity of the change in the tropics; and as a movement took place, they all knew that a final assault was to be given, and must go against them.

Then the spirit of Syd's family seemed to send a flush through him; he forgot his pain, the sickness passed off, and he turned to gaze on the torn and blood-stained men about him.

"French and English," he cried, raising his sword.

"Hurray!" shouted the brave fellows; and every cutlass flashed as they prepared to defend their tiny stronghold, built up for the very emergency in which they were.

"*Rendez, messieurs!*" shouted the French officer, half appealingly.

"*Non, non!*" shouted Sydney, excitedly.

"*En avant!*" rang out the order, and with a rush the men came on in the rapidly increasing morning light.

At that moment the rocks echoed and quivered as a heavy gun thundered forth.

Chapter Forty Five

The advance was checked, and a man ran up to the flagstaff, to reach it at last, and then he shouted down something in French, which the occupants of the upper defence could not make out.

A second gun rolled forth its summons, and, giving an order, the French officer led his men toward the lower battery, where about twenty were halted, and busied themselves in turning one of the guns, so that it was pointed toward the upper battery, while the rest went down over the wall.

"What does it mean?" said Syd. "Are they going to blow us out of here?"

"No," said Roylance, "I think not. It is to occupy the place and keep us at bay. I'd give something to see what it all means. We're so shut up here, and can see nothing," he said, fretfully.

And it was so. They had a good view of the sea right out toward the town, but looking back they could see along the gap to their guns, which with the breastwork completely hid the landing-place.

"I'd give something to know what it all means."

"That gun meant the recall," said Roylance.

"If I could get to the flagstaff," said Syd.

"I think I could slip over at the back here," said Rogers; "climb along, and then crawl up."

"No, no, my lad; you'd break your neck."

"Oh, no, sir. You trust me."

"He can climb like a monkey, sir," said another of the men, who was binding up a wound.

"Then try," said Syd, after a glance upward to see that the French were not there.

The man slipped over the back directly, and crept along a narrow ledge that made them all feel giddy, but he got along in safety, and then creeping and climbing to the left of the regular path he disappeared in a rift.

"He'll do it now," said Roylance, who stood nursing one arm. "I say, Belt, as soon as you can I should be glad of a little help."

"Yes, I'll come directly," said Sydney; "but where are our other fellows?"

"All wounded or prisoners. The French have had the best of it this time. We shall be prisoners of war, lad."

"I wouldn't care, only we've lost the place, Roylance. Oh, how could an English fellow be so treacherous!"

"Don't know," said Roylance, dismally. "There always was something wrong with Mike Terry."

"Ahoy!" came from above their heads; and they looked up to see that Rogers had reached the flagstaff, and had hauled up the British colours, which blew out in the morning air as a faint cheer came from the hospital, and an angry chattering from about the guns.

"Sail ho! *Sirius* in sight," shouted Rogers through his hands; "boat's gone back to the Frenchman. Hurray!"

He was answered by a cheer from the little group about Syd, as three of the French sailors ran up at a trot, and began to mount the flagstaff path.

"Look out, Rogers. Don't be taken."

"Not I, sir. I'm coming back," shouted the sailor; and he disappeared, leaving the colours flying, and climbing back into the sturdy little work in time to join his companions in a loud groaning. For the French reached the top and hauled the British colours down, one of the enemy waving them derisively at the Englishmen, and throwing the flag over his shoulder as he laughed at them, and then carried it down to the battery, where his comrades had been strengthening their works toward the English position, one man standing ready with a port-fire to sweep the gap should there be an attack.

Two hours' waiting ensued—two weary hours, with injuries growing stiff, wounds smarting, and a terrible feeling of thirst coming on. That was forgotten directly the heavy boom of a gun was heard, answered by another; and for a time, as report after report echoed among the rocks, the imprisoned party saw in imagination the *Sirius* coming slowly up and attacking the French frigate, which answered with shot for shot. But it was most tantalising; and again and again Syd was for climbing up to the flagstaff to see what was going on, duty to the men alone keeping him to his post.

Their patience was rewarded at last, for Roylance suddenly gave a cheer, which was taken up by the others, as they saw the French frigate, her sails dotted with shot-holes, forge into sight, firing hard the while.

"Why, she's beaten—retreating," cried Sydney.

"No, only manoeuvring," replied Roylance; "and, hurrah! my lads, here comes the *Sirius*."

Syd's heart gave a leap as his father's noble frigate came slowly into sight round the south end of the gap, bringing with her a cloud of smoke which was rent and torn with flames of fire. For the next hour, there, a mile away, the frigates lay manoeuvring and exchanging their broadsides, neither appearing to get the upper hand.

Two of the French officers were now up at the flagstaff, where they had hoisted their own colours, and they were eagerly watching the varying fortunes of the naval action, which, as far as the lookers-on could see, might result in the favour of either. The firing was terrific, and for the time being the occupants of the fort forgot their enmity in the excitement of the naval engagement going on.

A wild shrill cheer suddenly rose from by the flagstaff, answered by a shout of defiance from the English battery, as all at once the mizzen-topmast of the *Sirius* with its well-filled sails bowed over as if doubled-up; but the loss did not check the firing nor her way, and the shrill cheer was silenced. For in the midst of the French elation, and as the course of the frigate was changed so that she might cross the bows of the *Sirius* and rake her, two more of the officers had gone up from by the guns, and were mounting the path to the flagstaff to participate in the triumph. They were in time to see the mainmast of the French frigate, already sorely wounded, yield to a puff of wind and go right over to leeward, leaving the beautiful ship helpless like a sea-bird with a broken wing.

Captain Belton quickly took advantage of the position, raked the Frenchman from stem to stern, ran his own vessel close up under her quarter, and as the smoke rolled away a crowd of boarders were seen pouring over on to her decks, the shouts and cheering of the fighting reaching to the ears of the spectators.

"We've taken her," cried Roylance, exultingly, and he was about to call upon the men to cheer when a look from Syd silenced him.

"Quick, lads!" he whispered. "In two parties. I'll lead one, Mr Roylance the other. We'll divide and run down to the guns and take them before they know where they are. Hist, not a sound! Now!"

The officers were still gazing directly away at the concluding episodes of the fight, so that only one was down at the battery, whose occupants were so taken by surprise, that before the junior lieutenant left had given the order to fire the Englishmen were half-way to them. Then as a cannon sent its charge of grape hurtling up the narrow pass, the two little parties cheered, dashed on, jumped over the rough wall cutlass in hand, and in less than a minute the place was once more in English hands.

"More prisoners than we want," said Syd; but they were soon got rid of, being disarmed, and compelled to lower themselves down a rope to the foot of the great natural wall, where they were huddling together, a discontented-looking group, when Syd had taken the swords of the other French officers and sent the British colours flying once more from the flagstaff.

The French lieutenant shrugged his shoulders as he handed his sword to Syd.

"*Ah, vous anglais!*" he muttered, and then to one of his companions in French—

"It is of no use to try any longer. The men from the English frigate will be ashore directly. But to be beaten by that boy!"

He was quite right. Before an hour had elapsed two well-manned boats from the *Sirius* was at the landing-place to take possession and charge of the prisoners, while in another hour Syd was standing before his father, giving him an account of all that had been done.

Captain Belton listened almost grimly to his son's narrative, and when he had finished—

"Well, sir," said the captain; "and what have you to say for yourself? You went ashore without leave. Of course you will be punished."

"Yes, sir."

"Where are Mr Roylance and Mr Terry?"

"Ashore, sir, wounded both."

"And Mr Dallas badly, I hear. Tut—tut—tut! and I have a terrible array of losses to confront here. Well, you have something else to say?"

Syd was hesitating, for he had a painful duty to perform. Had he been the only holder of the knowledge of his messmate's treachery, he would have held his tongue: but it was known to all on shore, and he told everything.

"Go now," said the father, "I am too busy to say more. You can stay on board; I will give orders for a fresh party to occupy the rock."

Syd thought his father might have forgotten the captain a little more at their encounter, and given him a word of praise; but he smothered his feelings, and joined his messmates in the gun-room, for the middies' quarters were horribly occupied just then by the doctors.

He had stared aghast at the shattered aspect of the deck and rigging, and seen that the French frigate was no better, and then learned that which he was longing to hear.

It was a simple matter; the gale they had felt on the rock had grown into a hurricane outside, and in the midst of it both the *Sirius* and her consort were cast ashore on one of the coral islands far out of the regular track of ships.

There they had been ever since, till by clever scheming and indefatigable work, Captain Belton had got his frigate off, literally carving a little canal for her from where she lay to the open water. For his consort was a hopeless wreck, and he had the help of a second crew.

As soon as they were clear, Captain Belton made sail for the rock again, to arrive only just in time.

The wreck had given him one advantage, though: he had the crews of both frigates on board, and several extra guns which he had saved.

It was nearly dark when the boat from the shore arrived with the wounded and the remnant of the brave defenders of the rock, and a warm welcome was accorded them; the two little middies, Bolton and Jenkins, who had nearly gone mad over Syd, seeming to complete the process with Roylance, who got away from them as soon as possible to draw Sydney aside.

"Seen him?" he said, in a low tone.

"Whom—Mr Dallas? Yes."

"No, no; Terry."

"No; nor do I want to."

"Yes; go and see him, poor wretch."

"If I do he'll accuse me of being the cause of all his trouble."

"No, no; I've shaken hands with him."

"Shaken hands?"

"Why not? My father is a clergyman. I want to recollect something of what he taught me."

"But with a man like that, even if he is wounded?"

"But, poor fellow! he's dying."

"What!" cried Syd.

"Don't you know?"

Syd shook his head. He felt half suffocated.

"In that last scuffle when we took back the battery, he was one of the fellows we drove over the side. I didn't know it then. No one did till he was picked up from where he crouched. The doctor has gone to him now."

Syd hurried away, and after a time was able to find his old messmate lying where he had been left by the surgeon, side by side with one of the many wounded who filled the lower decks.

There was a lanthorn swinging overhead, and Syd started as he saw the ghastly change in the young man's countenance.

He could not think of enmity or treachery at such a moment as that, but went close up.

"Terry," he said, "I'm sorry it has come to this."

The midshipman's face lit up, and he feebly raised his hand.

"Better so," he said, in a faint whisper. "Good-bye."

Chapter Forty Six

They knew in the midshipman's little company that night how Michael Terry had died, and the frank-hearted lads joined in saying they were glad he had died from his fall, and not from a wound given by an English blade. And somehow, though it was known to all now, not a voice uttered a word about his treachery. The terrible fate that had overtaken him had come as a veil over all that.

For the next few days, as they lay there to leeward of the rock, Syd and Roylance used to look up at the colours flying from the flagstaff, and feel something like regret that they were no longer living in the gap; but there was endless work to do. The captain had transferred his less fortunate brother officer and crew to the French frigate, and on board both vessels the knotting, splicing, and repairing that went on was enormous, while the carpenters and their mates had the busiest of times.

One of the first things done after hospital tents had been rigged up in the gap, was for all the wounded to be transferred to the shore; the garrison was strengthened, provisions and stores landed, a surgeon put in charge, and the *Sirius* with the prize set sail for the nearest British possession to land their prisoners.

In a week they were back off the rock, and after communications, sailed on for Saint Jacques; the French frigate, in spite of being minus one mast, making fair way under the jury spar set up, and, thanks to the vigorous efforts made in the way of repairs, in excellent fighting trim, and with her crew eager to make up in the end for the loss of their own ship.

Syd had been out of the naval engagement, but he was now to witness a bold attack made upon a fortified port—a successful attack, the batteries being pretty well demolished, and the force of sailors and marines that was landed carrying all before them, so that in one short day the British flag waved over the town of Saint Jacques, and the island of La Haute became one of the possessions of the British Crown.

After refitting, the *Sirius* did good work in the western seas for two years before she was ordered home, where upon the captain landing at Shoreport, it was known that he was promoted to the command of a line-of-battle ship, while sundry honours were ready for his officers, notably for Mr Dallas, who had long been well and strong.

"Yes, Strake," said Roylance, "promotion for every one but the poor midshipman."

"Wait a bit, sir, wait a bit," said the bronzed old fellow. "'Tain't fault o' gover'ment, but fault o' natur'. Soon as you and Mr Belton here grows big enough you'll be lufftenants, and then captains; and if that swab of a boy of mine minds his eye he'll be a bo'sun."

"You'll lay up now, I suppose?" said Roylance.

"Me, sir? me lay up?" cried the boatswain, indignantly. "Not the man. No, sir, I hope to sail yet with young Capen Belton when the old capen's a admiral, as he's sure to be afore long."

"Seems a long time to wait for promotion," said Syd.

"Awful, sir, to a young gent who has only been two years at sea. But—whish, sir! Look!"

Syd, who was leaning over the side with Roylance, gazing at the town, started with pleasure, for in the stern-sheets of the barge, which was coming back from shore with the captain, who was returning to take leave of his officers before quitting the *Sirius* for good, was the grey-whiskered, florid face of Admiral Belton.

He came on board, bowing to the salutes given him, and then looking round sharply, he exclaimed—

"Now then, where's that doctor?"

"Here, uncle," cried Syd, merrily.

"Why! Well! Hang the boy, I shouldn't have known you. You have grown! Shake hands, you dog! I'm proud of you. I know all about it. I say," he said with a chuckle, "don't want to be a doctor now, eh?"

"Saving your honour's presence," growled a deep voice, "I dunno what we should ha' done if he hadn't been one."

"Hah! bo'sun, you there. Glad to see you. Do you follow my brother to his new ship?"

"Ay, ay, sir; please goodness, and Mr Belton here, too."

"No," said Captain Belton, quietly. "My son is going for a cruise with Commander Dallas in the sloop-of-war to which he has been appointed."

"Then, saving your honour's presence, and thinking of you as the best captain I ever served, if it could be managed, I'd like to sail under Mr Dallas too, and I'll take my boy."

"You shall, Strake; and I'm very glad."

So six months after Sydney Belton joined the sloop *Ariel*, and this time saw active, service in the eastern seas.